Only Murders in the Abbey

Also by Beth Cowan-Erskine

Loch Down Abbey

About the Author

Beth Cowan-Erskine wrote her first novel, *Loch Down Abbey*, during the pandemic, mostly because she had nothing better to do. There is only so much sourdough one can bake. Her second novel came about when her husband, sensing literary fame and an early retirement, moved her to the most depressing place in England so she could turn it into a series. Happily for him, Lady Georgina kept waking her up with plotline notes, and thus we have another book. Enjoy. The author now lives in the Scottish Highlands and there is no telling what will happen next.

Only Murders in the Abbey

BETH COWAN-ERSKINE

HODDER &
STOUGHTON

First published in Great Britain in 2025 by Hodder & Stoughton Limited
An Hachette UK company

The authorised representative in the EEA is Hachette Ireland,
8 Castlecourt Centre, Dublin 15, D15 XTP3, Ireland
(email: info@hbgi.ie)

1

A CIP catalogue record for this title is available from the British Library

Paperback ISBN 978 1 399 73931 3
ebook ISBN 978 1 399 73932 0

Typeset in Plantin Light by Manipal Technologies Limited

Printed and bound in Great Britain by Clays Ltd, Elcograf S.p.A.

Hodder & Stoughton policy is to use papers that are natural, renewable
and recyclable products and made from wood grown in sustainable forests.
The logging and manufacturing processes are expected to conform
to the environmental regulations of the country of origin.

Hodder & Stoughton Limited
Carmelite House
50 Victoria Embankment
London EC4Y 0DZ

www.hodder.co.uk

This one's for you, Dad

Only Murders in the Abbey

Introduction

Loch Down Abbey Hotel, Est 1933, is a grand hotel near the village of Inverkillen, which sits on the shores of Loch Down, deep in the Scottish Highlands. On the hotel grounds runs the River Plaid, source of the famous Abbey Whisky and Inverkillen Smoked Salmon. It was home to the Ogilvy-Sinclair family for six hundred years.

List of Characters

The Hotel Staff

Director of Operations – **Mrs Alice MacBain**

Head of Food and Beverage – **Mr Robert Hudson**

Head of Guest Services – **Mr Hamish Mackay**

Head of Sales and Marketing – **Mr Giles Lockridge**

Head Chef – **Mrs Eleanor Burnside**

Head Housekeeper – **Sadie Milne**

Head Porter – **Ollie MacNair**

Master Distiller – **Ross MacBain**

The Ogilvy-Sinclair Family

Lady Georgina – The Dowager Countess of Inverkillen, who resides in Thistledown Cottage on the edges of the hotel grounds. Her rose gardens are the pride of the hotel.

Her Children

Major Cecil Ogilvy-Sinclair – Her younger son and his wife **Eva**, who live in London with her parents. They are rumoured to be divorcing.

Lady Elspeth Comtois – Her daughter, who lives in France with her husband, **Philippe, Marquis de Clairvaux**, and their children: **Auguste**, **Hugo**, **Delphine** and **Florence**.

Lord Angus Inverkillen – Her eldest grandson, and current Earl of Inverkillen, who lives in Tangiers with renowned author, **Hugh Dunbar-Hamilton** and his three children, who have a very strict Nanny.

The Honourable Fergus Ogilvy-Sinclair – Her youngest grandson, Manager of the prestigious Loch Down Abbey Hotel, his wife **Imogen** and their first child, **Tessa**. They have two dogs, Grantham, and Belgravia.

Lady Annabella Martin – Her eldest granddaughter, née Inverkillen, ex-wife of **Hugh Dunbar-Hamilton**, now remarried to her second husband, the British Consul-General of Shanghai. They have fourteen maids.

Lady Iris Kettering – Her youngest granddaughter, who lives in London with her husband **Thomas**, the **Marquess of Drysdale**, their twins **Alice** and **Edward**, and her mother, **Flora**.

Prologue

Hudson was doing his rounds the morning after the ball. It was quiet in the Abbey, for which he was thankful. He might have had more whisky than advisable, and this morning he was feeling a bit queasy. He so rarely indulged but it had been the first ball in the Abbey in centuries; they had all been a bit giddy. However, it meant only three footmen and two housemaids reported for duty this morning. So Hudson, co-owner of Loch Down Abbey, and former butler, was carrying a tray, helping to clear up the abandoned glasses from the night before.

Next time, if there is to be a next time, he thought to himself sternly, *no staff at the ball.*

Hudson nodded as one of the footmen entered the hall from the Rose Drawing Room.

'Someone's broken a chair, sir. I'll send a hall boy up to fetch it now.' The lad was a delicate shade of grey.

Hudson nodded gently and hoped it wasn't one of the Chippendale chairs. There were so few remaining. He entered the Long Gallery and glanced at the Oak Room. The footmen, he noted, had failed to clean up the cards tables before taking themselves to bed last night. As he surveyed the damage, he calculated how long, and how many people it would take to put the room back together again. It was more than he could manage this morning.

He crossed the Long Gallery, plucking glasses from here and there, making his way towards the Small Library. They hadn't opened it for use, but people got up to all sorts at a ball and he felt it best to check the room. *Diligence dispels disgrace*, as he always said to the footmen when they attempted to shirk their duties. He turned the knob and crashed into the door. His head quietly whinged. Surely he wasn't so hungover he could no longer operate a door? He tried it again and growled in frustration. The door was locked.

Why is it locked? he thought, irritated. *It shouldn't be locked.*

They'd had no end of difficulties with lost keys and old locks when they'd taken over the Abbey. An official policy was taken that all public rooms were to be left unlocked at all times.

Well, perhaps Mrs MacBain locked it, he mused, *to keep people out during the ball.*

Mrs MacBain stumped for limiting the number of rooms people were allowed to use. One less room to clean in the morning, she had said. And now, with a skeleton staff, he understood the wisdom of that. But he remembered someone coming out of the room during the midnight buffet. Or perhaps going in? He couldn't have said; his attention was focused on the food, which was dwindling much faster than they'd planned. Running out would have been a catastrophe, one he was determined to avoid. But, he distinctly remembered the door opening and closing.

Hudson stepped back into the Long Gallery and grumbled. If he couldn't get into the Small Library from the main doors, he'd try the garden doors. He picked his way around the building, careful to stay on the pebble pathway. Today would be no easier if he soiled the cuffs of his livery. Standing in front of the garden doors, he tried the knob but found they too were locked. And the curtains were drawn.

Hudson huffed his frustration. He tried to peer in through the curtains but could see nothing.

Perhaps, just this once, he needn't check? *Thin edge of the wedge*, he told himself darkly. How could he expect the highest of standards from his staff if he let this slide? No, he really did need to get into that room, but how?

He made his way back into the Abbey and stopped to check his shoes and livery were clean. Once satisfied, his gaze fell to the doors of the Oak Room. *That might just do the trick*, he thought fleetingly, before crossing over and taking a brass key from the nearest door.

Hudson inserted it into the Small Library and turned the lock. One small victory for the morning, then. He opened one of the doors and stepped into the room.

There was a lamp by the sofa still on, giving just enough light to make his way to a side table, where he set his tray down and flung open the heavy damask curtains to the garden. The pale morning light entered the room slowly, as if it, too, had a hangover. Hudson reached for the silver tray, but his left hand missed its mark and ended up in a half-eaten plate of food. Grimacing, he reached for one of his six handkerchiefs – experience had long ago taught him it was best to be overprepared – and he turned to survey the room as he cleaned his hand. He twitched. There was a blanket on the floor in front of the sofa. He looked closer and then jumped. Not a blanket, a person. Someone was sleeping on the floor in front of the sofa.

Well, that explained why the door was locked, he supposed. But why sleep on the floor? Perhaps they'd been so drunk they'd fallen off? He shook his head, allowing himself this small display of disdain before questioning what he should do.

He moved closer, as silently as he could, debating whether to wake the sleeper or to slip out unnoticed. *What is the etiquette for this?* he wondered. Guests were politely requested to leave at three thirty, with the footmen instructed to sweep out any remaining stragglers at five. So who then, was this?

He needed to know exactly who it was before rousting them out of slumber. He wasn't up to being reprimanded by a lord this morning, but if it was a footman . . . He rounded the arm of the sofa and leaned over cautiously, only to issue a loud yelp.

His feet carried him to the main doors far swifter than his head liked. He flung one side open, stuck his head out, looking left and right for a footman. *Where are they? Never around when you need one!*

Carefully closing the door behind him, he hesitatingly stepped towards the Rose Room, hopeful a hall boy was collecting the broken chair. But for every step forward, he took a halting step back, as if to both advance and remain in place to protect the door. Just as his hand reached the brass knob, the door flew open and a hall boy leapt backwards, startled. He dropped the chair.

They stared at one another for a half-second, before Hudson finally barked an order at the boy.

'Go fetch Mrs MacBain. Bring her to the Small Library.' He pointed at the double doors across the way. The boy stared at him, unmoving. 'Now!' he barked.

'Yessir!' The boy picked up the chair again.

'No.' Hudson wrenched it from his hands. 'Leave the chair.'

He watched as the hall boy scurried out of the room and disappeared behind the green baize door. Looking to the chair in his hands, he sighed. *Of course, it was a Chippendale chair*. He set it down gently next to the vitrine of antique music boxes. The chair could be dealt with later.

Stepping back into the Long Gallery, he faced the double doors to the Small Library. He hesitated, unsure what to do next. Should he wait outside? Or inside? Surely it was best to wait outside. But then he remembered he'd opened the curtains and anyone in the garden – unlikely this early, yes, but still possible – would be able to see in. That would never do. He closed his eyes, took a deep breath, and entered the room swiftly.

He went straight to the windows and jerked the curtains closed. The room was plunged into darkness, but for a lamp by the sofa. He could just make out the shape of . . . it was too horrible. His head throbbed.

He crossed the room and locked the doors. How long would it take for Mrs MacBain to arrive? he wondered. He turned the chandelier on and surveyed the room, doing his level best not to look at the sofa again.

He was deep in thought; could they rearrange the furniture, or perhaps rotate the rug? The doors rattled and Hudson started violently, crashing into a nearby armchair. Staring at the knob, he held his breath. Another attempt to open the doors, and then he heard a soft knock.

'Mr Hudson? It's me.'

Hudson unlocked the doors and opened one just a few inches. 'Mrs MacBain, thank god it's you.' He stood aside to admit her.

Mrs MacBain stood still, looking at her business partner, confusion on her face. 'I was told you wanted to see me quite urgently.' She was dressed, as he'd expected, but clearly the hall boy had got her in the middle of her toilette. Her hair was down around her shoulders, something Hudson, in all his years at the Abbey, had never seen.

Without another word, he grabbed her arm and pulled her into the room, locking the door behind them. Mrs MacBain turned around, clearly offended at being man-handled, but then gasped. She was looking at the sofa in front of the fire.

'What is that? What's happened?' She rushed closer. 'Is that blood?'

Part One

July 1937

Fergus shut the door softly behind him. The baby had been up all night and Imogen, his wife, had only just got the girl to sleep. He loved being a father, but jeepers was he tired. Breathing deeply, he looked up and admired the deep blue sky.

Amazing weather today, he thought.

Setting off, he closed the gate and walked up the gravelled drive. In three minutes, he passed by the old family chapel and spotted Reverend Douglas. Waving across the churchyard, Fergus noted how plump the vicar had got in the past year, clear evidence the new wife was a good cook.

Continuing up the drive, under the ancient trees of the old Estate, he finally reached the forecourt and stopped under the arched yew trees to take in the scene.

Loch Down Abbey Hotel, once his family home, was a hive of activity.

They'd hosted a big shoot over the weekend, and the guests were leaving today. Porters were scrambling, weaving between people and dogs; bellboys were loading the trunks, guns, and hunting baskets onto cars; the doormen were settling the ladies into their seats and accepting handsome tips from the gentlemen. Fergus could see Lord Enderleigh trying to coax his new retriever out of the pond. Fergus shook his head slowly; that hound had caused no end of trouble on the shoot: barking, leaping through the bracken, charging a herd of deer. As the manager of the hotel, Fergus would have to discuss it with Lord Enderleigh before he left. The dog could not be allowed back until he was properly trained. It was a conversation he didn't relish having, but it had to happen. Shooting was a large part of their livelihood.

Fergus sighed and moved to the entrance, passing under the stone archway and stepping into the Armoury. It was buzzing with activity here, too. Ladies waiting for their cars to be pulled around; maids rushing to pour them tea or tidy a table; two clerks at the desk were settling bills with guests.

A short porter approached Fergus. 'Good morning, sir. Telegram for you.' Fergus looked at the porter with mild surprise. Telegrams were becoming rare in this day; most people simply telephoned. Taking the envelope from the silver tray, he nodded his thanks and opened it. The porter stepped back and waited. Fergus grimaced and looked to the boy.

'Where is she?' he asked.

'In Rowan Tree, sir, waiting for you as usual.'

'Thank you.' Fergus turned and strode across the Armoury. As he passed through, he nodded absent-mindedly at the guests who were having a late morning tea. He was stopped by Mrs McCready, a rather elderly woman, who was profuse in her thanks for keeping her usual rooms for her. It meant the world to her, she said, given it would surely be her last trip. She was, you see, dying of some vague never-quite-specified disease, but she still managed to come three or four times a year, much to the annoyance of her children, who watched in horror as their inheritance drained away. Fergus smiled and exchanged a few pleasantries before moving on. He passed to the far side of the Armoury, pausing to ask a footman to freshen her tea, and then continued to a small, panelled door under the stairs. A tasteful brass plaque read: *Rowan Tree*.

Mrs MacBain looked up as he entered the room. Alice MacBain, former Housekeeper of Loch Down Abbey, had been the driving force behind purchasing the Estate and turning it into a thriving hotel and shooting estate. She, and several of the other long-standing employees, had purchased the Abbey when the family had been forced to sell it to avoid bankruptcy. Fergus, as the only family member who tried to help keep the family Estate afloat, was kept on as manager of the hotel. They also housed his grandmother, Lady Georgina, in a cottage on the Estate, but the remainder of the family was scattered to the four corners of the earth.

Fergus crossed the circular room Mrs MacBain used as an Above Stairs Office. It had been a medieval ammunition keep and was now a small but cosy sitting room. She was seated at their usual chairs by the window, readying the tea.

'Good morning, Fergus. Is everything all right out there?'

Since taking over the hotel, she and Fergus made it a point to meet each Monday morning, before he met with the rest of the senior staff. Over tea, they discussed the coming week's business. When Fergus first started running the hotel, he'd found it quite overwhelming. The sheer volume of details involved, managing so many people – not to mention the guests, the shoots, the fishing, the Distillery – it all engulfed him. Fergus had been drowning when Mrs MacBain suggested weekly meetings, just the two of them, to discuss how she'd managed it all as Head Housekeeper. He would be forever grateful to her for helping him succeed.

Mrs MacBain offered him a cup of tea and noticed the telegram in his hand. Fergus sat down heavily, wordlessly, and handed the telegram to her. Mrs MacBain slowly set the teacup down, worry creasing her face. She reached for her reading glasses.

Shanghai invaded by Japanese.
Foreigners evacuated.
Expect arrival Marseille, 8 Aug, Imperial Airlines.

Mrs MacBain looked up, alarmed. 'Bella's coming home?' The incredulity in her voice was unmistakable.

Fergus nodded slowly, looking stunned himself. 'Bella's coming home.'

Mrs MacBain slumped back in her chair, breathing out slowly as she said it. 'Lord help us.' The pair sat for some moments in silence, their brains digesting the implications of the news.

Lady Annabella Martin, known to the family as Bella, was Fergus's sister, who lived in Shanghai. After her marriage fell apart – broken up by her brother Angus, of all people – she fled to Europe to escape the humiliation. It had been reported in the local paper, in gleeful and unflinching detail. While in Monaco, she found herself engulfed in a whirlwind romance with the very handsome Lord Edmund Martin, Consul-General of Shanghai. They married after two weeks, and Bella settled into her new life abroad, returning to Loch Down only twice in three years. Neither visit had been easy on the hotel staff.

'Where are we going to put her?' Mrs MacBain glanced at the telegram again, noting the date. 'She'll be here for the ball. We're booked up because of it. If it's just Bella and Sir Edmund, we can make do, but if she brings all those maids she's always bragging about . . . I just don't know where we'd find the room. How many were there at last count: fourteen? I don't know why any one person needs that many maids.' She tutted softly and set the telegram on the tea tray.

Fergus shook his head slowly. 'Because she can, Mrs MacBain. Simply because she can.' He was quiet for a minute, staring at the carpet. 'At least we have a few weeks to sort it. Can you brief the senior staff this morning? I'm going to see if I can get more information.'

She nodded and watched as Fergus stood and left the small room. Sipping her tea pensively, Mrs MacBain pondered the collective noun for maids. *A gaggle of maids*? A *pack*? *A bevy*, perhaps? If Lady Bella was coming with fourteen maids, surely a more military term would be necessary. Phalanx? Yes, *a phalanx* of lady's maids was about to descend on Loch Down Abbey.

August

Fourteen Days to the Ball

Mrs Burnside hummed softly as she began her day. As the Head Chef of the hotel, she was reviewing the number of trays that needed to be sent up to the rooms before her staff laid the main breakfast in the dining rooms. Glancing out the window into the service yard, she could see the village delivery van was just arriving.

Am I going mad, she thought to herself, *haven't they already been today?*

The van came every morning at six o'clock sharp bringing the post, the papers, and the milk. She glanced at the clock in the kitchen: six fifteen.

She walked to the kitchen door, noted the maids rushing about putting away the delivery and shouted, 'Have you forgotten something, Mr Russell?' Good nature showed though her smile. 'A second trip will throw your whole day behind schedule.'

Mr Russell, normally a chipper man, was silent with an inscrutable expression on his face. He jerked his head towards the back of the van. 'Special delivery.'

Mrs Burnside hesitated a moment, and then walked slowly around the van to the open doors. There in the back slumped a man and several small children, all fast asleep. Mrs Burnside looked between Mr Russell and the van several times, her mouth slightly open in confusion.

Mr Russell stood beside her and together they silently contemplated his passengers.

'Erm . . . ' was all Mrs Burnside could get out.

'They came on the milk train. Said I'd bring 'em up to the house. Figured it was too early for anyone to come fetch 'em.'

'On the milk train?' Mrs Burnside looked to the driver, confused. 'But, who are they? And why would you bring them here?'

'That,' he said darkly, 'is Lord Inverkillen.'

Upon hearing his name, Angus jolted awake. 'Oh! Have we arrived?' He looked around the yard, confusion rapidly clouding his face. 'Where are we?'

Angus Inverkillen, brother to Fergus and Bella, was the current Earl of Inverkillen. Loch Down Abbey had been the family seat for nearly six hundred years. When the Abbey was sold, he moved to Tangiers, Morocco, where he was helping raise Bella's children with her ex-husband. It was an arrangement that suited them perfectly but raised many an eyebrow when mentioned in Loch Down.

'Welcome home, Lord Inverkillen,' said Mrs Burnside, unsure if she should curtsey. She nodded her head instead. 'You're in the service yard, at the back of the house. I'm Mrs Burnside, the cook.'

Angus stared at the pair. He seemed deeply unsure of them.

'Ah yes,' said Angus, hesitation in his voice. 'Cook.' That seemed to be as far as he was prepared to go in the discussion. He struggled to get out of the van and woke the children as he did so. Mr Russell stepped forward to help them out. As they blinked the sleep from their faces, another figure got out of the van. Mrs Burnside stood staring at it, mouth agape.

'Who are you?' she finally asked loudly.

The most blazing pair of amber eyes stared back at her.

'She would be their Nanny,' said Angus, stretching his neck.

Mrs Burnside looked her up and down and then back to Angus. 'Why is she wearing a sheet?'

Angus yawned. 'It's how the native population dresses in Morocco.'

'Oh,' she replied, giving the Nanny another once-over. Looking into the van, she noticed their luggage. 'Are all those your cases?' It was a lot of luggage for a visit.

'What? Oh, yes,' he said. Stifling another yawn, he asked, 'What time is it?'

'Six fifteen. The house isn't quite up yet. Erm . . .' She wasn't sure what to do with them. 'Why don't you come with me, and I'll fix you some breakfast?' She ushered the group towards the door to the kitchen.

'Majida will settle the children in the nursery.' He turned to the Nanny and said something Mrs Burnside didn't recognise. The woman stared at him, and Angus pointed to the children, then to the top of the house and then snapped his fingers. The woman nodded deeply and herded the children to the door. Mrs Burnside twitched. The very notion of being snapped at offended her greatly.

Angus turned back to Mrs Burnside. 'Have a tray sent to my rooms. I'm aching for a bath.' He looked at the delivery van again with some distaste. After a moment, he strode off through the kitchen, looking left and right for a way out. The kitchens were a hive of activity. Maids and footmen rushing about with trays, kitchen maids getting fires and ovens going. Mrs Burnside chased after him, trying to keep up.

'It's just . . . I don't know what rooms to put you in, Your Lordship. I don't know how all that works.'

Angus stared at Cook as if she'd gone mad. 'I'll be in my usual rooms, of course. Now, how do I get out of here?'

'But, Your Lordship, I don't know if your usual rooms are free.'

Angus turned swiftly and stared at her, thunderstruck. It hadn't occurred to him that someone else might be occupying his old rooms. This damnable hotel idea! All he needed was a bath. And a change of clothes. And a cup of tea. Why was that so difficult a request? Frustration showed on his face.

'Look,' said Mrs Burnside slowly, noticing that Angus was stewing. She gently guided him to the staffroom. 'Why don't you have a seat here and I'll make some tea. The desk clerk usually gets here at a quarter to seven and he can sort rooms for you then.' She held the door open, pleading silently for Angus to just do as he was asked.

'You expect me to wait in the servants' hall? For someone to give me rooms in my own home?' Angus had swung from frustration to anger swiftly, and it wouldn't do to have her staff see her in a shouting match with Lord Inverkillen. Mrs Burnside pedalled furiously.

'I'm happy to bring you tea in the Armoury if you'd rather. I just thought, as you wanted a bath, you might prefer a more private place to wait, instead of being on show to anyone coming and going.' She held her breath and hoped he was vain enough to take the bait.

Angus digested this, and nodded once, curtly. Mrs Burnside held the door open again and Angus passed through, looking around, disappointment etched on his face.

'I'll have a tray brought into you in a moment, milord.' Mrs Burnside walked swiftly to the kitchen and breathed a deep sigh of relief, prayed that Mr Thompson, their usual morning clerk, would be on time that morning, and went in search of Mrs MacBain.

There was a pause at breakfast and both Fergus and Imogen looked up. The tap at the door was so faint, neither was certain they'd heard it. After a moment, it was more pronounced. Imogen looked to the mantel clock, Fergus to the watch on his wrist. It was before eight o'clock. People rarely came to the house, but they never arrived before eight o'clock. It was borderline indecent. Imogen shrugged and went back to feeding the baby. Fergus stood and walked to the front door.

Mrs MacBain stood on the little porch, looking apologetic. 'I hope I didn't wake the bairn. We had a bit of an early morning visitor, and I thought it best to come warn you.'

'Warn me? Bella finally show up, did she?' He stepped out of the way so Mrs MacBain could enter the little cottage – it was softly raining – and then ushered her through to the dining room.

'Ah, no. No. Quite the opposite, in fact. Good morning, Imogen. Sorry to burst in on you like this.'

'Not at all, Mrs MacBain! I'm just finished with the wee lassie and it's time to dress her. Please help yourself to tea. I'm afraid the toast's gone cold though.' She lifted the small child from her chair, beaming, and walked from the room, humming.

Motherhood suits her, thought Mrs MacBain. She turned her gaze to Fergus, who was pouring her some tea. *He looks tired*, she thought, *but happily so*.

'Now,' he said genially, 'what's the opposite of Bella invading? Oh, no . . . not Angus?'

'Angus indeed. With the children in tow, and some sort of a servant.' She went on to recount the story Mrs Burnside had related to her.

'The milk train? What on earth was he doing on that? And why is he here at all?'

'Well, that we're not sure about. Mrs Burnside didn't like to pry. But I thought it was best you knew before you arrived.'

'Yes, thank you.' He scanned her face. 'Something's bothering you.'

Mrs MacBain stood and looked out the window for a moment. Turning back, she looked regretful. 'They had a mountain of cases and trunks with them. I don't think he's here for a quick visit.'

'Right,' said Fergus slowly. He sat for some moments in silence, staring at the cold toast in the centre of the table.

The mantel clock chimed the hour and brought Fergus out of his reverie.

'Well, I'd better get up there and find out what's happened.'

'Knowing your family, you're going to need a plan. Or at least some options. I'll do the staff briefing; you take some time and come up when you're ready.' She stood and smoothed her skirts. It was a gesture Fergus knew well and he felt a surge of affection. 'I can see myself out.'

And then she was gone, leaving Fergus contemplating the return of his brother.

When Fergus finally found his brother in the dining room, Angus was attempting to eat breakfast and from what

Fergus could see, it wasn't going well. He was frowning and picking at his food with his fork.

'I heard we had an unexpected visitor!' Fergus said warmly as he approached his brother. He stood for a second, waiting for Angus to react.

'Yes, sorry about that, old chap. I couldn't face a night in Fort William and so we pushed on though.' He indicated the chair across the table.

Fergus sat and looked at his brother. He was tanned, and noticeably thinner than the day he left Loch Down, but he still had a cigarette case to hand and a slight look of boredom on his face. Some things never changed, apparently.

Angus motioned to the food between them. 'Is this breakfast every morning? I shall have to speak to Cook.'

Fergus surveyed the table. The half-eaten remains of his full Scottish breakfast were between them: fried eggs, roast tomatoes, baked beans, haggis, black pudding, tattie scones, kippers.

'You didn't get mushrooms, my apologies.' He moved to summon a waiter, but Angus shook his head.

'I do not need mushrooms, Fergus.' He pointed to the plate. 'Mushrooms cannot rescue this.'

'What's wrong with it?'

'What's right with it? All that brown on the plate and none it fresh. It's a grim start to the day.' He moved some beans around with a fork. 'And don't even get me started on the tomatoes. These things—' He speared a roasted tomato with a fork. 'I didn't know something as hard as a golf ball could also be mushy.' He dropped the fork, leaning back in his chair, sighing.

Fergus was annoyed. He'd hadn't expected Angus to leap to his feet with joy, but a polite hello wouldn't have gone amiss. 'Then tell me, dear brother, what would you have served me if I'd turned up on your doorstep, unannounced?'

Angus glared at his brother for a long moment. 'Firstly, we'd be on the roof terrace.'

Fergus rolled his eyes and stifled a sigh.

'We'd start with mint tea and bread with apricot jam. Then fresh fruit, goat's cheese, hmm . . . lightly fried eggs with olives, or maybe B'ssara, which is a bean soup, very delicate.'

'Soup? For breakfast? You're going to be hard pressed to find that in Scotland.'

'Don't I know it.' Angus scowled.

There was a dark pause. Fergus cleared his throat. 'So, how long are you staying?'

Angus slowly lit a cigarette and then looked to his brother. 'Not sure. Things have changed. Need to get my head around a plan of action.'

Fergus nodded slowly. 'Will Hugh be joining you?'

Angus's eyes flicked to his brother. Angus studied him carefully, and then exhaled slowly. 'No.' It was a curt reply followed by violent stubbing out of his cigarette.

Hugh was The Honourable Hugh Dunbar-Hamilton. Second son of their neighbour, ex-husband to Bella, and Angus's oldest friend. They'd been at school together. Hugh was an author, quite a successful one; however, no one in the family had ever bothered to read his books. When his marriage with Bella broke up, due to his life-long affair with Angus being discovered, he convinced Angus to move to Tangiers, where they could live together in the open. All the important writers and artists of the moment lived in Tangiers, he said, and Hugh wanted to be among them. As they packed to leave, Bella took her revenge: she fled to Europe, leaving Hugh with the children.

Fergus didn't know what to say, so he waited silently. Angus lit another cigarette and stared across the dining room.

'Hugh's gone to Spain.'

Fergus was startled. 'Spain? But there's a war on.'

'Yes, I know.' Angus turned back to the table and tapped his cigarette lightly against a crystal ashtray. 'He wants to be a journalist. Thinks no one takes him seriously because he writes novels.'

Fergus nodded as if he understood, but he wasn't sure he did. He had questions but Angus was in a dark mood, and he'd have to be careful, or it would erupt. The brothers contemplated in lengthy silence. Fergus was just starting to wonder if perhaps he shouldn't excuse himself and get to work when salvation arrived.

Lady Georgina burst into the room and made a beeline for the brothers. Fergus leapt to his feet and offered her a chair. She was breathless. 'I heard you'd arrived, but I hardly dared to believe it.'

How does she hear? Fergus wondered. She always knew the goings-on before anyone else seemed to know. Not for the first time, he wondered if she had spies in the hotel.

Angus rolled his eyes and sighed. 'Hello, Grandmama.' He stood to kiss her, but she waved him off.

'Why weren't we told you were coming? Does no one write anymore? Perhaps you did, and no one bothered to tell me.' She glared at Fergus accusingly.

Angus waved his hand. 'It was very last minute; there wasn't time to write or send a telegram. We've been in transit for days.' He yawned impolitely.

'Why? What's happened?' She settled into her chair and delicately pulled off her gloves. She glanced at Fergus and noted his discomfort. 'And where's Hugh?'

Angus bristled and turned his head away from the family. 'He's gone to Spain.'

'Spain? But there's a war on.' Lady Georgina looked between the brothers, confused.

'I'm well aware of that, thank you.' He stubbed out his cigarette only to immediately light another.

'I don't understand.' Lady Georgina leaned forward, placing her hands on the table. 'Why on earth would Hugh go to Spain?'

Angus stared at the table and sighed. 'He wants to be a war correspondent.'

Her eyes narrowed. 'A war correspondent?' Lady Georgina repeated flatly.

'Apparently, being a celebrated author isn't enough for him.'

Fergus raised his eyebrows. 'Celebrated is a bit of a reach, isn't it?'

'Now isn't the time, Fergus,' chided Lady Georgina. 'And what of the children?'

Angus drained his teacup and sighed heavily. 'I thought it best to bring them back here.'

'Yes.' She nodded sagely. 'Quite the right thing to do.'

Angus slumped forward in his chair and sighed heavily.

'Chin up,' said Fergus, 'it's not all as bad as that.'

'Yes,' chirped Lady Georgina, 'the worst is past. You're home now and the children are safely in the Nursery. You did bring Nanny, didn't you?'

Angus sighed heavily. 'Yes, I brought Nanny,' he said morosely.

Lady Georgina eyed him hawkishly. 'What am I missing?' she asked, steeling herself.

Angus could barely bring himself to utter the words. 'He emptied the bank account.'

'What?!' Fergus and Lady Georgina shouted in unison. The dining room guests stared at them.

'He left some ready money, which is what I used to get us here. But there wasn't much, and the exchange rate was appalling. We had . . .' He shifted uncomfortably. 'We had to travel third class.'

Lady Georgina dropped her teacup.

A waiter rushed forward to clean it up and she waved him off.

'How could he do such a monstrous thing?' She was seething. 'He left you with his children, penniless and in a foreign country? Third class. It's . . . it's positively Dickensian.'

'That's a bit dramatic, Grandmama.' It was Fergus's turn to tut. He was fascinated by his brother's story, but something was amiss. 'How did you end up on the milk train?' The milk train, being the service that transported milk, the morning papers, and other sundry goods, made third class look positively luxurious, as there weren't any seats.

'The milk train?' Lady Georgina gasped loudly. 'What if someone had seen you? The Earl of Inverkillen on the milk train.' The idea was too abhorrent, especially this early in the day.

'Oh, that.' Angus shifted uncomfortably in his chair. 'I was able to get us as far as Fort William and, well . . .'

'The money ran out.' Fergus nodded sympathetically, but Angus had never been so humiliated in his life.

'I tried to convince the ticket agent that you'd pay the fares when we arrived, but they just wouldn't hear of it. Not an ounce of respect for the aristocracy.'

Lady Georgina allowed herself a loud and derisive tut.

'And it was either sleep at the station and ring you first thing this morning or get on the milk train.' His shoulders slumped forward, and he hid his face in his hands.

Lady Georgina and Fergus stared at one another; she horrified, he bemused.

'Well, I dare say the children thought it a grand adventure,' Fergus said brightly. 'And well done for getting back. I think it's jolly resourceful of you.' He nodded encouragingly at Lady Georgina, who simply stared at her grandson sternly.

Angus sighed miserably, not looking at either of them. 'I think I'll just go and lie down for a bit.' He stood and walked slowly out of the dining room.

When he'd gone, Lady Georgina said briskly, 'Do you know, I never liked the Dunbar-Hamiltons. One could never count on them. Just look at what Hugh's parents did to the Estate: selling it on the sly, for a golf hotel. I've never seen worse ground for golf in my life.'

'What? Where did you hear that?' Fergus was alarmed. He'd heard various rumours as well, but Lady Georgina seemed to be privy to a vastly more detailed stream of gossip.

She waved a hand airily and sighed. 'Now, what are we going to do, then?'

Fergus shook his head. 'I don't know. If he hasn't any money, he can't stay in the hotel for long.'

'No, that's true. Well, he can stay with me in Thistledown Cottage, but I'm afraid it simply isn't suitable for the children.' She shuddered a little, recalling the chaos that ensued the first time the children were allowed into the dining room. 'Can they stay in the hotel Nursery?'

'For now, yes, but we'll need a longer-term solution,' said Fergus thoughtfully. He stood up. 'I'll discuss it with Mrs MacBain.'

'Why don't you go help Angus gather his things? Best to move him while he's fragile, before he has a chance to entrench. I'll breakfast and we can go to the cottage when I've finished.' Lady Georgina waved for a waiter. 'I only hope I'm not too late for the pastries.'

Mrs MacBain was passing though the Armoury, the central space of the Abbey, decorated with the arms and weapons of long-ago vanquished enemies of the clan. She was coming to see the guests from the overnight sleeper service had arrived, but all was not as she expected. A rather rotund gentleman was arguing with the Head Clerk. Normally unflappable, Thompson, the clerk in question, was clearly flustered. He spied Mrs MacBain and waved her over.

As she approached, she heard the man say something about Lady Annabella. Mrs MacBain involuntarily sighed. Forcing a smile on her face, she stepped towards the desk. 'Hello. Can I be of assistance?' she asked.

The gentleman turned and Mrs MacBain involuntarily flinched. His waistcoat was loudly and heavily patterned. It was nearly worse than the Inverkillen tartan. He looked her up and down once, *harrumphed*, and turned his back, demanding to speak to the manager.

'Allow me to introduce Mrs MacBain,' the clerk said, again gesturing to her. 'She is one of the hotel owners.'

The gentleman's attitude changed immediately. 'But of course. My apologies, it's been a long and tedious trip, and we were expecting to have rooms when we arrived. May I present Mrs Fenella Blackwood,' he gestured to an elderly woman seated on the bench, 'and Colonel Henry Lamont, at your service.' He bowed his head and then looked expectantly at Mrs MacBain.

'My apologies, Colonel, Mrs Blackwood, the reservation must be misplaced. Let me have a look. When did you make it?'

'We didn't. Lady Annabella asked us to stay. We travelled out of Shanghai together.'

Oh dear, thought Mrs MacBain, *the girl isn't even back and she's already causing trouble.*

'Yes,' she said slowly, looking at the ledger. 'Well, I dare say we'll find you a room.'

'Rooms,' said the Colonel. 'We are not together, we'll need separate rooms.'

Mrs MacBain looked at him. There was something hard in his voice. 'My apologies.' She looked at the woman who was sitting patiently in a chair, and then back to the Colonel, who was thrumming his fingers on the desk. *I don't know that I'd want to share a room with him either,* she thought. Returning to the ledger, she scanned for rooms. 'We're busy this time of year, what with Grouse Season just opening.'

'How many rooms does this place have, eh?' interrupted the Colonel, who didn't bother to wait for an answer. 'Surely there's room. Ah, what's that?' He strode towards a display of battleaxes.

'And I'll need a second room near mine, for my nephew,' said Mrs Blackwood. 'He's had to stay in London for a few days, on business. I expect he'll be here shortly.' A small, cold smile graced her face.

'Adjoining?' Mrs MacBain scanned the book. She wasn't seeing any free adjoining rooms.

'No,' came the quick reply. 'Not adjoining, but I do require him near me. Next door, perhaps.' Another small, more pleasant, smile from the woman.

'That we can certainly do.' Mrs MacBain scanned the book for a few quiet moments. 'Ah, I think I have just the thing for you. Three rooms together, you can choose which two would suit.'

She glanced up and started visibly; the Colonel was weighing up a broad sword in his hand. Thompson scurried over to relieve him of the weapon.

'What a collection! Any chance I could try some of them? I'd love to see how that crossbow handles. Is that a Lochaber axe? Always wanted to handle one of those.' He looked at Thompson with schoolboy eagerness. He was clearly going to be a handful. She wondered if he was planning a lengthy stay and hoped not.

'Colonel, I can put you in the Scott Rooms. It's very pleasant and overlooks the croquet lawn.'

He dropped the lance he was holding, nearly taking off Thompson's foot, and strode towards the desk again. 'Scott. Like the sound of that. Admiral Scott. Great man.'

'Ah no, the room is dedicated to Sir Walter Scott, the poet.'

'Poet?' The Colonel grimaced. 'He was a bit namby-pamby, wasn't he? All that romance and atmosphere. Haven't you something a bit more fitting for a military man?'

Mrs MacBain surreptitiously eyed the Colonel's strained waistcoat. 'I'm afraid all our war-themed rooms are occupied, Colonel. But the room is only named after Sir Walter. I think you'll be quite comfortable there.' She smiled back up at him.

The Colonel harrumphed a bit and seemed to settle. 'Fine.' He grabbed the pen to sign the register and when finished, put the pen in his jacket and glanced around the Armoury. 'When's the next train from London? I expect Lady Annabella will be on that. Shame we got separated. Well, she'll be all right, I dare say. Once you're in Paris, it's safe for a lady to journey alone.' He turned to leave.

'Alone?' Mrs MacBain asked sharply. 'Isn't her husband with her?'

'Lord Martin? No. Stayed behind to close the Consulate. Burn the classified documents, that sort of thing. Joining us as soon as it's finished, I gather.' He noted Mrs MacBain's look of concern. 'Standard protocol. Nothing to worry about. I'd have stayed myself, but he insisted I accompany the civilians, for safety.' Mrs MacBain obviously didn't look impressed enough, so he continued. 'Several of the stopovers are quite rough, no place for ladies.'

'Right,' was all Mrs MacBain said, once again eyeing up the Colonel's rather rotund figure. *Well*, she thought, *perhaps he's good with a pistol.*

'Now, what time are cocktails round here?' He strode off towards the coats room without waiting for a reply. Mrs MacBain, entirely nonplussed, motioned to a porter to deal with the Colonel's suitcase, as Thompson escorted him to the bar.

'Why don't I show you to your rooms now, Mrs Blackwood?'

Mrs Blackwood stood, and Mrs MacBain was taken aback. The woman was tiny, barely five feet, but she was beautifully dressed in a pale green travelling suit, with birds intricately embroidered in vivid colours. She leaned on a wooden cane with a carved green flower at the top. Mrs MacBain had never seen anything like it. The old woman noticed Mrs MacBain noticing it.

'Jade,' she said, holding the cane up for a closer inspection. 'It was wedding gift from my late husband.'

Mrs MacBain must have raised her eyebrows because Mrs Blackwood continued, 'Unusual, yes, but Shanghai was quite dangerous in those days, especially for a young Western woman, and he wanted me to feel I had a bit of protection as I went about my day.'

Mrs MacBain smiled but secretly wondered how effective the cane would have been, given Mrs Blackwood's petite stature. 'Well, it's beautiful. Your luggage, then?'

Mrs Blackwood indicated the two trunks at her feet. One was positively enormous, larger than Mrs Blackwood, in fact. Mrs MacBain waved for the porters, two of whom stacked the trunks then plucked them from the floor as if they weighed nothing. She caught a faint whiff of perfume as they passed by. It was at once musty and floral. She wondered briefly if that was what Shanghai smelled like.

'Will you be all right on the stairs?' asked Mrs MacBain, wondering where they could put her if she wasn't able to get to the second floor easily.

'Take no notice of this. Stairs I can manage. My house in Shanghai was five storeys and I managed them quite well.' She set off briskly.

'Well, if you're sure.' She nodded at the porters. 'You left Shanghai with Lady Annabella then?'

'Yes. I was lucky to get on the aeroplane. Sadly, I could only get two seats, so my maid had to stay in Shanghai. 'Twas a pity. It took so long to train the girl and she was quite efficient.'

'How long is the trip?' asked Mrs MacBain. She'd never left Loch Down, let alone Scotland.

'About twelve days. It's a rather tiresome trip, which involves ten overnight stops. They put everyone in the same hotel, so one does rather get to know one's travelling companions, good or bad.'

'I'd say,' murmured Mrs MacBain. She was trying to place her accent. It was quite unusual and not entirely English. But perhaps that's just what happened when one lived away from home for years. They reached the top of the stairs and to her credit, Mrs Blackwood had no trouble keeping up. 'It's just down this corridor.' They turned left and in two minutes were standing in front of a door marked *Mackintosh.*

'Here we are. I've put you in this room; it overlooks the grounds and gets morning light. Your nephew can take the room next door or across the hall.'

'Across the hall would be fine. Thank you.' She smiled sweetly again, and Mrs MacBain had a fleeting thought that her smile was more of a weapon than a welcome.

She opened the door with the key and held it open for Mrs Blackwood.

'Oh, this is lovely,' she exclaimed as she stepped in the room. 'I hadn't expected it to be so grand. Thank you.'

Mrs MacBain stood just inside the door. Being on the second floor, it wasn't the most impressive room. Cosy, certainly, but not grand. 'I'm glad you like it. It's always been one of my favourites.'

'I shall be very comfortable here.' The old woman moved to close the door, nudging Mrs MacBain towards the hall.

'If I may ask,' Mrs MacBain said hesitatingly, 'the Colonel said you and Lady Annabella got separated. How did that happen? I thought you were all together on the aeroplane?'

There was a momentary flash of irritation in her eyes and then the sweet smile replaced it. 'Ah, yes, that would be confusing.' She sighed softly. 'I don't think any of us could stand the idea of flying any longer, so we boarded a Blue Train in Marseille. The last I saw of her was at luncheon just before we arrived in Paris.' She started to close the door again.

Mrs MacBain frowned. 'How do you get separated on a train?'

There was no hiding the irritation this time. 'The journey changes to another train altogether when it reaches

Paris. Something to do with the size of the rails here in Britain, I think. At any rate, we switched cars and continued. I presumed she got lost in the station. Gard du Nord is rather larger than the station in Shanghai, so I can see how that would happen. She is awfully young to be travelling alone but I decided it was best to carry on and meet her here rather than wait in London, where we could easily miss one another.' She paused briefly, her face frozen with her unsettling smile again, a gloved hand on the door. 'Now, if you don't mind, I really do need a lie-down before luncheon. It was rather an exhausting journey with the Colonel.'

'Yes. Well, thank you. I appreciate the information. Luncheon is served from one o'clock. In the evenings, aperitifs are served in the Library from six o'clock. Dinner seating is either seven or nine o'clock. Seven usually includes children.'

The door snapped shut the moment she finished her sentence and Mrs MacBain walked swiftly towards the servants' stairs, her mind replaying the conversation. Something was deeply unsettling, but she couldn't put her finger on it.

Fergus and Mrs MacBain were in her Below Stairs Office, just off the kitchens. It had been her office when she was Housekeeper, and from this tiny room, with its dim light and the small fire, she actually ran the Abbey. It was her stronghold and she refused to give it up. But as she couldn't possibly bring a hotel guest downstairs, she used Rowan Tree on those rare occasions a hotel guest needed to speak with her in private.

'We can't keep them in the Nursery forever,' said Fergus. They were discussing what to do with the children.

'At least Angus brought their Nanny. We don't really use the Nursery much these days, so I'm not bothered. As long as Nanny keeps them under control, that is.' Mrs MacBain paused, thinking about it, and then continued, 'When is Bella due? Do we know?'

'Bella?' Fergus gave a sardonic laugh. 'Ha! You honestly think Bella's going to take charge of the children?'

'Well, they are her children.' Her tone was far from convincing.

'And she couldn't get away from them fast enough the first time around. She's not about to turn maternal now.' Fergus sighed heavily. 'Poor things. How must it feel to be abandoned by both of your parents?'

They were quiet as they contemplated this. Shaking her head, Mrs MacBain said, 'Regardless, have we heard anything from her?'

'No.' Fergus shook his head. 'I'm sure it's exactly as Mrs Blackwood said. She missed the connection and she'll be on the next train.'

'Perhaps.' Mrs MacBain didn't look convinced. 'It's very curious. I can't see her in a hurry to come home but Bella would have howled the station to the ground if she'd missed her train. All of Paris would have heard if there had been trouble.'

Fergus shrugged. 'True enough.'

Mrs MacBain sighed heavily. 'I'd like to speak to the Colonel again. Something doesn't quite feel right.'

Thirty minutes later, they found the Colonel in the Billiards Room.

'We travelled out of Shanghai together. Lord Martin personally charged me with her safety, so I took her under my wing, best I could. Some rough cities for ladies on the way here. Don't get me started on Baghdad. The stories I could tell you . . .'

'Yes, I'm sure you could,' said Mrs MacBain, 'but might we get back to Lady Annabella?'

'Oh! Right.' The Colonel looked a bit put out at being cut off. 'When we landed in Athens, half the party boarded the Orient Express and made their way back. Not many last-minute seats available, so the rest of us travelled on to Marseilles to board the Blue Train. I joined Lady Annabella on the train myself. I was due in London, for business, you see, but after the trouble with her maid, I felt it was my duty to get them back to Loch Down, safe and sound.'

'Her . . . *maid*?' Fergus dared to hope it was simply one maid. 'Just the one?'

'There was trouble?' asked Mrs MacBain.

'Yes, poor thing. Robbed by a street thug – Marseilles can be very dangerous – and in the tussle, she broke her wrist. Not much use as a Lady's Maid with only one arm. I have a few business associates in Marseilles, so I was able to sort out a doctor for her and push the ticket reservations back a day or two.'

'And Mrs Blackwood waited as well?' Mrs MacBain was puzzled. That bit confused her.

'Yes, she was very concerned about Lady Annabella travelling alone and insisted on staying in Marseille with her. Jolly loyal of her but entirely unnecessary. Women that age tend towards busybody.' He lined up a shot, and after great aim, failed to hit a single ball on the table.

'Yes,' said Mrs MacBain slowly. 'And yet, neither of you waited for her in London.'

The Colonel cleared his throat nervously. 'Ah yes, that would have been a sensible thing to do. Well, what's done

is done.' He lined up another shot, and then, thinking better of it, straightened and addressed Mrs MacBain. 'Any
chance I can get kedgeree for breakfast in the morning?'

The rest of the day passed without incident and that evening,
after dinner, Lady Georgina cobbled together a foursome
for bridge, as she did most evenings. Angus detested the
game and did all he could to avoid playing.

When they arrived in the Drawing Room, Lady Georgina
partnered the newest arrival, Mrs Blackwood, and they sat
down to the table with Lord Iverson and his sister, Lady
Buxton. Brother and sister were a poor pairing at cards, but
quite lucrative, so Lady Georgina never missed the chance
to play against them. Angus watched the first rubber and
then, bored, drifted to the footman who was pouring drinks.
It was a traditional tray of sherry, port, whisky, whisky and
soda, or whisky and water. He sighed. When he left Loch
Down, he'd stopped drinking altogether. He spent his days
dealing with the children, so Hugh could concentrate on his
writing. It didn't take long for Angus to realise the children
were easier to deal with if he wasn't hungover, so he went
teetotal. Without his family to deal with, it hadn't been difficult to give up.

The footman cleared his throat gently, and Angus took a
whisky. He drifted to the window.

Lifting the whisky to his nose, he sniffed gently. Much as
he hated to admit it, the whisky had improved tenfold under
the leadership of Ross MacBain. He swirled a glass, gazing
at the colour. Even that had improved. Plaid Whisky, as it
had been known under Angus's tenure, had always been

an uncomfortable shade of orange. Holding a dram again brought back all sorts of uncomfortable thoughts.

What if I'd listened to Fergus instead of Father? If I'd spent more time in the Distillery, would I have changed things? If we'd replaced old MacTavish sooner, would we still have the Abbey? Would Father have let me?

But he'd never know. It was yet another thing his brother had got right, that he, Angus, had got very wrong. He felt a surge of enmity towards his brother. Angus downed the whisky in one and walked to the drinks tray to grab another. He looked in on the cards again – Lady Georgina had a satisfied look; the Blackwood woman must be a capable partner – and headed to the Billiards Room. Perhaps there was more life there.

Thirteen Days to the Ball

The following morning, Lockridge, Head Chauffeur, had just arrived from the station with the guests who had come on the overnight sleeper from London. Mrs MacBain hurried to the Armoury. As much as she was hoping Bella was among them, she was more excited for the arrival of another. Stepping through the green baize door, she smiled at the bustling scene.

As expected, it was full of commotion, with people and porters, bags and trolleys. Sounds of hunting dogs came from the open door and one of the younger porters passed by with a large birdcage. But, in the middle of all the activity, stood her quarry: Lady Elspeth. Mrs MacBain made her way through the chaos and smiled warmly.

'Lady Elspeth, I'm delighted you could join us.'

Lady Elspeth was another of the Inverkillen family. Lady Georgina's only daughter, she lived in France with her husband and children.

Elspeth turned at the sound of her name and a smile crossed her face. 'I wouldn't have missed it for all the world! A Highland Ball at the Abbey! I never thought I'd see the day. Has the Abbey ever hosted one before?'

The women embraced lightly. They'd become quite close in the years since Mrs MacBain had taken over the Abbey. In fact, Elspeth had been very supportive, sending many of her friends to stay.

'As far as we know, only one ball has ever been held,' replied Mrs MacBain. 'Hosted by the Tenth Countess of Inverkillen.'

'Lady Morag?' Elspeth was agog. Lady Morag was the only woman in family history to have had her portrait painted and displayed in the Abbey. But since it had been done in the 1600s, no one had ever been sure what she had done to have earned such an honour. 'How amazing. This is truly an historic event!'

Mrs MacBain smiled demurely.

'Will Iris be joining? I've so been looking forward to seeing her.'

Iris Kettering was half-sister to Angus, Fergus and Bella. For years, she'd lived in the Abbey as a ward of the family, before her true parentage was discovered. It hadn't gone over well with some of the family members, and Lady Georgina had to order them to accept her, which some had done only grudgingly. Elspeth, however, had been delighted, and embraced her new niece enthusiastically.

'No, she won't be, unfortunately,' said Mrs MacBain, sidestepping a small child on a tricycle. 'Mr Kettering had unexpected business in, erm . . . Sweden, I think. He won't be back until after the ball and Iris didn't want to attend alone.'

'Oh, that is a shame,' replied Lady Elspeth.

Mrs MacBain glanced around. 'No children?' she asked, surprised to see Elspeth alone. Elspeth always brought her children when she visited.

'Delphine's taken them to the Nursery.' Delphine was Elspeth's eldest daughter. Just seventeen, she wasn't out yet, but Elspeth had decided to bring her to the ball regardless. 'I've come as early as I dared, so I can help. I know how much work a ball can be.'

Lady Elspeth looked around the Armoury and then leaned in, whispering to Mrs MacBain. 'Is Mama being unbearable?'

Mrs MacBain hesitated, groping for an answer. Lady Georgina had been trying to take charge and it was causing no end of grief.

'I'll take that as a yes.' Elspeth smiled knowingly. 'Well, I'll do what I can to mitigate her meddling.'

'Actually, there is one thing I might need some help with.' Mrs MacBain signalled to a nearby footman for tea to be brought to them in her office. They picked their way across the chaos of the Armoury. Closing the door behind them, the din faded away and they settled into the sofas by the fireplace. 'Angus is back.'

'The Prodigal returns. How wonderful!' Elspeth responded, surprise in her voice. She scanned Mrs Mac-Bain's face. 'Unexpectedly, I gather.'

The tea arrived and they waited for the footman to leave before continuing.

'It seems there's been a sudden and acrimonious parting of the ways between the boys.' Mrs MacBain readied the tea while recounting Angus's tale of woe. Elspeth listened quietly, letting her expressions comment on the events.

'Well,' said Elspeth as she accepted the delicate china cup, 'Angus can't be entirely faultless in this fiasco – I am well aware of his flaws – but, it does seem Hugh has most of the blame to shoulder.' She took a sip of tea. 'You've changed to Oolong?'

They sat for some moments sipping meditatively.

Elspeth shook her head and sighed, irritated at the entire situation. 'Angus should have known better than to rely on someone else for his financial well-being. He's clearly learned nothing. But the children – how could Hugh be so beastly?' She lifted the silver spoon and stirred her tea absent-mindedly. 'I presume Hugh's parents will step up and take the children?'

Mrs MacBain looked up in surprise. 'Oh, you've not heard!'

Elspeth stopped stirring. She didn't like the sound of it. 'Heard?'

'They've gone. Sold the Estate and moved abroad.'

'What? When?'

'A few months ago.'

'Mama never said a thing!'

'That's surprising; she was furious with them, and none too quiet about it.'

'What happened?'

'They were going on a long trip abroad and had the staff shutter the house. A week or two later, Lawlis came round, announced they'd sold the Estate and then paid the staff a week's wages before letting them go.'

Elspeth gasped. 'Only a week's wages?' She was shocked by the very idea.

'A summer wage at that.'

Elspeth was horrified. Wages for the staff were generally quite low when they lived in, but during the summers, when the family was abroad, it was customary to pay almost nothing but room and board.

'We took on as many as we could, of course,' said Mrs MacBain, 'but several have had to leave the village to go find work. It's been devastating.'

'I can't believe Mama made no mention of it. What a blow to the village.' She huffed a moment. 'And the house has been empty ever since?'

Mrs MacBain nodded her head wearily. 'Yes.'

'But . . .' Elspeth was shocked. 'Where did they go? And why? And who bought the place and where are they? Who are they? I can't believe it's just sitting there empty.'

'That's the mystery of it all. No one's come forward to claim ownership for some months and nothing's being done to maintain it.'

'So Hugh abandons his children while his parents abandon their Estate, and their staff, and the village?' Elspeth sipped pensively. 'I've never liked the Dunbar-Hamiltons, but this is quite beyond the pale. And now Angus is stuck here with Hugh and Bella's children? How extraordinary.'

'Well, that's the other thing.' Mrs MacBain hesitated. Elspeth felt her stomach lurch. 'Bella's on her way back to Loch Down.'

Elspeth thought about this a moment. 'Yes, well, given the news in that part of the world these days, it was bound to happen. Any idea when she's arriving?'

'That's the thing; she should be here already.'

Elspeth drew breath to speak and then thought better of it. She tilted her head, confusion washing over her.

Mrs MacBain explained the situation. 'She arrived in Paris, that much we know, but no one's seen her – or heard from her – since. Others from the Consulate arrived here, so she should be here by now.'

'That is worrying,' said Elspeth pensively.

'I have enough on my mind without chasing Bella, but it weighs on me.' She hesitated. 'Do you have friends in Paris?'

'Yes, of course I do.' Elspeth looked surprised but could feel where the conversation was going.

Mrs MacBain took a deep breath. 'Can I ask a favour? Could you get in touch and see if anyone has seen her?'

Elspeth shook her head. 'I'd be happy to, but everyone I know will have gone to their summer homes by now. Paris is quite empty in August.'

Mrs MacBain grimaced at the setback. 'Right. Well, I'm sure she'll turn up.'

There was a knock at the door and a footman poked his head into the room. 'Sorry to intrude, but Mr Thompson has asked for you.'

Mrs MacBain nodded and set her teacup on the silver tray. 'No rest for the weary.'

Elspeth watched her go and then nestled back into the sofa cushion. Mrs MacBain's hunches were generally sound, so if she was worried, Elspeth was as well. After another cup of tea, she made up her mind. If Bella didn't turn up by the end of the week, Elspeth would head to Paris herself.

It was quite late that evening, and Fergus was looking forward to going home. But Lockridge had gone, rather unexpectedly, to fetch guests from the last train, so Fergus agreed to wait with the Night Clerk and help settle them into rooms. As Fergus entered the Armoury, a voice filled the air.

'Nephew! How very well met!'

Fergus shuddered involuntarily. He had but one uncle.

'Uncle Cecil,' he said coldly.

Major Cecil Ogilvy-Sinclair glided across the room, his eyes cataloguing the changes to the Abbey, until he arrived in front of Fergus. 'All looks very successful and prosperous. My congratulations.'

Fergus stared at his uncle. They hadn't seen one another since the auction two – no, three – years ago, when Cecil ran off with Fergus's fiancée. *Time really does fly,* thought Fergus.

'I hear felicitations are in order.' He looked his nephew up and down appraisingly and picked an invisible hair from Fergus's lapel before straightening the flower in his button-hole. 'Being a papa suits you.'

'What? Oh yes, thank you.' Fergus sputtered. 'What are you doing here?'

'How could I possibly miss your first ball? I'd have stayed with Mama in Thistledown Cottage, but I wouldn't like to crowd her.'

Fergus was nonplussed. 'She has eight bedrooms.'

'Exactly. Positively bijou. No, I thought we'd all be more comfortable if I were in the Abbey. I presume you have room for your *oncle préféré*?' He sailed to the registration desk without waiting for an answer.

Fergus bristled and then followed him. *Who else is going to descend on us unannounced?* he wondered irritably.

Cecil presented a rather unassuming gentleman. 'May I present Mr Joshua Rosenthal, from New York. We met at Claridge's in London and when I told him about the Abbey, he simply had to see it.'

'I hope it's not too much trouble,' he said with an out-rageous American accent. 'I was under the impression we were expected.' The man was polite, nearly apologetic.

'It's not a problem, sir. If you'd like to sign the regis-ter here?' the Night Clerk responded, busying himself with settling Mr Rosenthal and leaving Fergus to deal with his uncle.

'How long will you be staying?' Fergus asked.

'Oh, I'm not sure,' Cecil replied breezily. 'When one travels this far, it feels as if one should stay awhile. Perhaps two or three weeks?'

'And will Mrs Ogilvy-Sinclair be joining you?' The emphasis on *Mrs* was bitter and Fergus regretted it instantly.

It was Cecil's turn to bristle. 'Ah, no.' He shifted uncomfortably and cleared his throat. 'Eva is staying London to fulfil some, erm . . . social obligations. Charity boards, that sort of thing. I'll be unfettered.'

The Night Clerk glanced up from his work and noted immediately that Cecil was lying. *He must be a lousy cards player*, he thought. Shaking his head slightly, he signalled to a porter. 'Thomas will show you to your rooms, Mr Rosenthal. Enjoy your stay.'

'Thank you.' He glanced around the Armoury and then mounted the stairs. 'See you at breakfast, Major?'

Cecil nodded and turned back to his nephew and smiled tightly.

'Right, two weeks.' He flipped through the reservation book. 'Yes, your old rooms are free.' He handed Cecil a pen to sign the guest book.

Cecil looked at his nephew, halfway to affronted. 'Haven't you anything on the family floor?' When they'd lived in the Abbey, the first floor had been reserved for the family bedrooms, the second floor for guests, not that they ever had any. It had always been a sore spot that Cecil's rooms had been on the second floor.

Fergus sighed irritably and flipped through the book again. 'I can put you in the Farquharson Suite.' Cecil raised a questioning eyebrow. 'Angus's old rooms.'

'Oh! Oh yes, that will be fine. Thank you.'

'We'll require payment in advance.'

'What?' Cecil was outraged. 'I never—'

Fergus stared at his uncle. Thompson stared at his boss, his eyebrows up to his hairline. He quietly shuffled backwards until he felt the hidden door to the back hallway, and then exited quickly. The Inverkillen family shouting matches were infamous in the village, and he had no desire to be involved in one.

'It's highly unusual for a gentleman to have to pay in advance. I'm hardly likely to disappear into the night.' Cecil was whispering angrily, his eyes darting around to be sure no one heard the exchange. 'I am family, after all.'

'You can always bunk with Grandmama.'

Uncle and nephew stared at one another for some moments, Cecil huffing softly. At last, he relented. 'Fine.' He reached for his wallet and Fergus readied his bill. When it was presented to Cecil, he merely stared at it. 'That can't possibly be correct.'

Fergus remained silent.

'For a week?' Cecil sneered. 'It's hardly The Dorchester.'

Fergus shot his uncle a warning glance.

'I had rather expected some sort of a, erm, family concession.'

'If you can't afford that I can always put you in your old rooms, which are far cheaper.' He said it loudly, which caused Cecil to blanch.

'Keep your voice down! I'm simply surprised you can get that much for a room here.' He counted the cash in his leather wallet. Fergus could see his uncle's growing unease and prepared a second bill, placing it without comment on the desk.

Cecil sighed and placed several notes on the desk and mustered as much dignity as he could, placing the wallet back in his coat. 'Let's call it a pique of nostalgia.'

'Yes, let's.' Fergus handed a key to the porter. 'The Serramuir Rooms, please, Ollie.'

As they stepped away, Fergus sighed heavily, staring across the Armoury. 'I shan't charge you for food and drink.'

Cecil froze for a moment, his back to his nephew. He turned his head back only enough to utter a soft thank you and then continued up the right-hand staircase to the guest floors.

Twelve Days to the Ball

The following morning was bright and crisp. Lady Elspeth stopped on the threshold of the Boot Room and took a deep breath. It was always good to be back in Loch Down. The air was sweeter, cooler than in France, and it felt more peaceful. She had just finished breakfast and wanted to get a walk in before the work for the ball began. She set out, happily humming a nonsensical tune. She wasn't the musician in the family.

When she reached the old, gnarled hawthorn tree she'd christened Sir Knotty when she was a child, she took a moment to savour the view. Of all the views here, this was her favourite, overlooking the Estate, down to the village and out over the loch. Just as she was about to leave, she noticed a puff of smoke from a clutch of trees to her left. She studied the area carefully and realised that it was near the bothy where she and Ross met in secret.

Ross MacBain, Head Distiller of Inverkillen Whisky, was the cousin of Mrs MacBain, and had been raised on the Estate with Elspeth and her brothers. He was, and always would be, the love of her life. When she came to Loch Down for visits, they met in the bothy after tea each afternoon. But today, it was barely nine o'clock. Why on earth would he be there that early? She scuttled down the hill as quickly as she could.

Forty minutes later, she was just coming up to the clearing where the bothy stood. She secreted herself behind a tree and observed for a few moments. The smoke had all but stopped. She didn't see any movement inside. There was only the single room, impossible for anyone to hide. The door was closed, and she started to creep up to the window. When a pigeon hooted, she nearly jumped out of her skin. She chided herself for being ridiculous. It was the middle of the day, what did she think was going to happen? Taking a deep breath and shaking her head, she walked to the door and opened it.

It was empty. She surveyed the room. The remains of a fire smouldered. Someone had clearly been here, and not so very long ago. She stepped in and studied the table. It had crumbs and scraps of food on it. Neither she nor Ross would have left it in that state, so it had to be someone else. Didn't it? But how could that be? No one – no one! – knew about the bothy except Ross and Elspeth. It had been their secret meeting place for decades. Elspeth walked to the fireplace and lifted an empty bottle of whisky. It was Ross's private blend, which no one knew about but her. It was named after her and he only drank it when they were together. She set it back down, puzzled, and then turned to leave. She stopped dead in her tracks. The bed that stood in the corner, their bed, was unmade. It had clearly been slept in.

Elspeth was in shock. She stumbled out the door and started walking in a daze.

It simply cannot be, she told herself. *There has to be another explanation.*

But try as she could, she couldn't come up with one. If only she and Ross knew about the bothy, then whoever had been there had been brought there by Ross. She had no right to demand it, of course, but she never thought Ross would stray. They were devoted to one another, weren't they? Then again, she had no idea what he got up to when she was in France. *With my husband*, she thought, and slowed her pace.

When the Distillery came into view, she stopped to look at it. They had smartened it some, repaired the roof at least, so nothing was growing out of it, but largely it looked as it had her whole life. The water wheel turned slowly in the river. The white paint looked a bit weatherworn. The Scotch pines formed a dark green backdrop. She walked a bit further and perched on a rock, warming herself in the sunlight.

What did she know about Ross's life when she was in France? Very little. They never spoke about the time they were apart. It made the distance between them all too real. But here, it seemed, was evidence of his life without her. Perhaps he was tiring of her, tired of waiting for her to find an excuse to visit. What if he wanted someone closer, some-one he could share his day with, someone he could plan a future with? Elspeth was none of those things.

She'd never really thought about their relationship from his point of view. She breezed in, stayed as long as she could, but then left without an idea of when she'd be back.

Of course he has someone else, she scolded herself. *Why shouldn't he? Men have needs. And those needs are more urgent than three or four times a year.*

Honestly, had she learned nothing from a lifetime in France?

Slowly, she rose from the sunny rock, turned her back on the Distillery, and walked towards the Abbey.

Ten Days to the Ball

A couple of mornings later, Mrs MacBain was on her way to see if Bella had arrived on the sleeper. It was getting tiresome to be worrying about her constantly. *Is this what motherhood is like?* she wondered. She opened the green baize door slowly and looked about the Armoury. As it always was when the sleeper arrived, the room was polite chaos. Her eyes swept the room for Bella and suddenly stopped on a man. She had never seen such a large figure. He made the woman beside him, presumably his wife – or maybe daughter? She was awfully young – well, he made her positively tiny by comparison. Stepping into the Armoury, she glanced around the room, shook her head and proceeded to the desk. *Where is MacPherson?* They always had two clerks in the mornings.

While Thompson was busy with another guest, the giant man drummed his fingers on the desk absent-mindedly and glanced around the room. Mrs MacBain stepped behind the desk and smiled up at the man.

'May I help?' she asked politely.

'Ah, yes please. Mr and Mrs Alistair Cooper. We have a reservation.'

'Welcome to Loch Down.' She opened the leather reservations book and searched for their name. She didn't recall them on the list of guests arriving today.

'We're a few days early, I'm afraid. Will that be a problem?' Mrs Cooper smiled sweetly at her. 'We were on our way to the Far East and had to change our plans.'

'Oh, yes, you would have to, wouldn't you?' said Mrs MacBain politely. 'Where have you come from?'

'We were in Paris,' said the woman. 'It's my first time abroad. It was swimmingly romantic. Have you been?'

Mrs MacBain smiled at the woman. She was little more than a girl, really, but she liked her. 'No, I'm afraid I've not been. Ah, here's your reservation. Yes, we have you in the Stuart Suite, which is—' she flipped a few pages back '—free. If you could just sign here, please?' She passed a pen, and the man took it, solemn and focused.

Mrs MacBain turned to Mrs Cooper. 'You said you were headed to the Far East?'

'Yes, first stop Hong Kong, and we hoped Shanghai. We're on honeymoon.'

Mrs MacBain smiled, a bit dreamy. 'A honeymoon in the Far East? How romantic.'

'See?' Mrs Cooper slapped her husband on the arm playfully. He harrumphed good-naturedly.

Turning back to Mrs MacBain she said, 'I studied Shanghai in school, back in Canada, and I've always wanted to visit. "Paris of the East" they say. So, when Alistair asked me where I wanted to go on honeymoon, it was the only place I could think about. The timing, I'll admit, wasn't ideal—' her husband looked down at her and shook his head slowly, sighing, which caused her to laugh '—but it'll make a great story for the grandchildren someday.' She placed her handbag on the desk and went to inspect the display of ceremonial daggers.

'That's wonderful, Mr Cooper, thank you.' Mrs MacBain took the pen back and signalled the porter to take the bags. 'Your first time in Scotland then?'

'Actually, yes. My grandfather hailed from the Highlands but emigrated to Canada before my father was born. Thought we'd see some of the Old Country while we're on this side of the pond.'

Mrs MacBain turned to locate the key to the Stuart Suite as she mused on the term he'd used. Old Country felt medieval, very Viking folklore. She wondered if that was most people's idea of Scotland.

Turning back, she handed him the key and wished him a pleasant stay. He started to follow the porter, hesitated and turned back. 'Did I hear you make your own whisky?'

'We do indeed. The Distillery is on the grounds, in the woods behind the Abbey.'

'Excellent, I'd love to see your operation.'

Mrs MacBain squirmed inwardly. 'Oh! Um, it's not really set up for the hotel guests, I'm afraid. It can be a bit dangerous at times. But you'll find some in your glass this evening before dinner.' She hoped that put an end to it, but Mr Cooper did not look satisfied.

Mrs Cooper linked her arm though her husband's. 'Great. We can see how it stacks up against yours.'

Mrs MacBain looked at the woman quizzically. 'Yours?'

'My husband makes whisky as well.'

Mr Cooper stiffened and shook his head. 'My grandfather brought the family recipe with him; he taught my father how to make it, and my father taught me. We've maintained as much of the authenticity as we could. Ontario is largely peatland, which is why my grandfather settled there, I suppose: reminded him of Alba.'

He pronounced the word with a nasally 'A' and it took her a moment to understand he was using the Gaelic name for Scotland. Mrs MacBain fought to keep from rolling her eyes. She feared Mr Cooper was going to be a tiresome guest. Though, not as difficult as the Colonel, certainly. She forced a smile.

'Ollie here will show you to your rooms.' She waved her arm towards the porter, who was standing with their bags.

'Thank you so much,' said Mrs Cooper. She backtracked and retrieved her handbag from the desk. 'Oh, and could you please tell Lady Annabella what room we're in?'

'Ah . . .' said the former Housekeeper tactfully, 'I'm afraid she's not arrived yet.'

'Oh, but she has; she came with us.' It was a simple statement, but she could see the impact it had on Mrs MacBain. 'We met her on the sleeper. Could have knocked me over with a feather when she said she was coming here.'

'Oh!' exclaimed Mrs MacBain. She groped inwardly for a moment and drew breath to speak when Mr Cooper called to his wife.

'Darling.' He was on the stairs, holding his hand out expectantly.

Mrs Cooper nodded gently and turned back to Mrs Mac-Bain. 'Apparently, her usual rooms are occupied, so your clerk has taken her to look for, um . . . suitable alternatives. She's very concerned about the size of her bathtub.'

Mrs MacBain looked at the woman and noted the merriment in her eyes. As she joined her husband on the stairs, Mrs MacBain felt it was hard not to like the woman.

Bella was settling into her rooms, soaking in a hot bath. Not her usual rooms, they were occupied until the end of the week, but rooms she agreed to accept until hers were vacated. It had taken MacPherson twenty minutes to convince her.

Sadie, the Head Housekeeper, was folding Bella's travelling suit.

'I can't abide to see that suit again,' Bella announced, as she slipped into her bath. 'Find me something else to wear and get rid of it.'

Sadie wasn't sure what to do about finding her something to wear. Did Lady Annabella keep a wardrobe here for her infrequent visits? No one had ever informed her of that. 'Shall I have it repaired, milady?'

'You can burn it for all I care. If I never see it again, it shan't be missed.'

Sadie stared at the suit. It was dirty, that much was true, and there were some repairs that needed to be made but they were minor. It was a perfectly fine suit still. *And such lovely fabric.*

'And the hat too. I have a sore spot on my head from where that flower was. I'm sure I left a few dresses on my last trip. Ask Mrs MacBain where they are.' Bella turned on the hot tap again and started humming. 'I'll need shoes, too!' she shouted as Sadie slipped from the room.

'Yes, madam.' Sadie nodded and closed the door behind her. She looked down at the suit again. It was a very nice suit; she was tempted to keep it for herself.

Honestly Sadie, she thought, *where are you going to wear a suit like this?*

She wondered what to do with it and then remembered Mrs Douglas, the vicar's wife, was always gathering things for the poor. Maybe she could find a home for it. Sadie looked up and took in Bella's maid.

The poor thing was dirty, dishevelled, and had one arm in a sling. She was standing against the wall, staring at a portrait of the sixth Earl.

'Oh dear,' Sadie said after a moment, 'looks to me like you could use a bath and a clean set of clothing more than your mistress does.'

The girl startled visibly, and then simply stared at the floor, silent.

'Right then,' she said in a clipped fashion, 'let's get you cleaned up and then I can find Mrs MacBain.'

More silence.

'Come with me,' Sadie said slowly, and pushed through the green baize door, up to the servants' quarters.

She was showing the girl her room when she realised two things in quick succession.

Firstly, the girl had nothing to wear but the robe – or was it a dress? Dress wasn't quite right – well, whatever it was she was wearing, it was the only thing she had to wear. Sadie sized up the girl, hoping to fetch her a uniform from the livery. She wondered if she could fashion a new sling from one of the aprons.

Secondly, and more worrying, was the fact she didn't speak English. Not a single word. That was going to be a Big Problem. Pantomime can only get you so far, especially in a busy hotel. They simply didn't have time to play charades every time Lady Annabella wanted something. And Lady Annabella, she recalled, constantly wanted things.

How the girl was going to manage with only one arm, well, that was one problem too many for the moment. *Get the girl bathed and into clean clothes*, Sadie told herself, *then find Mrs MacBain and get Lady Annabella something to wear*. Thankfully, Bella was renowned for lengthy baths. She'd have at least an hour.

Mrs MacBain was in two minds about Bella's arrival. The girl was safe; that was good. She had only one maid with her, which was more than they dared hope for; but the lack of clothing and a maid who couldn't speak English, well, that was just going to make trouble for everyone. She sent Sadie to clean and dress the maid, and said she'd take care of Bella herself.

Ten minutes later, Mrs MacBain and one of the hall boys were in the attic, sorting through the family trunks, trying to find Bella something to wear. After considerable effort and far too much dust – *I must get someone up here to clean* – they'd succeeded in finding some of her old clothes. She'd left them when she married and moved to Shanghai. *They'll do nicely*, she thought.

'I can't wear these! They're ages old!' gasped Bella, in Sadie's dressing gown, flicking through the clothing on the bed. 'And hopelessly out of fashion. Surely, I left some dresses here last time I visited.'

'I'm afraid this is all I can find, milady. They aren't so bad, are they? You used to wear this one frequently and it always looked so lovely on you.' Mrs MacBain held up a pale blue evening gown.

'I can't believe I used to wear this.' She looked disdainfully at what had once been her favourite evening dress. The colour was good at least.

'Try it on.' Mrs MacBain held out the dress and gave Bella a motherly look.

'Fine.' Bella slipped behind a dressing screen. 'Do you know, I had a new dress every single day in Shanghai. The seamstresses there are frightfully quick.'

'Is that so?' murmured Mrs MacBain, looking out the window and noticing the pond was a bit overgrown. She mentally added it to her never-ending To-Do List.

'No. No, this will never work.' Bella emerged, swathed in blue silk. 'It looks like I grabbed it from the dressing-up box.'

She was right. The gown hung limply on Bella, clearly a size – if not two – too large. Bella shifted slightly and the left strap fell down her arm.

'Oh dear,' tutted Mrs MacBain. 'Well, try on this day dress. It's not as fitted.' She handed a pale grey wool dress to Bella.

'Oh god, did I really wear such dowdy things?' She looked horrified. 'I can't. I'll be a laughing stock.'

'Well, it's this or your travelling suit, I'm afraid. Until Madam Elodie can get you something, I suppose.' Madam Elodie was the local seamstress. She was very good but speed was granted as a favour.

Bella sighed and stepped behind the screen. 'Where's my maid?'

'Sadie's getting her bathed and then dressed in a maid's uniform.'

'No!' Bella's head shot out from behind the screen. 'I don't want her in the hotel livery.'

'But her clothes are filthy. She needs something clean to wear and apparently, that's all she has.'

'Well, she can wash it herself, then.'

'With one arm?'

'Just get her something to wash with.' Bella was entirely unsure what equipment was necessary, but surely Mrs Mac-Bain would. 'And she'll be staying in my dressing room, not in the servants' wing. Can you bring her a mat or cushion or something to sleep on?'

'You want her to sleep on the floor of your dressing room?' Mrs MacBain had never heard of such a thing.

'She's used to it. It's how it's done in Shanghai. But she will need a mat of some sort. And a blanket, I suppose.

Although, with this heat, that might not be necessary. Can you arrange that?'

Mrs MacBain shook her head in frustration. *I'm not your servant and this is not your house anymore,* she wanted to shout. But she kept quiet and took several deep calming breaths. 'As you wish, milady.'

Bella re-emerged from behind the screen, wearing the wool dress, which resembled a lumpy sack more than a dress, even with the belt. 'Perhaps I'll ask our new maid to come up. She was a Lady's Maid before she came to us. A pinch here, a tuck there . . .' but she knew the dress would never fit as Bella wished. Wool wasn't silk and all Bella seemed to wear was silk.

Bella nodded mutely, staring at the clothes, one evening gown and two day dresses, all tweed and wool in muted Highland colours. Even the evening dress was drab by comparison to her Shanghai wardrobe. Well, she only had to manage until things started arriving from Paris.

Mrs MacBain went in search of Sadie. Bella hadn't been back an hour and she was already causing headaches for them. Maybe once she settled in, things would get easier. She chuckled at the thought.

'Ah, Sadie, there you are,' she said, entering the servants' dining room. 'Do you have the maid's clothing?'

Sadie was mending a pair of gloves. She shook her head. 'No, she refused to let me take them for laundry. I gave her the maid's uniform, but she wouldn't have it. She just got more and more upset. I wasn't sure what to do, frankly, so I left her in one of the bedrooms.'

Mrs MacBain's brow furrowed. 'Lady Annabella is insistent that she is not put in the hotel livery, why I cannot say. She wants the girl to wash her clothes herself.'

Sadie snorted derisively. 'With one arm?'

Mrs MacBain rolled her eyes. 'She wouldn't let it go. The girl's to stay in Bella's rooms, not the servants' quarters, and we're to take something to her so she can sleep on the floor.'

Sadie's head snapped up. 'On the floor?!' Even the family dogs, Grantham and Belgravia, slept in beds.

'It's how they do it in Shanghai, apparently.' Mrs Mac-Bain sighed. 'This is a battle I do not have time for. Can you get to the laundry and ask them for something that you can take to the girl?'

Sadie stood and nodded. 'I'll take care of it, Mrs MacBain.'

'Thank you.' She wandered off muttering about a one-armed maid doing laundry.

It was a new way of entering a room for Bella, trying not to be noticed.

How does one become invisible? she wondered.

In Shanghai, she was always the woman to watch. Bella had grown used to the room stopping when she entered. Being the wife of a prominent diplomat made her something of a celebrity, she supposed. But she had no wish for that here, *especially wearing this.* Bella stopped before the final stair, took a deep, strengthening breath, pulled her shoulders back, and entered the Armoury.

'Bella!' a voice rang out.

She cringed as Fergus came towards her, arms out-stretched, relief etched across his face. Several of the guests looked up and Bella could feel the judgement from the women.

I should have had a tray in my rooms, she thought.

'Hello, Fergus.' She tilted her head and leaned forward slightly.

Fergus stared at her; she seemed to be waiting for some-thing. After a heartbeat, when nothing happened, she bris-tled slightly, and huffed, 'How've you been?'

Fergus had decided to have a special dinner for the family, to welcome both his siblings back to the Abbey. As he escorted her to the Green Drawing Room, he chatted amiably. She gathered there had been a baby and he was exhausted but beyond delighted. The hotel was busier than ever. Something about Grandmama's roses . . . she wasn't really listening, in truth. She was watching the looks of the other guests as they passed by.

Oh, to have the earth open and swallow me whole!

'Here we are. Look who's turned up!' Fergus chirped.

A new dread replaced her sartorial woes. There, in the Drawing Room, were nearly all the members of her family. They were having sherry and whisky and waiting to be called to dinner, just as they had done every evening of her life.

It's bad enough to be back, she thought bitterly, *but having to eat together as well?*

'Bella!' cried Lady Georgina with obvious, but momen-tary delight. She looked Bella over from head to toe and then scowled.

'Hello, Grandmama. Auntie Elspeth.' She leaned over to dutifully kiss Lady Georgina on the cheek.

'Oh!' she cried, surprised to see Angus. They hadn't seen one another since Bella left the Abbey. 'It's the home-wrecker.'

Angus glared at his sister. 'Rich coming from the mother who abandoned her children.'

'Now, now,' chided Lady Georgina, 'you've not seen one another for some time. Let's try to be pleasant. Now Bella, what on earth are you wearing? You look like a monk in a cassock.'

Bella accepted a glass of sherry that Fergus was holding out for her, wishing desperately she was still in Paris. 'Mrs MacBain found some of my old things for me to wear.' She looked down at her dress and sighed. 'This was the best of the lot.'

'Why are you wearing your old things?' Lady Georgina asked, mystified.

'Because the only thing I have with me is my travelling suit.'

Lady Georgina was confused. 'What do you mean? What's happened to your luggage?'

'I have no luggage. Everything was lost en route, so I have absolutely nothing to wear.'

'How does one lose trunks while travelling?' asked Elspeth, baffled by the idea of it. She'd travelled a few times by aeroplane, and it had been quite straightforward. 'Surely the aeroplane staff is responsible for it's safekeeping.'

'They didn't lose it, it was stolen.'

'Stolen?' Lady Georgina exclaimed. Even Angus looked startled. 'But how did they manage to take all your cases without being noticed?' The only person who packed more than Bella for a trip was Cecil, and Cecil's rule of thumb was two cases per day, minimum.

Bella looked pained. 'Wretched company. To start with, we were only allowed a single case per person.' The room was outraged.

One case? But that's barely enough to get by a day. How does one even pack in a single case? My gloves alone take up a single case. I've never heard of anything so miserly.

'They didn't even bother to notify us in advance, so naturally, I showed up with all my bags and trunks, and they refused to allow me to board. They simply would not allow me additional cases. So disrespectful of them. I am the wife of the Consul-General; I should have been allowed more luggage than a mere secretary,' Bella continued. She glanced awkwardly at Imogen, who was a mere secretary. 'It took some doing, but I finally managed to convince them to allow me two cases plus my handbag. They counted my cosmetics case as luggage, if you can believe that!'

Someone tutted loudly.

'I boarded and left my maid to repack a case for me on the tarmac.'

'But, if you were only allowed one case,' asked Fergus, confused, 'and they counted your cosmetics case as yours—'

'Well, my maid hardly needed a case. Edmund paid for the tickets; I should have had that allowance as well. But of all the cases we took to the aeroport, she grabbed the suitcase of swimming costumes, stupid girl. I didn't know until we arrived in the first hotel, and by then it was too late.'

'How many swimming costumes does one need?' queried Cecil. Angus shrugged, looking mystified.

'You mean to say,' breathed Lady Georgina scandalously, 'you've been wearing nothing but your travelling suit since you left – what was it – nearly a month ago?'

Bella nodded and seemed to be near tears. Cecil handed her a handkerchief. Angus lit a cigarette.

Bella sniffed softly. 'As soon as we arrived in Paris, I went straight to the dressmakers and ordered some new clothes.'

'Ha!' barked Angus. 'I knew she was shopping.'

'Yes, thank you for that brilliant insight, Angus,' Fergus said dully. 'Continue, Bella.'

Bella glared at Angus and then continued. 'But of course, the seamstresses in Paris aren't nearly as quick at the ones in Shanghai, so I'm still waiting for my clothes to arrive.'

Cecil furrowed his brow. 'But, my dear, why didn't you go to the Galeries Lafayette and just buy some clothes?'

Bella stared at her uncle in horror. 'And wear off the peg?'

'She is a diplomat's wife, Cecil,' said Lady Georgina, equally horrified, 'not some common shopkeeper.'

'Sorry!' Cecil held up his hands in surrender and backed away. 'May I?' He indicated Angus's cigarette case and helped himself. Breathing deeply, he relished the foreign-ness of the tobacco. He missed travelling. Eva refused to leave London, quoting Dr Johnson whenever the subject came up. *When one is tired of London, one is tired of life.* Cecil always felt Dr Johnson was simply too poor to travel well, and thus never did.

Fergus furrowed his brow. 'So, the bag of swimming costumes was stolen in Marseille?'

'Yes. Some guttersnipe ripped the suitcase right out of my maid's hand on the street. Broke her wrist in the process.'

'But you still have your cosmetics case?' asked Lady Elspeth cautiously. Bella didn't have a daub of colour on her face, not even lipstick.

'Actually no. Someone broke into the hotel in Paris and stole that.'

'What?' Fergus was now truly alarmed. Once was unlucky but twice was something altogether different.

'Edmund told me it was dangerous to travel alone, but really, that was quite the last straw. What if I'd been in the room? Hm?' She shuddered and then continued, 'Anyway, I telephoned you, Auntie Elspeth, hoping to come stay at the Chateau – I hadn't known about the ball – and when they told me, I came home.' Better bored than in danger, she had reasoned at the time. Now that she was back, she wasn't so sure.

'Quite right,' someone murmured.

'How did you know my suitcase was stolen in Marseille?' she asked Fergus, processing that he'd known without her mentioning it.

'Oh, Colonel Lamont told us.'

'Colonel Lamont?' Her eyes flew open in surprise. 'That crashing bore? He's meant to be in London. What's he doing here?'

Fergus looked at his sister, a knot forming in his stomach. 'He said you invited him.'

'Oh lord. There is no shaking that man.'

Fergus was confused. 'He's here at your invitation, along with Mrs Blackwood.'

Bella looked to her brother, disturbed. 'What . . . No! With that ghastly nephew of hers? I most assuredly did not invite them.'

'Her nephew hasn't arrived yet,' said Fergus. 'He's in London, on business. But she's here.'

Lady Georgina looked up. 'She's a fantastic bridge partner; our winnings are approaching scandalous levels.' No one had ever heard her so gleeful about a bridge partner. Partnering with Lady Georgina generally ended with sniping and recrimination.

'I simply can't believe it,' Bella said breathlessly. 'I mean, no one really had firm plans for arriving back in England – well, the Colonel did; Edmund ordered him to report to the Foreign Office straight away – but the Blackwoods? I simply can't understand why they'd come here. Surely, they have lives to take up elsewhere.'

Angus gulped down the last of his whisky and waved the glass pointedly at a waiter.

'Well, if you're having another, I'll have one as well,' remarked Bella, setting her glass delicately on the silver tray proffered. 'Is this all? Sherry or whisky?' She grimaced and plucked a sherry off the tray before sailing over to the sofa, taking her customary seat.

Fergus followed her across the room. 'They are here, Bella, because you invited them,' began Fergus testily, 'which put us in a tight spot for rooms, I can tell you.' Fergus hadn't slept at all the previous night. The baby had cried endlessly until birdsong. He was overreacting and he knew it, but there didn't seem much he could do about it.

'Tight spot for rooms? Two of them in, how many guest rooms do you have? Honestly, Fergus, don't exaggerate. You should have just turned them away.'

'I couldn't turn them away, now could I? They were your guests!' he shouted, bring the attention of everyone in the room. 'Guests you didn't bother to tell us were coming!'

Bella's sherry froze halfway to her mouth. She stared at her brother for a moment and then tutted. 'If I didn't know they were coming to the Abbey, dear brother, how could I have possibly warned you?'

But then, suddenly, Bella had a flash of memory. One evening in – where was it? Someplace sticky, that she remembered – lounging over a piano with a Martini in one hand, she'd said, quite drunkenly in her defence, 'You all must come with me to the Abbey. It's so dreadfully dull. Can't bear the thought of it alone.' Sweeping the rose from the buttonhole of the pianist – where had they been? Baghdad? Delhi? No, but it had been early enough to still think everyone was lively and gay – she'd said, 'Do please say you'll come back with me? All of you?' She'd tossed the rose to the audience and then rolled off the piano, crashing to the floor. Ah yes, that was how the skirt had been torn.

She blinked at her brother, coming back to the present moment. 'In my defence . . .'

'Oh my god, Bella! Who is going to pay for those rooms?'

Bella squirmed in her seat. 'In my defence, it was simply one of those things you say. Like, I don't know, "Come to dinner next week" or "Wouldn't it be lovely to take a holiday house together?" One never takes it seriously unless an invitation arrives.' She waved a hand breezily.

'Quite so,' said Angus, strolling to the terrace with a smirk on his face.

Fergus glared at his brother. 'I'll thank you to stay out of this. You will pay for their stays, Bella.'

'That's hardly fair!' she retorted.

'That is entirely fair,' said Lady Georgina sharply, placing her sherry on the table, and fixing a stern expression on her face. 'Bella, you invited them, whether you meant to or not. They are your guests, and so you shall have to pay for them.'

'But . . .' she said, eyes darting between her brother and her grandmother, neither of whom looked likely to back down. 'Fine. But I expect the family rate.' She stood and stalked across the room, out the door that Hudson was holding open.

He gently cleared his throat. 'I believe they are ready for you now.' Standing to the side of the open door, he waited as the family crossed the room for dinner, feeling as if he'd travelled back in time.

Nine Days to the Ball

Angus was staring out the window, smoking pensively. Hugh had really dropped him in it. *Bastard.* What was he going to do now? He couldn't stay at the Abbey forever; that much was certain. Well, he could, but it meant being under Lady Georgina's thumb. Or his brother's. And there was no way he was going to do that. Angus shook his head. It was an indignity he shouldn't have to suffer. *Bastard.*

The door opened and Angus turned around. Bella crept in the room.

She put her finger to her lips to shush him and then shut the door as quietly as a human could. 'The Colonel is chasing after me. Cannot bear that man.'

She crossed the room and sat on the sofa across from Angus. 'So,' she said after appraising him for some moments, 'Hugh's left you, has he?'

Angus breathed in sharply and turned his head slowly to stare at his sister. He could see the malice in her eyes. Stubbing out his cigarette – shame, he was only two puffs in – he exhaled at his sister and then moved to leave.

'Now you know how it feels!' she called after him.

Angus turned sharply and in two quick strides was back at the sofas. 'How dare you!'

'How dare I?' Bella leapt to her feet. 'How dare you! Both of you! You set me up! Sending me into a marriage that was an absolute sham.'

'You knew going in that it wasn't a love match. Besides, you never wanted a husband, you wanted a maid.'

Bella gasped and then thought it over. It was true, but she needn't admit it. 'You humiliated me, for years—'

'Which part humiliated you, exactly?' he interrupted caustically. 'The affair or that he left you for me?'

Bella gasped again, aghast at his cruelty. 'I shouldn't have had to endure either! My lord, Angus, the amount of gossip I've had to suffer because of you.'

'Please, what gossip? You were on the other side of the world! How would anyone even know?'

'How? It got down to the village and then that little guttersnipe of an editor started a gossip column with it in the *Loch Down Star*. Then the Highlands knew, and then the whole of Scotland, which meant it followed me everywhere: London, Paris, even Monte Carlo.' She cringed, remembering the whispers and tittering as she walked through dining rooms and casinos.

Ooo, is that her? I heard her husband left her, for a man, ooo . . . Her own brother at that . . . ooo . . .

'I couldn't get away from it. People kept crawling out of the woodwork, trying to befriend me; only in the hopes of salacious details, mind you. There wasn't a single person I could trust until I met Edmund.'

Angus felt a pang of remorse. He hadn't thought about the gossip. The community in Tangiers was artistic and progressive. No one batted an eye at two men living together. He and Hugh had been welcomed, warmly and enthusiastically. They were celebrated, in fact, for being quite modern and raising children together. Not that he needed to admit that to Bella.

'Well,' he said pompously, 'I had to step into the breech after you bolted. You left your children without a second thought.'

'I left them with their father!' she shouted at full volume. Her voice rang off the walls and assaulted Angus. He stared at her with wide eyes.

'I seem to remember that you couldn't get out of here fast enough,' Angus sputtered.

'Well I couldn't have stayed; that much was certain.'

'Oh please.' Angus gave her a withering look of scorn. 'Don't be so dramatic.'

'You stole my husband!!' she shouted at full volume.

'He was mine first!' Angus roared back.

Bella grabbed the ashtray and flung it at him, scattering ashes and cigarette butts in the air. Angus deftly stepped aside and let it land some distance away. He heard it bounce twice.

'Did either of you, for a single second, consider what you'd done to me? Yes, *to me*. You destroyed my life, the two of you, my entire future!' Her voice bounced off the walls again, ringing in his ears. She sat down, tears threatening to spill. 'We both know the only future for women like me is marriage. You and Hugh doomed me to a life of dependence and begging.'

The siblings were silent for a long moment.

'Well,' said Angus at long last, 'that makes two of us.'

He sat down, pulled out his cigarette case and offered one to Bella. She glared at him before slowly taking one. After he'd lit both hers and his, they exhaled in unison.

'Hugh took all our money. I barely had enough to get us back here.'

Bella's jaw dropped open. 'That bastard! How could he do that to his own children?' She exhaled slowly, watching the smoke drift through the sunshine.

'I suppose it's not surprising, not really. Hugh didn't want to take the children to Morocco in the first instance. He planned to leave them with Grandmama.'

Bella's jaw dropped open again. 'He wanted to abandon his own children?'

'I couldn't do that to her. We fought about it for days. In the end, I brought them with us, and he pouted for weeks. Then we got Nanny and things got better. But honestly, he has very little to do with them.'

Bella was surprisingly unsurprised. Hugh could be cold at the best of times. There had always been something lacking in the Dunbar-Hamiltons.

'He really left you penniless?' It was unfathomable.

Angus exhaled slowly. 'Not a sou.'

'What are you going to do?' she asked hollowly.

'No idea.'

Later that day, Mrs MacBain was presiding over afternoon tea in the Library. She was checking all was going well, nodding and smiling at the guests. It gave her a chance to catch snippets of conversations she'd otherwise not hear. While it was, technically, eavesdropping, she had always found it instrumental to keeping things running smoothly.

How else, for instance, would she have known Lord Iverson was planning on leaving a week early, simply because they ran out of his favourite wine? That would have been a significant financial loss if he had gone. Luckily, she was able to smooth it over with a complimentary bottle of his second favourite wine, which he only drank during grouse season. She'd even convinced him to take an extra weeks' stalking.

'May I have a word, Mrs MacBain?'

A small voice came from behind her, startling her slightly. She turned in surprise. 'Of course, Mrs Blackwood. How can I help you?'

'I wonder if I may request a new dining table?'

'A new table? Is there something wrong?' Mrs MacBain was concerned. The guests were assigned a table for the duration of their stay, seated with other guests, at tables of four or six. Generally, she was a good judge of character, and it was the rare instance when the guests didn't like their dining companions.

'Not wrong, no. Lord and Lady Buxton are fine. Between us, it's the Coopers.' She wrinkled her nose in dislike. 'He's fine company, but I find Mrs Cooper exhausting. She's a bit, hmm . . . new puppy, if you know what I mean. Frankly, I'm amazed she's out of the nursery, she's so young.'

Mrs MacBain thought about it. She was young, yes, but not any younger than most upper-class brides. From what she'd seen, the worst that could be said about her was she could be quite shy. 'Of course, I understand. Let me put some thought into it. We should be able to place you somewhere more suitable.'

The woman smiled coldly. 'Thank you. If it's not possible for tonight, I'll dine in my rooms this evening.' She turned and left without another word.

Mrs MacBain was flummoxed. Well, she'd have a look at the seating charts when tea was finished. Perhaps she could put her with Lord and Lady Ruthven.

She continued through the room, smiling and nodding, eventually passing Lady Georgina, who was suffering through her weekly tea with the Vicar's wife. Lady Georgina felt it was her duty, as aristocracy, a pillar of society, to been seen doing good works with Church. It had been quite an empty task prior to Reverend Douglas being married, but now . . . Mrs Douglas seemed to have no end of good works that needed doing. *How they managed before I arrived*, she was fond of asking anyone within earshot, *is anyone's guess*.

'There are so many men out of work at the moment and families that need support.'

'Mmm . . . hmm . . .' said Lady Georgina, looking around the room for the pastry cart.

'It is getting desperate for some of them, you know. We simply must do more to help.'

'Yes,' she murmured, and picked up her teacup. Her gaze wandered to the chairs nearest them, where the Duchess of Idlewilde and Lady Buxton were engrossed in conversation. She wondered what they were talking about. It looked juicy. With Mrs Douglas across from her, it was difficult to hear anything else; the woman never stopped talking.

'What was that?' She'd missed something that she felt was crucial. Last time that had happened, she'd inadvertently agreed to an afternoon of home visits in the parish. It had been four interminable hours of weak tea – in mugs no less – and ghastly cottages. At one point, a small child tried to crawl into her lap.

'I've started a collection box for donated clothing. I wondered if you had anything you might want to pass on?'

'Pass on? No. I shouldn't think I have. Nothing suitable, at least.'

'Every bit helps, you know.' Admonished the Vicar's wife.

A wry look crossed Lady Georgina's face. 'Even the best millinery can't save the world.'

There was an awkward pause as both women sipped their tea, smiling rather tightly to one another. When the cups were set down, Mrs Douglas tutted.

'Well, I must say, it's quite generous of Lady Annabella to take tea with Mrs Cooper.'

Lady Georgina's gaze followed hers. 'Whatever do you mean?' she asked, guardedly. When Mrs Douglas showed interest, good rarely followed.

'I doubt very much they have anything to say to one another. A diplomat's wife chatting with a convent girl? It will be very one-sided, I should think.'

'No, no, you're quite wrong there,' corrected Lady Georgina, waving her finger. 'Not the convent, Canada. Mrs Cooper is Canadian.'

Mrs Douglas looked at her in surprise and then reappraised the girl. 'Canadian she may be, but the Ecclesiastical air lingers.' She paused and sipped her tea. 'Yes . . . I'm sure it's the same old story.'

'Story?' asked Lady Georgina, her hackles rising.

'You know the one: an illicit affair, a child out of wedlock, and the nuns take her in to save some grand family's reputation. Happens the world over, you know. So disgraceful.'

Lady Georgina set her teacup down forcefully.

'That is quite enough, Mrs Douglas.' Lady Georgina's tone was sharp. Sharper than usual, which embarrassed Mrs Douglas, who immediately stammered apologies. 'Gossip, from the Vicar's wife? I expected better.' She didn't. She relished it, in fact. Lady Georgina stood and tossed her napkin on the table.

'I think that's enough good work for one day.' Before Mrs Douglas could reply, Lady Georgina was halfway across the room and out into the Armoury.

Mrs MacBain watched as Lady Georgina stalked out of the room, each step announcing her indignation. She glanced at the Vicar's wife, who was awkwardly sipping her tea, trying to pretend nothing had happened.

What's gone wrong there? she wondered. Well, it mattered little; she had a room full of guests to deal with. Putting it out of her mind, she re-engaged with the room.

Ten minutes later, Mrs MacBain was pouring tea for a young couple from the Borders, when her ears perked up.

'Your hotel room?' asked Mrs Cooper, eyes wide, voice scandalised.

Bella set her teacup down and looked at her companion. 'Yes. You'd think a hotel of that standard would have better security. Luckily, I was at a dress fitting when it happened. But after all the trouble on the train, you can understand why I was spooked.'

'The train?' asked Mrs Cooper, her eyes wide. Mrs MacBain wondered about that as well. She moved to a nearby sofa and picked up a cushion, plumping it slowly and silently.

'Mmm, yes,' said Bella, munching a lemon and ginger biscuit. She swept the crumbs from her lips. 'Between Marseille and Paris, my compartment was broken into. The room was thoroughly savaged. My maid had quite a time putting it back together with only one arm.'

Mrs MacBain picked up a second cushion. *Broken into? What on earth were they talking about and why couldn't they have been by the windows?* Dressing curtains could take quite a lot of time if done slowly enough.

'Wait, you mean to tell me you've been broken into twice since you left Shanghai?' Mrs Cooper was incredulous. 'I can scarcely believe it.'

Mrs MacBain couldn't believe it either. She felt sure she needed to hear more, but there were no more cushions to be plumped. Her hands fell on a potted fern.

'For a woman with scant possessions, I'm having the most deplorable luck,' lamented Bella. 'You know, this never would have happened in Shanghai. It almost makes me wish I'd never left.'

'Golly,' murmured Mrs Cooper, sipping her tea.

Golly, indeed, thought Mrs MacBain. Maid injured, bags stolen, rooms broken into. It was all too unbelievable. *Is Bella exaggerating?* she wondered. Well, she had no luggage, that was true enough. But how was Bella so blasé about it all? She'd once sacked a housemaid after the girl placed Bella's sleep mask under the wrong pillow. Something was not right.

Mrs MacBain was jolted from her thoughts by a footman discreetly waving from across the room. He needed her assistance with Mrs McCready, who'd sneaked in a flask of brandy, again. She sighed and went to his rescue.

Bella smiled at Mrs Cooper demurely. She was a great audience, which was mollifying. Bella's family hadn't been nearly so sympathetic when she related the tale to them.

'So now you have nothing to wear?'

'Not a stitch. Well, a few ragged pieces I left here, but that's all.' She waved to the dress she was wearing. 'I ordered clothes when I was in Paris, of course, but until they arrive . . .' She delicately shrugged her shoulders and took a sip of tea.

Mrs Cooper made some sympathetic noises and then scrunched up her face. She set her teacup down and looked critically at Bella. 'Well, you must borrow some things – until yours arrive, that is. Alistair was incredibly generous with my trousseau. I've never had so many lovely clothes before!'

Bella was embarrassed. She hadn't been expecting Mrs Cooper to do anything more than commiserate. 'Oh no, I couldn't possibly,' she murmured. She couldn't help but size up Mrs Cooper's dress; it was good quality, that couldn't be denied, but she did wear an awful lot of pink. 'It is incredibly kind of you, but I couldn't possibly accept.'

'Nonsense! You must have something to wear, something that fits—' she glanced at Bella's dress, which was clearly too large, despite the belt '—and I have so much with me. We're not even on honeymoon long enough to wear it all. Oh please? You must borrow a few things while you wait.'

Bella paused and tried to get over the uncomfortable feeling of charity. But then Lady Buxton passed by, wearing a green dress that was much too young for her and far too expensive for words. Bella felt a stab of jealousy, which easily overcame her misgivings.

Mrs MacBain arrived at Bella's room just after the dressing gong sounded. She knocked softly and was let in by the maid, who was wearing her garb still. It was clean at least.

'I hope I'm not interrupting. Oh!' cried Mrs MacBain.

Bella was standing on a small stool, with a woman kneeling on the floor.

'I didn't realise you were having a fitting. My apologies.' She turned to leave.

'Not at all, Mrs MacBain. Mrs Cooper lent me a dress and it's a bit long. Auntie Elspeth suggested Delphine give it a go. She's quite a whizz with the needle, apparently.'

Delphine peeked around and smiled, pins in her mouth.

'Oh, well, that's erm . . . Right. I wonder if I could have a word, Lady Annabella?'

Bella made a noise indicating she should continue.

Mrs MacBain took a deep breath. 'I overheard you speaking to Mrs Cooper at tea this afternoon. Forgive the intrusion but it sounded like someone broke into your room? Was that here?'

Delphine gasped and Mrs MacBain hoped she hadn't swallowed a pin.

'Oh, that,' said Bella lazily, 'not here, no. Someone broke into my hotel in Paris and took my cosmetics case.'

'And someone was in your train compartment as well? Do you have any idea who it could have been?'

'I presumed it was local ruffians. Edmund warned me that travel was dangerous.'

'Both your bags were stolen, your maid's arm was broken, and two of your rooms were broken into. Doesn't that concern you? I concerns me.'

Bella turned from the mirror and faced her. 'I hadn't thought of it like that. But I'm home now and I haven't anything left to steal.'

'Be that as it may, I'd feel much better if you were in a room closer to the main stairs, where the footmen can look out for you.' A footman was permanently stationed at the entry of each corridor leading off the main stairs. Mostly it was to direct the guests when they inevitably become lost, but she couldn't help now thinking about sentinels on castle walls.

'Move rooms? I'd hate to give up my bath, though.' Bella hesitated and then considered Mrs MacBain carefully. 'Do you really feel I'm in danger?'

'I don't know,' she said slowly, 'but I can't believe it's a mere coincidence that you've been robbed, broken into on several occasions, and that your maid's been hurt.'

Bella looked at her maid and then back to Mrs MacBain. Her voice wasn't quite as confident. 'Well, if you insist. My maid can pack while I'm at dinner. But I'll still need a dressing room, and the bath must be at least as big as this one.' She turned back to the mirror and adjusted a strap on the dress, blissfully unconcerned.

Mrs MacBain could have slapped her.

Dinner had been yet another exercise in bland food, bland conversation, and not nearly enough wine. Angus had forgotten how narrow the diet was here. He'd struggled to find anything with actual flavour on the menu. Roasted game, fine enough but heavy; fish in a citrus and dill sauce, quite nice now that he thought about it; the usual vegetables, slightly overdone and terribly starchy; cheese and oatcakes followed by sugary puddings. It was the same as every dinner he'd ever had in this house. *Hotel,* he checked himself. Angus was slumped in the window seat of the Drawing Room, watching the guests mingle over their sherry. He wondered how much more he could take.

Being ten o'clock, it was just dusk, and Angus could see the dahlias were in bloom. He'd forgotten about flowers. Tangiers was vibrant and colourful and loud, but it lacked the lush green of Scotland. A sigh escaped his lips. Here less than a week and he was already contemplating the flora. Life was going to be very dull here. No music, no raucous debate over politics or art or literature.

'Aren't you bored? I'm so bored. How did we do this for so long?' Bella complained to Angus. She had flopped down beside him, watching the scene in front of them.

'You've only been here two days,' sniped Angus. 'I've been here weeks.'

'Five days, according to Grandmama.'

He glared at her and then tried to remember how long it had been. Had it only been five days? It felt like he'd been here for years. Long, dreadfully dull years.

'It's so quiet. Was it always this quiet?' Bella asked. 'We need, I don't know, something. Anything to make it a bit jollier. There was never a dull evening in Shanghai, you know. People demanded to be entertained. Music, cocktails, dancing. If we weren't at the opera, we were at dazzling parties; if there wasn't a party, we were at the Club. All the women in gorgeous silk gowns, jewels sparkling in the candlelight. It was all so glamorous.' She sighed mournfully. 'And now look at us: awash in tweed and sherry.'

Angus let out a heavy sigh. 'And haggis. One would have thought MacBain would have tried to modernise when she took over; make something noteworthy, interesting even. But no, it's just the same old people, having the same dull conversations, eating the same bland food, year after year after year. Not an ounce of imagination.'

Bella glanced at him; he was awfully bitter.

Across the room, Fergus looked up from pouring sherry to an old dear and saw his siblings chatting in the window. Angus had a dark look on his face. *Oh, that looks like trouble*, he thought. *Best to nip that in the bud.*

He set down the decanter and bounded up to his siblings. 'Anyone fancy a game of charades later?'

'Oh, Fergus,' sighed Bella, sliding out of the window. 'How can you be so hopelessly entertained?'

'Honestly, Fergus, this is the dullest evening imaginable. I think I'll retire with a book.' Angus stood and placed his whisky glass on the windowsill. It wasn't even empty.

Fergus was taken aback and gaped at his brother. *Angus going to bed early, with a book?* 'But, this is what we do after dinner. What's wrong with it?'

Bella tutted. 'There's no life here. It's all so tired. Look at that scene and tell me you don't want to yawn.' She waved an arm towards the room.

Fergus turned to survey the group and saw nothing out of the ordinary. The Coopers were in the corner playing chess. Mr Rosenthal and Uncle Cecil were smoking cigars, the Colonel braying loudly at anyone who would listen. Grandmama and Elspeth were sitting by the fire chatting. Old Mrs McCready was trying to read a book that was upside down, and in Latin, if his eyesight wasn't failing. It was a normal evening.

Oh.

He didn't want to ask but the question fell out of his mouth. 'What would you suggest then?'

'Music would be a good start. It's so unnaturally quiet.' Bella could see her brother starting to object. She held up a hand to stop him. 'I'm not saying get an orchestra but someone at the piano would be an improvement.'

'Sure.' Fergus nodded. 'We could have someone at the piano. Maybe we can have a singalong.'

'Or,' suggested Angus pointedly, 'we find the old gramophone and play something that doesn't make us want to drown our sorrows.'

Bella perked up. 'We should have cocktails. Drinks with actual flavour. Or champagne, if you haven't any gin.' She looked down at her port glass and set it down with a sneer. 'This is just so musty.'

'Now hang on, you two. Most of our guests are Old Guard and they like a traditional evening.'

'Yes, but not everyone does!' cried Bella. 'And not everyone here is Grandmama's age.'

'What happens when the Old Guard dies out? Hmm? Who's coming to stay then?'

Fergus hadn't ever thought about that. It was disquieting, to say the least. The average age of their guests was firmly in the 'golden years'. What would they do?

'Look, there are dozens of rooms in this place,' continued Bella. 'Surely you can find one spare room for the livelier guests?'

It was an interesting idea, he had to admit. 'All right,' Fergus said. 'Leave it with me.'

Bella rolled her eyes, entirely unsure it was safe to leave it with him. She turned to say something to Angus, but he'd left their company. *Was he really going to bed early? What was the world coming to?*

Angus had just reached the doors to the Drawing Room when the Colonel grabbed his arm and yanked him into a group of men.

'I say, a tour would be wonderful! Shall we do it tomorrow?' He looked around eagerly, nodding to the group. 'What say you, Lord Inverkillen? Care to join?'

'Join what, Colonel?' asked Angus, letting his irritation show. He couldn't think of a single thing on the Estate that was worth touring. The man was clearly drunk.

'The Distillery of course,' answered the Colonel.

Mr Cooper spoke up. 'I'd love to see that. Shall we go after luncheon tomorrow?'

The Colonel nodded excitedly. 'Yes. Would love to see how the warehousing stacks up against the warehouses in Shanghai. I'm sure I can improve upon the efficiency of it all. Seen a lot of warehouses in my time in the Orient, you know.'

'I'd be interested to see that,' said Mr Rosenthal hesitatingly. 'I've never been to a distillery before. Could be exciting.'

'Can you get that arranged for tomorrow?' the Colonel barked at Fergus across the room, garnering scolding looks from Lady Georgina. She was in a foul mood; bridge had been cancelled when Mrs Blackwood begged off. Her nephew had finally arrived, and they were having a quiet dinner together in her rooms.

The Colonel continued, without apologising or waiting for an answer. 'Just a small group, five or six of us,' he shouted to Fergus, 'with possibly a tasting after? I hear what comes from the barrel is quite different to this.' He raised the cut glass crystal and swirled the liquid in the light.

Fergus's head was spinning. Taking a group to see the Distillery was the last thing he wanted to do. He had enough on his hands as it was. How was he supposed to lead a tour group? The idea sparked and was out of his mouth before he had time to consider it. 'Angus can take you. He used to run the Distillery, you know.'

Angus shot his brother a murderous look. *A tour guide. Can my life get any worse?*

'Capital!' cried the Colonel, looking around the room. 'Anyone else?'

'It's settled then,' said Mr Cooper. 'We meet in the Armoury tomorrow at three.'

Ross won't be happy, reflected Fergus, *but at least Angus will bear the brunt of it*. The thought made him smile.

Seven Days to the Ball

Bella waited for exactly two days for Fergus to produce the gramophone. When it didn't appear, she took matters into her own hands. Grabbing a houseboy and a torch, she headed to the attics. After a long and filthy afternoon of searching, they managed to find the old gramophone in the West Attic, and some records in a remote corner. They weren't the best records for a party, admittedly, but they would have to do. She'd order some others next time she went into the village.

They waited until Fergus left to change for dinner and then Bella had the footmen drag it all downstairs and install it in the Blue Drawing Room. Once finished, she proceeded to teach the bartender how to make a Martini and went to dress for dinner, eagerly anticipating the evening.

When pudding arrived, Bella excused herself, mentioned she had a surprise for them and left the Dining Room with a smug look on her face. Curious eyes went round the table, but no one hazarded a guess.

She could have left us a hint, thought Lady Elspeth.

Once Bella was in the Drawing Room, she fired up the gramophone, instructed the footmen to circulate in the room, with trays of Martinis. Standing in the bay window, waiting for people to arrive, Bella looked very much like a child at Christmas.

People filtered in, some bemused, some confused. But as the Martinis started to circulate, laughter and chatter slowly filled the room. Angus was the last to arrive. He sauntered over to Bella, who was chatting with Mrs Cooper in the bay window.

'I've got to hand it to you, Bella, this is a huge improvement.'

Bella basked in an altogether too rare compliment from her family.

'I'm just telling Mrs Cooper she's had a lucky shave, not playing cards against Grandmama. I don't think she quite believes me.'

Lady Georgina had tried to get a table together for bridge, and Mrs Cooper had volunteered eagerly. But when Lord and Lady Ruthven volunteered to play, she was roughly put aside, and she was feeling quite bruised.

Angus set his glass on the table and lit a cigarette. He was running out of his Moroccan supply. What would he do when he had nothing but English cigarettes? It was a shame that Philippe, Elspeth's husband, hadn't joined. He always had generous stash of Gauloises. Well, it didn't bear thinking about.

'Grandmama's a bit of a brute when it comes to cards,' he said quietly. 'And partnering with that Blackwood woman, well, you've saved yourself a fortune, from what I hear.'

Mrs Cooper looked between the siblings. 'I suppose you're right. It seems like something I should learn how to play.'

'Oh!' exclaimed Angus. 'If you don't even know how to play bridge, do not, under any circumstances, play against or with Grandmama. She will eat you alive.'

'She doesn't allow chatting,' interjected Bella, 'and snipes if you take too long to bid. Between you and me, she's quite unpleasant to play against. You've dodged a bullet, trust us. Let me get you another Martini.' She waved for a footman.

Angus looked up from Mrs Cooper to see his grandmother rushing up to them. 'I thought you were playing cards tonight, Grandmama.' He wondered if she'd heard what they'd just said about her.

'We've finished early.' Lady Georgina was clearly exasperated. 'It was a disaster.'

'Where's Mrs Blackwood?' asked Mrs Cooper, glancing around the room.

Lady Georgina tutted and waved a hand, irritation showing. 'She's gone to bed.'

'Oh,' said Mrs Cooper, disappointment in her voice. 'I've been wanting to get to know her, hear about life in Shanghai. It all seems so glamorous.'

Bella was slightly offended. Her life in Shanghai was glamorous and yet Mrs Cooper hadn't asked a single question about it. 'Did you lose?' she asked Lady Georgina, who looked cross.

'Certainly not. The very idea of Lady Ruthven prevailing at cards . . . it's laughable. But the American, my word. What a fiasco.' She gave Mrs Cooper a shrewd look. 'You were wise not to sit down with him, dear.'

Mrs Cooper, still smarting slightly, smiled shyly.

'He chattered incessantly. Onlookers are meant to be silent. I don't approve of talk at the games table, let alone a running commentary from the room.' It was, they knew well from experience, a cardinal sin. "Lemme . . .", "Hey lemme", "Lemme ask". Who speaks like that? Tsk . . . After two rubbers of his inane chat, I quit the table.'

Bella and Angus were shocked. No one was ever allowed to leave the table early when Lady Georgina was playing.

She said it showed weakness of character. He must have rambled quite a bit to get her to retire early.

'Ah, there you are. Lost you for a moment.' Mr Rosenthal handed a cocktail to Lady Georgina. Bewildered, she reluctantly accepted it. After a moment, she set it awkwardly at the base of the palm with a grimace.

'Good evening, Mr Rosenthal,' said Bella.

Angus merely nodded in greeting.

'Swell party!' He gestured to the room. When no reply came, he continued, 'Lemme ask you something: loch means lake, right?'

Angus hesitated for a moment. 'Yes.'

'Then why isn't it called Lake Down? Seems like you'd get more tourists if they knew it was on a lake.'

Bella and Angus stared at the man, unsure if he was sincere in his query. Lady Georgina turned and offered them a look that patently said, *I told you he was insufferable.*

Angus pulled himself up as tall as he could possibly stand, gazed down at Mr Rosenthal, and replied in a slow and dangerous voice: 'Lakes are English, Mr Rosenthal. Lochs are Scottish.'

There was just the slightest moment of tension before Mr Rosenthal burst out laughing. 'Oh! Oh, that's fantastic!' He bent over himself and slapped his knee. 'I'll have to remember that.'

'If you'll excuse us, Mr Rosenthal,' interrupted Bella, who said nothing more but grabbed her grandmother by the elbow and led her across the room.

'Oh yes. Yes, of course,' he replied. They watched as all three of the women crossed the room and settled down by the fire.

He turned back to Angus. 'Your sister throws a hell of a party. I understand this is her doing?' He waved his arm towards the room, which Angus did have to concede was a lot livelier than any evening he'd ever had in the Abbey. 'I don't know that I could have taken another evening of sherry and "Animal, Vegetable, Mineral".'

Angus was confused for a moment. 'You mean "Bird, Beast, Flower"?'

'Yes!' Mr Rosenthal snapped his fingers and pointed at Angus. 'That's the one!'

Angus chuckled but had to agree with him. 'It's a bit of a slower life here in the Highlands.'

'Mmm, yes.' Mr Rosenthal nodded as he took a sip of his Martini. 'Damn, that's good. So, did I hear correctly? Her children live with you?'

He's well informed, thought Angus. *Uncle Cecil? Grandmama?* He couldn't decide who was more likely to have let that one slip.

'Yes. Shanghai's really no place for children, so it was felt they were better with their father.'

'In, where was it? Morocco?'

Angus nodded. 'Tangiers.'

'I stayed in a great riad in Marrakech. Amazing food.' He hesitated. 'So, where's their father? I mean, if the kids are here, why isn't he?'

Angus bristled. 'He is in Spain.'

'Spain? There's a war in Spain.'

'Yes, that's rather why he's there,' said Angus dryly. 'He's a writer, reporting on the war.'

'He's a journalist? Wow. So, she went to Shanghai, and then he went to cover the war, leaving the kids with you?' He issued a low whistle. 'That's not a story you hear every day.'

'Yes, well . . .' stammered Angus, feeling a bit helpless.

'Well, good for you. Better to keep them in the family. Ha! I guess he should be paying you child support, huh?

Since you're in the charge of them now.' He downed the rest of his cocktail, scooped up Lady Georgina's discarded one, and wandered off, leaving Angus to his thoughts.

Late that evening, Mrs MacBain was looking over the list of tasks for the ball. There was still so much to do. She was just questioning the number of reels when the door to her office slammed open, startling her.

'It's happened again! But this time, I'm sure of it.' Mrs Burnside came into the office in the middle of her rant. She threw a towel over her left shoulder and leaned both arms on the back of a chair.

Mrs MacBain was confused. 'What's happened? What are you talking about?' She had no idea what had happened, but taking in the visage of Mrs Burnside, it was big.

'Someone's been stealing food from my cold larder.' She harrumphed and shook her head. 'Wasn't sure the first couple of times—'

'First couple?' Mrs MacBain didn't disguise her surprise. It was unlike Cook not to notice even the minutest detail in her kitchen.

Mrs Burnside shifted uncomfortably. 'Well, there's so much food in there now, and on any given day up to a dozen kitchen maids, cooks and footmen go traipsing in and out. But this time, it wasn't just a Scotch egg, it was a game pie!' She looked strangely triumphant for a woman who was being robbed. 'They took an entire pie. Just imagine walking out with one of those!' Her gaze drifted into an unseen distance, a satisfied smile on her face.

Mrs MacBain wondered briefly if the woman had lost her grip on the situation. Theft was not a good sign in the kitchens, but she couldn't see any of their staff taking an entire pie. A slice of ham or a sausage roll now and again, yes. But given the size of Mrs Burnside's game pies, and the sheer weight of one, well, it would take some effort to sneak that out unnoticed.

'Could the children have taken it? You know how they are when they're bored.' But the moment it left her lips, she remembered Nanny. Silent and a bit ominous, but from what little she'd seen, she had a grip on them that would have made Napoleon proud. No, they wouldn't dare to slip away from this one. 'What would you like me to do about it?' she finally asked.

Mrs Burnside blinked and looked at her colleague.

'Do?' she asked. 'I've no idea. There's little to do about it unless we lock the larder and sign food in and out. I just thought I was losing my mind for a moment, and this is proof I'm not.'

The women stared at one another for a moment.

'Right,' said Mrs Burnside briskly, 'now you know. I'll go have a word with my staff before they turn in for the night.' She spun on her heels and left as quickly as she'd entered, leaving Mrs MacBain to wonder why she'd come in the first place.

She glanced down at the accounts again, realised her concentration was broken, and gave up the ghost. It had been a long day. Mrs Boyle had fallen in the woods and twisted her ankle. Two of the footmen had got into a shouting match and refused to speak to one another, making dinner service nearly impossible. And then Lord Thornton spent an hour hectoring her to change her staff – her staff, mind you – into his personal livery for the duration of his stay. What she needed was a nice cup of tea and her book.

She decided to make one last pass of the ground floor before turning in for the night. As she crossed the threshold to the Armoury, she heard furious whispering and instinctively, stepped back into the recess of the doorway. She tentatively glanced around the room and then up to the timber walkways. There, on the guest floor, was the Colonel, red-faced and gesturing wildly at – could it be? – a rather stoic-looking Mrs Blackwood.

What on earth is going on there? she wondered.

She stood still, not wanting to disrupt them, and listened. When the Armoury was empty, it could be quite an echo chamber, but she was on the wrong side of it, and she was only just able to hear the odd word or phrase.

'But . . . how is that possible?' the Colonel sputtered, looking rather like a small child who'd lost a favourite toy.

Mrs Blackwood murmured something she couldn't make out.

'I'm not putting my neck on the line that way!' the Colonel exclaimed. 'I'm in deep enough as it is.'

'*Mumble, mumble, mumble* . . .' She placed a hand on the Colonel's arm. '*Mumble,* or else *mumble, mumble.*'

The Colonel's eyes widened. 'You wouldn't dare!'

Mrs MacBain watched as the old woman smiled coldly at the Colonel and then turned, making her way across the walkway towards her room. The Colonel stood huffing for some moments before stomping the opposite way to his room.

What on earth was that about? Mrs MacBain wandered slowly back to her room, turning the snippet of conversation over and over in her mind. The Colonel was clearly out of sorts, his usual posturing and bluster nowhere in sight. *What wouldn't she dare?*

By the time she was crawling into bed with her book, she'd resolved to put it out of her mind. A guest had left the latest Ngaio Marsh novel and she was very much looking forward to reading it. It was set in New Zealand! Oh, to be far away from Loch Down, even for just a few hours. After settling into her bed with a cup of tea, Mrs MacBain immersed herself in her book and let the day fall away.

Six Days to the Ball

Bella walked slowly to the Nursery. She hadn't been here in years. *Smells the same*, she thought absent-mindedly; it was a curious mixture of furniture polish, talcum powder and fear. Nanny had been a fierce disciplinarian. *Why on earth does Angus want to meet here?*

As she entered the room, the sound of chairs scraping the wooden floor bounced off the walls. Bella was immediately engulfed by the children, who sprang from their lessons, sprinting towards her, shouting delightedly.

Auntie Bella! Auntie Bella's here! They were leaping around her like small, excitable puppies.

Bella stared at them and then glared at her brother, patting a child on the head. 'Auntie? They call me Auntie?'

Angus had been perched in the window. He shrugged, pointed at the children, snapping his fingers. From out of nowhere, a figure in white appeared and shouted something entirely incomprehensible. The children paused for the merest of seconds before scrambling back to the table like well-trained hunting dogs.

Rather admirable, Bella thought.

Angus escorted Bella to the far side of the room.

'I'm their mother, not their aunt,' she began again, once they were out of earshot.

'It was easier than explaining,' he said dryly. He reached into his jacket and pulled out his cigarette case. 'But that's not what I wanted to speak to you about.'

He offered a cigarette to his sister, who refused, and he snapped the case shut. When he'd exhaled the first puff of sweet smoke, he began.

'I've been thinking about Hugh and the children, and this is how I see it. You, at least, left them with their father. He, however, abandoned them, penniless in a foreign country. I managed to get them back here, only just, but what happens to them now? I haven't a bean to my name, and neither do you.'

She started to object, but Angus wagged a finger at her.

'Edmund's in a war zone, Bella. If he makes it back, you're sorted. But if he doesn't, your only choices are a widow's pension or a new husband.' He paused and took another drag, exhaling slowly towards the ceiling. 'And I doubt very much a government pension would stretch further than your hair appointments.'

Bella reached into his jacket pocket and took out the silver case, helping herself to a cigarette.

'So, here's what I think we should do,' Angus continued languidly.

'We?' Bella repeated.

'Yes, *we*. We will need to be united on this or we haven't a hope in hell.'

He detailed his plan and when he'd finished, he sat back in his chair and looked intently at her face, trying to gauge her thoughts. Was she in? Did she think he was crazy?

Bella took a deep drag of the cigarette, exhaled slowly, and then stubbed it out on the floor. She could hear Nanny chiding her from beyond the grave. 'What do we do first?'

Angus smiled. 'First, we go see Lawlis.'

Elspeth stepped out of the door, giddy with anticipation. She'd been in Loch Down for several days, but she hadn't had many chances for a walk. She'd been helping Mrs MacBain with the details for the ball, and it was endless decisions about table arrangements, flowers, linens. Not to mention refereeing between her mother and, well, pretty much everyone who tried to help. This morning had been a humdinger.

Fergus was initially delighted Lady Georgina wanted to help, but quickly realised she meant to take over. She handed him her handwritten guest list, all four pages of it, and then announced she'd open the ball with Hamilton House. The first reel was always the privilege of the host, choosing the tune and the others in the set.

Elspeth and Fergus exchanged guarded looks.

'Grandmama, it's not your ball. It's the Abbey's ball,' insisted Fergus. 'Mrs MacBain will choose the first reel.'

'Hotels do not give balls, Fergus. That is a ghastly a modern convention, now that so few houses have ballrooms.' Lady Georgina waved him off. 'A ball is always hosted by a family, in this case, our family. I shall greet the guests at the door and then open the ball with the first reel, as is proper. A member of the aristocracy always opens a ball, and I am head of this family.'

'After Angus, you mean,' said Elspeth gently.

'Angus being back does not automatically confer him head of the family status.' She glared at her daughter. 'It is I who live at the Abbey.'

'In Thistledown Cottage,' said Fergus, gently, but firmly, 'not in the Abbey.'

Lady Georgina snorted in derision and plucked an invisible thread from her skirt. 'Are you trying to get yourself cut out of my will?'

'Grandmama,' began Fergus carefully, in what he hoped was a conciliatory voice. 'Mrs MacBain is hosting this ball. It was her idea; she's in charge of the menus, the staff, the setting up and the tearing down, ordering supplies, auditioning bands, checking the livery. Unless you're willing to do all of that, Mrs MacBain will choose the participants for the first reel.'

Lady Georgina sat up even taller in her chair, indignation at the ready. 'And who's going to partner her? Hmm?'

'I don't know,' said Fergus, exasperated. 'Hudson? Lockridge?'

Lady Georgina blanched. 'I can't see Lord Neasden taking kindly to that. It's not a servants' ball, you know.'

Fergus sighed heavily. 'They aren't servants, Grandmama.' He gave Elspeth a sidelong look. They knew a losing battle when they saw one, but they fought on for at least another hour.

Now, however, Elspeth was outdoors and had three glorious hours before tea. Setting off across the service yard, she relished the crunch of the gravel underfoot. By the time she was across the drive and into the woods, she had a broad smile on her face and the squabbles of her family were a thing of the past. She walked for a while in happy silence, until she heard some crashing in the woods, and then cursing.

'Oh!' she exclaimed when she rounded a yellow rhododendron. 'Hello. Do you need help?'

A man had fallen and was struggling to get back up on to the path. She held out a hand to help him and braced herself to take his weight.

'Thank you,' he muttered glumly.

'It's Mr Blackwood, isn't it?' She stood watching as he dusted himself off. He was dressed entirely wrong for

Scotland. His suit was white, and the fabric was quite thin, but his shoes were the real liability; he was wearing brogues with smooth leather soles. The man was clearly not an outdoorsman.

'Are you lost?' she asked after some moments, unsure why he was even there.

'Ah, no. I was just, erm . . . Took a wrong turn to get to the, erm . . . croquet lawn. Suppose I am a bit lost,' he finished sheepishly.

'The croquet lawn? Those are on the other side of the house entirely. Shall I show you?' She started to walk back along the path she'd just come from.

'No, thank you.' He'd said it so brusquely, Elspeth stopped in her tracks and stared at him. 'You needn't bother yourself, just point me in the right direction . . .'

'It's no bother. Besides, it's quite easy to get lost out here.' She looked down at his shoes and back up again. 'Perhaps you should go this way. The service yard is just through this hedge. Easier terrain.'

He looked to where she was pointing, issued a gruff thank you, and scurried on his way. She watched him go, to see he went the right way to the house. When she heard the scrunch of the gravel drive, she continued her own walk, wondering what on earth he'd been doing there and why he'd lied to her.

Lawlis was speechless.

As the Inverkillen family solicitor, he'd weathered decades of strange legal demands from the family; some were unusual but legal, some were simply crazy. But this time, he wasn't sure he understood the request. He stared at the pair of them and shook his head slowly. 'Let me get this straight: you want to sue Hugh, for what the Americans call 'Child Support'?'

'Yes,' said Bella evenly. 'He's their father, and he cannot be allowed to run away from his responsibilities.'

Lawlis nodded thoughtfully and looked over to Angus. 'But they'll continue to live with you, not with their mother?'

'Correct,' answered Angus.

Lawlis shook his head. Bella and Angus had come to his offices and proposed the most audacious idea he'd ever heard. Hugh, as a father, had a duty to provide for his children. That much, they could agree upon. But since Hugh had abandoned the children with Angus, and couldn't be contacted, Bella wanted Hugh's publisher to settle funds on Angus, who acted as de facto guardian.

'If Hugh is earning money from his writing, that money should be supporting his children. I simply want his publisher to send it to Angus, as a matter of some urgency.'

'His brother-in-law.' Lawlis said hesitantly.

'With whom he left his children,' countered Angus pointedly.

'But not to his ex-wife, the mother of the children?' This was what Lawlis couldn't understand.

'Were I to open a bank account, Mr Lawlis, it would be in the name of my father, who is dead, my husband, who is absent, or . . . my brother.' She waved a hand towards Angus.

Lawlis covered his mouth with his hand and drummed his fingers on the desk. It was all terribly unorthodox. He couldn't think of a single precedent for it. If the publisher refused, which they were likely to do, well, there wasn't much Lawlis could do about it. *Why is it never easy with this family?*

'Leave it with me,' he said after a long pause. 'I'll approach the publishers and see how they react. Let's try a friendly approach first. More flies with honey, that sort of idea.'

Bella and Angus exchanged dark looks.

'I think you should prepare for a fight,' Angus countered. He reached into his jacket pocket and deposited two bank books on the desk. 'He cleaned out the household account before he left and removed my name from the British account. This wasn't a spontaneous act.'

Lawlis nodded and reached for the books, flicking through the pages. He'd never liked the Dunbar-Hamiltons.

Mrs Douglas was at the front desk with a suitcase. Mrs MacBain did a double take. Why was the Vicar's wife checking into the hotel? Curious, she crossed the room and called out her name.

'Mrs Douglas. What brings you here?'

Gladys Douglas turned and gave a small huff of frustration. 'I'm trying to get this young man to tell me which room Lady Annabella is in, but he simply won't.'

Mrs MacBain caught the clerk's eye and gave him a small nod. 'I'm afraid he's not allowed to divulge such information. Perhaps you can wait in the Morning Room, and I'll send someone to fetch her?'

But Mrs Douglas was not going to be put off her mission. 'He's already said that, but it simply won't do. You see, I have all these clothes for her, and she'll need to try them on.' She lifted the suitcase and tilted her head.

'Clothes?' What was she on about? Mrs MacBain glanced down at the tattered brown case and felt her stomach clench.

'Yes. I went through the donations last night and picked some suitable things for her.'

'Suitable things?' She replied slowly, sensing trouble.

'Yes. I'm given to understand she's lost her luggage and hasn't a thing to wear. I've come to help in her hour of need.' Mrs Douglas looked both exasperated and pleased with herself.

Mrs MacBain breathed in deeply. *Ooh, boy,* she thought, *how do we handle this?*

'Well, that's very kind of you, Mrs Douglas, very kind indeed. Why don't you leave it with me, and I'll bring back anything she can't use?'

But Gladys Douglas was determined to have her moment in front of Lady Annabella. She gave Mrs MacBain a stern look and then huffed again. 'That simply won't do. How can I effectively minister if I am not present?'

'It's just, Lady Annabella is quite a private person, Mrs Douglas,' began Mrs MacBain, her brain whirring, searching for plausible excuses.

'Which is exactly why I need to see her in her rooms.' Mrs Douglas was not going away; Mrs MacBain could see that. And it wouldn't do to anger the woman. She had many virtues – probably – but discretion wasn't one of them. She was the biggest gossip in the village, a fact that made it increasingly difficult for her to minister to the parish.

'Very well. This way please?' Mrs MacBain plotted a very circuitous and lengthy route to Bella's room, hoping that Mrs Douglas would never remember how to get there. She only seemed to flag once on the trip and was clearly not used to carrying her own suitcases. When they finally arrived and were waiting to be admitted to Bella's rooms, she glanced around the corridor with a bewildered look on her face. Mrs MacBain smiled; she had done her job well.

The door opened and Bella's maid stood to one side to admit them, head bowed slightly. Unfortunately for her, she couldn't hide it from anyone, let alone Mrs MacBain. In addition to her broken wrist, she now had quite a welt on her cheek, as if she'd been hit by something.

'Oh my! What's happened to you?' Mrs MacBain exclaimed, turning to examine the girl.

Mrs Douglas froze in her tracks and gazed in fascinated horror at the girl. 'Oh my goodness!' she cried, and stared at the maid, who started to curl into herself with embarrassment. 'Is it safe to have her here?'

'She's not a wild animal, Mrs Douglas,' replied Mrs MacBain, somewhat tersely. Turning back to the maid, she tried to see the welt more clearly. 'What's happened to her cheek, Lady Annabella?'

'I've no idea. I came back from an appointment in the village, and she was in a heap on the floor, her cheek bright red. There are times I wish I spoke her language, and this is certainly one of them.'

Mrs MacBain held the girl gently by the shoulders and examined the injury. 'It almost looks as if someone punched her. Or slapped her, but really quite hard. Who would do such a thing?'

'Ahem!'

It irritated Mrs MacBain, who summoned as much calm as she could before she turned around. 'Yes. This is Mrs Douglas, the Vicar's wife. She wanted a word, Lady Annabella.'

'How do you do?' replied Bella politely, confusion evident on her face.

'I'll just fix her a cold compress, shall I?' asked Mrs MacBain, walking towards the bathing room.

A flash of irritation crossed Mrs Douglas's face – she hated to be interrupted – but it was quickly replaced by a bright smile. She glanced at the sofa, but Bella didn't invite her to sit. Undaunted, Mrs Douglas moved to the end of the bed and set the shabby case on the bed throw, placing her hands on the clasps.

'Now, I hope you won't find it shocking, but I was having tea with Lady Georgina the other day, as I often do. We meet once a week, you know. She's an inspiration to us all.'

'The only shocking part of that statement,' Bella interjected wryly, 'is Grandmama being inspirational.'

'Oh, but she is!' replied Mrs Douglas. 'I can assure you, she is tireless in helping the less fortunate.'

Bella and Mrs MacBain exchanged looks. Mrs MacBain applied the cold compress to the maid's cheek.

'Well, while she was pouring – I do wish you'd go back to British tea, Mrs MacBain. With so many men out of work, we should be supporting British industry.' Mrs Douglas paused and groped for her original train of thought. 'Where was I? Oh yes. Lady Georgina was pouring the tea, and I couldn't help but overhear part of your conversation. Please be assured, I was not trying to eavesdrop; the words simply floated into my ears. You'd be amazed how often the Almighty sends conversations into my ears. I believe it's how he shows me where to minister. And when I overhear someone in need, well, I simply must act. So here I am, Lady Annabella, at your service.'

'My service?' stammered Bella, who hadn't really been listening to the woman.

Mrs Douglas threw the case open with a flourish and stood back. She looked as proud as a cat bringing a dead mouse to its owner.

Bella looked at the case. Mrs MacBain looked at the ceiling. This wasn't going to be pretty.

'I don't understand,' stammered Bella, looking from the case to Mrs MacBain and back again.

'I have spearheaded a drive in the parish to collect clothes for the needy. One must help where one can, and I've been tirelessly visiting and collecting for months. I don't mind saying to you that it's been more difficult than I'd expected. But we have been quite successful, and we can now minister to those in need. Of course, I never thought the Almighty would bring me here, but he does work in such mysterious ways.'

Is the woman incapable of speaking plainly? wondered Mrs MacBain.

'And . . . you want me to . . . donate something?' Bella asked, thoroughly confused.

'No, not at all! I brought these clothes for you.' Mrs Douglas smiled broadly. 'I pulled out several pieces that would be appropriate for a woman of your station, but of course there aren't many grand houses left, and those that do remain were jolly difficult to get donations from, I don't mind saying. But, I've done the best I can. This suit, for example,'

'That's my suit!' exclaimed Bella. She moved to the bed and grabbed it from Mrs Douglas. 'Yes, that's my travelling suit.' She looked down at the rest of the case, desperately hoping it was somehow filled with the rest of her clothes from Shanghai. The penny still hadn't dropped.

'How extraordinary! Then this must be your hat as well!' She pulled the hat from underneath a baby-sick green tweed skirt. 'It's awfully heavy. I wonder that it didn't give you a headache.'

Bella dropped the suit and grabbed the hat. 'Yes! Where did you find this?'

'One of the housemaids brought it to the church and donated it to our clothing drive.'

Bella stared at Mrs Douglas, and the horror of what she was suggesting sunk in. She lowered the hat slowly. 'Are you suggesting I wear other people's cast-offs?'

'Well, I wouldn't have put it that way,' stammered Mrs Douglas, entirely unsure why she wasn't being thanked. 'You haven't anything to wear and we have all these clothes at the church.'

'I am not *needy*, Mrs Douglas. My husband is the Consul-General of Shanghai. I do not need charity.' Bella shuddered at the very prospect.

Mrs Douglas was stunned. She rooted though the clothes for a moment. 'They've been laundered, and they're in perfect condition, I can assure you. This dress, for instance, would look lovely on you.' She held up a drab brown and white polka dot dress.

'I'm not wearing that!' shouted Bella.

Even Mrs MacBain thought it was hideous. She took a step towards the bed and gently took the dress from Mrs Douglas.

'Mrs Douglas, it was very kind of you to think of Lady Annabella. And she appreciates your generous offer.' She gave Bella a stern look and then folded the dress and placed it back in the case. 'But Lady Annabella has ordered some things and is simply waiting for them to arrive. Perhaps, for the time being, you should keep these.'

Bella snatched her suit from the bed and handed it to her maid. She cleared her throat gently. 'Thank you, Mrs Douglas, for returning my suit to me. It was a mistake that you got it in the first place. I apologise for the confusion.'

Mrs MacBain offered Bella the hat and then placed it in the case when Bella shook her head. She snapped the case shut and ushered a mute Mrs Douglas to the door.

People are usually so thankful, Mrs Douglas thought. *Why did this go so badly?*

After dinner that evening, they gathered in the Drawing Room for drinks. Lady Georgina approached Fergus and Bella, an aggrieved look on her face.

'I simply cannot have another conversation with that man. You must move him tomorrow.' She patted the bun at the nape of her neck and did a double take when a footman proffered a tray of cocktails. 'And what, may I ask, is this?' Dinner had clearly put Lady Georgina in bad form.

'Martinis, Grandmama. They're all the rage in Shanghai,' replied Bella.

Lady Georgina picked up a glass tentatively and sniffed, wrinkling her nose. She grabbed the footman's arm and handed him the offending glass. 'Yes, well, what rages in the East most certainly does not fly in the Highlands. We are a traditional people. Bring me a sherry.'

'Don't I know it,' murmured Bella.

'What was that?' asked Lady Georgina sharply. She would not abide being mocked, especially by her granddaughter.

Fergus jumped into the fray, hoping to defuse the tension. 'Who did you want moved, Grandmama?'

Lady Georgina stared reproachfully at Bella for another two ticks and then turned to Fergus. 'The American. He's positively painful at table.'

This surprised both siblings. They all rather liked Mr Rosenthal, didn't they? He was a bit loud, yes, but weren't all Americans? He was, on the whole, genial company.

'What's happened?' asked Fergus.

'His table manners are simply atrocious.' She shook her head at the memory. 'He was on my left, so I had him for starters, and he was lovely company, asking about my roses. We had quite a discussion, I can tell you. He's more knowledgeable about horticulture than one should be coming from New York.'

'You love talking about your roses. What was wrong with that?' asked Bella.

'Nothing at all. It's what happened after the first course.' She stared into the distance and gave a little sigh. 'When the footman came round with the butter, rather than taking some on to his plate, he tore his bread roll in two, with his thumbs, and proceeded to butter both sides of it while the footman stood there. Neither the footman nor I knew where to look. I'm surprised his arm didn't cramp.'

The siblings exchanged glances and tried not to smirk. Bella hid behind her drink; Fergus coughed lightly.

'Then the soup was served, and Mr Rosenthal failed to turn. Failed to turn; can you imagine? Poor Mrs Cooper and Lord Ashdown had no conversation for the better part of the meal. Well, that's not so bad where Mrs Cooper is concerned; she's a bit quiet, but Lord Ashdown is a renowned raconteur, and I was quite looking forward to his stories.' She tutted and shook her head. 'Quite honestly, who doesn't know to *turn*?'

The Abbey had long observed the tradition of alternating speaking partners with the courses of the meal. The ladies speak to the gentleman on their left during the first course, the gentleman to their right for the second course and so on. It was a faux pas, certainly, not turning. One, that under Country House Rules, would have been the social kiss of death. But as a hotel, it was difficult to enforce. One simply could not pack the bags of an offending, paying guest and have the chauffeur take them to the train station.

'Perhaps they do it differently in New York, Grandmama,' said Fergus.

'He spent the best part of three courses holding forth on that Simpson woman. Seems to think she is marvellous and cannot understand why we can't accept her. As if we'd have a divorcee on the throne. An American one, at that.'

'Well, he is entitled to his opinions, Grandmama,' said Fergus.

Bella glared at him, as if to warn him not to egg her on.

'Not when they are the wrong opinions.' She scowled at him and then turned to see Mrs Blackwood and her nephew entering the Drawing Room. 'Ah, wonderful! Time to raise a table for cards.'

She cast an enquiring glance at the siblings, both of whom shook their heads.

'Just as well,' Lady Georgina responded and sped off before anyone else could lay claim to Mrs Blackwood as a partner. Fergus and Bella watched in silence for some moments, as their grandmother shamed and hectored people into playing bridge.

'Do you know,' said Bella after some moments, 'the more I watch them, the less I understand them.'

Fergus followed her gaze. Mrs Blackwood sitting by the fire, her nephew hovering just behind her, as he always seemed to do. 'What do you mean?'

'Well, I love Auntie Elspeth to bits, but since that nephew arrived, he's followed Mrs Blackwood everywhere; he's always at her side. And to have that sort of slavish devotion to Auntie Elspeth that he seems to have to Mrs Blackwood . . . I just don't think I could do it.'

Fergus thought about it for a moment and then shook his head. 'No. Neither could I.'

'They're decidedly odd.' Bella paused and then twirled to take in the whole room. 'Ah, there's Mrs Cooper. I must ask her what colour she's wearing to the ball. If she says blue, I shall have to shoot myself.' And with that, Bella sped off, leaving Fergus to his thoughts.

When she was gone, one of the bartenders approached, now that Fergus was finally alone, and handed him a slip of paper, his hand shaking slightly. Fergus stared at the figure in disbelief. 'This can't be right,' he said softly. The bartender blinked innocently. Fergus looked to the slip of paper again. He was looking at Angus's bar tab. It was enormous. 'He's been here less than a fortnight.'

Fergus left the room, muttering darkly. He marched straight to the Billiards Room where he knew Angus would be. By the time he'd arrived, he was enraged and had startled several of the guests with his angry muttering.

Stepping into the Billiards Room at last, he glanced about quickly and then positively stomped to the table and slapped the bill on the green baize, directly in front of his brother's shot.

'Just what do you propose to do about this?' he fumed as quietly as he could. There were a few guests in the room, and he didn't want to cause a scene. More of a scene, that was, than he already had.

Still leaning over his cue, Angus raised his eyes to his brother. Sighing heavily, he rose and leaned the cue against the table. 'If you'll excuse me a moment, Mr Rosenthal.'

Fergus flushed and stammered an apology to the man. Mr Rosenthal set his cue down and backed away politely, but sensing a fracas was imminent, stayed near enough to jump in, if needed. He knew from experience how ferocious siblings could be with one another.

Angus lazily walked to the side of the table and picked up the paper.

'What are you on about now?' he asked loftily. But his casual disdain was pierced when his eyes found the total. *God, does it really cost that much to drink here?* Recovering quickly, he cleared his throat and handed it back to Fergus. 'Relax, Grandmama will take care of it.'

'Grandmama?' Fergus was scandalised. 'You can't possibly expect her to clear this!'

'Why not? It was her gift to me.' He leaned over to line up the shot that had been so rudely interrupted. Fergus snatched the cue ball away.

'You can't possibly accept. We are not children. This isn't a trip to the sweet shop.' He glanced around the room and lowered his voice. 'She hasn't any income, Angus.'

Angus placed his cue on the table and leaned on the bumper, crossing his arms casually. A wry smile crossed his face.

Fergus could feel his blood boiling and he struggled, and failed, not to shout. 'Are you trying to bankrupt her? The money she has is just sufficient to keep her comfortable. She hasn't anything for luxuries, Angus. Paying for you, she simply cannot afford.'

Angus laughed sharply. 'She keeps a cook, a maid and a gardener, dear boy. Trust me, she has the money.' He held out his hand for the cue ball.

In truth, Fergus had always wondered how she afforded three servants. The maid lived in, which was less expensive, but the cook and the gardener were daily, and he quickly calculated what the hotel paid for those positions. Confusion clouded his face.

Angus studied his brother slightly amazed. 'You really don't know a thing about her, do you?' He chuckled. *Fergus can be so dense.* He took the cue ball. 'Shall we resume, Mr Rosenthal?'

The man nodded mutely, eyes wide as saucers. No one in the room spoke.

'What does that mean?' demanded Fergus. 'Of course I know her.'

'Look,' Angus barked, losing his temper, 'she offered, I accepted. I didn't ask for it. I didn't hint around until she took the bait. She offered, all on her own. She's allowed to spend her money how she sees fit. And if she wants to pay for my drinks, I don't see why that's a problem.'

'Because you are an adult! You should be paying your own way, not living off the generosity of others. My god, you're no better than Uncle Cecil!'

Angus crossed the distance in two steps and stood toe to toe with his brother, jabbing his finger in his fist. 'You take that back!'

'Prove me wrong,' Fergus seethed.

'Boys, please,' Mr Rosenthal stepped up and parted them. 'As much as we're all enjoying the drama—' he glanced around the room pointedly '—let's stop short of actual bloodshed, shall we?'

Fergus shook himself and stepped back, taking a seat on the leather benches that lined the long wall. Angus leaned back on the billiard table again, straightening his waistcoat.

'Now,' said Mr Rosenthal reasonably, 'if you'll allow me?' He glanced at the brothers, who nodded curtly, still angry with each other.

'Seems to me, you are both correct.' He held up his hands to stave off any objections. 'Fergus, you cannot dictate how your grandmother spends her own money. Unless she's losing her marbles – I met her; she's sharp as a tack – she gets to spend her loot anyway she sees fit. He's not a fortune hunter, he's her grandson.'

Angus smirked at his brother sanctimoniously. Mr Rosenthal turned and scowled at him.

'As for you, Lord Inverkillen,' his words were sterner, which mollified Fergus, 'your brother is right. You are an adult and even though it was a gracious offer, you shouldn't have accepted. Be a man, pay your own way.'

'And just how am I supposed to do that?' spat Angus, spinning the cue ball across the table.

Both Fergus and Mr Rosenthal stared at him; Fergus incredulously, Mr Rosenthal innocently.

'You could get a job,' Mr Rosenthal suggested gently, shrugging his shoulders.

'What?' Angus's voice was cold. He drew breath to object further but was cut off by his brother.

Fergus turned to stare at Mr Rosenthal. 'A job?' His voice was filled with wonder.

'I am the twentieth Earl of Inverkillen, a Peer of the Realm,' said Angus. 'The aristocracy do not have . . . *jobs*.' He sneered the word.

Mr Rosenthal waved a hand towards Fergus. 'May I present your brother?'

'A job . . .' Fergus said again, staring into the distance.

'That is entirely different. He—' but Angus got no further.

'We could use a tennis coach,' Fergus interrupted, speaking to Mr Rosenthal.

'There you go!' Mr Rosenthal clapped his hands together. 'A tennis coach. A way to earn and still be a man of leisure. Perfect!' He looked pleased with himself, as he nodded at both men.

'You can start tomorrow morning.' Fergus was looking decidedly lighter. 'I'll have Thompson round up a few
people for you.'

'I . . . what?' sputtered Angus.

'You can coach from ten in the morning until luncheon and then resume until teatime. Perhaps we can have
a tournament at the end of each week.' Fergus's mind was
spinning. It could be a nice little earner for the hotel and,
frankly, the only job he'd trust his brother to do. He needed
to speak with Thompson, to get it sorted properly. He
grabbed the bar bill. 'I must go. Thank you, Mr Rosenthal.
You were most helpful.'

'Happy to be of service,' replied Mr Rosenthal, bowing
his head.

Fergus scurried from the room.

'Wait!' shouted Angus after him. Turning back to Mr
Rosenthal, he asked, 'What just happened?'

True to his word, the following morning at ten, Fergus had
two guests on the tennis courts warming up: Lord Bryden
and his eldest son. Fergus sent a footman at half past nine
to fetch Angus, just to be sure he showed up. Pacing nervously, he surveyed the weather. September was one of the
best months to be in Scotland. They could have at least six
weeks of tennis before the weather turned. Looking towards
the main house, he spotted the footman, with Angus behind
him, in his tennis whites. He was scowling and sullen, but
he was there. Fergus breathed a sigh of relief.

Five Days to the Ball

Mrs MacBain was in her office, bright and early that morning, trying to bring a maid to task for mistaking Lady Monkhouse for the Duchess of Auldwilde. It had been a harmless mistake – they did look quite similar – and Mrs MacBain thought it was ridiculous to have to discuss it. But Lady Monkhouse was very touchy about these things and had insisted the girl be fired. She doubted very much Lady Monkhouse could pick the maid out of a line-up, but a guest complaint needed to be taken seriously, so here they were, discussing how very touchy wives could be when mistaken for the husband's mistress.

'You must be more careful, and if there's any doubt in your mind, use madame instead of a title.' Mrs MacBain stopped herself mid-chide as a man wandered past her office. 'Who was that?' She got to her feet quickly and rushed into the hall after him.

'Excuse me. Colonel? Is that you?' She chased him for a few yards before he turned around, looking slightly chagrined. 'Colonel, what are you doing down here?' She was confused and irritated. Guests did not belong in the kitchens, especially ones as tiresome as the Colonel.

'Ah, Mrs MacBain! I'm . . . erm . . . I'm looking for Cook. Wanted to see if she can make a special dish for me.'

Mrs MacBain shook her head, unsure how to respond. 'A special dish?'

'Not special really, more like, especially for me. Toad-in-the-hole. Haven't had one for years and I have to say I've got quite a craving for it.'

'Toad-in-the-hole? I'll see what I can do, Colonel,' she replied wearily. She escorted him back to the staff stairs.

'Rather speak to Cook about it myself,' he said portentously. 'I'm particular about my sausage to batter ratio, you know.'

'I'm afraid you can't be down here, Colonel.' She motioned to the stairs, saying nothing more.

'I really must insist,' he blustered.

'And so must I,' countered Mrs MacBain firmly.

He looked offended and then slowly mounted the stairs, mumbling petulantly about standards and gravy.

She shook her head slowly and walked to her office. When would that man leave? She was trying to decide if she should speak to Mrs Burnside about it when a voice called her name.

'Ah, Mrs MacBain, good. I got here fast as I could.' It was the village doctor. He was dressed in plus-fours, which Mrs MacBain eyed curiously. 'I was just headed out the door to do some golfing when Thompson rang me. Stroke of luck there, no pun intended. Now, where's the girl?'

'The girl?' Mrs MacBain repeated blankly.

'I gather a kitchen maid's taken a tumble down the cellar stairs and is quite badly hurt.'

'What? Oh dear!' she exclaimed. 'This way.' She rushed past him, through the kitchen, towards the service-yard door, stopping in a small vestibule. A timber door, normally kept closed, stood ajar. Opening it fully, she peered into the darkness. She could hear Sadie murmuring softly.

Oh lord, please not Sadie, she thought. *We'd never manage without her.*

She followed the doctor down the stairs, praying as she went. But as they got to the bottom, and her eyes adjusted to the dim light, she could see it was not Sadie, who had tumbled, but Bella's maid. She was ashamed of the relief that flooded her.

'Now, what's happened?' asked the doctor, kneeling beside the women.

Sadie moved aside and addressed Mrs MacBain. 'The door was open, which is quite unusual, so I came down and found her in a heap.'

'If she went down those,' he said nodding at the rough timber stairs, 'she probably has concussion.' He gently brought the maid's face to his and looked into her eyes.

'It's her leg that worries me,' said Sadie, pointing to the girl's foot.

'Oh dear, that's not in the right place, is it?' he said. 'I need to lift your skirt to see it properly. This might hurt a bit but try to hold still.'

'She doesn't speak English,' Sadie said quickly.

The doctor turned to look at her. 'Well, that complicates things.' He shifted position and then reached for the skirt. 'I LIFT SKIRT NOW,' he shouted slowly, and pantomimed moving her hem. 'MIGHT HURT, HOLD STILL.'

'Doctor! She's Chinese, not deaf,' Mrs MacBain said caustically.

'Works on the Continent,' he snapped huffily.

'I'll wager it doesn't,' she mumbled back.

He prodded her leg as gently as he could and then sighed heavily. 'We need to get her out of here and down to my surgery. I've got to reset that leg and then get it in a plaster cast quickly. But we'll need some strong lads to help. And something for her to bite down on; this won't be painless for her, I'm afraid.'

'Right.' Mrs MacBain nodded. 'I'll go ring Ross. I don't think the hall boys could manage. What can we do in the meantime?'

'Nothing. Just keep her as still as possible.'

Ross arrived immediately with a few large lads in tow. It didn't take them long to size up the situation, get the poor girl up the stairs and into the waiting ambulance. When the door was shut, Mrs MacBain slowly went back inside.

What else can possibly go wrong for the poor girl? she wondered.

On the other side of the kitchens, three kitchen maids had stopped their various tasks and rushed over to the serving counter, peering down at something. That something was Mrs Burnside, on her back on the floor, flailing about like an upside-down turtle. Quite an angry turtle. They quickly righted her and helped her onto a stool, assessing the situation. She had an angry bump on her forehead that resembled the soft-boiled egg she'd trod in.

'How the bloomin' heck did that get there?!' she raged at the maids, who could only stutter and stammer in terror.

'What on earth is going on in here?' Mrs MacBain asked sharply, rounding the prep table in the middle of the room. 'Loud enough to be heard in the village. Oh!' She started violently when she caught sight of Mrs Burnside. 'What's happened?' She looked to the three maids who stood back, meekly staring at the floor. 'Well don't just stand there useless. Go fetch a cold compress. You, clean up that mess. And you—' Mrs MacBain pointed to the youngest maid '— in my office, in the top left-hand drawer of my desk, you'll find some headache powder. From the looks of this, she's going to need it.'

The maids scurried off to their tasks. Mrs MacBain turned back to Mrs Burnside, who was blinking back tears of pain. It must have been quite a fall. Mrs MacBain had seen her burn her fingers and arms without so much as a flinch.

'First the maid, now you. What on earth is happening down here today?' She gently turned Cook's face to the light. 'Now, let me have a proper look. Oh dear, that's going to bruise badly, I'm afraid. You'll need some arnica as well.'

'Boiled egg on the floor,' declared Cook, angry at the thought of an untidy kitchen. 'I was looking over the inventory sheets and didn't see it. Next thing I know, I'm on my back and lucky my clipboard missed my eye.'

'A boiled egg?' Mrs MacBain looked around, confused. This was where the breakfast trays were prepared, but it was, as usual, absolutely spotless. 'How did it get there?'

Mrs Burnside harrumphed, 'Must have fallen off a breakfast tray.' She touched the growing bump on her forehead and winced. 'But I don't see how. We cover those trays soon as they're complete. It's that new girl from next door. I warned you the Dunbar-Hamilton maids weren't up to scratch.'

'I know she wasn't your first choice, but I dare say she knows enough to pick up an egg if she dropped it,' she chided Cook gently. 'But how is it no one complained about a missing egg? I'll check with Thompson.'

The cold compress and the headache powder arrived just as Mrs Burnside stood up and immediately toppled to the floor. Mrs MacBain grabbed her and signalled for a nearby hall boy to help.

'Take her up to her room, please, Andy. The kitchen can manage without you for an hour or so,' she said when Mrs Burnside started to object. 'Go lie down and get your bearings back. This place is dangerous enough as it is.'

She watched as Andy guided Cook towards the servants' stairs. When the door shut, she rounded on the kitchen maids, a severe look on her face. 'Now, what happened at breakfast?'

Cecil's breakfast tray was late that morning, but he hadn't noticed. He was still trying to decide what to wear. Standing in front of the mirror, holding suits in front of his dressing gown, he sighed.

Without a valet, again, Cecil, he thought morosely. *Life should be easier than this.*

Well, he only knew one way out of it. He chose the dark grey tweed with the russet waistcoat and a crisp white shirt, always a favourite with the ladies. There was precious little joy in choosing for oneself. He missed Georges. Strictly speaking, that wasn't true. He had always felt Georges was smirking behind his back, disapproving of him in some way. He missed having a valet; he didn't miss Georges.

A knock at the door brought him out of his reverie.

'Breakfast, sir,' came a common little voice from outside the room.

Cecil let out an aggrieved sigh and then remembered that this was no longer a home but a hotel. And stepping into a bedroom unannounced was now impolite. Although he couldn't help but notice the fires were lit each morning by some unseen fairy.

He crossed the room – annoyed once again by having to fend for himself – and held the door open as a young maid carried a wooden breakfast tray into the room. She bobbed a perfunctory curtsey and looked enquiringly at Cecil. 'Good morning, sir.'

Cecil pointed to the table and wondered if he was supposed to give the girl something, or if, as in the old days, one merely left something in an envelope upon departure. Why was it that everyone suddenly expected a tip for every little thing? *Open the door, tip please. Carry your bags, tip please. Here's your hat, tip please.* It was exhausting, and frankly, expensive. He thought of Mr Rosenthal, working his way across the Armoury, handing out shillings like they were pennies. Honestly, Americans ruined everything. Cecil nodded at the girl as she bobbed another perfunctory curtsey and disappeared though the door.

Closing it behind her and still thinking badly of the Americans, he wandered over to his tray and took the chair facing the garden. As he tucked a napkin into his dressing gown, he realised he was famished and quite looking forward to Cook's black pudding. She didn't have much of a repertoire, but her black pudding was, in his opinion, unsurpassed. Uncovering the tray, he felt a jolt of irritation.

They forgot it, he thought petulantly. No black pudding, no bacon, no egg. But what was this? Cecil picked the object up and turned it over in his hands. How curious, he thought. He set it down and then gasped, realising that it might just be the best breakfast he'd ever had at Loch Down.

Four Days to the Ball

Mackay was sitting in his office, which they'd created in an old safe room on the family floor. As a former valet, he now spent his time assisting the personal servants of the guests on this floor. These were the most important guests in the hotel, and they bent over backwards to accommodate them. He dealt with lost gloves and smashed perfume bottles that needed to be replaced quickly; he supplied preferred reading materials, forgotten hot water bottles, or specific stationery. He arranged excursions, visits to local gardens or picnics by the river. If a guest wanted a clandestine tryst in a bothy, he made the necessary arrangements for the valet in question. It was more or less what he'd done as a valet to the previous Lord Inverkillen, but he was no longer required to dress or launder clothes. That much he didn't miss. Lord Inverkillen had been unpredictably moody and highly ticklish, which made brushing off any stray lint from his suits particularly difficult.

In the days leading up to the ball, Mackay found himself increasingly busy with guest requests. Many needed new clothes for the ball or wanted specific people at their tables. He was even starting to organise the dance cards for people. But today, at this moment, everyone was at tea, and he could relax with his crossword puzzle. He was struggling with twelve down: *Name of Napoleon's Mother, 5 then 7 letters* when he heard footsteps in the corridor.

Unless they appeared at his door, he generally ignored it. Switching to sixteen across, he tried to recall the name of Charles II's Lord Chancellor. *Had he even had one?* Mackay shook his head in frustration. History had never been his strong suit.

Murmuring to himself, he took a sip of tepid coffee. He'd left it slightly too long.

Suddenly, he heard voices from the corridor, indistinct but sharp and then a rather irritated voice barking loudly: 'Get back here!'

Rising from his chair, he went to the open doorway and peered out. He could see two men, neither of them from this floor, squaring off in anger. The older gentleman had his finger on the chest of the younger man in the white suit.

Lord, that suit needs a proper pressing, he thought involuntarily.

The younger man swatted the finger like an irksome fly and tried to walk away. He managed a single step when the older gentleman grabbed his shoulder and roughly yanked him back. The next thing Mackay knew, the two of them were nose to nose, seething at one another, the younger one grabbing the lapels of the older man's suit.

'If you're not satisfied,' young man said, 'find it yourself.' He threw the old man backwards.

'You're lying!' The old man tumbled into a chair and fell to the floor. 'And your loyalty is wasted on her. If anyone can give you what you want, it's me.'

The men glared at one another, a fist forming in the young man's hand. Mackay wondered if he should intervene.

'You don't even know what I want,' he hissed, 'how could you poss—'

'Su Ying.'

The young man looked as if he'd been doused in cold water. He stood, frozen in place, staring at the old man on the floor, gulping for breath.

'Find it.' The old man got to his feet, a nasty smile on his face. He straightened his suit and descended the stairs, leaving the other to collapse against a console table. He'd gone as white as his suit and started to rock back and forth with his head in his hands.

Mackay stepped back into his office, thinking about what to do. He scraped his chair loudly against the floor and then walked determinedly into the corridor, as if nothing had happened. The man leapt to his feet and stared at Mackay for a moment.

'Can I help you, sir?' Mackay asked, in as light a tone as he could, trying to look surprised to see the man.

'Erm . . .' stuttered the young man, looking slightly panicked. 'No.'

And then he scurried down the stairs without another word, leaving Mackay to wonder if he should report it to Mrs MacBain.

Clarendon! The answer came to him in a flash. The Earl of Clarendon was the Lord Chancellor. He walked back into his office, putting the fracas out of mind.

Lady Georgina was incensed. She was standing in front of the seating plan for the ball. She had presumed her table would be at the far end of the room, in front of the fire, under the portrait of the fourteenth Earl of Inverkillen. It was the best spot in the room and should have been reserved for the family. But staring at the seating plan, it was clearly marked 'Duke of Auldwilde'.

How can Mrs MacBain be so thoughtless?

She tutted and threw her gloves on to the table next to her. She'd simply have to arrange them properly herself. Plucking the Duke off the board, she moved Inverkillen under the ribbon at the fireplace and relocated the Duke to the table to her left. Which meant the Monkhouses needed to be relocated. *And for more than one reason*, she thought archly. Mrs MacBain had no idea of the skill and delicacy involved in putting together a seating plan. Lives could be at stake, not to mention reputations.

Twenty minutes later, she was just about to finalise the new plan when Fergus opened the door to Rowan Tree, looking for Mrs MacBain. The surprise on his face was quickly replaced by a shrewd look.

'What are you doing, Grandmama?' He closed the door behind him and sauntered over to the plan.

'Correcting the seating plan,' she said. Raising a hand to stay his objection, she continued. 'Mrs MacBain has many skills; I am the first to admit she is exceedingly capable, but seating plans are not her forte. She's put the Auldwildes and the Monkhouses next to one another and that simply cannot happen.'

Fergus closed his eyes and gently shook his head. They'd spent days discussing the layout. How much had she changed? he wondered.

'And the Ruthvens simply cannot be on the same side of the room as the MacGregors or you'll have bloodshed. They're still arguing about ownership of that wretched barn. It's little more than rubble at this point.'

Fergus conceded the mistake. He'd not remembered that when they placed them together. Stepping closer, he cast an eye over the changes. Noting that his family was now in pride of place, he took a deep breath, only to be cut off again.

'And the Menteiths cannot be anywhere near the bar. You know what those sons of his are like. Absolute disgraces when the drink is flowing. If only they'd play more cards . . .' She moved them to a spot near the Oak Room, which they intended to use as a cards room for the gentlemen.

The entire plan had changed, he could see and, frankly, with her intimate knowledge of the families, their feuds, the grudges – not to mention the current gossip – perhaps she was best placed for this task. He smiled, kissed her gently on the head, and then left the room, continuing his search for Mrs MacBain.

Three Days to the Ball

Mrs MacBain was in her office downstairs, having a moment of silence. Things below stairs were getting increasingly frantic as the ball approached. This morning they'd had to clean scrambled eggs off the stairs after a display of Speed the Plough spun out of control. Poor Ollie had to rush to change his livery and wash his hair. How were they going to get everyone to focus?

A soft knock at the door interrupted her.

'Ah, Ross, come in.' She indicated the chair by the fire, but he didn't sit.

'Not much time, I'm afraid.'

'What can I do for you?'

Ross looked at his cousin a bit sheepishly. 'I need you to speak to Mr Cooper for me.'

Her eyes shot open in surprise. Ross never interacted with the guests. 'Mr Cooper?'

He nodded heavily. 'I keep catching him sneaking around the Distillery. I've told him several times already that he's not allowed to be there, but I keep catching him. Today, he was in the barrel room.'

'In the barrel room?' she asked, aghast. The barrel room, where the casks were stacked for ageing, was heavily secured. Mrs MacBain had never been in there. 'How did he get in?'

'Don't know, but I had to throw him out and I was none too polite.' He grimaced apologetically.

'Right,' she said, 'I'll have a word with him.'

Ross nodded his thanks and turned to leave.

'Oh, I wanted to ask,' she said suddenly, 'when you bring the whisky for the ball, can you leave it as close to the opening as possible? The staff's a bit over-excited and if we set it out too early . . .'

Ross chuckled and nodded his head. 'I'll bring it up when the doors open.'

'Thank you. You're coming to the ball, yes? I expect a dance.'

Ross bowed and then left. *And now,* thought Mrs Mac-Bain, *I need to find Mr Cooper.* She knew he was going to be a bothersome guest, but this was not how she envisioned it.

Two Days to the Ball

The ambulance showed up in the service yard with no warning. Mrs Burnside was thrown.

'No one told me about this. We aren't prepared, you understand?' she shouted at the two young lads who were trying to unload Bella's maid. 'You can't just leave her here.'

A houseboy was sent to fetch Fergus. They waited, the four of them, in the sunshine. One of the lads kicked a stone. They heard footfall on the gravel and turned, but instead of Fergus, it was a hotel guest, clearly lost.

'Can I help you?' shouted Mrs Burnside. The man was visibly startled, asked for the croquet courts, and then retreated before he got an answer, leaving the group in an awkward silence.

'How's your mum doing, Jamie?' Mrs Burnside asked.

'Oh, she grand now, Mrs Burnside,' Jamie said brightly. 'Thanks for sending all them pies. It was a big help.'

'Well, we all need a hand now and again,' said Mrs Burnside kindly. 'I'll send one of the girls down tomorrow to fetch the laundry.' Jamie's mum had just had her fifth child in as many years.

It was silent again and Mrs Burnside looked the maid over. There was a nasty bruise on her forehead, far worse than the one Mrs Burnside was sporting. In addition to her arm in a sling, the maid now how a cast on her leg and she was seated in a wheelchair. The wheelchair would be useless with only one arm. *What on earth are we going to do with her?* Mrs Burnside wondered. Thankfully, it wasn't her call.

Fergus arrived at long last, took in the scene and sighed heavily. Mrs Burnside scurried for the door. 'Well, I'll leave you to it.'

Jamie stood to attention behind the maid, hands on the wheelchair. 'Where do you want her, sir?'

'Erm . . .' But Fergus didn't know.

'You put her where?' Mrs MacBain was shocked.

Fergus squirmed. 'It was the only place I could think of that was on a single level.'

'There are plenty of places on a single level, Fergus. You didn't need to put her in the back end of nowhere.'

'Really?' countered Fergus combatively. 'You tell me where I can put her that has a lavatory near, and I'll move her myself.'

Mrs MacBain drew breath to speak and then hesitated. 'Well, how about . . . erm . . .'

Fergus cocked his head and waited with a slightly smug look on his face.

'Well, erm . . . we could put her . . .' She waved her arm and then lowered it. 'No that won't work. How about . . . Oh, that won't work either.'

Fergus let her stew for a few minutes. He was enjoying seeing her flummoxed. It was rarer than a Nessie sighting. He nearly giggled.

'You win,' she said at last. 'But who's going to take care of her? The old servants' quarters are a long way from the daily routine of the staff. With the ball, we don't really have a set of hands going spare.'

'Ah yes,' said Fergus bleakly, 'that's the rub.'

He'd found her in the music room, playing a rather tricky Chopin piece he remembered from his childhood. When she finished, he walked into the room properly.

'I didn't know you still played,' he said.

'Thought I was alone.' Bella turned, startled at the voice. 'I play occasionally. It's a good way to rescue a dull party.'

Fergus couldn't be sure, but it felt like a stab at his attempt at entertainment. Shaking it off, he steeled himself for the task at hand. Crossing the room slowly, he perched on the sofa arm. 'Your maid's back from hospital.'

'Oh thank heavens! It's been so difficult without her; I just don't know that I could have gone on much longer.'

'Ah . . .' Fergus cleared his throat nervously. 'The thing is, Bella, you're going to have to do without her a while longer.' Bella's head snapped up. 'She's in a wheelchair and with her broken wrist, she's not at all mobile.'

Bella sighed and looked to the ceiling with closed eyes. Fergus briefly wondered if she was praying.

'Oh, you have got to be kidding me!' she finally said, irritation unmistakable in her voice. 'What else could possibly go wrong? This has been the worst month of my life. I'm obviously cursed.'

Fergus was appalled. *She can't possibly be this selfish, can she?* he wondered. But as he was thinking of something to say, Bella snapped the piano shut and turned to face her brother.

'Bella,' he began to remonstrate with her but honestly did not know how to begin.

She counted on her fingers. 'Divorced. Lost my home to war. Husband absent. Wearing my cast-off clothing. And now, crippled maid. There simply must be a curse on me.' She viciously picked the leaves off a potted plant. 'My god, it would be funny if it weren't true.'

It took everything Fergus had not to slap her. He stood, breathing slowly, and then walked away from the display of marble busts. They were the composers his mother had most admired, and they were quite heavy. If a person could wield one, well, it didn't bear thinking about.

'Bella, how can you possibly be thinking about yourself at a time like this?' He managed to keep his voice nearly under control.

'Excuse me, but I'm the one whose life has been destroyed.'

'Your life has been destroyed?' Fergus shouted it. A passer-by flinched and scurried away from the double doors. Fergus moved swiftly to close them. No point in making a public scene. 'What about your maid? That poor girl has been wrenched from her home, and dragged halfway around the world to a foreign country.'

'It's Scotland,' she said scoffed, 'it's hardly foreign.'

'That's because you're Scottish!' he bellowed. How on earth could she not see it? 'She can't even speak to us. And now she's bedridden, body mangled, all because you dragged her here. And I am certain you did not give her the option of refusal.'

'Excuse me, but I did not drag her. She's my servant. It is her job to be where I am.' She flicked a nasty look his way and snorted, 'And if you think I want to be here, you'd best think again!'

'Feel free to leave at any time, Bella, because I can get a lot of money for those rooms I'm letting you have at a discount.'

Bella looked as if he had slapped her. Her mouth gaped open, wordlessly. 'I'm family! I shouldn't have to pay at all!'

'It's a business, you halfwit!' Fergus dropped his head in shame. 'I'm sorry. I . . . ' He moved to put his hand on her arm, but she jerked it away.

'How dare you speak to me like that!' she snapped.

Any regret Fergus felt was swept away by her statement. 'You're lucky I'm not turning you out altogether. You and your maid will lodge together in the old servants' hall, until she is able to get about by herself.'

'I am not sharing a room with my maid!' Bella shouted.

'Bella, be reasonable. Someone needs to take care of her,' implored Fergus.

'I am not sharing a room!' she shouted. 'Surely you can get someone here to take care of her. Maybe just leave her in hospital? Or you could hire a nurse.'

'Are you going to pay for that? Because she's not my maid, I'm not paying for it. I'm willing to bet you're too cheap to spend any money on someone other than yourself!'

Bella's gasp and expression told Fergus he had gone too far, but he just couldn't give in, even if Bella was weighing up the brass and walnut metronome.

'I'm not switching rooms,' she said through gritted teeth.

'You most certainly are!' He crossed to the bell pull to summon a footman and nearly tore the cloth from the wall. 'I run this hotel and if I want to move someone to another room, by god, it happens.' They glared at one another for a few moments, huffing and circling the room.

'You wouldn't dare,' hissed Bella.

'Try me,' he said though clenched teeth. The door opened. 'Ah, good, Ollie.'

Ollie's eyes flicked between brother and sister, both red-faced and glaring. He'd heard the shouting from the corridor and suddenly wondered if he shouldn't move the fire pokers. And the candlesticks. Was she holding an ashtray?

'You rang, sir?' he asked cautiously.

'Yes, please escort Lady Martin to her rooms and help her pack her belongings. She is moving rooms.'

Ollie moved towards Bella, doing his best to nonchalantly come between the siblings. 'Certainly, sir. Would you care to come with me, milady?' He leaned down to take the ashtray from her hand. After a brief struggle, he placed it on the piano and gestured to the doors.

Bella gave Ollie a black scowl and then turned to her brother. 'What a brute you've become. Give a man a bit of power and you see his true character.' She swept from the room, reminding Fergus strongly of his grandmother.

After Ollie closed the door, Fergus sat down on the sofa, hands shaking, heart thundering in his chest. He hadn't shouted at anyone like that in years. And frankly, he didn't miss it. He strode out the French doors into the garden and stomped to the woods. He needed to calm down before he spoke to another human.

Over at the Distillery, a knock at the door irritated Ross. He was studying the books. It was the part of the job he least liked – accounting, numbers, debits and credits – but he didn't feel they were ready to take on a numbers person just yet. Work was hard to come by these days, but he wasn't sure they could afford another worker. Which left him doing it himself, stuck at a desk, poring over numbers that made his eyes ache.

A lad from the yard stuck his head in the office. 'Begging pardon, sir, but there's something I think you should come and see.'

Ross happily gave up the books for a chance to stretch his legs and get some fresh air. 'What is it, McAllister?'

'I'm sure it's nothing but, someone's been in the peat store.'

Ross sat back down. 'Someone's always in the peat store.'

'Not through this door, sir.'

Curious, he stood and followed McAllister through the Distillery, out the yard and over to the peat barn. But rather than go in though the main door, McAllister led him round the side, to the very back, where a door stood just out of sight, covered by trees and scrub. He opened it for Ross to see. 'It was open when I found it.'

Ross looked at him, through the open door, and then stepped in, to the back of the peat barn. He couldn't see anything amiss. McAllister shone a torch on the floor. Footprints that looked, to Ross's eyes, fresh.

'Anything taken?' he asked, but knew the answer would be no. Who would steal peat, especially when they could dig it out of the ground?

'Not that I can see. Honestly, I didn't even know there was a door here.' Ross glanced at him. 'I was chasing one of the dogs.'

Ross nodded. It was a favourite game for Grantham and Belgravia: sneak in, grab something that looked important, and wait to be chased. Not for the first time, he wondered if it was too late to train them as gun dogs.

'I'd lock it but there doesn't seem to be a lock.'

Ross surveyed the dim interior critically. All looked in order, but it was a bit unsettling. 'Did you check the other buildings?'

McAllister nodded. 'Nothing out of place. What should be locked, was locked. Maybe someone just needed a roof over their heads one night?'

Ross glowered at the thought, unconvinced. 'Too many bothies on the Estate. Well, let's see if we can get a lock fitted somehow.' He stepped back through the door and surveyed the surrounding area.

'Yes, sir.'

Ross walked slowly back to his office, pondering the discovery. He hadn't known about the door either and wondered if it was Something or Nothing. When he sat back down to his desk, he decided it was probably Mr Cooper again. But he'd have McAllister keep an eye on it, regardless.

It was worse than Bella could have imagined. When Fergus said the old servants' hall, he meant the old pigsty, which had been repurposed as servants' quarters sometime in the Georgian period and connected to the main house by a small, dark stone corridor sometime in the Victorian era. They were at the very far end of the East Wing of the house and quite a long walk from anything worthwhile. Bella had not even known this part of the house existed. Ollie had only been here once. His first day on staff, he'd taken a wrong turn and got himself turned around. All the servants' halls looked alike and until you knew where you were going, it was a maze. When he finally found his way back to the kitchens, he was forty-five minutes late and Mr Hudson was not impressed. It had taken Ollie years to undo the damage to his reputation.

Bella stared around the room, horrified, and then sat down roughly on one of the four small metal beds. The frame rattled and the springs squeaked loudly. She suppressed tears. Ollie had unrolled the mattress for her and went to fetch linens. Other than the beds, there were two small bedside tables to share, a washbasin sitting on a pine table, and a single ladderback chair.

For god's sake, she thought, looking at the empty ceiling, *the room is still lit by candles.*

The grey stone walls were unadorned, and the floor had rough flags. Her eyes landed on the four chamber pots stacked in the corner.

No, she thought, staring at them with dread. *I cannot. I simply cannot be expected to use a chamber pot.* Bella mentally retraced the journey here. Had they passed a loo anywhere? Surely there was one nearby. This was inhumane.

By the time Ollie returned from the linen store, Bella was pacing the room in an absolute panic, muttering wildly. 'He can't mean for me to stay here!' she spat at the footman before he'd even had both feet across the threshold. 'Angus might be this callous, but not Fergus. I cannot possibly stay here! Has he seen these rooms?!'

Ollie looked around the room. It was so bare it couldn't even be called Spartan. 'Ah, not to worry, milady. We didn't know you were moving rooms, so no one's had a chance to, erm, get it ready. When we're finished, I'm sure you'll be quite comfortable.'

A maid walked into the room and stopped dead in her tracks, gawping in horror at the surroundings. Ollie pointedly cleared his throat and she scurried to make up the bed.

'Erm, what furniture do you need, exactly?' he asked cautiously.

'Electricity for a start.' Bella surveyed the room. 'There had better be a loo nearby as well. I am not holding a chamber pot for her.' Bella paused, looked around the room and began a litany of furniture she would need.

Twenty minutes later, Ollie wished he had never asked.

Fergus had just returned from his walk in the woods, calming himself after his fight with Bella, when, bizarrely, he'd run into Mr Cooper in the service yards, looking like he was lost. His face was red with exertion and there were twigs in his hair. Fergus escorted him to the front of the Abbey and then peeled off. He had just reached the baize door in the Armoury when his name rang out sharply. Turning, he came face to face with his grandmother, and Lady Georgina looked to be in a dangerous mood. 'A word, please?' It was not a request. Whatever it was, he felt sure the Armoury didn't need to hear it.

He guided her to Rowan Tree and closed the door behind him.

'Angus has to go,' she said, before either of them even sat down. 'I simply cannot have him in Thistledown Cottage any longer.'

'Why? What's happened?'

'God knows I've tried, but this was the last straw.' She twisted a handkerchief in her hands.

Last straw? What was the first straw? he wondered.

'He's completely disrupted my household. He keeps no consistent schedule to speak of, except for breakfast, which he demands at nine thirty. Nine thirty! Who has breakfast that late? No one, that's who. Cook has to stop her work to prepare his breakfast, which puts luncheon behind schedule.'

'Don't you have luncheon with us most days?'

She scowled at him. 'That is not the point. He has no routine, so the maid never knows when she can make up his room. He walked in on her the other day, gave the girl quite a fright, chased her out, and then had the audacity to complain to me that his bed wasn't made up.'

Fergus shook his head. It sounded exactly like his brother. 'I don't know how I can help. You're the only one he listens to. Bring him to heel.'

'It's not just the schedule,' she lamented, 'it's the late nights. He comes in well after midnight, stomping, banging, crashing about. I haven't had a full night's sleep since he's been back. Do you know, he hosted a cards evening. Didn't even have the courtesy to ask. They just showed up after dinner, with the Colonel and that American. It's difficult enough to sleep this time of year, but one doesn't need the sound of gentlemen underneath one's bed.'

Fergus tried not to smirk at the image of a miniature Angus playing poker underneath Lady Georgina's antique four-poster bed.

'But this morning—' She broke off and suppressed a sob. She grabbed Fergus's hand for strength and lifted her handkerchief to her eyes. 'This morning was the last straw. I was in the garden with my gardener – we're preparing for the village show, you know; it's a very tricky moment for the roses, with this heat – and we checked on my prize-winning *Rosa spinosissima*. Care to guess what we found?'

Fergus had an idea but knew better than to answer.

'Cigarette butts! Everywhere. Tossed, carelessly, into every single rose bed. I tell you, it's the last straw. The boy must go. You simply must find a room for him at the Abbey. Tonight.'

Fergus tried not to laugh. He didn't succeed.

'I don't see what's so funny. My life has been turned upside down.'

Fergus took a deep calming breath. 'Well, I don't have a room for him in the Abbey, but perhaps . . .' Fergus thought about it for some moments and began to warm to the idea. It meant he couldn't be late for lessons, which guests had been complaining about. And he could send a maid down each morning to tidy. *Yes, that wasn't a bad idea.*

'All right, Grandmama, I'll move him into the Tennis Pavilion this afternoon. But . . .' he hesitated and looked at her sternly '. . . you have to tell him.'

In the Drawing Room after dinner, Angus was brooding in a corner. Again. Bella was rather sick of it and crossed the room to speak with him.

'What's wrong now?' she asked dryly.

'I can't take this much longer,' he said sullenly. 'Lawlis needs to pick up the pace. It's bad enough I have to *work* for Fergus, now he's making me stay in the Tennis Pavilion!'

Bella rolled her eyes. Angus had spent years in the Tennis Pavilion. She couldn't understand why it was suddenly beneath him.

'Lord Ashcroft is staying,' Angus went on, 'and he came for a tennis lesson. We were at school together, for heaven's sake! When he worked out who I was . . . it was humiliating.'

'Oh boo-hoo! So you have to give him tennis lessons. It's hardly a train crash.'

'You, of all people, should understand the indignity of it.'

'Indignity? Of playing tennis? Please. I'm stuck nursing my mangled maid because Fergus won't let me pinch a maid off him. Do you have any idea what that involves? I have to take her to the lavatory, Angus! Help her on, then help her off. I have to bathe her and dress her. And that's before breakfast has arrived, which I have to go get, by the way. Back and forth to the kitchens, three times a day. The kitchens! Do I look like the sort of woman who should be in the kitchens? It's like having a child again. That, my friend, is undignified. You have nothing to whine about.'

Angus scoffed at her. 'I've been taking care of your children for the past three years!'

'Oh, please. We both know Nanny does all the work.'

Lady Georgina looked up to see her grandchildren sniping at one another. Again.

When will they learn to get along? she wondered. She swept across the room to intervene.

'Please, could we have just one evening without a disgraceful scene? Hmm? You are adults, both of you. At least try to project dignity while we're in public.' She smiled tightly. Bella and Angus shuffled, chastened. 'Now, what's the issue this time? No. No, I don't want to know.'

Mr Rosenthal bounded up to them, saving Bella and Angus from further scolding.

'Good evening!'

The man radiated joy, which thoroughly disgusted Lady Georgina. It simply wasn't normal to be that happy all the time. Sensing the tension between the Inverkillens, Mr Rosenthal continued, 'Lemme ask you something . . .'

'Excuse me, Mr Rosenthal,' began Lady Georgina swiftly, 'I must go rescue Mrs Blackwood.'

They turned to look at the fire, where Mrs Cooper was chatting amiably. Mrs Blackwood looked decidedly uncomfortable.

'Mrs Blackwood doesn't care for Mrs Cooper,' she said gravely.

'Really? How strange,' responded Mr Rosenthal. 'I find her delightful.'

Lady Georgina appraised Mr Rosenthal sharply. 'Yes, well, Mrs Cooper is rather young and still feels as if everyone ought to get along. She doesn't yet understand the joy in thoroughly disliking someone.'

Mr Rosenthal looked at Lady Georgina with delighted shock.

'Bella, shall we? Good evening, Mr Rosenthal.'

The men watched as the ladies swept to the fireplace.

'Your grandmother doesn't like me much, does she?'

'Erm . . .' hesitated Angus.

'It's okay,' he said, bemused, 'I'd hate to deprive her of her joy. Billiards? I hear the Colonel has some new cigars for us.'

One Day to the Ball

Cecil had been summoned to the Map Room and could clearly see from the threshold that Angus was agitated. His nephew was pacing to and fro, muttering to the dogs on the sofa. The dogs, for their part, listened lazily, in case there was a treat was in the offing.

Cecil watched for a moment, wondering what Bella had done this time, and then gently cleared his throat. 'Nephew,' he said brightly.

Angus jumped and turned towards the sound. He nodded and crossed the room, motioning to the snug under the catwalk.

Cecil made his way across the room. As he settled, his eyes fell on the painting over the sofa in the main part of the room. It was a seascape rather than the nude that had hung there for decades.

Probably for the best, he mused. He turned his attention to Angus. Cecil waited a full minute in silence. Angus, it seemed, was in no hurry to speak. But Cecil was; he had a haircut in half an hour. 'You wished to see me?' he enquired at last.

'Um, yes.' Angus hesitated. He stubbed out his cigarette and shifted uneasily in his chair. 'Erm . . . the thing is . . .' He cleared his throat and reached for his cigarette case. 'I'm rather in a spot of trouble, hmm . . . and I could, um, use some . . .' Again he paused. 'Well, I could use some advice.'

Cecil was taken aback. No one in the family had ever come to him for advice. Which wine to serve, yes. What key a particular sonata was in, absolutely. But advice about life, my word, that was unprecedented.

'I see.' He let a puff of air escape his lips. 'I'm only too happy to be of assistance, dear chap. What seems to be the trouble?'

Angus nodded, staring at the floor, still uncomfortable. He swallowed hard and then twirled a small brass figurine on the table next to him. Whatever it was that was bothering him, it was big, Cecil surmised. After several false starts, a few seating positions tried and rejected, Angus finally spoke.

'There's a claim against my honour.' He took out his cigarette case and fiddled with the latch. 'Gaming debts, you understand?'

Cecil nodded sagely, covering up his surprise. He hadn't thought of his nephew as a gambler.

'I've rather lost a packet to that Blackwood woman and, well, she's being none too pleasant about collecting it.'

An involuntary grimace crossed Cecil's face. 'Yes, she doesn't strike me as sympathetic. Exactly how much, if I may?' Cecil took out his own cigarette case and started to tamp one on the silver exterior.

Angus watched, a bit forlorn, and then quietly stated the amount. It rolled across the coffee table like a dense fog, engulfing Cecil in a haze. The cigarette fell in slow motion.

'How on earth did you lose that much?' he sputtered. 'You've only been here two weeks!'

Angus looked chagrined and reached for the fallen cigarette. Handing it to his uncle, he shrugged, looking like a schoolboy caught sneaking out of quarters past curfew.

Cecil was staring at him, aghast. 'How? You're reasonably proficient in billiards and I've never seen you sit down to cards after dinner. Not once. How is this even possible?' Cecil had accrued his fair share of gaming debts in his day, but this was positively reckless.

Angus stared at brass figurine, breathing deeply, clearly steeling himself.

'Angus,' Cecil said sternly, 'how did you lose this much money?'

Elbows on knees, Angus covered his mouth and breathed out deeply, staring at the floor. 'Backgammon.'

Cecil drew breath to speak and then held it as his brain processed the new information.

'Backgammon?' His voice was rife with confusion. 'But you hate Backgammon. You've always been rubbish at it.'

'I have improved greatly since moving to Tangiers!' Angus shot up out of the chair and paced, irritation evident in every step.

'Clearly not enough. How did this all come about?'

'I was in the Sun Room one day after luncheon, messing about with the board. The Blackwood woman come in, saw me, and asked if I wanted a game.'

'And you said yes?'

'I didn't see the harm in it.' Angus sighed petulantly. 'So, we played. The first few games, I won, rather easily. The final one was close run, but I still won. I excused myself and thought nothing more of it. The next afternoon, a footman delivered a handwritten invitation to another game. It seemed rude to refuse, so I accepted. But when I sat down, she insisted we wager on the game.'

'And she won?'

'No, she lost. Badly. And then insisted on trying to win her money back the following day.'

'And that's when she started winning?' Cecil hazarded, a shrewd look on his face.

'Yes. Before I knew it, it was a guinea per point, and then she brought out the doubling cube.'

Cecil issued a low whistle.

'Six games later I finally left the table, very much in her debt.'

Cecil nodded, deeply engrossed in the story.

'And now she's demanding the winnings, which—' he paused and resumed the squirming of earlier '—I haven't got.'

Cecil's head snapped up in shock.

'You wagered without the capital to back it up?' Cecil was horrified. He might have been reckless in his day, but he always had a way to pay his debts. Well, nearly always. But he'd never lost this much.

Angus sighed, resigned to tell his uncle the entire truth. 'I haven't a bean to my name. Hugh took care of everything. I was hoping to make a bit of cash. I'd beaten her so easily, it never occurred to me I'd lose.'

'Which is precisely how people lose their fortunes!' Cecil huffed and stood up, glaring at his nephew. He crossed the room to pour them each a whisky and walked back slowly, gathering his thoughts. Handing one to Angus, he asked, 'Any chance she cheated? This feels like a set-up.'

Angus shook his head as he reached for the whisky. 'I don't see how.'

'Dropping her handkerchief and then rolling just as you lean down to retrieve it? Or perhaps distracting you some-how and moving the pieces while your back is turned?'

Angus thought for a moment and then shook his head. 'No, none of that. And it's Bella's old board, so nothing's funny with the dice.'

Their father, Hamish, had given Bella a pale blue and white leather set one year for Christmas. They'd been playing on a tatty old set in the evenings, and he felt she was rather good, for a young girl, so he bought her a new set. But Bella was more than good. She was gifted, and ruthless, and as the holiday wore on, tantrums, tears and gloating clouded each day and most of the evenings. Things came to a head on Hogmanay when Fergus – Fergus! – threw the board across the Drawing Room, knocking the sherry glass clean out of Lady Georgina's gloved hand. They had been forbidden to play another game, and a footman was charged with hiding the board. Unfortunately, that swiftly led to an epic search effort, resulting in several broken pieces of Wedgwood and a badly damaged chandelier. Hudson finally locked it in the silver vault.

'Perhaps you should have Bella play her,' Cecil suggested. 'Avenge the family honour.'

Angus grimaced. 'But then I'd have to explain it to Bella, and I'm not sure I'd prefer being in her debt to the old woman's.'

Cecil silently agreed. 'How long is she willing to hold your marker?'

'That's just it; she refuses to hold it.'

'What!' Cecil sputtered into his whisky. 'That's positively unsportsmanlike. No gentleman of any standing would demand such a thing.'

'Yes, well, I'm starting to understand that she's no gentleman.' Angus stood and started pacing again. One of the dogs raised a head in hope of a walk. Disappointed, he swiftly resumed his afternoon nap. 'If I don't pay her immediately, she's threatening to go to the police.'

'To report you for a gaming debt? That's ridiculous.' Cecil pulled a face and dismissed the idea. 'I sincerely doubt our bumbling police constable would take that seriously.'

Angus had gone deathly pale as he gulped his whisky. His hand shook slightly as he poured another. Cecil studied his nephew carefully. 'Why are you so concerned? It's a gaming debt. It's large, yes, but these things happen.'

'Somehow, I don't know how, but somehow, she knows about Hugh.' He let the statement hover in the air, hoping his uncle would understand without having to explain it further.

But Cecil was confused. He cocked his head to one side, thoughts circling in his brain.

Angus stared in disbelief. 'She has his books.'

Uncle and nephew stared at one another, one knowing full well the books were enough evidence to condemn; the other confused, having never read a single volume.

'Oh for god's sake!' Angus swore and slammed his glass on the table. 'I could go to prison! Oscar Wilde ring any bells?'

Cecil screeched like a small girl, leapt to his feet, and sprinted across the room to lock the Map Room doors. The dogs sat up, eager to watch the drama unfold. With the perimeter secure, Cecil swiftly crossed over to Angus, grabbed him by the arm and whispered angrily, 'My dear boy! Such things must never to be said aloud. You know Mama's penchant for magically appearing at the most inopportune moment.' He threw Angus into a chair with surprising strength. It was Cecil's turn to pace.

'Surely you knew?' implored Angus.

'Knowing and acknowledging are vastly different things,' he said coldly. He continued to pace, deep in thought. 'This is very serious. Money aside, a scandal of this nature would ruin the family. And we've only just managed to repair our reputation after the bankruptcy.'

'Damn the family reputation, I'd be facing prison!'

Cecil hesitated in his pacing long enough to nod. The worry of it rounded his shoulders. 'How long have you got?'

'I'm to give her the money at the ball.'

'Right,' he said tentatively. The Highland Ball was the following evening. Cecil would have killed for a deck of cards. He always thought best when his hands were busy. Instead, he paced.

He did have a way to raise the funds. It would take a few days to bring to fruition, and he'd never make it in time for the ball, but it could – theoretically, at least – be done. Cecil hesitated. This was not how he envisioned things would play out, however. If he did this, to save his nephew, questions might be asked, and that was the last thing Cecil wanted.

He glanced at his nephew, sitting on the sofa, looking for all the world as if his life was over. If the truth about Angus and Hugh were to come out, however, Angus's life – and freedom – would most certainly be over. Just how serious was the woman? he wondered. He sighed deeply, wondering just how much love for his family he truly had.

'I might have a solution.'

Angus's head snapped up, his face full of unbridled hope.

'We're not out of the woods yet,' cautioned Cecil. 'I want you to think carefully before you answer this question: Is she more interested in the money or the scandal?' Money could always be found, but if she was more interested in causing chaos, then there was precious little anyone could do about it.

Angus considered. 'I don't know. He only spoke about the money.'

Cecil held up a hand and shook his head. 'He? Who's he?'

'That nephew of hers.'

'Oh!' he cried. 'So she's sent the nephew to do her dirty work, has she? She's no amateur, then. Describe to me exactly how it happened.'

Angus thought back, glancing out the window at the trees. 'I was changing for tea this afternoon, and there was a knock at my door. Stupidly, I invited him in.'

Cecil closed his eyes and tried to picture the scene.

'I hear you're none too good at Backgammon, Lord Inverkillen. I've come to collect Mrs Blackwood's winnings for her.'

'I'm afraid you've wasted a journey.' It was a haughty reply, which Angus often relied on to gain the upper ground. 'I've not had time to get to the bank and I simply haven't that amount on my person. She'll have to wait.'

'No, no,' Lawrence responded, waving a finger, 'that's not how the game is played. You lose the money. We ask for the money. You give us the money. They're rather simple rules. Even you should understand them.'

'Kindly put that down,' said Angus in his coldest voice. Lawrence had picked up a cigarette case that Hugh had given him. 'It's a considerable sum to raise quickly . . .'

No response. He merely turned and looked at Angus.

'I don't keep that much as ready cash,' Angus spat, angered that this wretched man, so clearly not a gentleman, didn't understand he was being dismissed. 'Especially not when I come to visit family.'

Lawrence offered a cold smile and placed a small parcel on the bed. 'She expects the money before the end of the ball.'

'And if I can't raise it by then?' asked Angus, a tiny note of panic entering his voice.

The nephew turned and gave Angus a strangely sympathetic look. 'She wants the money. I suggest you find it for her. She's

*not a woman to be underestimated.' He pointed to the parcel on
the bed and then left.*

Angus was staring out the window and shook himself back
into the present. He turned to look at his uncle. 'When he'd
gone, I opened the package. It was one of Hugh's books.'
Angus sat back in his chair, spent from reliving the memory.

Cecil issued a low whistle. 'She's got you foxed. Who
would have suspected that tiny creature of being so calcu-
lating? Well, she's clearly after the cash, not the scandal,
which bodes well. We can work with that.'

'Can we?' asked Angus, delighted to hear 'we'.

'Yes. Money can always be found, dear boy. But sadly,
with what your dear brother extracted from me for my
rooms, I haven't much on my person. I think,' he said
slowly, 'that you should spend the day in the Billiards
Room. Be ruthless, as ruthless as your sister would be, and
take as much off the Colonel and Mr Rosenthal as you can.
And anyone else you can find.'

'I can't possibly make enough before the ball.'

'No, but every bit helps. The rest, we'll have to win at
cards tonight and at the ball. Let's hope some heavyweights
show up, like Lord Cosgrove. Get him tiddly and you might
be in black before the third reel.' He turned to stare sternly
at his nephew. 'But – and this is imperative – absolutely no
drink. Not until you've paid her. You have one chance, or
you'll be asking Mama for the money.'

'No!' Angus shrieked. 'That's why I came to you. I don't
want anyone else to know. Grandmama would murder me.'

'Indeed, she would, my boy,' Cecil muttered darkly. 'Well,
you'll have to scrape together as much as you can. I'll help.
Something is better than nothing and we can see about the
rest over the next few days. She'll just have to accept that.'

'And if she doesn't?'

A sigh escaped Cecil. 'Let's cross that bridge if we come to it. Now go.'

Angus scurried out to fleece the Colonel and Mr Rosenthal, leaving Cecil to wonder what life without family would be like. *Peaceful*, he decided.

After dinner, Lady Georgina convinced Mrs Blackwood to play bridge, despite her 'headache'. She was increasingly begging off each evening and, quite frankly, she was too good to go to bed early. Lady Georgina had never had such a strong partner and she wanted to take full advantage while the woman was still in residence. What had the American said? *Get while the gettin' was good.*

'Don't just stand there scowling, Angus,' said Lady Georgina impatiently, waving at the chair next to her. 'Come and sit down.'

Angus's eyes darted to Cecil, who was fussing with sheet music at the piano. 'I don't think I shall, Grandmama.' He walked towards the drinks tray.

Mrs Blackwood looked up at him coyly. *Is she smirking?* he wondered.

'Nonsense, come sit down.' Lady Georgina issued the command without looking up from her shuffling. 'Mr Rosenthal, whist or bridge?' She had no intention of asking him to join. Asking invited refusal.

Mr Rosenthal looked surprised but simply nodded. He glanced at Angus. 'Fair warning, I'm not the strongest player.'

But Angus, who had lost quite enough to Mrs Blackwood, had no intention of playing – or losing – anything else.

'Erm . . . no, I erm . . . I don't think I shall. Perhaps you can find someone else. Mrs Cooper, perhaps?'

At the mention of her name, Mrs Cooper looked up and smiled, eager to join the table. 'I'll happily join, Lady Georgina,' she volunteered. 'Darling, shall we play?'

Mr Cooper didn't look terribly enthusiastic, and Mrs Blackwood even less so. She started to make noises about retiring for the evening, which was something Lady Georgina would not allow.

'Angus, come and partner Mr Rosenthal. What's got into you, this evening?'

'No, I won't!' Angus shouted. He hadn't meant to bring the room to a halt, but he did. They all stared at him in surprise. Lady Georgina stared daggers at him.

'I'll join, Mama,' called Cecil from the piano, glancing knowingly at his nephew. 'I'm feeling rather lucky tonight. If you don't mind, Mr Cooper?'

'Not at all,' came the reply. Mrs Cooper looked at her husband with disappointment.

'Thank you, Cecil.' Lady Georgina spent another few seconds glaring an etiquette lesson at her grandson, and then promptly refocused her attention on the cards. 'Now, bridge or whist?'

Angus felt a surge of relief, nodded his thanks to his uncle and continued to the drinks tray, hastily grabbing the nearest whisky. He would have to be careful until the old woman left. Lady Georgina might have taken no for answer tonight, but next time might really irritate her. And the last thing Angus needed was Lady Georgina angry with him. As he was ruminating, the Colonel burst into the room, blustering inanely about something or other – a horse, perhaps? Who knew? The man simply spoke at anyone who was near to hand. He grabbed a whisky from the bar, downed it, and then shuffled off with a second and third in hand. He barged in on the conversation Mr Rosenthal and Cecil were having.

'What ho! Billiards chaps?'

The men turned to look at the Colonel.

'Ah, no thank you, Colonel,' Cecil began politely, 'we're sitting down to cards this evening.'

The Colonel's interest was instantly piqued. 'Cards? Oh, you mean bridge. Yes, well.' He shuffled in a bit closer. 'I'd be careful with those two, if I were I you.' He nodded at Lady Georgina and Mrs Blackwood, who were settling into chairs.

Mr Rosenthal looked surprised.

'Don't let the old lady guise fool you, man. They took nearly ten pounds off me the other night. Not an ounce of mercy between them. Lady Georgina's all right, but that Blackwood woman, she's vicious. Well, good luck!' he called cheerily as he bounced out of the room, leaving Cecil and Mr Rosenthal to stare at one another, entirely unnerved.

'What did we get ourselves into?' Mr Rosenthal asked hoarsely, his eyes wide with fear.

Cecil struggled for a moment and then managed to compose himself. 'Pay him no mind. I've played against Mama for years. I know all her tells and signals. We'll be fine.'

They turned to the women, who were smiling, but not warmly. *Like wolves*, thought Cecil.

It took the ladies three-quarters of an hour to bankrupt the men and they had difficulty in getting away from the table. The Colonel had been right; they were a formidable pair. Lady Georgina had always been a strong bridge player, but what Cecil had just witnessed was an altogether different level of skill. If the Blackwood woman played backgammon half as fiercely as she played bridge, it was no small miracle that Angus only owed her a small fortune instead of a large fortune.

Mama must be making a killing partnering Mrs Black-wood, he thought to himself as he walked slowly to the billiards room. If only he could find a way to convince Lady Georgina to pay off Angus's debt without explaining it to her. There simply had to be a way.

The Morning of the Ball

It was the morning of the ball and, regrettably, nothing short of chaos. The staff were giddy beyond belief. Today, they had extra duties to perform and were rushing about as if they were all new to service. Several collisions had already taken place and a crystal vase shattered.

Hudson was upstairs in the Ballroom with the footmen. The room needed to be set up with chairs and tables laid out along the perimeter of the dance floor, dressed in flowers, candles and dance cards; new candles for all the candelabras, with the flowers trimmed so as not to catch on fire; carafes of water on the tables with crystal glasses.

In the Oak Room, games tables were set with score pads and pens, chips for games, and dice. Sofas and chairs were brought into the Rose Drawing Room for the ladies. The Yellow Lounge adjacent was stocked with handkerchiefs, headache powder, sewing kits, perfumes and smelling salts.

Downstairs, extra staff from the village came to help in the kitchens. Mrs Burnside was shouting orders rapid fire, standing on a stool in the middle of it all. Pasties, pies, terrines, and all sorts of delectable goods were being prepared for the supper. They'd spent a week prepping for today, but still ran short of some items. Houseboys ran back and forth to the village most of the day. Three of the lads from the Distillery oversaw roasting the meats – venison, boar, pheasant and quail – just to help.

Sadie spent the morning running back and forth to the laundry, checking on table linens, making sure they had tablecloths and napkins to spare. In the afternoon, she wrangled staff, two by two, to the livery room to get them outfitted for the evening. Starched shirts, bleached gloves, perfectly clean aprons and bonnets. Everyone needed to look their best.

When not running to fetch things from the village, the houseboys were tasked with polishing silver. Trays, tableware, punchbowls, candleholders. They'd been slowly working on the task in the evenings, but there was still much to do. The smell of silver polish was so strong, they had to open the windows and take turns leaving the room for fresh air.

Mrs MacBain watched nervously. If the ball was a success tonight, then most likely it would become an annual event. It might be easier if one did this regularly, she mused, but she couldn't escape the notion they needed more hands on deck.

She heard another crash in the hall. Summoning up her patience, she went to investigate.

Upstairs, Elspeth asked the ladies of the family to gather in her rooms after breakfast. She had a surprise for them. They gathered, tittering with excitement, awaiting Bella.

'What is it, Maman?' asked Delphine, entirely overexcited for her first ball. Elspeth was a bit concerned how she'd manage to get through the day if the girl was this excited at ten o'clock.

'Just a hint?' asked Lady Georgina, eyebrows raised in curiosity.

'No, not a word, nor a hint, until Bella's here.'

They made small talk, laughing as Lady Georgina regaled them with scandalous tales of balls she'd attended in the past.

'Lady Worthington, do you remember, Elspeth, tripped on her sash at the Colquhoun Ball – her brooch had broken during a turn – and fell face first into the lap of her husband's best friend. She wasn't seen in public for at least a year.

'A chartreuse gown with pink Chantilly lace,' she continued. 'I ask you, who wears chartreuse? It is universally an unflattering colour.'

Then: 'They were discovered in the summer house, in a scandalous state. The Countess was, of course, livid and had to be restrained from attacking her son. He was always a bit of a rogue. We were at their wedding three weeks later. The flowers were disgraceful, it was so hastily arranged.'

Bella finally walked in the door. 'Wretched maid,' she said by way of excusing her tardiness. 'I dropped her again and it took me ages to get her back up onto the bed.'

She flopped down on the sofa, a sour look on her face, hair dishevelled.

'Well, now that we're all together,' Elspeth chirped, her eyes twinkling. 'A ball means jewellery and I won't have Clan Inverkillen outshone by anyone.'

She walked to her wardrobe and retrieved a large Hermès case. Setting it gently on the dressing table, she unlatched it and threw the doors open to reveal drawers and drawers of jewellery sparkling in the daylight.

A hushed awe filled the room.

'I want every one of you dripping in jewels. Mama, I brought the tiara you saved for me. I thought you should have it back.' She tenderly handed a box to her mother.

Lady Georgina was moved beyond anything she'd ever felt. She opened it and smiled. 'Your father always wanted you to have this. It belonged to his favourite sister.' She fingered the centre stone gently. 'I hadn't thought I'd see it again. Thank you.'

Elspeth smiled indulgently. It was fun playing Father Christmas. 'Imogen, I wasn't sure if you had a tiara to wear, so I erred to the side of caution. Please don't be offended.'

'Not at all!' she cried, eyes wide in disbelief. She'd never seen a jewellery display like this before and the idea that it all belonged to Elspeth was nearly too much to process.

Elspeth selected a navy-blue box. 'This one is for you. You're wearing peach tonight, yes?'

Imogen nodded mutely.

'I thought perhaps this might work well.' It was a gold bandeau woven to resemble lace and lined with ivory pearls and a citrine centre stone. 'I thought it would look beautiful in your dark hair.'

Imogen was speechless with shock.

'It belonged to my husband's great-great-grandmother. She wore it to the court of Louis the Sixteenth.'

'That's always been my favourite,' exclaimed Delphine.

'Then you should wear it!' cried Imogen, handing it to the girl. 'I don't need a tiara, honestly.'

'No, no,' said Lady Georgina in a soft rebuke. 'Unmarried ladies do not wear tiaras.'

'Well,' said Elspeth, guiltily, 'I did bring one for her.'

'She's not even out, Elspeth!' Lady Georgina was shocked. 'She shouldn't be at the ball in the first place, let alone in a tiara. It is a serious breach of etiquette.'

'I know, Mama, but I figured it wouldn't do any harm. She'll be courting in France, not Scotland. What happens here can stay here.' She smiled at her daughter indulgently.

'However, I didn't know Bella would be here for the ball, so we're a tiara short.' She looked apologetically at Bella.

'She can have mine, Maman!' Delphine volunteered, keenly aware she needed to court her grand-mère's good favour, or she'd be sitting in the Nursery with silent Nanny all evening.

'Are you sure, Chérie? I chose it especially for your dress.' It was Delphine's first ballgown, which she'd sewn herself, and Elspeth had taken great care to choose a tiara for it.

Delphine nodded and Elspeth handed the box to Bella.

Bella opened it to find platinum leaves with flowers of blue and pink sapphires. Bella fought back tears and struggled to keep her composure. 'Well, I suppose it will have to do. Since mine was stolen.'

Elspeth and Imogen exchanged conspiratorial glances.

'Now, I've got several brooches to choose from and as much jewellery as Philippe would let me travel with. Let the choosing begin!'

It was, Elspeth felt, a great start to the day.

'Sir?' Thompson called softly to Fergus as he walked through the Armoury. Fergus waited while Thompson finished with Lord Follett. Seemed the man wanted to try his hand at falconry. Standing behind him, Fergus motioned a silent 'No' to Thompson. He was a slight man, Lord Follett, and one of the ghillies had already pulled him out of the river after a salmon caught his fishing line. The idea of him with a bird of prey was more than Fergus could handle.

'Leave it with me, milord, and I'll see what we can arrange.' Thompson waited until the man was a judicious distance away and then leant across the desk to Fergus. 'We've had more complaints.'

Fergus sighed. He had an enormous To-Do List for the ball that evening. Dealing with his errant brother was the last thing he needed.

'I was able to smooth things over with nearly everyone, but word is spreading.'

'I can't understand it.' Fergus shook his head and took a deep breath. 'Is he there now?'

Thompson nodded and stepped back to his post.

Fergus headed to the front door, his task weighing on him. He walked the long way around, partly to gather his thoughts, but mostly so he could approach without being seen. He needed to see what was happening for himself.

As he crept round the corner of the Tennis Pavilion, he could hear Angus shouting at Mr Gibson.

'Not like that. Have you learned nothing?' Angus crossed the court and stood behind his pupil. 'Feet like this.' He kicked the man's feet apart. 'And swing when it's at the top of the arc. Top. Of. The. Arc.' Grumbling, he took his place on the other side of the net. Mr Gibson did as he was bid and served the ball to Angus. *That looked all right,* thought Fergus. But then Angus fired it back to 63-year-old Mr Gibson who cowered in the corner of the court.

'Again,' barked Angus. Mr Gibson's face was flushed with frustration. 'And do try to volley this time. It's not much fun for me otherwise.'

Mr Gibson ran like a frightened puppy to gather the tennis balls from the far side of the court. Angus watched, spinning his racquet in his hand, looking both bored and annoyed. As Mr Gibson took up position to serve again, Angus called to him. 'Remember, top of the arc.'

Mr Gibson nodded, looking for all the world like he was about to defuse a bomb. After a tense moment, he gently tossed the ball aloft and started to swing.

'Foot fault!' erupted Angus.

Mr Gibson was so startled he dropped his racquet and narrowly missed hitting himself with it. He gathered himself together, and carefully standing behind the line, served the ball to Angus. It didn't have much force in it. Fergus didn't play tennis but could have easily returned it. He watched as Angus swung and missed the ball entirely. Mr Gibson looked jubilant. Angus muttered darkly.

Another serve went straight to Angus, who clearly wasn't expecting it, and he launched it over the enclosure into the woods. This went on for several exchanges and Fergus could barely believe his eyes. When Angus did manage to return the ball, it was either dangerously strong or wildly out of control. But the rest of the time, he missed the ball altogether.

Fergus was shocked. *Could it be? No . . .* He watched a few minutes more as the realisation solidified. But, all that time, the hours, the days spent at the Tennis Pavilion with Hugh through the years. How on earth could this be? They started each day with tennis. In the summer, they returned after luncheon and played until the dressing gong. How could it possibly be that *Angus couldn't play tennis?*

Fergus stood with his mouth agape for some minutes, feeling the earth tilt underneath him. *No wonder people are complaining*, he thought.

Angus shouted at Mr Gibson again and sent a ball careening towards him. Mr Gibson leapt out of the way, throwing himself on to the ground. The poor man needed rescuing.

Fergus approached the court, shouting, 'Hold fire, Angus!' He stepped on to the court, holding his hand up to his brother, and unconsciously bracing in case he got hit. 'Mr Gibson, would you mind terribly cutting things short today? I need Lord Inverkillen for something.'

Mr Gibson looked at Fergus with relief in his eyes. 'Thank you!' And he scrambled to collect his things, hurrying up the steps towards the Abbey.

'Sorry to cut it short,' said Fergus casually.

'Please. God himself couldn't help that man.' Angus walked to the Pavilion and sat down, pouring himself a glass of water.

'That didn't look like a great time for Mr Gibson.'

'It's not my fault the old boy can't play.'

'Actually, it is your fault. You are supposed to coach him.'

'I tried!' shouted Angus defensively.

'No, Angus, you didn't. You tried to beat him. He signed up for a lesson, not a match. Your job is to be helpful. As a paying guest, he was supposed to come out of this feeling good, not injured.'

'It's not my fault I'm a better player than he is.' He pouted and hastily poured himself some more water, slopping some on the table. 'Someone must lose the match. It's not football.'

What a child, Fergus thought. *How were we raised by the same parents?*

'Angus, this isn't about winning! It's about giving the customer what he wants. They need go away happy.'

'I play at a particular level and if he can't handle that, I don't know how to help.'

From what Fergus had witnessed, that level was quite low. 'This is not about you, Angus. It's about them.'

'So I'm expected to dumb down my game, to pander to his level, so he can feel like a bigger man?'

'Yes!' cried Fergus. He wracked his brains. How to explain to him, a man who had never thought of anyone by himself, that his raison d'être was now others' happiness? He sighed and tried again.

'You're here to help them. To improve their backhand or explain how the scoring works; whatever they want. It's about them feeling like you've helped their tennis game. It's only ever about them. You are simply here to fulfil their needs.'

Angus snorted. 'I am not a servant.'

Fergus arched his brow.

'I am aristocracy,' Angus said forcefully.

'Aristocracy without means,' Fergus enunciated slowly.

The brothers glared at one another for some moments.

Fergus back-pedalled. 'You're not a servant, exactly.' He had to get through to him. 'More of a professional, like, erm . . . Bill Tilden.'

'American,' sneered Angus.

'Twice Wimbledon champion. He's made a fortune from tennis. Plus, he wrote that book, which I know you've read several times.'

Angus begrudged this. It was a tremendous read and, admittedly, one of the only books, other than Hugh's, that he'd read. 'I just don't see why I have to do this,' he grumbled, aimlessly tracing the pattern on a linen tablecloth.

'Because it's this or sobriety. Take your pick.'

They were silent for some moments. Fergus watching closely to see if he'd got through, Angus contemplating life in Loch Down without the benefit of cocktails.

'Now look,' Fergus continued, 'you've got Lady Gill and her daughter coming in thirty minutes. I've seen them play; it won't be entertaining. It will be tedious, in fact. Be gentle with them; the ball is tonight, and they need to be unbruised.' He stood and looked to his brother, who didn't look at all happy. He went quickly, leaving Angus to mumble something about life not being fair.

The Loch Down Highland Ball

Mrs MacBain was inspecting the room one last time. If she were honest with herself, she was nervous. She'd never been to a ball, so the input of Lady Georgina, while tedious, had been a godsend.

The Inverkillen Ballroom was a long room with six pairs of French doors along one side leading to a terrace. An enormous fireplace commanded the far wall, with a famous portrait of the fourteenth Earl looking down on the room. The walls were inky blue with ornate gilt panelling. Crystal wall lights dotted around, lending a soft glow to the room. But the star of the show was undoubtedly the ceiling. Rather than the expected neo-classical fretwork, the fourteenth Earl had opted for something altogether different. Three enormous chandeliers, twinkling with candlelight, hung beneath a painted fresco of the night sky, spectacularly coloured by aurora borealis.

The band was warming up, sitting in the gallery above the entrance. Footmen dressed in special livery were placing decanters of whisky on the tables. Ross's pale gold whisky gleamed in the candlelight. Every available surface was covered in candles, and Lady Georgina's roses graced every table, ledge and windowsill. Mrs MacBain had to admit the woman was a spectacular gardener. Or at least her gardener was.

It was, on the whole, a breathtaking scene. Mrs MacBain nodded in satisfaction and went to change her clothes.

Lady Georgina arrived fashionably late to the ball. The Inverkillens did not arrive on time, even for their own ball. She was always precisely twenty-two minutes late. Late enough to make a statement, but not late enough to be hostile. As she entered the double doors to the Ballroom, she stopped dead in her tracks, her mouth falling open.

'Hudson! What on earth are you wearing?'

Hudson was dressed in a vivid turquoise robe, with a wide collar of fur down the front, and rows of alternating violet and mustard-coloured tassels covering the lower third. He wore a matching tricorn with the Inverkillen coat of arms.

'Good evening, Your Ladyship.' He bowed deeply. 'May I say you look lovely.'

'Yes, thank you.' She continued to stare at him and then waved her hand up and down, questioning his garb.

'This is the traditional Beadle's Robe, featuring the colours of the Inverkillen tartan. And you'll recognise the staff of office, no doubt, crafted after the siege of 1632, from the weapons of the fallen clansmen.'

'Erm . . . yes.' She eyed him critically. He had sweat on his brow. The Inverkillen tartan was garish, but it was tartan; all tartans were all inherently garish. The robe, however, was a queasy six-foot-tall nightmare. 'Perhaps the robe needn't be worn this evening. It is quite warm, after all. I hadn't remembered the fur. Is that stag?'

'Rabbit, I believe.' He handed the staff to a footman and removed the robe, secretly relieved to be shedding the awful garment. 'Tricorn as well?'

'Yes, I think so. Oh, I must say, that's much better.'

Hudson pulled himself to attention and stepped to the edge of the stairs.

BANG! BANG! BANG!

Lady Georgina started violently and stumbled to the side, a footman catching her before she hit the floor. Hudson banged the staff loudly again on the floor before announcing: 'MR AND MRS ALEXANDAR KINCADE AND MISS KINCADE.'

She hadn't appreciated this portion of her role as hostess. While she'd been to many a ball and had herself been announced to the room, she'd never acted as hostess. It was the host's duty to stand with the Beadle and greet the guests as they arrived. One didn't enter the Ballroom until one's name had been announced. As a guest, Lady Georgina had never been next to the Beadle when her name was called and she hadn't quite understood just how loud the announcement, and the staff, would be. One, she felt she could manage, but not both. As she spotted the doctor and his wife arriving, with their four daughters in tow, she stayed Hudson's arm.

'Perhaps we need only announce the guests of note?'

'Guests of note, milady?' asked Hudson, confused. Tradition dictated each guest be announced.

'I mean the aristocracy. One only cares about the titles in attendance, not about the little people.'

Hudson gave her a dark sidelong glance.

'And it will save your voice,' she hurriedly responded. 'We don't want you hoarse tomorrow, now do we?'

Well, he thought to himself, *it is early, and my throat is starting to itch*. He capitulated.

As the guests poured into the Ballroom, the tediousness of greeting so many strangers started to wear on Lady Georgina. Who knew so many from the village would attend? She should have brought a spare pair of gloves; these would surely be filthy by the first reel. She wondered if she should send a footman to Thistledown Cottage. After ten minutes, she spotted Mrs MacBain, and waved her over.

'I can't possibly stand here any longer. It's like standing beside a cannon.'

'Yes, well,' hesitated Mrs MacBain, 'I did try to talk you out of the staff, you'll remember.'

'Thank you for reminding me. Any other lapses of judgement you'd care to highlight? Hmm?' Lady Georgina was in no mood to be scolded. Between Hudson, the staff, and her tiara – which she'd not worn for some time and was finding strangely heavy – a headache was brewing. 'I'm moving to centre of the dance floor.'

'But how will people see you? It's getting crowded and it's early still.'

Lady Georgina scowled and then waved a footman over. 'Gather a few of the others and make a pathway from the door, so people can see me when they enter.'

And with that, she took up her post in the centre of the Ballroom.

BANG! BANG! BANG!

'THE EARL AND COUNTESS OF BUCHAN.'

Fergus had arrived early, to be sure everything went off smoothly. It had, of course, being under the watchful eye of Mrs MacBain. But as this was their first ball, he didn't want to leave anything to chance. Standing in front of the band, he prayed there would be no disasters.

BANG! BANG! BANG!

'THE HONORABLE MRS OGILVY-SINCLAIR.'

Fergus whirled around and caught his breath. Imogen, his lovely Imogen, had arrived. Resplendent in a peach silk gown, she blushed as she was announced. Fergus crossed the room quickly and took her hand, escorting her to the centre of the room.

'I'm so sorry!' he stammered. 'They were supposed to tell me when you'd arrived so we could enter together.'

'It's fine, Fergus. I just wanted a peek at the room, but Hudson announced me before I could ask him not to.'

'But it's our first ball and I want it to be magical.'

She stopped and looked up at her husband, a dreamy smile on her face. 'It is. Don't worry.'

They approached Lady Georgina, who surveyed Imogen's gown critically.

'Imogen, you look lovely,' she exclaimed. Her approval had clearly been granted. Imogen breathed a sigh of relief. Lady Georgina gently touched the diamond brooch fastening Imogen's sash to her gown. It had been a wedding gift from Lady Georgina. 'I'm so delighted it's getting an outing. Do enjoy the ball.' She handed Imogen back to Fergus and moved to the next guests in line.

Fergus escorted Imogen across the Ballroom.

'That ceiling!' she gasped.

Fergus looked up and then smiled. 'Yes, the fourteenth Earl – that's him above the fireplace – had it painted to recreate the night sky of his birth. He felt being born under the Northern Lights was a good omen and foretold of his greatness.'

'And was he great?' Imogen stared at the portrait.

'Erm . . .' Fergus groped for this part of his family's history. 'If memory serves, he was shot while in bed with a nun. I think he might have kidnapped her.'

Imogen looked to Fergus, horrified.

'But wait until it's dark,' he continued cheerfully, 'the candlelight bouncing off the jewels makes the aurora look as if it's moving. It's quite special.'

They arrived in front of the fireplace where the family had gathered. Elspeth and Imogen embraced. 'You look wonderful, Imogen.'

'Thank you, Elspeth. So do you.'

'Are you nervous?'

'A little, yes,' said Imogen nodding.

'Don't be. You were perfect this afternoon.'

'This afternoon?' Fergus asked, a bit confused, looking between the women.

Elspeth looked coyly at Imogen, who flushed. 'Elspeth and Delphine have been giving me dancing lessons. It's my first ball. I didn't want to embarrass you.'

The breath left his body as if he'd been punched. It was her first ball and he'd had no idea. He'd volunteered her for the first reel, which the entire room would watch, without asking her. It never occurred to him she didn't know how to dance. Everyone he knew was raised attending these events. *But she wasn't*, he castigated himself.

He took her hands in his. 'You could never embarrass me.'

A blush spread across her cheeks, and she looked away shyly, her gaze landing on Delphine.

'Delphine! Look at you! That dress is spectacular!' She wandered over to the girl.

Fergus sighed and turned to Elspeth. 'Auntie Elspeth to the rescue, once again. Thank you.'

'It's Delphine's first ball as well. I wanted them to be prepared.' Elspeth shrugged modestly. 'But to be honest, they weren't my primary concern.' Elspeth's gaze travelled to Lady Georgina, who was holding court and positively radiating pride.

'Yes,' said Fergus slowly, 'that was probably the right call.' They burst into laughter.

'Oh look, the children are here!' she cried, waving up to the Gallery that overlooked the room.

It was Highland tradition for the children to come for the first few dances, and they were as excited as Delphine had been. They'd been practising different reels in the Nursery all week, with Strip the Willow being the hands-down favourite. Ranging in age from twelve to six, they presented adorably, dressed in tiny kilts and white dresses with Inverkillen tartan sashes. They crowded to the balcony and peeked over and through the railings, waving wildly at Elspeth and Fergus. A few people whispered and pointed, no doubt at Nanny, who was backed against the wall, shrouded in her customary white garb. *In a dark room, she would look like ghost*, mused Elspeth.

The staff came down heavily, six times in quick succession, bringing the room to order.

'MY LORDS, LADIES, AND GENTLEMEN,' Hudson began. 'PRAY MAKE WAY FOR CLAN INVERKIL-LEN.'

It was time to open the ball.

The ladies had acquitted themselves well. Imogen hadn't put a foot wrong. Giddy with success, she asked Lawlis to give her the next dance. Cecil and Angus moved to the Drawing Room to play cards the moment the final bow was taken. Lady Georgina basked in the applause of the guests.

The Dashing White Sergeant was the first reel on their dance cards. Elspeth partnered Cecil and Mr Rosenthal, who apologised in advance, while Bella and Delphine had drawn the short straw and were partnered with the Colonel. As badly behaved as Lord Enderleigh's retriever had been on the shoot, the Colonel was worse on the dance floor.

He charged into the other dancers, sending people flying into neighbouring groups. He twirled Delphine into a table, to which Lord Ruthven took umbrage, and demanded satisfaction. Before they could decide on swords or pistols – Lord Ruthven unfairly dismissing the idea of poleaxes – Fergus reminded them duelling had been outlawed in the 1840s. Peace restored, they swept through to the next group, the Colonel charging forth exuberantly, nearly ripping Bella's arm from its socket. Huffing and puffing, he was nearly doubled over when it finished.

Elspeth watched with trepidation. *Is it wrong to pray for a heart attack?* she wondered. She desperately needed an excuse to cancel the next dance with him. Perhaps she could hide in the Ladies' Lounge? Or submit herself to the midges on the terrace?

He accosted her before she could decide.

'Ah, Lady Elspeth. I think . . . hooo . . . stitch in my side. I think . . . ha! . . . I think I've quite had enough dancing tonight. Would it be terribly rude of me to beg off? Not as fit as I once was.' He patted his waistcoat, as vibrant and unappealing as Hudson's robes had been, and continued to breathe heavily.

'What a pity, Colonel, but of course I understand,' she said, trying to disguise the glee in her voice.

Bella nearly snorted. 'Reeling is a young person's game.'

'Indeed, it is.' The Colonel mopped his brow with a handkerchief. 'I beg your forgiveness and bid you good evening.' He bowed deeply, nearly fell over, and went in search of cards, limping slightly.

'The whole of the Highlands just breathed a sigh of relief,' said Bella when he'd gone.

'Bella!' chastised Elspeth. Bella merely raised her eyebrows. Elspeth grabbed two glasses of champagne. 'Let's go up to the Gallery and say goodnight to the children. Then we can decide who has the worst gown.'

The ball was in full swing, and Mrs MacBain decided to check in on the Drawing Rooms. As expected, the ladies congregated in the Rose Drawing Room, for cards and gossip. They had a view of the dancing though the open double doors that dotted the length of the long wall. Lady Georgina was holding court at the fireplace, looking every bit the Countess of the Abbey she had once been. It was, Mrs MacBain reflected, good to see again. It had been difficult for her to adjust to life after leaving the Abbey. She had her cottage, and her flowers. She had luncheons and dinners in the Dining Room frequently and was a fixture at the bridge tables in the evenings. And while she was established, she wasn't quite flourishing, Mrs MacBain suddenly realised. Perhaps they needed to find a more social role for her. *For the woman who had famously refused to entertain guests*, thought Mrs MacBain wryly. Wandering through to the Oak Room, she was assaulted by the cigar smoke that clung to the air. *This will need a good airing out tomorrow.* She waved a hand in front of her face. Deciding to stay on the periphery of the room, she could see Angus playing against Lord Cosgrove and Cecil at the table next to him. A raucous table caught her attention. The Colonel, it would seem, had won a large hand.

All was well, and she carried on. Coming out into the corridor, she was surprised to see a footman exiting the Small Library. It wasn't a room they'd planned to use that evening.

'Colin, isn't it?' she addressed the young man, who nodded once, eyes wide. 'Everything all right?'

'Yes, ma'am. Just checking all was well. I saw some, erm, revellers, in this part of the hall and I know this room is off limits tonight.'

'Well, off limits is a bit strong, but yes, if we can keep people out, that would be good. Thank you.'

He nodded and continued to stand. There was an awkward pause. 'I would think it's best to head back to the ball now.'

Colin continued to stand.

'I'm sure Mr Hudson will need you.' She took a step back and held her hand out to escort him.

Colin hesitated and then shuffled off. Mrs MacBain couldn't shake the feeling he was irritated with her. It wasn't a feeling she normally got from the staff. Turning around, she spotted one of the kitchen maids peeking out the baize door. Upon seeing Mrs MacBain, the girl squeaked like a frightened mouse and disappeared.

Of course, Mrs MacBain smiled to herself, *it's a ball, why shouldn't young love be flourishing?*

The Foursome Reel was announced, and she sped off. She'd promised this one to Mr Rosenthal.

The breakfast buffet had been laid at midnight, and people were crowding the silver dishes of food in the Long Gallery. Mrs MacBain watched from the entrance to the Ballroom, smiling and nodding as people came past with plates of sausages, tattie scones, eggs and haggis. Hudson was pacing the length of the table like a general, keeping a keen eye on food levels. They would not, under his watch, run low on anything.

Her attention was caught by Lawrence Blackwood. She hadn't seen him at all that evening and was pleased they'd come to the ball. Mrs Blackwood had demurred earlier in the week, saying she hadn't a suitable gown for a ball, but here was Mr Blackwood, dressed in his white linen suit, as always. Perhaps she'd changed her mind as well.

Mr Blackwood walked quite far up the line and tapped the Colonel on the arm. They exchanged a few words, and the Colonel, plate in hand, sausage suspended from his lips, got out of line and followed Mr Blackwood to the Small Library.

What's that about? she wondered. But before she could process any further, a voice was in her ear.

'Oh, there you are! Where did you set up our table? I couldn't remember.'

Mrs MacBain turned to see Lady Georgina looking at her expectantly. 'I'm sorry, what?'

'The family table. Where did you put us?'

'I don't understand.'

'The host always withdraws to a private supper,' Lady Georgina said portentously.

Mrs MacBain looked at her blankly. This was the first she was hearing of it.

'You can't expect us to stand in line. Next to common-ers.' Lady Georgina was truly irritated. 'Never mind. I'll have a footman set something up in the Music Room.' She swept off before Mrs MacBain had a chance to respond.

Of all the things she'd done for this ball, a private supper for the family had never once been mentioned.

How was I to know that was the custom? she thought, irritated. *I've never been to a ball in my life. Not even a servants' ball. And it's my ball! If anyone should be having the private supper, it should be me!*

She breathed out slowly and counted to ten. She would not let Lady Georgina ruin what was, in her opinion, a wonderful evening. After a few deep breaths, she approached a footman. They had a table to set.

'You've been avoiding me,' Ross said quietly.

Elspeth whirled around and looked up at him. 'There's been a lot to do. I haven't really had a spare moment.' She hesitated and touched his clan badge. 'Have you, erm . . . missed me?'

Ross bowed his head in greeting to someone behind her and then looked deeply into her eyes. 'I always miss you, but it's easier to miss you when you're in France. Knowing you're this close . . .' He paused, choosing his words carefully. 'It's been difficult.'

Elspeth stared at him, searching his face for answers to questions she didn't want to ask. Instead, he grabbed her hand, pulled her behind a pair of stone columns, and kissed her deeply. 'We could disappear. No one would notice.' The twinkle in his eye returned.

Elspeth was tempted. But the image of the unmade bed in the bothy floated to the surface. 'I shouldn't. It's Delphine's first ball. She might need me.'

They glanced round the columns to the dance floor, where Delphine was laughing as she twirled, showing off her gown to several local girls.

'She's fine,' said Ross, a smile on his face. 'Belle of the ball, I'd say.' He nodded towards a group of four or five lads, all watching her.

Elspeth couldn't help but smile. What a magical night her daughter was having. Ross took her hand.

'I'm not sure, Ross. Besides, I'd never make it to the bothy in this dress. Let's just have a dance instead, shall we? We've never danced together.' She stepped back into the Long Gallery and walked straight into the ball, leaving Ross to wonder what had changed.

Mrs Cooper came off the dance floor, beaming, despite Reverend Douglas clumsily throwing her on the floor during the Gay Gordons. Mrs MacBain was checking her dress hadn't been damaged.

'I think things are going swimmingly, Mrs MacBain.' She was breathing heavily. 'You should be quite proud.'

Mrs MacBain smiled up at Mrs Cooper. 'Oh, thank you. That's very kind of you to say.' She took in the young woman. She was clearly having the time of her life. 'Well, I can't see anything amiss. You should be fine. But I'd avoid the Reverend, were I you. It's too beautiful a dress to risk it. I do love seeing a full skirt on the dance floor. It swishes in a way the modern gowns don't.'

'Oh, thank you. I was worried it was a bit young for a married woman.'

'Not at all. You are a young bride, after all. Now, where's your husband?'

'Oh, he went to bed after the breakfast.' She fanned herself with her dance card. 'He doesn't do late nights. And I think the dancing exhausted him.'

'Yes, it can be quite demanding.' Looking over the young woman's shoulder, Mrs MacBain noticed Lady

Beaumont slipping out of the Small Library. She looked flushed. Mrs Cooper noticed the look on Mrs MacBain's face and turned to follow her gaze. A moment later, the door opened again, and Mr Blackwood slipped through.

'I thought the Blackwoods weren't coming to the ball,' said Mrs Cooper, curiously.

'They weren't. Mrs Blackwood didn't feel she had a suitable gown. It appears they've changed their minds.'

Mrs Cooper looked at Mrs MacBain, who was staring at the door of the Small Library still.

'What's wrong, Mrs MacBain?' She cocked her head and asked, 'Is he not supposed to be in there?'

'What? Oh, no. It's just, erm . . . we hadn't planned on using that room this evening, so it was never prepared. I'm just surprised to see people going in there.' She tried to say it as lightly as she could.

What is happening down there? she wondered. *First the footman and now . . . oh.*

Her mind at ease, Mrs MacBain turned back to Mrs Cooper, who was now watching Mr Blackwood with some interest. When he disappeared into the Oak Room, she turned back to Mrs MacBain and smiled.

They announced the next reel.

'You'd best get in there. Only two more reels, you know.'

'So soon? Tonight flew by. Well, I'd best go check on Alistair.' Mrs Cooper took three steps forward and then turned back. 'Thank you, Mrs MacBain. This was a wonderful evening.'

It had been a wonderful evening. Mrs MacBain went in search of a dance partner.

The Morning After the Ball

Early the next morning, Mrs MacBain was sitting at her dressing table, sleepily brushing her long auburn hair and reflecting on the previous evening. The ball had gone spectacularly well, and she congratulated herself. If she was honest, she'd not been sure they'd pull it off. But they had! She was as close to bursting with pride as she would allow herself. She set the brush down and rummaged in a drawer for her hairpins.

Her door erupted in furious pounding, causing her to start and knock over a bottle of hair tonic.

'Just a moment!' she called irritably, mopping up the tonic with a handkerchief. When it was under control, she went to the door and opened it. A hall boy was huffing slightly. He'd clearly sprinted to her rooms. 'Jimmy! What's happened?'

'Mrs MacBain,' he huffed between gulps of air, 'Mr Hudson needs you straight away. He's in the Small Library.' The boy took a deep breath and turned to allow her passage.

'The Small Library?' she asked, instinctively on guard. 'What's happened?'

'Dunno, miss,' the boy said, gently pulling her by the arm, 'but he didn't look good, and he shouted.' Hudson never shouted, especially above stairs, as a matter of principal. No one was to shout above stairs. It was something they were reminded of each and every staff meeting. '*Decorum always*' was Hudson's motto.

Mrs MacBain nodded and shut the door behind her, following the boy through the labyrinth of hallways, doors, stairs and passages to get to the East Wing. *No wonder he was out of breath*, she thought when the Ballroom Wing came into view. She had a stitch in her side.

As they neared the Long Gallery, the hall boy stopped, doubled over to catch his breath, and waved an arm at the Small Library. Mrs MacBain approached with trepidation.

She turned the handle and was surprised when the door didn't open. Why was it locked? She turned back to the hall boy who shook his head vigorously. She tried again and then knocked softly.

'Mr Hudson? It's me.'

The door opened, just a few inches. 'Mrs MacBain, thank god it's you.' He stood aside to admit her.

Mrs MacBain stood looking at her partner. He had lost all colour in his face. She felt her stomach lurch. 'I was told you wanted to see me quite urgently.'

Without another word, he grabbed her arm, pulled her into the room and locked the door behind her. Mrs MacBain turned around, offended at being manhandled, but then gasped. Her gaze fell to the sofa. 'What is that? What's happened?' She rushed closer. 'Is that blood?'

Hudson nodded gravely.

'Oh! Oh, dear lord. What's happened?' She leaned in for a closer view, gasping. 'Mrs Blackwood?'

Part Two

The Morning After the Ball

Mrs MacBain knelt by the body of Mrs Blackwood, careful not to touch anything. She held her hand in front of the old woman's nose, just to be sure.

Hudson shook his head. He doubled over and tried to breathe deeply. He was dizzy. 'That's how I found her.'

Mrs MacBain stood and looked around the room. There was a moment of silence and she nodded sharply. 'Right. Did you touch anything? Is the room exactly as you found it?'

Hudson thought carefully. 'Yes. Erm, no. I'm not sure.' He was very pale and Mrs MacBain fleetingly wondered if he was going to faint. She took him by the shoulders and pushed him into an armchair, his back to the sofa, so he couldn't see Mrs Blackwood.

'Pull yourself together. We need calm, clear heads.' She straightened up, noticing the curtains at the garden doors. 'Were those drawn?'

'Yes,' he replied after a quick glance to see what she was looking at. 'And the little lamp was on. And both sets of doors were locked.'

'Locked?' She glanced at him, wondering if the shock was clouding his judgement. 'If the room was locked, how did you get in?'

He held up a brass skeleton key with a small silk tassel attached. 'When I couldn't get in through the garden doors,

I remembered the doors to the Oak Room have a key, so I tried it.'

Mrs MacBain stared at him, bewildered. She stared at the brass rim lock on the door. 'They open this door as well?'

Hudson nodded. 'These old Georgian locks aren't terribly sophisticated, so practically any key can be used to open them. It just needs to be the right size. When I was a footman, I carried various skeleton keys with me at all times, just in case.'

Mrs MacBain shook her head. The man had been destined to be a butler; that much was certain. She resumed walking slowly around the room, scanning intently for, well, she wasn't entirely sure.

'Did you tidy anything? Pick up any glasses, fluff the cushions?' She glanced at his tray, which was half-filled with champagne coupes and a dirty ashtray.

'Erm . . . well, not in here.' He pointed to the tray. 'I set it down to open the curtains. When I turned around, I saw . . . I thought someone was sleeping.'

Mrs MacBain nodded. What a discovery that must have been. She walked slowly around the sofas and looked at the fireplace; there was fresh ash in the grate. *She had a fire?* How odd. It had been incredibly warm last night. They'd had to open every available door and window at the ball just to keep people from fainting.

'Should we ring for someone?' Hudson asked thickly. 'The doctor, perhaps?'

'What? Oh, yes.' Mrs MacBain snapped out of her reverie. 'I suppose we should ring the police as well.'

'What?!' Hudson spun round to face her. 'Whatever for?'

'She didn't do this to herself, Mr Hudson.' She said it quietly, gently.

The implication rendered him silent. He looked at Mrs Blackwood, crumpled on the floor in a pool of blood and back to Mrs MacBain.

'No,' he said at length, 'no she didn't. The poor woman. I'll go and ring from my office. Shall I have Cook set up a breakfast buffet in the servants' hall?'

The question caught her off guard.

'If I feel this bad this morning, I'd wager there isn't a lad in the village without a headache today. They'll need something in their stomachs to deal with this. Lock the door behind me.'

Mrs MacBain reflected on his statement and then smiled faintly; immeasurably glad he was there.

Fergus had been asleep when the maid banged on the front door of the gatehouse. He wasn't pleased to see her, she'd woken the baby. His mood was dark as he stomped down the hallway to the Small Library.

Whatever it is, he thought, *it had better be genuinely important or heads will roll.*

He was close to fuming when he rounded the corner and noted that the main Ballroom hadn't been cleaned yet. Across the Long Gallery, the Small Library came into view. His anger faltered. It was being guarded by a police constable.

'I've been asked to come,' he told the constable, unsure what to say.

The constable, who couldn't have been more than twenty, nodded gently, and opened a door to admit Fergus. It was unfortunate timing. Just as Fergus entered the room, the doctor rolled the body of Mrs Blackwood on to her back, so he could get a better look at the wound. Fergus's legs buckled but Mrs MacBain grabbed him, setting him on the arm of a nearby chair, close to Hudson. She stared intently at the pair of them. Fergus looked woozy and Hudson was still chalk white. She felt sure they'd need smelling salts before too long.

'What happened?' Fergus asked hoarsely, not daring to look back at the scene.

'It's Mrs Blackwood,' Mrs MacBain answered him. 'Mr Hudson found her this morning while tidying up.'

'That must have been a nasty shock,' he said gently. Hudson gave a weary nod.

'Yes, as I suspected,' said the doctor. He was crouched over Mrs Blackwood, inspecting the wound, and now sat back on his heels. 'She was stabbed.'

'Stabbed?' Mrs MacBain was incredulous. 'No! Are you sure? Could it have been something else? Please say a gun-shot.'

Fergus and Hudson stared at her, a bit disturbed at her questioning.

Shaking his head, the doctor stood and looked at her. 'Sadly, no. It was a quite a sharp blade. Bit of a problem there.'

'I'll say,' replied Mrs MacBain, sighing heavily.

'A bit of a problem?' Detective Inspector Jarvis looked bewildered. He was head of the Loch Down police force, which never failed to amaze Mrs MacBain. The man wasn't the sharpest axe in the shed.

Mrs MacBain looked to the doctor, who shook his head in disbelief.

'You are aware, are you not, that we had a Highland Ball here last night?' Mrs MacBain started slowly. She couldn't recall if he'd attended or not.

'Yes,' answered Jarvis, even slower. 'What of it?'

'Nearly every man here was in Highland dress.'

The room was quiet as Jarvis digested this news. From the unchanging look on his face, the statement meant nothing to him.

Mrs MacBain huffed and continued in a sharper tone. 'You are a Highlander, for god's sake! Surely you recall that formal dress includes a *sgian-dubh*?'

Comprehension dawned very slowly over his face. 'Which is a sharp blade.'

'Yes,' said Mrs MacBain wearily, 'and there were hundreds of them in the Abbey last night.'

'Which,' Jarvis said as the penny dropped, 'is a bit of a problem.'

'Yes,' said Mrs MacBain, relieved he'd finally got there. *How is this man in charge of anything?* she wondered, not for the first time in her life.

'Right.' Jarvis nodded, sagely. He paused for a few moments and then said, 'Guess I'll be needing your guest list then.'

They all stared at him in mute disbelief.

'Why?' asked Fergus, hoping the man wasn't going where Fergus suspected he was.

Jarvis, sensing he was about to be challenged, pulled himself up to his full height and puffed out his chest. 'Whoever killed her is on that list. I'll need to speak to each guest. Well, the male ones, at least.'

'You can't be serious,' Fergus said, nearly laughing. It was such a ridiculous idea. 'The entire county was here last night!'

The doctor could see his morning slipping away and interjected swiftly. 'I'd quite like to get the lads here to take her down to my surgery, if you're finished, Inspector?'

Jarvis, who had been glaring at Fergus, looked first to his constable, who nodded, and then to the doctor. 'Yes, we're finished. Get me a time of death as soon as you can.'

'I shall. And I strongly feel this discussion should be held in another location.' He nodded to Hudson, who was swaying dangerously.

'Yes, of course,' replied Mrs MacBain, crossing over to steady him. 'This way, Mr Hudson.'

'If you go through the kitchens, you can grab a bacon butty on the way out.' Hudson's voice was thick and slow. His legs buckled dangerously. Another moment and he might be on the floor.

Ten minutes later they were in Mrs MacBain's office. Hudson had been dispatched to lie down. Tea had just been set on the desk and Jarvis was noisily pouring himself a cup. It was making her head ache.

'Now,' he said, turning around to face Fergus and Mrs MacBain, 'I'm quite serious about wanting the guest list. We need to know who was here last night.'

Fergus tutted loudly, strongly reminding Mrs MacBain of his grandmother. 'Between the staff and the hotel guests, the gentry, and anyone who wandered up from the village, there must have been nearly three hundred people. We can't possibly account for every name!'

'We've got to start somewhere, and one of your guests killed that old woman last night. Where do you suggest we start?' Jarvis was starting to lose his temper. He really didn't like being second-guessed. And he was quite hungry. Since Hudson mentioned bacon butties, it was all he could think about.

Mrs MacBain stood silently for a moment. 'I'll get you the guest list, if that's what you want. Far be it from us to tell you how to run your investigation, Roddy,' she said, and then helped herself to tea.

'But?' asked Jarvis, a bit cautiously.

'But I find it hard to believe someone from the village murdered that poor woman.' She returned to her office chair and continued, tea balanced in her hands, the rim to her lips. 'Mrs Blackwood only arrived here a few days ago. She told me she's lived in Shanghai since she was a young bride, so what, forty years? And she's only been here a couple of weeks. What could anyone from the village have had against her? She was a complete stranger.'

'Exactly,' said Fergus pointedly.

The room was silent for a moment. 'Homicidal maniac?'

Fergus made an impolite noise. Mrs MacBain glared at Jarvis. 'I find it even less likely there's a homicidal maniac in Loch Down.'

'You think one of the people travelling with her killed her?' Fergus asked Mrs MacBain.

'Well . . .' Mrs MacBain shrugged. 'It's more likely than, say, Robbie from the chemist's shop killing her, don't you think?'

Fergus thought about it and nodded slowly. *Did people kill complete strangers?* He jokingly thought about killing his family on many occasions, but a stranger? He thought it improbable.

'Besides,' she continued, 'you don't really want to conduct hundreds of interviews, do you, Roddy? Spend hours studying the dance cards to be sure no one was lying? It would take ages!'

Jarvis thought about it. The paperwork alone would take weeks, and he really wanted to get in on the first flush of grouse this season. 'So what do you suggest?' It came out harsher than he'd meant it to, and Fergus shot him a warning glare. Jarvis held up his hand. 'Apologies.'

Mrs MacBain was staring at the empty grate, miles away from Loch Down. 'I think trouble would have followed her from Shanghai, not found her here. She was travelling with people who knew her, who knew her life there; it's far more likely one of them killed her.'

Jarvis nodded slowly. 'All right. Let's suppose that's true. Who does that give us?'

'The Colonel,' answered Mrs MacBain, 'and her nephew.'

'And Bella.' Fergus's voice was hollow as he mentioned his sister's name.

Jarvis stared at Fergus, unsure what to say.

Fergus was staring at the wall, taking deep breaths to quell his panic. 'If it was someone on the trip with her, why do it here?' said Fergus, pacing the room, trying to dispel his anxiousness. 'I mean, the Colonel is always banging on about how unsafe the journey is.'

'True,' answered Mrs MacBain, thoughtfully. 'All those stops along the way, there must have been dozens of places to kill her and evade suspicion. The plane would continue and could be weeks before anyone knew who she was.'

'And if they found her,' Jarvis interjected, 'it would be put down to local ruffians. You'd be a thousand miles away, beyond reproach.'

'If you'd been planning on killing her, that's a safer solution, yes? So why not take it?' Mrs MacBain sighed with frustration. 'Why wait until she's in Loch Down, a tiny hamlet with a lot of prying eyes and gossiping old hens? It doesn't make sense. It's almost reckless to do it here.'

They were quiet for long time. The clock chimed the hour and a small knock on the door revived them. Jarvis's constable poked his head in and announced they were finished and ready to leave. He nodded gravely.

'Did you find the knife?' Jarvis asked.

'Erm . . . the knife?' mumbled the constable, suddenly worried he'd messed up.

'The knife that killed her. I had stupidly hoped we'd find it under a sofa or something.' He looked hopefully at his constable.

'Um, no. We didn't find a knife.'

'Well,' said Jarvis slowly, 'that supports you *sgian-dubh* theory. Thank you, Constable.'

He turned to leave.

'Oh, Constable, a moment?' said Mrs MacBain. 'Did you find Mrs Blackwood's cane?' All three men stared at her in confusion.

'Her . . . cane?' he asked slowly.

'Yes, her cane. Mrs Blackwood walked with a cane. It has a carved jade flower on the top. It's quite valuable, I'd imagine.'

'You think this is a robbery gone wrong?' asked Jarvis with scepticism.

'No. No I don't.' Mrs MacBain looked troubled. 'I just don't recall seeing it in the room, which I find odd. She was never seen without her cane, so where did it go?'

Jarvis stared at her for a long moment, and then slowly replied. 'Best go check again, Constable.' He hated it when she was right.

The constable nodded and left the room and they settled into thoughtful contemplation.

'The question is, why was she in there in the first place?' she muttered quietly, mostly to herself.

'What's that?'

'Oh, I was wondering why she was in the Small Library. She told me, in no uncertain terms, that she wouldn't be attending the ball. So why was she in the Small Library?'

'Erm . . . Maybe she wasn't at the ball. She could have come down after the ball.'

Mrs MacBain gave it a moment's thought. 'I'm not convinced by that,' she said slowly. 'I saw her nephew at the ball, and they were rarely apart. It does make me wonder . . .' She stood and absently-mindedly rearranged a few trinkets on the mantelpiece. When she'd spotted Lady Beaumont, she'd presumed they'd gone into the Small Library for a tryst. Lady Beaumont was rather famous for her dalliances while her husband was at cards. She'd also seen him escort the Colonel into the room but, as she searched her memory, Mr Blackwood had stayed outside the room. A new picture started to form in her mind's eye.

What if Lady Beaumont hadn't been there to see Mr Blackwood, but his aunt? Mrs Blackwood, who hadn't wanted to be at the ball, but spent the evening near the ball. Adjacent to the ball. Where no one saw her, unless they went into the Small Library. With the loud music, and all the comings and goings of a ball, no one would notice a quiet little assignation, even if it got a bit shouty.

Jarvis waited. He'd long ago learned to interrupt her as little as possible when she was in this state. Staff were starting to report for duty and the hum of the kitchen was increasing. It was soothing, he thought, peaceful in a way.

Mrs MacBain took a deep breath, seeming to have come to a decision to share her thoughts. 'I overheard a conversation a few evenings ago, between Mrs Blackwood and the Colonel.'

Jarvis raised his eyebrows. 'Overheard?'

'It was late, and I was making my final pass for the evening. They were up on the first landing, and you know what the sound is like in the Armoury when it's empty.'

Jarvis nodded. It echoed loudly, a terrible place to spill secrets.

'I didn't get the entire conversation, and, at the time, I didn't think much of it. But now, I can't help but wonder if she was threatening him.' Mrs MacBain turned to face him. 'She had the upper hand and he was very unhappy about it. I wonder . . .' She trailed off.

Jarvis stared at her a moment, waiting for her to finish her train of thought. When she didn't, he asked, testily, 'You wonder what?'

Mrs MacBain looked at him, as if she'd forgotten he was there. 'I wonder if she was blackmailing him.'

'Blackmail?!' Jarvis was shocked at the very idea. 'That sweet little old woman?'

Mrs MacBain noted how quickly Jarvis had given the woman a personality. Was it because she was old or because she was tiny? 'She was many things, Roddy, but sweet wasn't one of them.'

Jarvis was sceptical, which was written all over his face.

'The Colonel was sort of barking at her,' she continued. 'He said he wouldn't risk his neck, that he was in deep enough, and she responded with "something, something, or else". You don't generally say "or else" unless you're giving someone an ultimatum, do you?'

Jarvis screwed up his face, thinking swiftly. 'Erm . . . can't think of another situation.'

'And the Colonel responded with "*you wouldn't dare*".'

'She wouldn't dare *what*?'

'I don't know. But she definitely had the upper hand in the conversation.' She stared into the empty grate of the fire, trying to concentrate on the memory. 'It was very odd, because the entire time they've been here, I've not seen them speak to one another. On this side of things, I now wonder if they were actively avoiding one another.' She sighed and slipped back into thoughtful reverie. If she was blackmailing the Colonel, might she have been blackmailing the others as well?

The mantel clock chimed the hour and brought Jarvis back to the situation at hand. He stood and picked up his hat. Mrs MacBain looked at him, confused.

'I need to go tell her nephew before word gets round,' he said by way of explanation.

Yes, thought Mrs MacBain heavily, *word will spread quickly*. 'Shall I come with you?'

Jarvis nodded. This wasn't a part of the job he enjoyed.

They knocked on the door of Lawrence Blackwood's room and waited as he shuffled to answer it. He was fully dressed but for his shoes. A toe poked out of his left sock. He looked at Mrs MacBain with surprise and eyed Jarvis uncertainly.

'Can I help you?'

'Excuse me, Mr Blackwood,' Jarvis began nervously, 'I'm sorry to call so early, but it's rather urgent. May we have a word?'

He looked between them several times and then wordlessly opened the door. Mrs MacBain surreptitiously glanced around. His bed was unmade but otherwise the room was untouched.

'What can I do for you?' he repeated.

'This is Detective Inspector Jarvis, of the Loch Down Constabulary,' Mrs MacBain began, speaking quietly. 'He'd like to speak to you about your aunt.'

'My aunt?' His voice was cautious. 'Nothing wrong, I hope?'

Jarvis looked around the room, set his hat on a small table, and squared his shoulders. 'There's no good way to say this but, erm, I'm afraid your aunt has, erm, passed away.'

Confusion clouded Mr Blackwood's face. 'I'm sorry, did you just say she's died?'

'Erm, yes.' *Lord*, thought Jarvis, *how do you say this?* 'Well, erm . . . not quite.'

Mrs MacBain looked to the floor and sighed softly.

'How can someone not quite die, Inspector?' His voice was disdainful.

'She was . . . ah . . . *found* this morning by a servant while clearing up from last night's ball. Someone killed her.'

Lawrence inhaled sharply and then his brow furrowed in confusion. He looked out the window and nodded slowly. They held the silence while he digested the news.

Mrs MacBain watched him carefully. If he'd known, he wasn't showing it. In fact, he wasn't showing much reaction at all except confusion. He huffed a bit and then turned back to look at Jarvis. 'Someone's killed her?' He emphasised each word, as if he wasn't sure the English was correct.

'Yes, sir.'

He let out a long slow breath and sat roughly on the end of the bed. 'Didn't see that coming.'

Jarvis and Mrs MacBain looked at one another. Callousness or shock, she couldn't tell, but it was a decidedly odd reaction.

'My condolences for your loss,' said Jarvis, hesitantly.

Lawrence barely acknowledged it.

'I realise you're still getting your head around it, but we need you to answer a few questions. We need to move swiftly if we're going to find out who did this.' Jarvis said it gently, and then ventured a query. 'Do you have any idea who would have done this?'

'What?' Lawrence shook his head, his face neutral. 'Oh, erm, no.'

Jarvis waited, hoping he'd continue. When he didn't, Jarvis broke the silence. 'You and your aunt came over from Shanghai, I gather. Fleeing the war?'

'Yes. We were lucky to get seats on the flight. If we'd waited another day, we'd have been on the boats.' He grimaced as he said it.

'And that's bad?' asked Jarvis.

'Considering one of those ships ended up in the earthquake in Manila, yes.'

'I see.' Jarvis nodded. 'What brought you to Loch Down?'

He hesitated briefly. 'Um, Lady Annabella invited us.'

'She did.' Jarvis made it sound like a statement rather than a question.

'Yes, while we were in, erm . . . somewhere. Can't quite recall where.' He shook his head and then continued, 'But during the trip, Lady Annabella spoke warmly of the hotel, and the Highlands. When she invited all of us to visit, well, it seemed a charming idea.'

Well, that was a lie, thought Mrs MacBain. Bella had never in her entire life spoken warmly of Loch Down, and she certainly never referred to the Abbey as a hotel. She hoped Jarvis realised it.

'Where were you headed before you detoured here?'

'London.'

'London's home then?' asked Jarvis gruffly.

'London is merely a place to start over.' His voice was cold and distant.

'Where's the rest of the family?'

'Family? Erm, there is no family.'

'You're it? Just the two of you?' Jarvis was a bit envious. He still lived with his mother and three sisters. The house was constantly filled with gossiping women ordering him about. 'Then you'll no doubt inherit everything she has. Interesting.'

Lawrence's eyes flicked to Jarvis instantly. He could see exactly where Jarvis was headed with his statement. 'Let me assure you, Inspector, if I had wanted her dead, I'd have done it in Shanghai.'

His voice was hard and there was something in the statement that bothered Mrs MacBain greatly.

'Besides, there is nothing to inherit.' His tone was bitter. 'We're refugees, remember. We fled with the clothes on our backs and what little we could carry.'

Jarvis nodded, feeling foolish. There was a tension in the air and Mrs MacBain could feel they were losing any chance to get honest information from him. She decided to wade in herself.

'Did you enjoy the ball last night?'

He looked at her, a bit startled. It pleased Mrs MacBain immensely to have caught him off guard.

'I presume your aunt joined you?'

Lawrence looked decidedly unsettled by the question. When no answer was forthcoming, Mrs MacBain pressed her advantage. 'I don't recall seeing her there, but I do remember you.'

He considered her for a moment. 'We watched the opening dance and stayed for the first number. Bewildering display.' He shook his head. 'We found seats in a room nearby.'

'You didn't dance at all?' Her voice sounded surprised.

He shook his head. 'No. It just looked too difficult. I mostly tended to my aunt.'

'That must have been a bit lonely. But perhaps you had company? Everyone likes a bit of a gossip at a ball.'

There was a slight flicker in his eyes, which he quickly got under control. 'We had a quiet evening together.'

He didn't lie, but he didn't answer her either. He was deliberately evading her. Why?

'And how did the Colonel and Lady Beaumont fit into your quiet evening?'

Lawrence appraised her slowly, and then reached for a cigarette case. He took a long slim brown cigarette out of it, slowly tamped it down, said nothing.

'Mrs Blackwood was meeting people, wasn't she? In the Small Library. I saw you fetch the Colonel out of the breakfast queue. What did she want with him?'

He lit the cigarette and took a long drag, exhaled it slowly, never once letting his eyes stray from Mrs MacBain. If he thought he could out-wait her, get her to speak out of nervousness, he greatly underestimated her. Mrs MacBain, as a former domestic servant, could hold her silence for hours, if the occasion called for it.

Jarvis, however, had no such discipline. 'We have a witness who says she was blackmailing people.'

Mrs MacBain wanted to slap him. The man had no sense of nuance.

Mr Blackwood twitched with surprise, staring at him. 'A witness?' he asked caustically. His eyes narrowed and he leaned forward. 'Who?'

Jarvis stirred uncomfortably and cleared his throat. Mrs MacBain tried not to roll her eyes.

'That's confidential,' he said at last. 'Were you aware she was blackmailing people?'

Lawrence considered Jarvis for a long moment and reached a decision. 'Yes.'

Jarvis looked jubilant.

'Do you know what she was using as blackmail?' asked Mrs MacBain cautiously.

'No. She never told me, I never asked.'

Mrs MacBain arched an eyebrow.

'Too much information can be dangerous in Shanghai,' he responded, and took another puff of his cigarette. 'The fewer questions you ask, the longer your life expectancy.'

She considered him for a moment. *Blackmail. Life expectancy.* Here was proof that the Blackwoods existed in a dark and dangerous world in Shanghai, and that he clearly expected it to follow them to Loch Down.

'But you knew who she was dealing with?'

He nodded. 'I was tasked with fetching and delivering, that's all.'

'And in the chaos of the ball, no one would notice a quick absence.'

'Correct.'

'Who did she see last night?'

He hesitated, trying to decide if it mattered or not. The old woman was dead, after all.

'It's going to come out eventually,' barked Jarvis. 'Better if you cooperate and tell us now.'

Mr Blackwood scowled at Jarvis, looked back to Mrs MacBain, and then began. 'First was Lady Matthews, followed by Lord Pakenham, then a footman named Colin, Lady Beaumont, one of the sons of the Earl of Carrick, Mrs McCready, and then Lord Burridge.'

'She was blackmailing all of them?' Mrs MacBain was flabbergasted. 'You haven't been here that long. How on earth did she uncover so many secrets in so short a time?'

'What do you think the footman was for?'

It hit her like a ton of bricks. 'Of course,' she whispered softly. Who better to know the goings-on than the staff? He'd have to be sacked, today if possible. She couldn't have a member of their staff – no, the Dunbar-Hamilton staff

– spying on the guests. *How dare he?* But her outrage would have to wait.

'Any others?' Jarvis asked gruffly.

'Just one.' He took a long drag of his cigarette and blew a smoke ring. 'Lord Inverkillen.'

Mrs MacBain's heart stopped. She hadn't expected to hear Angus's name on the list; it reverberated to the deepest core of her being. Lawrence could see the panic in her eyes, and he sat back in the chair, smiling with pleasure.

Mrs MacBain struggled to keep her composure. The last name she thought she'd hear was Angus's. Luckily, Jarvis took over and she had a dim recollection of the rest of the interview.

Mr Blackwood had left the ball at about two thirty, just after delivering Angus. Mrs Blackwood had one further interview that evening, she said, and then she'd retire, but he didn't know who it was with. He thought it was unusual, but she sent him to bed and he did as he was told. He passed the desk clerk, who was reading a book, but no one else that he could recall, and he'd been in his room ever since.

They were back in her office, but Mrs MacBain couldn't remember the journey. Sitting down in her chair, she looked at Jarvis, who could read the shock on her face.

'We have to go interview him,' he said gently. 'If she really was blackmailing Lord Inverkillen, that makes him a suspect.'

'You will never be able to convince me that Angus killed that woman.'

'Right now, I just want to establish if Mr Blackwood is telling us the truth. There's nothing about him that I trust.'

She exhaled slowly and nodded her head in agreement.

He stood. 'Shall we go find Lord Inverkillen then?'

Looking at her watch, she realised it was quarter to nine. 'He won't be awake for a while yet. Let's start with the people we have in the Abbey.'

Jarvis appraised her carefully. It had been quite a shock, and he needed her steady on her feet. 'Okay,' he said, nodding his head. 'Who'd you have in mind?'

When the Colonel finally answered his door, he was still dressed in his clothes from the ball.

He yawned widely. 'Mrs MacBain. Good morning. What can I do for you?'

'May we come in, Colonel?'

The Colonel looked between the pair of them, quizzically, settling his gaze on Jarvis.

'Allow me to introduce Detective Inspector Jarvis, from the Loch Down Constabulary.' Was it her imagination or did the Colonel flinch?

'A Detective Inspector? In a village this size? I'd have thought a local magistrate would be sufficient.' He looked Jarvis up and down, evidently found him lacking authority, and then turned to Mrs MacBain, and nodded. 'Come in. How can I be of service?' He stood aside and they entered his suite.

They settled on the sofas, Jarvis and Mrs MacBain across from him. The Colonel's room, she couldn't help noticing, was in tatters: clothing strewn about, overflowing ashtrays on every table she could see. He had at least three breakfast trays stacked by the door. Why haven't the maids tidied? she wondered.

Jarvis took the lead, clearing his throat. 'I believe you knew Mrs Blackwood in Shanghai?'

'Mrs Blackwood? Yes. What of it?' The Colonel looked between them, a guarded look on his face, as if he was bracing himself for something.

'What was the nature of your relationship?'

'Relationship is putting it a bit strong. Knew one another, yes. The expat community is small, you understand. Spend any amount of time there and you'll meet the lot. I was there nearly thirty years. Very few I don't know or know of.'

'And did you know Mrs Blackwood or know of her?' Mrs MacBain ventured. *Oh yes*, she thought, *he reacted that time. He clearly doesn't like speaking about her.*

The Colonel cleared his throat. 'We ran into one another from time to time. At the races or a drinks party. Can't say if I was ever seated next to her at dinner, but I must have done. She isn't the type you remember the next day, if you know what I mean.'

The statement cemented Mrs MacBain's dislike of him, and it took every ounce of her resolve to keep smiling pleasantly. 'It's just,' she began hesitantly, 'I get the distinct impression you did know one another, quite well, in fact.'

The Colonel was offended. 'You calling me a liar?' he demanded.

Mrs MacBain smiled sweetly and offered a small shrug of her shoulders.

The Colonel leaned forward and pointed at her. 'See here! I work in a consulate and, not to put too fine a point on it, I'm quite important. I go a lot of places and meet a lot of people in my day-to-day, and sometimes one simply cannot recall the faces or the specifics of every meeting. I long ago realised it was easier if I treated everyone like old chums. It's called diplomacy.' He scowled at Mrs MacBain for a moment, reassessing his opinion of her. *Middle-aged women can be such busybodies*, he thought.

She continued, entirely unruffled, 'But I've seen you speaking to one another, in quiet corners, here and there around the Abbey.'

That rattled him and he glared at her for a long moment before abruptly addressing Jarvis. 'What's this about, exactly?'

'I'm afraid that Mrs Blackwood was found dead this morning.'

The Colonel's bluster left him. He looked between them as he digested the statement, then slowly shook his head. 'Pity. Not the warmest woman, but still, no one deserves to go out that way.'

'And what way is that, Colonel?' Jarvis sat forward on the sofa.

'In my experience, the police don't come round to ask questions when someone dies peacefully in their sleep.' He said it rather matter-of-factly. Mrs MacBain wondered what exactly he'd done at the consulate.

'Did you dance with her at the ball last night?' asked Jarvis.

'What? Oh, no. Not much of a dancer these days.' He patted his rumpled waistcoat and gave Jarvis a knowing smile. When Jarvis's face didn't change, he hurriedly added, 'I partnered Lady Annabella for the first reel. Hadn't wanted to, but she practically begged me; wouldn't take no for an answer. Poor manners, if you ask me.'

Poorer manners to come to ball and refuse a lady a dance, thought Mrs MacBain.

'And the next reel?' Jarvis prodded.

'Left the Ballroom. I don't care for reeling. Does my head in, all that spin here, gallop there. No, I was at the cards table most of the night.'

'Define most.' Jarvis's voice was steely.

'I sat down after the second reel and didn't get up until the midnight buffet.' He glanced at Mrs MacBain. 'Excellent kippers, by the way. Perfectly seasoned.'

Jarvis pointedly cleared his throat.

'Yes. Let me think. After the kippers, I sat down before the next reel and played until the footmen turfed us out.'

'You didn't leave the table at all?' Jarvis leaned forward eagerly. 'Or visit one of the other rooms?'

'Might have got up once or twice to answer nature's call, but otherwise, no.' The Colonel looked between them, confused. 'When you're winning, and I was, you don't leave the table.'

'Who were you playing against?' Jarvis asked, pulling a notebook from his jacket pocket.

'Ah. There you have me. Terrible with names, can't ever seem to remember them.'

Jarvis looked up, unimpressed. 'Try.'

The Colonel sighed and then squinted at the ceiling. 'Right. Next to me was a gent who made whisky. Can't remember his name. Seemed an unlikely sort at a ball, a bit rough, if you know what I mean. Across were two local lads who went out quite quickly. I suspect the stakes were too high for them.' He nodded knowingly at Jarvis, who merely blinked at him. 'Who else? Erm . . . that Canadian chap. He had quite a discussion with the whisky man, lots about peat and whatnot. Bored the pants off me, frankly, so I left them and joined another table across the room.'

'Was that before or after the breakfast buffet?'

'What?' asked the Colonel. 'Erm . . . during. It was a good excuse to leave the table.'

'Okay, so who was at this next table?'

'Let me think. I took quite a packet off Lord something-or-other. He stormed off about quarter past three. And then there was a local lad, might have been called Jerome? Or Roger, perhaps. Does something with forestry, I gather. And then . . .' His brow furrowed. 'Nope. Can't remember.' He looked expectantly between Mrs MacBain and Jarvis, as if expecting a prize.

'So, to recap,' said Jarvis slowly, 'you played against Roger – or Jerome – who does something in forestry, someone who makes whisky, that Canadian chap, and an unnamed Lord.' Jarvis was irritated and he didn't bother to hide it.

'With due respect, Colonel,' interrupted Mrs MacBain gently, 'I'd have expected a diplomat to be better with names and faces.'

'There was a lot of whisky last night, as you well know.' He huffled indignantly, as if this explained everything. 'See here, I've done my best. Now, if you'll excuse me, I have a tennis lesson in half an hour and I need to change my clothes.'

Without waiting for an answer, he leapt up and strode towards the door, holding it open for them. Reluctantly, they rose and walked to the door. Jarvis was only millimetres across the threshold when the door snapped shut.

'Well, he's definitely lying about last night.'

'Yes,' Mrs MacBain said slowly. 'He is. Which makes me wonder if they knew each other before they arrived here. Did she know something about his life in Shanghai that she was holding over him, or did something happen after they left?'

'How do we find that out?'

'We should go have a word with Lady Annabella. She knows the Colonel and she might have known Mrs Blackwood as well.'

An involuntary shudder ran though Jarvis. Every encounter he had with Lady Annabella had gone badly, leaving him feeling like a foolish child. It didn't go unnoticed by Mrs MacBain.

'Never fear, I'll do the talking,' she said kindly.

They found Lady Annabella in her rooms. Jarvis thought it a very strange place to have rooms, especially for someone so grand; it was miles from the main part of the Abbey. Well, it felt like that, at any rate. He wondered if the family had a private wing to separate them from the rest of the hotel.

'My apologies for calling so early, Lady Annabella, but may we have a word?' Mrs MacBain asked gently when the door cracked open.

Bella pulled her dressing gown tighter around her. She glanced at Jarvis, giving him a head-to-toe inspection that didn't appear to find favour, and then turned to Mrs MacBain. 'What's this about?'

'You'll remember Inspector Jarvis? He'd like to ask some questions about Mrs Blackwood.'

'Inspector Jarvis?' Bella was confused. 'Mrs Blackwood?'
'She was killed last night.'

Bella gasped and then looked at Jarvis again, understanding why he'd come to ask her questions. 'Give me a moment to put on something more appropriate.' She closed the door quietly.

Mrs MacBain paced some way up the hall, clearly lost in thought. Jarvis glanced around. It wasn't nearly as posh as other bits of the house he'd seen. 'It's a bit grotty, isn't it? I pictured the family somewhere grander.'

Mrs MacBain looked at him and didn't reply. Jarvis's mind drifted back to breakfast. He was about to suggest he could pop to the kitchen for a bacon butty when the door opened again. Bella, fully dressed in a sombre grey, held the door open for them. 'Do come in.'

Mrs MacBain went first and managed three or four steps into the room before she stopped abruptly, Jarvis running into the back of her.

This is the old servants' quarters? She hadn't been there in some time, and when Fergus said he was going to lodge Bella there, her misgivings were rife. But this was not at all what she was expecting.

There were carpets on the floors, pictures on the walls, including a tapestry on the exterior wall, which kept the chill at bay. Bella had created a seating area in front of the small, ancient oven, and managed, somehow, to hang a small chandelier, which was lit by six or eight taper candles. The room was divided in two by several free-standing room screens, which the tenth Countess and her daughters had embroidered for the Dining Hall one winter when the Abbey was under siege. Mrs MacBain peeked around and could see a brass bed, and Bella's old Regency dressing table. All in all, the room was warm and, well, cosy.

'My word!' Mrs MacBain cried, astonishment in her voice. 'I can't believe this is the same room. You've transformed it!'

Bella gestured to the sofas, indicating they should sit down. She perched on one and addressed Mrs MacBain. 'Now, what can I do for you?'

'What do know about Mrs Blackwood?' began Jarvis. His voice bounced off the stone ceiling, making the women wince. Bella glared openly at him until he shrunk back in his coat, vowing not to speak again.

'Did you know her in Shanghai?' asked Mrs MacBain.

'No. Not really. I knew *of* her, obviously.'

'Obviously?' queried Jarvis, who startled himself with the question.

Bella looked at him, and then back to Mrs MacBain. 'The expat community is small, and uncomfortably close knit. Not as claustrophobic as Loch Down, but similar. One can know who someone is without ever meeting them.'

Mrs MacBain nodded. This she understood perfectly, having lived in a small village her entire life. 'And you'd never met in Shanghai?' she asked.

'No. Absolutely not. Scandalous woman. Edmund forbade me to socialise with her.'

'Really? Why is that?' Mrs MacBain could hardly believe a world where Bella did as she was told, especially when she was forbidden. But looking around the room, she wondered if she knew anything about Bella any longer.

'To be honest, I didn't ask. I was new to Shanghai, terribly naive, so I presumed he knew best. You meet the wrong sort in the beginning and life becomes very difficult. But it wasn't long before I started hearing stories and realised Edmund was right about her. There had been an almighty scandal when she was much younger. The whole of the international community knew about it. I seem to think it caused a diplomatic row of some sort, not just a run-of-the-mill society scandal.' Bella shook her head. 'Whatever it was, her reputation never recovered, and she was never accepted into polite society after that.'

'Any idea what the scandal involved?' Mrs MacBain asked.

Bella shook her head. 'You know how gossip is: a thousand stories, none of them true. The most popular story is that her husband caught her having an affair with her bodyguard and the husband had him killed.'

Both Mrs MacBain and Jarvis gasped. Her recitation had been entirely blasé, as if she were recounting what she'd had for luncheon one afternoon.

'It's absolute tosh, of course,' Bella continued, entirely satisfied by their shock. She smiled coyly. 'Another is she owns the largest jade quarry in all of Asia, staffed entirely by nude male slaves. Erm . . . ah, she poisoned a rival's horse because it kept beating hers; she's Chiang Kai-shek's mistress; she runs a high-class brothel frequented exclusively by diplomats. That one would cause an international scandal.' She shook her head lightly and then smiled. 'Oh, and my personal favourite: she controls a fleet of international assassins, which she contracts to warlords and governments. It's all nonsense but, because of the gossip, one simply doesn't socialise with her.'

Jarvis nodded, scribbling notes in his pad.

Bella stood and pulled a plaited cord next to the door. 'Shall we have some tea? My head is still a bit fragile.'

Jarvis's head snapped up, hoping to ask about a bacon butty but he didn't want to speak again. She never seemed happy when he did. A houseboy arrived quickly and was dispatched with the order and a coin.

No wonder they're never around when I need them, Mrs MacBain thought to herself.

The trio settled back into the sofas, Bella leaning back into the plump cushions rather casually.

'Tell me about Colonel Lamont,' Mrs MacBain said lightly.

'Oof.' She sighed. 'What a liability! Always has been. Absolute bane of Edmund's existence. He used to say that a monkey would be a better deputy than the Colonel. But of course, he couldn't sack him.'

'Why not?'

'He's been in the diplomatic core for ages. He has very powerful friends, very high up.'

Mrs MacBain nodded. 'What does he do at the consulate?'

'And, if I may ask,' ventured Jarvis, plucking up his courage, 'what happens at a consulate? Is that different to an embassy?'

'Ah, yes, it's all very confusing. Took me ages to work that out. The embassy is all about national and international governments, very political; world affairs, the sort of thing you read about in the papers. The consulate, however, is about local relations and supporting British business and British citizens who live or visit there. Visas and passports, notarising paperwork, translating official documents. Domestic, but equally important.'

'What was the Colonel's role?' ventured Mrs MacBain

'That's less clear. According to Edmund, he did very little. I do know he helped secure a lease on a warehouse for a friend's husband, but what his official role is, I couldn't say.'

Mrs MacBain thought for a moment. 'What else do you know about him?'

'Not much. He's been in Shanghai for nearly thirty years. Knows absolutely everyone.'

'Hang on,' said Jarvis, confusion on his face, 'he's been there for thirty years and he's only a deputy?'

'What I could glean from Edmund is that he's failed in every position they've put him in and finally the Foreign Office sent him to Shanghai, hoping the lifestyle would keep him out of trouble.'

'The lifestyle?' asked Jarvis.

'Cards, cocktails, horse racing, swish restaurants, the opera. Shanghai's terribly glamorous. Edmund says he's never even seen the Colonel before eleven in the morning. Calls him The Vampire.'

'Cards and horse racing . . .' Mrs MacBain thought for a moment. 'He's a gambler? A serious one?'

'He's an absolute fixture in betting circles.'

'Any good?' Jarvis asked. Having met the man, he was guessing no.

'Mixed reviews. He seems to keep on the right side of his winnings. You can't survive in Shanghai long if you're out of control. It's not a forgiving society, from what I understand. But most people meet their downfall in the casinos, and the Colonel wouldn't be that stupid.'

'There are casinos in Shanghai?' asked Mrs MacBain. She'd never thought much about Shanghai, let alone what sort of entertainment they had. Casinos sounded glamorous indeed.

'Loads, but they're strictly off limits to government staff. Instant dismissal if you're caught in one.'

'Why's that?' Jarvis asked. He'd know many men who'd lost everything by picking the wrong horse. Casinos didn't seem that different. Not that he'd ever been in one.

'Because the casinos are owned by the gangsters.' She said it simply, as if he should have known. 'And we can't have members of government offices in debt to gangsters.

Just think how they could leverage that. It'd be an absolute disaster. No, the track is fine, private gaming is fine, but the casinos are strictly forbidden.'

Mrs MacBain's head was reeling. She glanced at Inspector Jarvis, who looked as gobsmacked as she felt. This was not where either of them thought the conversation would go. Thankfully, there was a knock at the door.

'Oh good,' said Bella, as the hall boy entered the room, 'the tea's here.'

Bella waited for the hall boy to leave and then expertly poured three cups. She leaned back and pulled the cup to her lips. 'There is nothing like a cup of Earl Grey in the morning.'

They sipped in silence for a few moments before Mrs MacBain asked, 'Were the Colonel and Mrs Blackwood friendly on the journey here?'

Bella looked surprised and then thoughtful. She shook her head slowly. 'I wouldn't have said that, no. Nothing springs to mind, at any rate.'

'It's just, she mentioned something about close quarters and getting to know each other. And so I wondered . . .' She left the query unfinished. 'Did they know each other in Shanghai, or do you think they met on the trip here?'

Bella scanned her memories and slowly shook her head. 'No idea. They were none too chummy on the trip, that's about all I can say for certain. But that nephew of hers kept most of us at bay. Deeply unpleasant man.'

'Yes,' murmured Mrs MacBain. Something in the back of her brain flickered. She continued, 'How did she end up here, at the Abbey?'

Bella squirmed. She'd thought a lot about that since the run-in with her brother. The Colonel, she at least had known in Shanghai, and he'd attached himself to her after the incident in Marseille. While she'd been grateful for his help at first, he exhausted her by the time they boarded the train. He was boorish in the extreme, braying about his plans for a new foreign assignment. *So why is he here?* she thought suddenly.

As for Mrs Blackwood, well, that simply defied explanation. Bella had spoken to her on the journey, much as one must socialise with everyone at a small dinner party. Bella had worked hard to keep her distance, but the wretched woman seemed determined to befriend her. Any time she turned around, there was Mrs Blackwood, with that unsettling smile of hers, followed closely by her horrid nephew.

'It's strange, really. Both the Colonel and Mrs Blackwood singled me out on the trip. Colonel Lamont insisted on attending to me, saying Edmund personally dispatched him to keep me safe, which is ridiculous. Edmund doesn't trust the Colonel in the least. And if he had sent someone to protect me, it most assuredly wouldn't be the Colonel.'

Mrs MacBain agreed wholeheartedly. Even Jarvis nodded in agreement.

'And Mrs Blackwood felt I was too young to travel alone, bless. She insisted on keeping a watchful eye.' Bella paused and huffed, irritated by the memories. 'I couldn't shake them for anything.'

'And yet you did,' said Mrs MacBain, 'when you got off the train in Paris.'

'Yes, but they didn't know I was stopping in Paris. It was a spur-of-the-moment decision.'

'When did you decide to stop?'

'Just outside of Paris. I couldn't face another few days in my travelling suit and since we were there, it seemed a godsent opportunity to order some new clothes.'

'And you didn't tell anyone?'

'No.' She looked horrified. 'I was afraid they'd follow.'

Mrs MacBain nodded, her eyes squinting into the distance. 'They disembark in London, find you missing, and then both, separately, decide to come to Loch Down to wait for you. It's such an . . . odd decision. Especially if the Colonel believed he was sent to protect you.'

'Well, the Colonel should have reported to the consul in London as soon as he hit UK shores. Edmund gave him strict instructions. He's risking a lot by being here. But Mrs Blackwood . . .' She paused and tapped the rim of her teacup with her ring, sending a trill into the room. 'I don't understand that. Perhaps she had nowhere else to go.'

Mrs MacBain looked at her uncertainly.

'She has been in Shanghai for a long time, and, not to put too fine a point on it, she wasn't young. There might not have been any family left. Someone's got to be the last man standing.'

'Then who does her nephew belong to?' asked Jarvis.

Bella looked at him and considered this. 'Orphan? How should I know?' She poured herself another cup of tea and sat back meditatively. The room was quiet until Jarvis spoke.

'Why would someone want to kill her?'

Bella winced. The man's voice made her eyes ache. 'No idea. If it had been me, I'd have killed the nephew.'

Cecil awoke to the hammering on his door.

Surely no one is awake at this hour.

No one rose early after a ball. No one of good breeding, that was. He rolled over and the banging stopped. He drifted into a hopeful sleep, but the pounding started again, and he realised there would be no peace until he answered it.

There really is no rest for the wicked. It was inhumane. He'd only been asleep for, looking at the clock on the mantel, four hours. Nothing could be this important.

But he pulled on his dressing gown and tied the sash as he stumbled to the door. Perhaps he'd forgotten to cancel his breakfast tray.

'Yes, yes,' he called, 'give me a moment.'

Cecil had just barely opened the door when someone rushed past, nearly knocking him over.

'She's dead! Oh my god, she's dead and I'm going to prison.'

The shock of being rudely woken, then pushed out of the way into his own rooms, by a maid no less, was cause for outrage. But as Cecil turned, he realised it wasn't the breakfast tray. It was Angus.

'What? Who's dead? What are you talking about?' He yawned as he said it. His brain was a bit fuzzy. Had Angus said *dead* or *bed*? Why was he frantically pacing the room? And what was that smell? It was simply too early for all of this.

Angus stopped and fixed a serious gaze on Cecil. 'Mrs Blackwood was killed last night.'

'My god. When? What?' He shook his head, as if that would ward off the fatigue of a long night of cards. If Cecil had been sleepy before, he was now wide awake.

'One of the servants found her this morning, and now the police want to speak to me. They must know.' He resumed his pacing, crashing into an armchair and not bothering to right it.

'Calm down, please, and do stop pacing.' He placed his hands on Angus's shoulders and guided him to the offending chair. 'Sit. Take a deep breath. Start from the beginning.'

Angus did as he was bid and breathed out slowly. Moderately calmer, he began. 'I was giving a tennis lesson to the Colonel.'

'At this hour?' Cecil interrupted, caught the glare from Angus and continued meekly, 'Yes, sorry. Not important. Please go on.'

'And the Colonel told me she was found dead this morning. Mrs MacBain and, erm, that police chap had already spoken to him. Then I got this note from Inspector Harv-something—' he glanced at a piece of note paper '— Jarvis. He's asked me to meet him in the Rowan Tree room "at my earliest convenience". I'm going to prison.'

He shoved a piece of the hotel's stationery at Cecil. Written in a childish scrawl was the request. Cecil tsk'd involuntarily – *What self-respecting adult uses pencil?* – and skimmed the note. Still holding it, he sat heavily on the bed.

'Well, if he'd wanted to arrest you, he'd hardly have sent a note asking you to come see him. He'd have been in your rooms.'

Angus stopped pacing and looked at his uncle, a glimmer of hope in his eyes. 'That's true. But why would he want to speak to me then? What if he knows about the debt?'

'Well then, you've nothing to worry about,' said Cecil, waving the disbelief away. 'You have a debt of honour, which is in no way illegal in this country. I dare say the largest part of the ruling class has the same debts.'

'But—' whimpered Angus.

'But nothing. You owed the woman for a bad run of cards.'

'Backgammon,' corrected Angus.

'Whatever. And now she's turned up dead before you could pay the debt. A debt which you intended to honour.

It's unfortunate timing but it's hardly damning. You're an Earl for heaven's sake. You're quite above reproach.'

'But I went to see her last night. And if that despicable nephew of hers decides to say something about it . . . ' He hesitated. 'I'd be the prime suspect. I'm probably the only suspect . . . ' He drifted into a new chain of horror and collapsed into the chair, nearly sliding out the bottom.

'Was he in the room when you met with the woman?'

'No, but he was outside, so he knows I was there. What if he mentions the blackmail? Or the reason for the blackmail?'

'Then it's his word against yours,' replied Cecil firmly. Angus looked at him sceptically. 'Let's remember, he is a henchman, a common thug. You are a Peer of the Realm. You spoke with her about paying your debt; nothing more, nothing less. As for the other, well, there will be dozens of people – important people, people who matter – who will speak on your behalf.'

Angus stood and walked to the window as he digested this, pulling the curtain to one side delicately and staring at the grounds. *If only I'd stayed in Morocco*, he thought bitterly.

Cecil stood and sighed heavily. 'Go and bathe, change your clothes. I'll meet you in the Armoury in thirty minutes. Let's see what the police want from you before we panic.'

Thirty minutes later, there was a sharp rap on the door of Rowan Tree.

'You ready?' Jarvis asked Mrs MacBain. She nodded. 'Come in,' he called.

The door opened swiftly, and Angus strode into the room. He was the picture of aristocratic confidence.

'Major.' Mrs MacBain's voice was higher than usual. Cecil was behind Angus, making his way across the room. She gathered herself before continuing, 'We weren't expecting you.'

'Well, Angus mentioned he needed to stop for a little tête-à-tête before we had breakfast together. Who am I to make a fuss?' He sat, quite deliberately, in the chair furthest from the door.

'Ah, yes, well . . .' She stumbled for words. 'It's, erm . . . it's a bit of a sensitive topic.'

'I shall be the soul of quietude.' Cecil nestled so far into the chair she worried they'd have to prise him out with a tractor.

Angus seated himself across from Mrs MacBain and Inspector Jarvis and looked expectantly at the policeman. 'You asked to see me?'

'Ah, yes, Lord Inverkillen, thank you for coming.' Jarvis sat down, perching on the edge of his seat. 'I'm afraid I must be the bearer of sad news.'

'I already know about Mrs Blackwood, Inspector.'

Word travels quick in this house, Jarvis thought. 'You do?'

'Yes. Colonel Lamont told me when he came for his tennis lesson this morning.'

Mrs MacBain pulled a face. 'He really had a tennis lesson? I thought he was making that up.'

'So did I.' Jarvis nodded in agreement. 'Who schedules a tennis lesson the morning after a ball?' He was baffled. *These people*, he thought, *never cease to amaze me*. Imagine, running on a court with a pounding headache. The thought of it made him want to vomit.

'Yes,' said Angus lazily, 'well, he clearly hadn't thought about the timing. Now what can I do for you?'

Jarvis shuffled in his seat, adjusted his tie for a moment and then began. 'We understand you had a meeting with Mrs Blackwood in the Small Library last night.'

Angus hesitated. 'I called in on her, yes.'

'What did you speak about?'

Angus looked at Jarvis for a moment and then slowly, deliberately, looked down at the man's shoes. They were dusty from the walk up and a shoelace was undone. Angus looked back to Jarvis pointedly, and lazily replied. 'I owe her a gambling debt and we were agreeing on the terms of payment.'

'I see.' Jarvis tucked his shoes under his chair and made a mental note to have his sister polish them this evening. 'And how much is this debt?'

Angus gave him a withering look. 'A gentleman does not disclose his gaming debts.'

Jarvis hesitated a moment. 'I need to know how much.'

'It wasn't significant, I can assure you.' Angus gave him a scornful look and pulled his cigarette case from his pocket.

Jarvis raised his voice, just below shouting. 'A woman is dead! I'll be the judge of what is and isn't significant. Now, how much was it?'

Angus, entirely unaccustomed to being shouted out – by others than his family, at least – shrank back in his seat. 'About four hundred pounds.'

Jarvis's eyebrows shot up into his hairline.

'Angus!' The word slipped from Mrs MacBain's mouth before she could help herself. 'That's a tremendous sum!'

Cecil gently cleared his throat and spoke. 'If I may? It's not such a large sum, in our world, Inspector. I've routinely lost that of an evening.'

Of an evening? Jarvis didn't make that much in year. He looked to Mrs MacBain, who shrugged subtly.

Angus resumed his haughty demeanour. 'As I said, we were agreeing on the terms of repayment.'

Jarvis looked back to Angus, blinked several times, and shook his head. 'And did you?'

'Did I what?' spat Angus, letting his full irritation show.

Jarvis glared at him for a moment and said, though gritted teeth, 'Agree on terms of repayment?'

'Erm . . . ' His eyes flicked to Cecil, who nodded slowly. 'Yes. As a matter of fact, we did. I have until the end of the month.'

'But now,' said Jarvis pointedly, 'you owe no one. Rather convenient, isn't it?'

'Now see here, you impertinent swine,' seethed Angus, 'if you think I killed that woman, over something as tawdry as money—'

'People kill for a lot of reasons, Lord Inverkillen.' Jarvis was unruffled being insulted. It was hardly the worst he'd ever been called. His eldest sister could be particularly creative when she was angry.

'What time did you meet her, Lord Inverkillen?' Mrs MacBain jumped in, hoping to change the mood. Jarvis settled back into his chair.

Angus turned his head towards her but kept his eyes on Jarvis until he spoke. 'The Eightsome when I went in.' He paused. 'And Duke of Perth when I came out.'

Mrs MacBain did some quick calculations. The Eightsome was the third reel after the buffet, so two thirty, say. The Duke of Perth was the final reel, which meant three o'clock. 'Did you see her nephew when you left?' She held her breath.

Angus thought for a moment. 'I didn't go back into the ball.'

'Where did you go, then?'

'I went out through the French doors to the Tennis Pavilion.'

Jarvis pulled a face. 'The Tennis Pavilion? Why there?'

Angus looked at him and said in a rather aggrieved tone, 'It's where I'm staying.'

'Did anyone, anyone at all, see you after you left the Small Library?' Mrs MacBain's voice was anxious, and Jarvis found himself holding his breath. Even Cecil was leaning forward on his chair.

Angus hesitated. He'd been so upset with the wretched woman, he'd walked back to the Tennis Pavilion without realising where he was going. She'd refused to give him more time and was going to ring the police in the morning. This morning, as it happened. And here the police were, asking not about Hugh, as he'd feared, but about Mrs Blackwood. Which, he wondered fleetingly, was the worst of the two to be accused of?

Angus's eyes registered his increasing panic as he tried to remember his movements. He went out a French door on to the terrace, which had been empty, the Duke of Perth being one of the more popular dances. He'd slipped into the darkness behind the braziers on the terrace and made his way to the Tennis Pavilion.

Angus's voice was hollow and hoarse. 'No.'

'I don't care what you say, Angus did not kill that woman.' Mrs MacBain was watching Jarvis pace in front of the window. They'd been arguing for well over an hour. He was ready to arrest Angus. She was trying to talk him out of it.

'But he has no alibi, he was in the room, and he owed her money. A lot of it, as it happens.'

'To us, yes, but to these people, four hundred pounds isn't a lot of money. Not a devastating amount, at least.'

'You said he was flat broke.'

She sighed. *Now he's paying attention.* Well, better late than never, she supposed. Although he was barking up the wrong tree. Of that, she was certain.

'The simple fact is, someone would have given him the funds. Lady Georgina, or Fergus, or . . . the Major, well, no, not the Major, but someone. I can't see him killing the woman to avoid paying her.'

'He had motive, he had opportunity. And he was in full Highland dress; he had a *sgian-dubh*.'

Mrs MacBain gasped lightly. 'I hadn't thought of that.'

Jarvis was infinitely pleased with himself. 'Can we go arrest him then?'

'Erm . . . not yet.' The absurdity of him asking her permission to arrest someone was lost in the flurry of activity that came next. Mrs MacBain leapt up and practically sprinted to the door. 'I need you to go find the Colonel. Ask him what Angus was wearing when he showed up to his tennis lesson.'

'What? What does that have to do with anything?' He gaped at the empty door, and then recoiled when she came back through it.

'And then meet me at the Tennis Pavilion, quick as you can.'

He bolted to the door and called after her. 'Where are you going?'

'To check the laundry.'

Mrs MacBain played out various scenarios as she flew to the laundry. She was trying to imagine what she would do, if she'd just stabbed someone. There would be blood, quite a lot of it, she imagined. On Miss Blackwood, on the floor, on the knife, and most certainly on her own clothes. And with blood on her clothes, she'd want to change out of them as quickly as possible, so no one would see. And it was perfectly possible to get from the Small Library to the Tennis Pavilion without being seen by anyone, especially if you knew your way around the grounds, as Angus did. But what would Angus do with the soiled clothes after he changed? That was why she was headed to the laundry.

'Oh, miss, we weren't expecting you!' The ladies looked up from their work as Mrs MacBain entered the laundry house.

'It's just a quick question.' She took a deep breath to steady her nerves. She tried to keep her tone light. 'I don't suppose Lord Inverkillen brought his laundry to you this morning? Or perhaps there was something waiting for you when you arrived?'

She could see from their confused faces that he hadn't. 'Well, I just wondered . . .' she began.

The ladies quickly recovered from their shock and began laughing, mocking the very idea of a member of the aristocracy delivering their own laundry.

Lord Inverkillen? Here? Can you imagine? Yes, milord, we'd love to do your socks. Do you even know what he looks like? Doubt he even knows where the laundry is. Probably thinks fairies take care of it.

Relieved, Mrs MacBain slipped out the door and left them to their morning banter.

Well, it was a long shot, but worth taking, she told herself. She hurried to the Tennis Pavilion, hoping she would beat

Jarvis there. She wanted to look around before he arrived, just in case. But her heart sank when she rounded the hedge, and saw the tell-tale overcoat of Jarvis, pacing outside the Pavilion. Well, regardless of what she found, she'd have to tell him about. She just hoped finding it would clear Angus.

'Ah, there you are,' called Jarvis, looking slightly sweaty and more than a little grumpy. 'Laundry all sorted then?'

'Yes, thank you.' She ignored his sarcasm and moved past him, reaching for the doorknob.

'It's locked,' he said, with just a hint of glee in his voice. 'Now what?'

She hesitated, unsure she wanted to show him. But as they were in a bit of a race against time, she had little choice. She dragged a teak garden chair and placed it in front of the door. Standing on the edge, she lifted a slate tile to reveal a small compartment, just large enough to hold a key. Jarvis gaped at her as she crouched down, unlocked the door, and returned the key to its hiding place. She gratefully accepted Jarvis's hand to dismount from the chair.

'When we took over the Abbey, I had spare keys made for all the outbuildings. We had to have several of them changed, in fact, because the keys were long missing. So now each building has a hidden spare.'

The woman was, Jarvis marvelled, prepared for everything. 'Were you a Girl Guide?'

She smiled. 'No. I was already in service here when they started. Shall we?'

They entered the Pavilion, and it was immediately clear that Angus had been there. The ashtrays were filled with his brown cigarettes, an empty bottle of whisky stood on the central table, a second lay on its side. And there was an almighty stench to the place. Mrs MacBain opened the doors wide to air it out.

'What did the Colonel say?'

'What?' Jarvis was looking through a bookcase. *Who keeps books in a sports pavilion?* he wondered. 'Oh, the Colonel, yes. He said Lord Inverkillen was in tennis whites.'

Mrs MacBain looked dismayed. 'Was he positive about that or was he conjecturing?' Jarvis looked at her oddly. 'After hearing his stories, I can assure you he's not the most reliable witness.'

Jarvis chewed on this for a moment, nodding. 'He didn't hesitate, seemed to think I was barking mad even for asking, openly mocked me for being too common to play tennis. So yes, I think Lord Inverkillen was wearing tennis whites. Why does it matter?'

Mrs MacBain nodded, a grim look on her face, and began silently rifling through the Pavilion, opening every cupboard door she could lay her hands on. Jarvis stood still, watching her.

Mrs MacBain turned around, irritation all over her face. 'If you've nothing better to do, perhaps I should fetch you a cup of tea and a paper?'

Jarvis blushed and walked sheepishly across the room and began searching the window seat Lord Inverkillen was using as a bed. But what he was looking for, he wasn't sure. He carried on with the desk. Every drawer was filled with spare tennis balls, chalk for the scoreboard, books on tennis, and a pair of old, very well-used plimsolls.

Mrs MacBain had exhausted the cupboards, and moved to uproot the cushions on the sofas, then checked behind the curtains, and emptied the log basket. Finally, she came to a stop in front of the fireplace.

After a moment's hesitation, Mrs MacBain knelt in front of the fireplace. There had clearly been a fire that morning. *Oh, Angus!* She poked around the ash a bit, hoping to find an unburned scrap. What she would give for a bit of tree bark. But no, it had all thoroughly burned to ash and there no telling if it had been logs or his Highland dress. She sat back on her heels and took a deep steadying breath.

It wasn't looking good for Angus.

Elspeth was on her way downstairs. She'd slept badly after the ball, knowing that she should have spoken to Ross about the bothy. But she didn't want to speak to him in so public a place, and if she were brutally honest with herself, she didn't want things to be over. But if he needed more, wanted more, she would have to let him go. He deserved more and she couldn't give that to him. This was not a walk she wanted to take, but while it was still quiet, it might be their best chance to speak.

She was walking slowly, imagining how the conversation would go; what she would say, how he would respond. In one scenario it was a tender parting, in another it was acrimonious, and it brought tears to her eyes. She shook herself to the present and realised she'd taken a wrong turn. Glimpsing the stairs to the Armoury at the far end, she walked towards it, gently cursing herself, both for imagining the worst and for getting lost in her childhood home.

As she neared the stairs, she came to a stop in front of one of the rooms. The door was open. Wide open, which allowed her to see it had been completely torn apart. Elspeth looked up and down the corridor, saw she was quite alone, and cautiously stepped in and looked around. Clothes were strewn every which way, drawers had been left open or thrown on the floor, even the mattress was off the bed frame. Whoever had searched this room had done quite a thorough job. Whose room was it? she wondered. She needed to tell someone and hoped one of the clerks had reported for duty this morning. She left swiftly, heading to the desk in the Armoury, then doubled back, realising she'd need the name of the room: Mackintosh.

Mrs MacBain and Jarvis trudged back up to the house and installed themselves in her office, just off the kitchens. Jarvis couldn't believe she kept the same office from her days as Head Housekeeper. He'd have taken a much better one, he thought, if he owned the Abbey. That Rowan Tree room had been nice. He wondered why she didn't use it.

They settled into chairs and were silent for a moment. Jarvis collected his thoughts and couldn't come up with a single reason why he shouldn't arrest Lord Inverkillen. Mrs MacBain collected her thoughts and couldn't come up with a single reason why Angus would burn it, unless he was guilty. What to do? And how to get rid of Jarvis so she could think?

'Well—' he began gravely.

She interrupted him. 'We need to speak to Lord Inverkillen again. There might be a perfectly rational explanation.'

Jarvis considered her for a moment. Rational explanation for *what*? What had they been searching for? He didn't want to admit that he didn't know.

'Well, let's find him and ask,' he said with more confidence than he felt. 'You know him well enough to know if he's lying, I suspect.'

Mrs MacBain thought about the statement. She did know Angus well, but not quite the way Jarvis thought. She knew Angus's likes and dislikes, his habits, his routine. She knew his favourite shaving soap – Trumper Eucris – and that he preferred cloves to lavender in his wardrobe. His good mood was signalled by a Windsor knot, a bad one by a Four in Hand knot. If given the choice, it would always be raspberry jam over orange marmalade, boiled eggs over scrambled, but never, ever fried. She had been his servant. It had been her job to know these things.

But they weren't intimates; they weren't friends. She'd never even had a proper conversation with him. She had with Fergus; she had with Elspeth. But Angus was different. He was an Earl and she, even as the owner of the hotel, was still beneath him. Would he lie to her? Almost certainly. He'd hidden a lot of things when he lived in the Abbey; some small, like stealing cigarettes from his brother-in-law, and some large, like his relationship with Hugh. But that was nothing compared to murder.

She stood slowly, deep in thought, and rang for a hall boy. When he arrived, she asked him to find Lord Inverkillen and bring him to Rowan Tree. Would she know if he was lying to her? They were about to find out.

Angus was not happy to be summoned again. He was especially disturbed to see Jarvis still in residence. Mrs MacBain tried to get him settled into a chair, but Angus refused and stood by the fire. She watched him closely. He was visibly agitated.

'Lord Inverkillen, I'd like to go over your movements last night again.' Jarvis said it slowly, reasonably, as if he were in charge. But when Angus glared at him, he stammered like a schoolboy. 'If, erm . . . you don't mind.'

Mrs MacBain sighed softly.

'I do mind, actually. We've been over it. I've nothing more to tell you.' He shifted the posy vase on the mantel.

'You left Mrs Blackwood in the Small Library just as the Duke of Perth began?'

Angus sighed. 'Yes.'

'And you left through the French doors in the Small Library?' Mrs MacBain asked. 'Not the ones in the Long Gallery?'

Jarvis looked at her quizzically.

Angus replied, somewhat off guard. 'Yes.'

'You're positive about that?' she asked, urgency in her voice.

'Yes,' snapped Angus. He couldn't see why it should matter how he left the room.

Jarvis couldn't either. The man had been in the room and that was good enough for Jarvis. 'And you went to the Tennis Pavilion, without being seen by anyone, correct?'

'I have no idea if anyone saw me, *Constable*. It was dark. Someone could have been lurking, but I certainly didn't see anyone.' His voice dripped with disdain.

'Why didn't you go back to the ball?' Mrs MacBain asked, trying to keep her voice light. She'd been very curious about that. If he hadn't murdered her, and he really did have the time to pay her, why leave the ball?

Angus started and then stared at her. He really hadn't been expecting the question. 'Erm, because, erm, I needed a moment of quiet.'

He hasn't thought about this, Mrs MacBain reflected. *That bodes well. He doesn't have a cover story yet.*

'A moment of quiet?' she asked, eyebrows raised. Angus had never in his life needed 'a moment of quiet'.

He shuffled from one foot to the other. 'Yes. Can't a chap gather his thoughts in peace?' He really hadn't thought about why he'd run there. He'd just ended up there. He should have gone back to the tables and won as much money as he could have, but she'd been so cruel . . .

Jarvis drew an irritated breath, but Mrs MacBain cut him off. If they angered him, they'd never get to the truth. She gently placed a hand on his knee to stall him.

'Angus, I don't think you killed that woman. I really don't. But Inspector Jarvis does and he's desperate to arrest you.' Angus looked at Jarvis, panic etched on his face. 'As he rightly says, you had motive, you had opportunity and, as she was stabbed, you had a weapon.'

Angus blanched, and his knees started to give out. *Dear god, how had it come to this?*

'Angus, we need to know exactly what happened in that room,' she continued gently.

They waited as Angus stared at Mrs MacBain. She looked back, as encouragingly as possible. Jarvis held his breath. The clock on the bookcase chimed half-past the hour. He blinked and sat down roughly, head in his hands, voice hollow.

'She didn't give me to the end of the month. She wanted the money right away, but I simply don't have it. I offered her what I did have but she just laughed.'

'All title and no money? I should have known. The number of times I've had this conversation. How honourable is it to gamble without the capital to back it up? Nobility just isn't what it used to be.'

'Now look here, I've done my best. I've raised nearly half in the day you've given me and as of tonight, I'm only short by

forty pounds. If I could return to the card tables, I'll have won all of it by the morning. I can pay you by teatime. You have my word.'

'Please. As if I'd take the word of a gentleman. You know, had this happened in Shanghai, they'd have taken you out back and shot you by now. Lucky for you, that's not how I play. But I shall be speaking to the police in the morning. You've left me no choice.'

'They'll put me in prison!'

'Yes, and it will be humiliating, to be seen for what you truly are, but I think we can agree it's better than being shot and dumped in the river. Now, you have two options, Lord Inverkillen: come with me in the morning and turn yourself in or wait to be arrested in front of your beloved Grandmama. Which is it to be?'

'I'm only forty pounds short! Why are you doing this? I've never done anything to hurt you!'

'One must face the consequences of one's actions, however unpleasant it may be.'

Angus cleared his throat and moved the posy vase again. 'That's when I left. I was so angry; I didn't really pay attention to who might have seen me or not. I just wanted to get out of there. But she was alive when I left!' His eyes were pleading with Mrs MacBain. 'I never touched her, I swear. You must believe me. I didn't even go near her.'

Jarvis sat in his chair, entirely confused. Why on earth would he have arrested Angus for a gambling debt? It was large, yes, but as far as the law was concerned, it was hardly a matter for the police. Gambling wasn't illegal. What had she expected him to do?

'Where was she sitting?'

Angus thought for a moment. 'In the chair facing the doors to the Long Gallery.'

Mrs MacBain cocked her head. 'Was there a fire going?' she asked.

'A fire?' He was caught off guard by the question. 'Erm . . . no. I don't remember one.'

'Did she have her cane with her?'

Angus shook his head and thought. 'Yes,' he said slowly, 'she was leaning on it. Why?'

Mrs MacBain nodded, painting the scene in her mind. 'Where were you standing?'

'Just inside the French doors.'

'Were the curtains closed?' She held her breath.

Angus thought for a moment. 'No. The French doors were open to the garden.'

Mrs MacBain breathed out slowly. That narrowed down the time of death.

Angus reached in his coat for his cigarette case, opened it and groaned. It was empty.

Mrs MacBain stood and walked to the small demilune table at the door. Picking up a silver box and opening it, she offered it to Angus. 'They aren't your fancy Moroccan ones, I'm afraid.' Angus nodded his thanks and took an English cigarette, grateful for any tobacco in this moment.

He and Mrs MacBain stood by the windows, Angus smoking and staring at the garden.

'What was she holding over you?' she asked quietly.

Angus exhaled and looked at Mrs MacBain, entirely forgetting Jarvis was there. 'I didn't touch her; I swear to you.' He let out a stuttering breath and his hands shook as he said it. 'She had Hugh's book.'

'Oh my lord above.' Mrs MacBain's head was reeling. 'How did she know?'

Angus shrugged. 'I don't know, but she knew.'

'Knew what? What's happening?' asked Jarvis, coming to the windows. They were having a quiet conversation between themselves, and he didn't like it one bit.

Mrs MacBain sighed heavily. Colin the footman's face floated to the front of her memory. It enraged her further. 'Well, how she found out isn't important. She knew, and she knew enough to use it to blackmail you.'

'What did she know? What are you two talking about?' Jarvis demanded. It was his investigation, after all, and Mrs MacBain was being too secretive about things. It was like they were talking in code.

'Angus, this bit is very important.' She held her breath. 'Where are your clothes from last night?'

For a moment, he was confused and then Angus blushed deeply and made a face, groaning at the floor.

'Angus?' She prodded it as gently as she could. 'It's quite important we see your kilt. Do you understand? It's the only way we can prove you're innocent. Did you burn it?'

He looked confused. 'No. Why? Oh, the fire. Uncle Cecil told me to burn Hugh's book.'

Relief flooded her and she nodded at him encouragingly. 'Where is your kilt?'

'Does he have to hear this?' He looked pained and nodded to Jarvis.

'I'm afraid so.'

He sighed heavily and looked near tears. 'When I got to the Pavilion, I opened a bottle of whisky. I had a drink and then I had another. And then I opened another bottle. Next thing I remember, I hear the Colonel shouting for his tennis lesson.' He paused and blushed even deeper than before. 'And I'm lying in a pool of my own sick.'

Jarvis had the good grace not to guffaw, but it was difficult. He spun round and covered his mouth and coughed.

'I changed into whites and used my kilt to wipe up the mess.'

'Where is it now?' she asked urgently.

'I didn't have time to do anything with it, so I tossed it out the back window on to the wood pile.'

'Oh, thank the Lord!' she shouted. She could have kissed the boy. Turning to Jarvis, she said eagerly, 'Let's go get it before anything happens to it.'

The constable carried Angus's kilt in an evidence box, held at arm's length, down the drive to the police car. Sitting in the sun had done it no favours. Mrs MacBain had never been so delighted to find something so putrid. But it did exonerate him from murdering Mrs Blackwood. There wasn't a speck of blood on it and his *sgian-dubh* was so blunt it couldn't have sliced butter.

As she walked back to the house, Jarvis fell into step with her. 'Well, that puts him in the clear. You must be pleased.'

Mrs MacBain nodded, a slight smile of relief on her face. 'Yes. And now we know he was telling us the truth about the timings and the room. She was killed after three and whoever did it locked that room, lit the fire, and made off with her cane.'

Jarvis processed this. 'So, she did have one last visitor, as Mr Blackwood said. Okay. Let's go over the timeline. What time did things finish last night?'

'Weren't you there?' She had a distinct impression he had been, but she couldn't quite recall seeing him.

'I popped in after it started, had a couple of reels, but then Mother said she was exhausted, and we left before the breakfast.' Which had been a shame, he'd felt, knowing it would have been quite a feast. His stomach rumbled and he hoped they'd go back though the kitchens. It was time for lunch, and he was starving.

'Ah, well, she is getting on, I suppose. What is she now, seventy-eight?'

Mrs Jarvis was not a hearty woman, and Jarvis's sisters were, by all accounts, harridans of the highest order. Jarvis had been henpecked his whole life, particularly by his eldest sister. Mrs MacBain didn't doubt the daily toll of it weakened an already delicate woman.

'Seventy-nine next month – good guess,' Jarvis responded. 'What time then?'

'Oh yes. Doors opened at eight and the ball was officially opened at nine with Hamilton House done by the Inverkillens.'

Jarvis arched a brow. 'It was your ball. Shouldn't that have been your honour?'

Mrs MacBain smiled modestly. 'Well, normally, yes. But Lady Georgina insisted on being part of the set and I thought, as they were all here, it might be easier to have them open the ball.'

Jarvis shook his head. 'Okay, the Inverkillens opened the ball at nine and the first reel was at nine thirty?'

'Yes. Breakfast buffet at twelve. Carriages at three thirty – not that there are carriages any longer, I suppose; I do miss the sound of the horses – and the footmen were instructed to shut the doors to the cards room at five o'clock, chasing out any and all stragglers.'

Jarvis stood aside and opened a gate for her. 'And now that we know both Lord Inverkillen and Mr Blackwood were telling the truth, that puts the murder between three and five o'clock.'

'Do we know that?' she asked, picking her way carefully up the stone stairs to a terrace near the Tennis Court. 'We know Mr Blackwood told us the truth about leaving her at two thirty, but how do we know he didn't come back down and kill her after her last appointment left? We only have his word that he was in his room all night.'

A puff of air escaped Jarvis's lips. 'We could search his room for the cane? He seems a bit to canny to keep those in his room, though.'

'Agreed. But what bothers me is that I can't see any reason that he'd want to kill her. What possible motive could he have?'

Jarvis shrugged. 'If he's from Shanghai, he'd know how valuable the cane is. And it's like he said, they escaped with what little they could carry. Maybe he wanted to start over on his own, and the cane made that financially possible.'

Mrs MacBain was silent as she contemplated this. Could it have been a simple robbery? It seemed mad, but desperate people did desperate things. 'Let's say he did kill her for the cane. Why would he still be here? He could have taken off on foot last night, hopped on the milk train at five thirty, and be who-knows-where by now.'

It was, Jarvis conceded, a good point.

'Perhaps we need to have a chat with all the others she was blackmailing.'

They reached a side door to the Abbey and Mrs MacBain stopped to look at him. She was sure it would be futile, but they had little else to go on. 'All right, who do you want to speak to first?'

Fergus was on his way back from the Small Library. Jarvis's constables had done a thorough search of the room and hadn't found either the knife or the cane. Mrs MacBain wasn't going to be happy.

He had just entered the Armoury on his way to the kitchens, hoping to find her, when MacPherson called his name. Fergus changed course and walked to the desk, forcing a polite smile on to his face.

'Yes?' he asked genially.

Thompson was standing with two men, one of whom was staring at the fourth Earl's suit of armour. As he approached, MacPherson indicated, and the men turned their attention to him. They surveyed him critically in silence. Then the taller of men spoke quietly. 'We'd like to speak with Lady Annabella Martin.'

It was Fergus's turn to do the surveying. The men were dressed in grey suits with black ties and bowlers, all very tasteful, but they were not here for a holiday, which was evident, and they certainly weren't Bella's friends. Fergus suddenly had a bad feeling in his stomach.

'I believe she's usually in the Ladies' Morning Room this time of day, Mr . . . ?' He fished for a name. When none came, he sighed inwardly. 'Well then, would you care to follow me?'

'If you could just tell us where to find her, that would be best.' It was a polite but firm request for privacy.

'That's a bit tricky as it's quite easy to get lost on the way. Best if I show you there.' As he mounted the first stair, he paused, turned back and said, 'This way, gentlemen.'

Three minutes later, he passed through a set of double doors marked with a tasteful brass plaque reading *Ladies' Morning Room*.

'Ah yes. Bella,' Fergus called as they crossed the room. Bella was sitting on a pale-yellow sofa next to the windows. 'You have some visitors.'

Bella looked up from *Tatler*. 'Visitors? Who?' She eyed the men and then frowned slightly. They were not her sort of people. She stood and smoothed her skirt.

'Lady Annabella Martin?'

'Yes. And who you are?'

'We're from the Foreign Office. Perhaps we should move somewhere quieter.'

'Do you have news of Edmund?' Bella asked anxiously.

'Erm, no,' said one the men. 'We lost communication with the Shanghai offices some time ago.'

'Oh. Well if there's no news, what are you doing here?' she asked suspiciously.

They seated themselves, without invitation, on the sofa. Bella watched, and then looked at Fergus affronted by their lack of manners. Fergus merely shrugged. Bella seated herself on the opposite sofa.

The taller of the men cleared his throat. 'We're here for the money and your receipts.'

Bella paused. 'What?' she asked, clearly confused.

'The money you were handed when you left Shanghai. We need that back.'

Fergus felt his stomach flip and he eyed Bella nervously.

'Whatever for?' asked Bella sharply.

The men shifted in their seats like schoolboys. 'It belongs to the government, madam,' came a soft reply.

'It most certainly does not.' Bella looked offended.

Fergus was utterly confused but quite alarmed by the exchange. 'Bella, what money? What are they talking about?'

'You don't understand,' said Bella. 'Edmund went to the bank the morning I left. He closed our Shanghai accounts and sent me home with the money. Our money.'

'Erm,' began the man, unsure how to go on. He had never dealt with civilians before. 'Actually, Lady Martin, the money Sir Edmund gave you to travel with was from the Consul safe.'

'Are you saying Edmund stole from the Consul?' asked Fergus

'No, not at all. We keep cash in embassy and consul safes for exactly this purpose. Sir Edmund was following standard protocol. But we're tasked with collecting what's left after everyone arrives back safely.'

'That can't be right.' Bella looked at her brother, confusion and irritation in her eyes.

The man addressed Fergus. 'Lord Martin sent word that he couldn't raise enough cash in Western currencies to get everyone home safely. There had been runs on the banks, which we had expected. His next move was to use the money in the safe. Normally, this is given to the senior staff member accompanying the group, but . . .' he hesitated and gave a sidelong glance to his colleague, who nodded surreptitiously '. . . given the Colonel is his deputy, he sent the money with Lady Annabella instead. And we're here to collect it.'

'No! That is my money. If you take it, I'll be left with nothing!' She looked to Fergus, panic on her face. 'I've ordered clothes! How am I meant to pay for that?'

'That's not really my place to say, madam. But the money must be returned.' He didn't sound in the least bit sympathetic to her plight.

'And if I refuse?' asked Bella, defiantly.

'I'd think carefully about that, Lady Martin.' They slowly rose to their feet, in unison. 'The money belongs to His Majesty's government, and I shouldn't think you'd like to tussle with them.'

There was a shocked silence. Fergus marvelled at the courage of anyone who threatened Bella. But then another thought filled his brain. Knowing how Bella tended to spend money, he doubted any was left. 'What if she hasn't any left?'

'As long as we have receipts to square the books, it's fine.' The man chuckled. 'But she couldn't possibly have spent it all in a month.'

Fergus could feel his legs buckling already, but he had to ask. 'Exactly how much was it?'

Suddenly serious again, the man stared at Fergus, then Bella, and then looked about the room to be sure no one was eavesdropping. He said it quietly, but he may have well shouted it. 'About forty thousand pounds in various currencies.'

When Jarvis and Mrs MacBain finally reached her office, a footman was waiting for her. Thompson needed to see her urgently, he said. He was to escort her straight away. As they climbed the servants' stairs, her apprehension mounted. Finally, they turned the corner to the guest rooms, where Thompson and Lady Elspeth waited about halfway down the corridor.

'What's happened?' she asked.

Thompson opened the door for her, and her breath left her.

'What on earth?' Mrs MacBain walked in slowly, dazed by the destruction.

Jarvis walked behind her, gawping.

'When did you find this?' she asked.

'Perhaps we should shut the door? I doubt we want anyone seeing this,' Elspeth said quietly. Thompson agreed to stand guard outside. When the door was closed, Elspeth continued, 'I found it this morning as I was heading out for a walk. I ran for Thompson and since then, one or both of us has been at the door.'

'Did you enter the room?' asked Jarvis, looking around.

'Initially. I could see from the hall that it had been ransacked, so I stepped in to see if anyone was hurt.'

Mrs MacBain and Jarvis exchanged dark glances.

'What?' asked Elspeth anxiously.

'Do you know whose room this is?' Mrs MacBain asked cautiously.

'Not a clue. A woman, but that's all I know.' She pointed to a drawer with a strand of pearls hanging carelessly over the edge.

'It belonged to Mrs Blackwood.'

'Belonged?' Elspeth's arms went numb, noting the use of past tense.

Mrs MacBain ushered her to the door. 'Let's go to my office, shall we?'

They had settled into Rowan Tree, with Mrs MacBain pouring tea and explaining. Elspeth was quite shocked, so Mrs MacBain added a wee nip of brandy to hers.

'That poor woman,' she mumbled. She accepted the tea mechanically, thinking only of what she had just heard. 'And you have no idea who could have done it?'

Mrs MacBain sat down and frowned. 'No,' she said unhappily. They slipped into silence for some minutes.

'My money would be on that nephew of hers,' Elspeth said unexpectedly.

Jarvis looked over the rim of his cup. 'Oh yeah? Why's that?'

'Oh! Did I say that aloud?' Elspeth shook her head and looked embarrassed. 'My apologies. I hadn't meant to speak. I should think the last thing you want are unsolicited opinions. Ignore me.'

Mrs MacBain thought it interesting that Elspeth went immediately to Mrs Blackwood's nephew. He was top of her list, too. 'What makes you suspect him?'

Elspeth looked between the pair of them. 'Really, it's nothing. I wasn't thinking.' When Mrs MacBain looked at her encouragingly, she set her teacup down. 'It's just that, well, there's something sneaky about him. He's always turning up in places where he ought not be.'

'Such as?' asked Mrs MacBain, scrutinising Lady Elspeth carefully.

'I've seen him in the woods several times, near the service yard behind the Distillery, heading up to the ridge.'

'And why shouldn't he be there?' asked Jarvis. 'If you're allowed to be there, why isn't he?'

'He's perfectly welcome to roam, Inspector, but I'm dressed for it, and he never is.' She looked to Mrs Mac-Bain. 'I've only ever seen him in that suit of his, which is completely improper for walking in the woods.'

Jarvis harrumphed.

'Inspector, if you were going out into the woods, you'd put on proper clothing. At the very least, proper footwear.

You'd never go out in the shoes you're wearing now, would you?'

They all looked at Jarvis's shoes. Worn, black standard-issue leather shoes, with a smooth leather sole. They were, he had to admit, the last thing he would wear to go walking.

'His are very similar and they have no traction whatsoever. I had to help him up an incline one afternoon, because he kept sliding backwards.'

'So he doesn't have outdoor clothing. Doesn't make him a murderer.' *Why am I defending this man?* he wondered. With Lord Inverkillen in the clear, the nephew was his number-one suspect. Or maybe the Colonel. Perhaps Lady Annabella? He really wasn't at all sure.

'No, but it does make him suspicious,' Elspeth shot back. 'I told him to borrow things from the boot room and he simply never did. His suit is white, for goodness' sake. I can't understand how he's keeping it clean. So why does he keep going out improperly dressed?'

They stared at one another for a few moments before Jarvis reached for a second ginger nut. 'Maybe he was tired of being harangued by his aunt and needed a moment's peace,' he said testily.

That brought Elspeth to silence. She stared at Jarvis for several moments. 'All I know is, there were plenty of people on that trip from Shanghai.'

Jarvis finally said, 'Could have been any one of them. Lady Annabella, for instance.'

Elspeth choked on her tea. 'You can't be serious!'

'She didn't know the woman, Roddy,' said Mrs MacBain, transferring the strainer to her cup for a second cup. It was definitely a two-cup discussion.

'So she says,' Jarvis countered. 'But we only have her word for it.'

'Bella would never have risked her reputation and position,' Mrs MacBain said firmly.

'But if she was being blackmailed—'

'Blackmailed?' Elspeth was aghast. She had missed a lot
of their discussion, she suddenly realised.

Mrs MacBain sat back in her chair, delicately balanc-
ing her teacup. 'I sincerely doubt the woman had any
cause to blackmail Bella. She herself said that Edmund
wouldn't let her go anywhere alone; she always had a
guard with her.'

'Ha! You think she wouldn't get to up to no good
because of the guard?' Jarvis set his teacup down roughly,
sloshing tea over the side. 'It's like you always say, isn't it:
these people, peers and whatnot, they live by different rules.
Servants are just *things* to them, like furniture or animals.'

There was a shocked pause as Elspeth slowly looked at
Jarvis, who suddenly remembered she was in the room.

'I mean, erm . . . Ugh . . . ' he stammered furiously, trying to back-pedal his statement.

Elspeth looked slowly at Mrs MacBain. 'Is that what you
believe? That I think of you as an animal?'

Mrs MacBain blushed and shifted in her seat. 'It is rare
to find someone like you or Fergus, who treat us as people.
"Know your place" is still a common refrain.'

Elspeth chose her words carefully. 'I am aware that many
in the upper classes behave abominably towards those in
the lower classes. But I have always tried not to be one of
them.' She paused and took a sip of tea. Looking at Jarvis
again, she said, 'And while Bella thrives on having servants
to order around, she is not the sort to court trouble. It's not
how she's made.'

Mrs MacBain breathed a quiet sigh of relief. The last
thing she wanted was a rift with Lady Elspeth. She said

carefully, 'Edmund was worried about Mrs Blackwood at the outset. When Bella arrived in Shanghai, he forbade her from socialising with her. He wasn't being a controlling husband; it was important to his job; she was a scandalous person, remember. He absolutely would have instructed his guards to keep them apart. So I think there is little chance their paths would have crossed, especially in secret.'

'So as far as motives, she's out?' grumbled Jarvis.

'I think so, yes.'

They sat in silence for a few moments. A clock chimed softly in the hall outside. The Armoury was slowly coming back to life. She heard someone ring the front desk bell for attention. She glanced at her watch. It was time for the luncheon service.

'What about the Colonel, then?' Jarvis asked.

'Well, he says he was at the cards tables all night. We can ask the footmen to verify that. Not that I doubt him; that man's done nothing here but gamble and eat. But he did visit the Small Library, and he's not admitted that to us.'

Jarvis made some murmuring noises.

'Mr Blackwood, however, that's trickier.' Mrs MacBain stared into the distance, slightly shaking her head. 'He said he went to bed and left her there, for her next visitor. But how do we prove he didn't come back?'

'It's like you said, what possible motive could he have?' asked Jarvis, spitting crumbs of his ginger nut into the air. Mrs MacBain could see them drifting in the sunlight and sighed. Well, the room needed dusting as it was.

'He's not inheriting anything,' continued Jarvis, 'why would he want her dead? The others, at least, had a motive: blackmail. But she's not likely to blackmail her own nephew, now is she?'

'Why not? People do far worse to their family,' Elspeth said. 'I can think of three – no four! – people who've done just that.'

Jarvis conceded the point – suddenly thinking about his eldest sister – and took a large sip of tea. He carefully reached for a third biscuit. Mrs MacBain wondered if she'd need to send for more.

'Okay, so let's say she was blackmailing him.' He dunked the ginger nut into his tea, which made Elspeth grimace. Jarvis watched it slowly dissolve, waiting for the right moment to pop it into his mouth. 'How would he pay her? Everyone else had the means to pay her but he's a refugee, remember. He's only got a suitcase and the clothes on his back.'

Mrs MacBain looked at Jarvis suddenly. 'What did you just say?'

'Me?' asked Jarvis, startled. 'I said he's only got a suitcase,'

'And the clothes on his back. Oh, how did I miss that?' Mrs MacBain stood up abruptly.

Jarvis blinked, and she was gone. Looking back to his teacup, he swore softly. His biscuit was at the bottom of his tea.

Fergus was reeling. Forty thousand pounds? It was a tremendous amount of money. What if Bella had spent it all? Could she have spent it all? He wasn't sure. Bella had never been thrifty.

One of the Foreign Office men cleared their throat. 'If you could get the money for us, Lady Martin? We're booked on the early evening train.'

Fergus felt his stomach drop, for an entirely different reason. 'I'm not sure you're going to be able to catch that, gentlemen.'

They glanced at him curiously. They had checked with the station manager before starting out to the Abbey: there was a service at six o'clock that evening. Plenty of time to conclude business and get back to the station in time.

Fergus cleared his throat, suddenly nervous. 'You see, we've had a bit of an incident last night and the local police have asked us not to let anyone leave the hotel or its grounds. Technically, you shouldn't have been let on to the Estate.'

'An incident?' Both men raised their eyebrows.

'Yes, a woman was, erm . . . killed last night, and the local police are investigating.'

'Killed?' The man issued a low whistle. 'Well, that's nothing to do with us. We've only just arrived. We can show our train tickets as proof. Now, the money please, Lady Martin.'

'I think we should ask Detective Inspector Jarvis before we make any decisions. I'm sure he will have no qualms with you leaving, but I would like to be sure. It is a murder inquiry; it is quite serious.'

The men held a silent conference and then nodded. Having a deep respect for protocol and titles, as bureaucrats so often do, they would speak with Jarvis and abide by his decision.

'Bella, why don't you take them through to the Library – we've set out a cold luncheon – and I'll go find Jarvis?'

The men stood and followed Bella out of the room. Fergus let out a heavy sigh.

Bella settled the men into a corner table at the far end of
the room and then joined Lady Georgina, who was in her
usual place by the fire. She had been joined by Cecil and
Mr Rosenthal. Angus stood nearby, smoking a cigarette.

'There you are, Bella,' said Lady Georgina as she
approached. Bella sat heavily on the sofa beside her grandmother, shock written all over her face. 'You look terrible.
What's wrong?'

Bella looked at her grandmother and blinked, unsure how
to begin her latest tale of woe. Before she began, a voice
came from behind her.

Mrs MacBain burst into the room – followed by Jarvis
and Elspeth – and marched resolutely to the Cards Room.
'Mr Blackwood, a word, if you please?'

It hadn't been, they noted, a request. Wide-eyed, the
family looked to Mr Blackwood, who stared back for a
moment and then slowly stood to follow the trio.

Angus moved quickly and prevented the door from
closing properly. This he simply had to hear. Lady
Georgina, horrified that her grandson would stoop to
listening at doors – in public, no less! – scowled at him
and waved him away from the door.

'I think it's time you told us the truth, Mr Blackwood,'
said Mrs MacBain determinedly. 'Although, that's not your
name is it?'

Angus turned a scandalised face to the family. It was all
Cecil needed; he leapt to his feet to join his nephew. Lady
Georgina tutted loudly, and wondered, as she often did,
where she'd gone wrong with the family.

'What are you on about, Mrs MacBain?' asked Jarvis,
thoroughly confused.

'He's not Mrs Blackwood's nephew.' She and Mr Blackwood stared at one another intently.

Cecil motioned frantically to the family to come to the door. In a moment, they were all crowded around, shamelessly eavesdropping. Mr Rosenthal stifled a giggle at the scene.

'Okay, if he's not her nephew, who is he?' asked Jarvis.

Mrs MacBain cocked her head and waited with an expectant look on her face.

He stared at them for a moment. 'Parker. My name is Lawrence Parker.'

'And you're not her nephew, are you?' she continued. 'You're her servant. If I had to wager, I'd say you were her bodyguard.'

His eyes narrowed as they looked at her, and she could see the calculations he was making. Would he tell her the truth?

He said at last, quietly but clearly, never taking his eyes from her. 'Not so much "servant" as "paying off a debt".'

'Indentured servitude?' she asked, hoping she was wrong. But he nodded.

'I knew he was dodgy!' shouted Angus, bursting into the room. The family poured through after him, filling the room with noise.

Not her nephew? How the deuce do you know that? What do you mean he's not the nephew? Why would you lie about being her nephew? Does this have anything to do with her death? We've been socialising with a servant?

Startled by the intrusion, Mrs MacBain spun round and uttered an oath.

'All right, all right!' shouted Jarvis, throwing his arms up. 'Quieten down! This is official police business and I'm going to have to ask you to leave.'

They had the grace to fall silent, chastened under the glare from Mrs MacBain. But if Jarvis thought for one second they'd shuffle out of the room quietly, he was sorely mistaken.

Mrs MacBain crossed the small, now crowded, room and shut the door. 'Not a single word from any of you. Understood?'

The family nodded mutely.

She returned to Mr Blackwood and continued her queries.

'How did you know?' he asked, equally pained and curious. This woman, he realised, was formidable. He could learn a lot from her.

'Your suit.'

'My suit?' He glanced down at his clothing and then back up at her, confused. 'What's wrong with it?'

Cecil murmured something indistinct, and Mrs MacBain shot him a stern look.

'Nothing is wrong with your suit. But much like Bella's maid, it's the only one you have.' She turned to look at the family. 'Everyone leaving Shanghai was allowed a single bag. Bella kept both cases for herself, because Bella's things were more important than a change of clothes for her maid.'

All eyes fell on Bella, who huffed indignantly. 'We paid for the tickets . . . '

Mrs MacBain turned back to Lawrence. 'When Mrs Blackwood arrived, she had two rather large trunks with her, but you only have one suit. She obviously took your suitcase for herself and wouldn't even give you the smallest amount of space for a change of clothing. That's not something you'd do to a nephew, but you'd do it to a servant.'

He gave her a small smile and tilted his head in confirmation.

'You got all that from a suit?' Jarvis asked, incredulous. She never failed to surprise.

Mrs MacBain perched on the chair opposite Lawrence, so they were nearly eye to eye. 'She's not just a little old lady, is she?'

To this, he sighed, heavily, as if a great burden was smothering his body. 'No. She runs—' he corrected himself '—she ran Shanghai's largest opium den.'

The family gasped and started to twitter again. MacBain turned her head and issued a sharp threat of expulsion if they refused to be quiet, and then returned to Mr Blackwood.

'Why was she here?' Her voice was more urgent but still quiet. 'You know why she came to Loch Down, don't you?'

Lawrence stared intently into Mrs MacBain's eyes. *She doesn't know*, he thought. This was one secret he could keep. *She's dead, what does it matter anymore?* he thought. He said it quietly.

'She was after the ruby.'

Ross walked up to the ridge to clear away the cobwebs from the night of the ball; both the whisky and his conversation with Elspeth were weighing on him. He was just approaching the old osprey's nest when he spotted a thin curl of smoke from the area near the bothy. He glanced at his watch; it wasn't quite teatime, but it had to be Elspeth at the bothy! His heart soared and he scrambled down the ridge, making his way through the woods as quickly as he could.

But when he finally arrived, he stopped for a moment. The smoke had dissipated but the smell clung to the air. Whatever had been burned, it hadn't come from the Estate. Ross walked to the door, noticing there was a pile of juniper branches to one side. Juniper burned quickly and produced very little heat. It also produced a tremendous amount of smoke, which is why he could see it from the ridge. But Elspeth knew better than to use it. Something was amiss.

'Hello!' called Ross. 'Anyone about?'

Nothing happened.

He walked to the window, the smell intensifying, and he peeked in. The fire had died out. A bottle of his private reserve sat on the table, half drunk, next to a partially eaten game pie. Crumbs and ants were everywhere. Looking to the far corner, he started at the sight of a figure lying in the bed. He looked about and didn't see a rucksack. In fact, he saw no possessions of any kind. *Must be a vagrant*, thought Ross. He approached the door nervously.

'Hello?' he called, hoping to wake whomever it was in the bed. But the figure didn't move. In fact, he couldn't see that the figure was even breathing. Ross waited for a long moment and then opened the door. Walking to the bed, he reached out, pulled the shoulder over, blanched white, stumbled back a few steps. The man was dead, all right, but what he hadn't counted on was that it was Hugh.

'The ruby? What ruby?' Fergus had just come into the Cards Room, after noticing several hotel guests silently crowded by the Cards Room door. The family turned to look at him, but not Mrs MacBain, who kept eye contact with Mr Parker.

'What ruby, Mr Parker?' she asked.

'The Ambrose Ruby. It's the largest ruby in existence. It's been in the Chinese Imperial collection for generations.'

His speech slowed to a deliberate cadence. 'Until a month ago.'

Comprehension dawned on Mrs MacBain's face. 'Of course,' she said softly and then turned to look directly at Bella.

'What?' said Bella, uncomfortably, as the entire room followed Mrs MacBain's gaze towards her. 'I . . . I don't own rubies,' she sputtered uncomfortably.

Lady Georgina glared at her. 'Now is not the time for subterfuge, Bella.'

'But I don't own rubies, Grandmama. Red doesn't suit me, you know that.'

'Not rubies, plural,' spat Lawrence, clearly exasperated by Bella, 'ruby, singular. Your husband stole it and you smuggled it into England for him.'

Bella? Smuggling? You must be mad. Edmund stole it? He's a thief? I thought he was a diplomat? You can never trust foreigners.

Bella looked outraged and practically shouted. 'I don't know anything about a ruby. He's lying. Edmund wouldn't steal anything!'

'It was you who stole her suitcase in Marseilles, wasn't it?' asked Mrs MacBain. 'Searching for the ruby.'

Lawrence nodded.

'And again in Paris?'

Another nod.

'You stole my luggage?!' Bella crossed the room before anyone could process that she'd spoken. The slap made a resounding *thwack*! across his cheek. The hotel guests, watching through the open door, tittered with delight and shock.

'Whoa!' cried Lawrence, stumbling back, more from the shock of it than anything.

*Bella! Lady Annabella! Someone stop her. That is no way
for a lady to behave.*

The family chastised her as Bella pounded her fists about
the shoulders and chest of Lawrence.

'Hey! Hey, lady!' he sputtered, cowering away from the
blows.

Bella continued to deliver a barrage of blows, adding oaths
and curses into the mix when Fergus and Angus finally
jumped in to restrain their sister. They each managed to
grab an arm and hauled her backwards off Lawrence, who
was now nearly doubled over, protecting his head.

Bella howled, fighting hard against her brothers. 'You've
no idea what you've done to me! You've bankrupted me!
How dare you!'

Lawrence stood up and looked at her, confused. 'What's
the big deal? It was just a bunch of swimming costumes
and make-up.'

The kick landed squarely in his chest, knocking him
backwards over a chair and into the fireplace.

'Nice technique, Bella,' uttered Elspeth, admiringly.

Angus and Fergus still had firm hold of Bella's arms and
struggled to pull her further away.

By now, the entire Library was watching, unabashedly
staring, and Cecil and Mr Rosenthal jumped in to help
Lawrence off the floor and into a chair. Bella wrenched
herself free from her brothers and threw herself into a chair,
glaring at Lawrence and muttering darkly.

Once the combatants were separated, Mrs MacBain took
control of the group again. Standing in front of Bella, but
just out of harm's way, she spoke sternly to her. 'What was
that all about?'

Bella sighed deeply and unsteadily, her shoulders slump-
ing forward in . . . defeat? Surrender? Surely not.

'You idiot,' she spat at Lawrence, still enraged, 'my jewels were in that case.'

Gasps went out from the women; Angus snorted delightedly and lit a cigarette. Lawrence looked uncomfortable. 'No,' he said, hoarsely. 'There were no jewels in them. I did a thorough search.'

'Then clearly, you didn't spot the false back,' Bella said caustically. 'Some thief you are.'

Lawrence blanched. 'False back?'

Bella spat the words slowly. 'My jewels were tucked neatly in that case, hidden in a compartment behind the drawers of my make-up case, opened by this key.' She fished a key from inside her dress, which hung on a delicate gold chain.

'Now wait a moment.' Lady Georgina was confused. 'We've seen you wearing your jewellery, Bella. The other night you wore that stunning sapphire necklace.'

Bella smiled ruefully. 'Paste.'

The room gave a collective gasp.

'Well, I could have told you that,' muttered Cecil. All turned to glare at his remark. 'Of course, it's very good paste. One could wear it with nary a soul realising. Well, if you need proof . . . ' He waved his arm at the group.

Bella continued. 'Edmund insisted I wear paste while travelling, so he had a few pieces made for the trip. I was meant to wear them at dinner each night. You make a big deal about putting the paste in the hotel safe, while the real jewellery is hidden in your room. If anyone breaks in, well, who steals make-up?' She glared at Lawrence again, who had blanched whiter than Lady Georgina's gloves. Clearly it hadn't dawned on him to check for hidden compartments.

'What did you do with the case, after you searched it?' asked Mrs MacBain. She had a nasty feeling she knew.

Head in hands, Lawrence groaned, defeated by his over-sight. 'I might have pawned it.'

'What?!' Bella had slipped her brother's guard and was raining blows and oaths on Lawrence Parker again. It took considerable effort to pull her back. 'That was a bespoke Asprey! White ostrich leather, which is very rare! How dare you sell it in a common pawnshop.' She drew breath to continue when Lady Georgina turned and issued a cold hard glare of reproach until Bella froze and sat down meekly.

Mrs MacBain had Bella seated in a chair slightly fur-ther away this time. She turned back to Lawrence Parker, who looked forlorn. 'You pawned it? That seems a strange move.'

'Clearly he wanted the money,' remarked Angus, haugh-tily.

'No. Well, yes, but not the way you think.' He glanced up to see superior and disgusted faces staring back at him. 'I'd finished checking the case and was about to throw it in the river when this woman approached me. Girl, really, working the streets.'

'Working the streets?' asked Lady Georgina, a confused look on her face. 'What do you mean; she was selling flow-ers or some such?'

Lawrence gaped at her in disbelief. 'She was a prostitute.'

The room gasped and Fergus leapt to Lady Georgina's side, as she swooned. Never had anyone dared to mention that word in front of her.

'Steady on, old man!' chided the Cecil. 'These are genteel ladies, you know.'

Lawrence shot Cecil an exasperated face, then decided to ignore the room entirely and spoke solely to Mrs MacBain.

'She couldn't have been more than fourteen or fifteen; scared out of her wits. I could see she'd been roughed up by her pimp,'

'Now see here,' Cecil interjected, 'there's no need for that language!' He pointed to Lady Georgina, who had recovered from her shock and was listening with horrified fascination.

Lawrence sighed. 'Her, erm, handler, then.' He glanced to Cecil for approval. He nodded. 'He was a nasty piece of work, I can tell you. Such a wretched little thing she was, trapped in this horrific life. She just reminded me of . . .' His voice faded.

'Of?' Mrs MacBain prompted gently.

He shook his head, as if to rid it of ghosts. 'She deserved a better life than that, and I had that case in my hand. That quite valuable case. So I hired her—'

Cecil interrupted. 'You couldn't possibly have sold it for something so base. What a—'

Lady Georgina turned and glared her son into silence. 'Continue, please, Mr Parker,' she said, quite recovered from her earlier shock.

'I hired her, took her into the first pawnshop I found, and sold the case. We went out the back door of the shop, and I had a taxi take us to a train station on the outskirts of Paris. I gave her the cash and put her on a train back to her family.'

'You gave her the cash?' Cecil was incredulous. 'But she could have spent it on drink. She might have gone back to her . . . handler.'

Lawrence looked at him. 'She might have, yes. But she'd be dead in a month, and I think she knew it. I couldn't leave her to that fate, if I could help in any way. I did what I could; my conscience is clear.'

The room was silent – for once – in deep thought. But Mrs MacBain was staring at Mr Parker, a searching look on her face.

'Who was it you couldn't save?' she asked it quietly, subdued enough that very few heard it.

He looked up, surprised again, that this woman seemed to know so much. How?

He let out a shuddering sigh and said it softly. 'My wife.'

A gasp when up from the women.

'She worked for Blackwood in the dens.' Remembering that none in the room had ever been in an opium den, he explained. 'Opium dens are like clubs. A bit like this room. People would be escorted to a daybed; the handlers would bring the pipes and the opium. My wife brought trays of tea, helped clients hold their pipe, or removed them when they fell asleep. I met her my first day of being Blackwood's bodyguard. She was the most beautiful creature I'd ever seen. I married her, in secret, three months later. It took me a while to realise that she was an addict.'

'Why continue to work there?' Mrs MacBain asked. 'Surely there were other jobs available?'

A mirthless laugh escaped him. 'My wife wasn't a servant.' He looked at her scathingly. 'She was a slave. Blackwood owned my wife.'

This caused an uproar.

'It's all too common there. Her family was poor – malnourishment and starvation poor – and she was an expense they couldn't afford. Girls can't farm, so they can't earn money. It's another mouth to feed. So when someone offers to buy them . . .' He shrugged and sighed. 'Blackwood routinely sent men to the countryside to buy girls, one of whom was my wife.'

Elspeth's eyes were wide open in shock. Bella shifted uncomfortably in her chair, suddenly wondering how her fourteen maids were acquired.

'Blackwood put her to work in the dens, where she slowly became addicted to opium. She was breathing it in for years, just going about her duties. It wasn't until she lost the baby that I realised just how sick she was, and I knew we needed to get out.' He stood suddenly and crossed to the window, staring out at the trees. His voice turned bitter. 'I went to Blackwood and offered to buy her. And she agreed, as long as I did something for her.'

'The ruby.' Elspeth said it gently with a bit of awe in her voice. 'The ruby for her freedom.'

'Yes. She knew Lady Annabella was going to bring it to England, so Blackwood moved heaven and earth to get us on the same aeroplane. The last thing I wanted was to come to England, and leave my wife behind, but I had no choice. I had to get the ruby.'

'I don't know a thing about this ruby,' protested Bella. 'She had to have been mistaken.'

'So where's the ruby now?' asked Jarvis, entirely unsure it existed. It was too fantastical to be real.

'I don't know. I didn't find it in the luggage, and I stopped looking after Paris.'

'You stopped looking for it?' Mrs MacBain inhaled sharply. 'Your wife died?'

'Three days after I left. I got word when I arrived in London.'

The room was sombrely silent. Lawrence bowed his head and wept softly.

'Well,' said Jarvis, nervously, 'if that isn't the best motive for murder, I don't know what is.'

Lawrence's head snapped up. His face was red with tears. 'What? No. I didn't kill her.' Turning to Mrs MacBain, he pleaded, 'You must believe me. I did not kill her. The last thing I wanted was her dead.' Grief turned to bitterness quickly. 'Death was not good enough for that woman.'

'No, I don't believe you killed her. As you said, you've have done it in Shanghai, if you'd wanted her dead,' Mrs MacBain said, staring at him intently. 'But if your wife died, why did you keep working for Mrs Blackwood? Why not stay in London and make a fresh start?'

'Revenge, pure and simple. I wanted revenge, I won't lie. But death, death was too easy. She destroyed people's lives, my life, and profited from it. I wanted her to suffer. I wanted her to spend the rest of her days miserable and frightened.'

'Keep your enemies closer,' someone mumbled.

'Something like that, yes.' He nodded gently.

'And so your plan was?' asked Mrs MacBain.

'Come here, find the ruby, keep it from them.'

'Them?' asked Mrs MacBain sharply. 'Who's them?'

'Blackwood and Colonel Lamont.'

'Colonel Lamont!' exclaimed Mrs MacBain. 'What does he have to do with all this?'

'He's her business partner.'

Ross stood in the middle of the bothy and carefully looked around. The small table in front of the fire had a half-drunk bottle of milk that had curdled. In the grate was a peat log that hadn't burned entirely. But it didn't smell like a peat fire. Maybe he combined the juniper with it? Hugh wasn't a great outdoorsman. He probably needed it to light the peat. It wasn't, as he held his hand out, warm. The fire must have been out for some time. Why would it still smoke then?

Ross sighed heavily and shook his head. It didn't really matter. He needed to let people know. He the set about securing the bothy, pulling the curtains tight, then bolting the door, and began the walk back to the Distillery. He'd ring the doctor from there.

His walk back was consumed with thoughts of Hugh. *Poor sod*, he thought. They'd never been friends, but this was a bleak end, and he felt for him. However, he was more devastated by the inevitable loss of the bothy. It had been Ross and Elspeth's secret for decades and now everyone would know it existed. They wouldn't be able to meet there any longer.

Life always moves forward, he mused, whether we're ready for it or not. Except for Hugh. Hugh's life had stopped moving. In the bothy, of all places. *What on earth was he doing there?*

Colonel Lamont and Mrs Blackwood were business partners? The entire room was shocked.

'But they didn't like one another,' insisted Mrs MacBain. 'Why would they go into business together?'

'That was a ruse. They've been working together for decades.'

Mrs MacBain pulled a troubled look. 'What was this business?'

'They were planning on opening a club in London, a very exclusive and high-class—' his eyes flicked to Lady Georgina as he paused; there was no other word for it '—brothel in St James's. But she needed the ruby to secure the townhouse. Without the ruby, she didn't have the money.'

'Didn't have the money?' cried Jarvis. 'According to you she was the largest opium dealer in Shanghai. Surely, she had buckets of cash lying around.'

An irritated look crossed his face. 'Imagine crossing a border in a corrupt country and the guards open a suitcase full of money. What do you think they'd do with it?'

'Good point,' Jarvis conceded.

'Besides, money can always be raised.'

'Blackmail.' Mrs MacBain said it quietly.

'Yes, and cards.' He nodded to Angus. 'Or backgammon. You shouldn't drink while you play, by the way; her dice were loaded, and you didn't even notice she'd switched them.'

'I knew she cheated,' said Angus, hollowly, 'I just couldn't figure out how.'

'How much is this ruby worth?' asked Jarvis.

Lawrence gave a small shrug. 'Hard to say. Half a million? Maybe more.'

Jarvis issued a low whistle.

'Well,' Lady Georgina sniffed. 'She certainly wasn't going to make that playing cards here.'

'What happens if she doesn't get the ruby?' asked Elspeth.

'No townhouse.' Mr Parker shrugged nonchalantly. 'If they didn't kill her, that is. She was dealing with gangsters.'

'How could so much evil come in such a tiny unassuming person?' asked Lady Georgina. 'It's mind-boggling. Opium dens, brothels, blackmail, all washed up on the shores of Loch Down.'

'What's the Colonel's part in all of this?' asked Mrs MacBain.

'She's the brains; he's the influence. It's his contacts that have the townhouse. It's his influence that gets them permission to run a private club. It's his friends that will frequent the place.'

'The Colonel's not *that* influential in London,' Bella said, disdainfully. 'He's been in Shanghai for ages. How could he possibly know anyone in London, let alone gangsters?'

'What do you think he's been doing for thirty years? He's been fixing documents for every shady diplomat, businessman, and politician in the City. How do you think Blackwood got her opium den in the first place? The Colonel knew her husband. No Westerner gets anything in Shanghai unless the Colonel gets it for them.'

Bella immediately thought of her friend, whose husband had suddenly secured a warehouse last year. They'd been struggling for months to find something, and then, like magic, the Colonel had something for them in a matter of days. *No wonder she started wearing her old dresses.*

'My head is spinning. If Edmund was sending this ruby to England and Bella didn't know about it,' asked Mrs MacBain, 'how did Mrs Blackwood find out?'

'You don't think she had eyes and ears in every house of consequence in Shanghai? Please.' Lawrence lit another cigarette and inhaled deeply. 'She had maids, cooks, valets, gardeners, laundresses on her payroll. She knew everyone's secrets. And when word reached her about the ruby, the Colonel pulled some strings and got us all on the same flight as Lady Annabella.'

All eyes turned to Bella.

'Are you suggesting one of my maids was a spy?' she asked haughtily.

'No, not one,' Lawrence replied coldly, 'two of them.'

'Impossible!' shouted Bella. 'Every one of my maids came with impeccable references. They were from some of the best houses in Shanghai.'

'In the beginning, sure,' Mr Parker agreed, 'then we replaced them. That's the thing about servants. If you never look at them, you don't notice when someone new arrives.'

'How dare you!' Bella leapt to her feet, enraged at the accusation that everyone in the room knew was truth. 'I'm very close to my maids.'

Mr Parker instinctively lurched back with his arms crossed in front of his chest. 'Please. You didn't even realise your wardrobe mistress was colour blind.'

At that, Bella stopped in her tracks, shocked. Confusion and fury competing for her expression. 'But . . . but I was told those were traditional colour combinations in Shanghai. As worn by the empresses.' Horror dawned slowly. 'You mean I've been badly dressed all this time?!'

'That's what concerns you?' He gave her a scornful look. 'Your husband used you as a mule, two of your maids spied on you, but you're upset about your clothes?'

Bella gave him a scathing look and Mr Parker instinctively jumped back.

'We need to speak with Colonel,' Mrs MacBain said quietly. Jarvis nodded. He stood and cleared his throat. He had no idea what to say. Mrs MacBain saw it and took over. 'If you can all wait here, please? We need to have a word with the Colonel.' She glanced at Mr Parker. 'I don't think we're quite done with you yet.'

He nodded once and sat on the chair again. He didn't look lighter from his confession. Then again, the entire family was staring daggers at him.

Mrs MacBain walked swiftly to the door and out to the Armoury, Jarvis close behind her. They walked up the stairs in silence, each processing the idea that Mrs Blackwood and the Colonel had come here to open this business together. And they'd deliberately hidden their connection. Well, the Colonel had. They hadn't had a chance to ask Mrs Blackwood.

As they approached the door, Mrs MacBain struggled with how to proceed. They needed the Colonel to confirm that Mr Parker was telling the truth. But if he did, it would make him the prime suspect, something that surely wouldn't escape his attention.

She knocked on the door and waited, trying to supress her nerves. She was just about to knock again when a voice came from the door. 'Who is it?'

The Colonel sounded small and uncertain. That was quite unlike his usual bluster.

'It's Mrs MacBain, Colonel.' She stilled Jarvis's arm when he drew breath to speak. The door opened only enough to afford a view of the Colonel's latest garish waistcoat.

'Ah, Mrs MacBain. How can I help you?' He was not going to let them in; that much was clear. The sight of Jarvis caused him to flinch slightly.

'May we have a word?' she asked, doing all within her power to sound light and carefree.

'Ah, I'm a bit indisposed at the moment,' he said nervously. 'Perhaps I can come find you before dinner is served?' He moved to close the door, but Jarvis was having none of it. He put his foot in the door and held it open with a single hand.

'We'll speak now, Colonel.' He steadily pushed the door open, which to Mrs MacBain's surprise, the Colonel didn't fight. 'Not later.'

They stepped into the room and Jarvis closed the door quietly. The Colonel didn't ask them to sit down this time, but instead snapped his wardrobe door shut and walked to the opposite side of the room, putting the bed between them.

'Good tennis lesson, Colonel?' Jarvis asked coldly, poking the Colonel's tennis whites, draped over a chair by his wardrobe.

'No, as a matter of fact. Lord Inverkillen ran off before we started. Mind you, he was rather green around the gills; I doubt he would have been up to scratch.' He nodded at Mrs MacBain. 'I'll be expecting a refund, of course.'

She tried not to sigh and merely nodded and said, 'Tell us about your business venture with Mrs Blackwood.' She sat down on the edge of the bed, her eyes never leaving his face.

The Colonel had a flash of panic in his eyes and quickly snuffed it out.

'No idea what you're on about. I hardly knew the woman.' He shifted from one foot to the other a few times. It belied his nervousness, even to Jarvis.

'That's not the story we heard,' said Jarvis gruffly.

'Someone's been telling you porky pies then.' The Colonel pulled himself up a bit taller, glaring at Jarvis.

'Mrs Blackwood told me you were opening some sort of a members club together.' Mrs MacBain hoped he'd fall for her lie. 'A townhouse in St James's, wasn't it?'

He gasped, softly, but loud enough for Mrs MacBain to hear. She had him.

'Ah, that.' He shifted uncomfortably. 'That was, erm . . . banter. Yes, just a bit of banter. Something to keep our spirits up while on the road.' When neither Jarvis nor Mrs MacBain replied, he continued, his speech gaining speed with each phrase. 'People were fleeing; it was all a bit sad. Someone need to boost the morale, so I started asking people what they wanted to do when we reached London. New beginnings, hopes and dreams, that sort thing. I mentioned needing to find a new club, and she said perhaps she'd open one. We chatted about it. That was all it was, a bit of banter to get us through the dark times.'

Silence descended as they stared at one another. Mrs MacBain could hear water running in the adjacent room.

'Well, she may have been serious, but I certainly wasn't. I'm a diplomat. I'll be assigned to another post as soon as I get back to London.'

'And why aren't you in London, Colonel? Surely, you needed to report back when you arrived?'

'I told you: Lord Martin personally charged me with seeing Lady Annabella back to Loch Down.' He was starting to seriously dislike Mrs MacBain. A capable woman, clearly. He strongly disliked capable women.

'She's been back for some time now, Colonel,' she said. 'Surely your duty has been discharged.'

He glared at her for a moment but said nothing.

'So, why are you still here?' she asked boldly. Some of her frustration with him came out in the question. It felt good.

He man looked offended. 'Can't a chap enjoy a bit of time off? Not that it's any business of yours.'

'Actually, Colonel, it *is* my business.' Jarvis pulled himself up as tall as he could and walked nearer to the Colonel. 'Why are you here?'

'As it happens—' the Colonel cleared his throat '—I was planning on leaving this morning.'

'You're not going anywhere, Colonel,' Jarvis said. 'Not until I say you can. Now tell us why you're here.'

The Colonel was silent, but his eyes flicked around the room in panic.

Jarvis continued calmly. 'I have men posted at the gates and at the exterior doors. The Abbey is under lockdown until I figure out who killed Mrs Blackwood.'

It was, upon reflection, the longest silence Jarvis had ever endured. But he was determined not to speak. They had the Colonel backed into a corner.

'You are out of your depth, Inspector.' It was a cold reply, accompanying an even colder stare. Mrs MacBain got the distinct impression they'd finally met the real Colonel Lamont. 'A lowly backwater policeman shouldn't be meddling in diplomatic affairs. I am here at the request of my superiors and that is all you need know.'

'And would you like to explain to your superiors why you've been arrested for Perverting the Course of Justice in a murder inquiry instead of reporting to them?'

'You can't do that!' The Colonel was outraged. 'I am a diplomat. I have immunity.'

'You may have, but unfortunately for you, I'm just a humble backwater copper from the Highlands. I don't know anything about diplomatic immunity. Your superiors will have to come and explain it to me. Perhaps they'll use small words, so I can understand. Now—' Jarvis gritted his teeth, emphasising each word slowly '—why are you here?'

After some length, the Colonel breathed out and allowed his shoulders to slump forward. 'I'm not here to protect Lady Annabella. I'm here to recover a stolen artefact.'

Jarvis looked stunned. He hadn't actually expected the Colonel to tell them. Mrs MacBain could have burst with pride.

Just under an hour later, Ross led the small contingent to the bothy. Thank heavens it was summer, the sun didn't set until nearly eleven which gave them plenty of daylight still. The doctor was struggling as it was, but in the dark, he would have found it impossible.

'In all my years, I had no idea this was here,' he said to no one in particular. He looked around, bewildered. 'We're still on the Estate, though?'

'Aye,' said Ross, standing and coming to greet them. As the former Gamekeeper, he knew the boundaries better than anyone. 'There's a stream about five minutes' walk that way, and that's the edge.' He unlatched the door and stood aside, waving the doctor into the bothy.

The doctor knelt by the bed, inspecting Hugh carefully.

'Can you tell what killed him?' Ross asked, trying not to look at Hugh. 'I thought it might have been a heart attack.'

'Well, I wouldn't rule it out, but I'll have to do a post-mortem to establish what happened. My guess is poison.'

Ross, surprised, repeated, 'Poison?'

'If he was scavenging for food in the woods . . .' The doctor left the sentence unfinished. No more needed to be said.

'I can't see Hugh foraging in the woods, not with the house so close by.' Ross looked down at the pie, thoughtful. 'I heard someone was stealing food from the house.'

They looked at Hugh again, silent, and then the doctor covered him with a blanket. 'I don't think we should wait for Jarvis; he's got his hands full as it is.'

Ross looked at him quizzically. The doctor had finished explaining Mrs Blackwood's death. 'I'd wager he's still up at the house. Lads, let's get Hugh down to my surgery.'

They began the long and arduous process of carrying Hugh back to the Keeper's Cottage, which was the closest they could get with the van.

Ross followed them out of the bothy and watched them disappear into the trees.

'I'll lock it up so nothing's disturbed.' He shook the doctor's hand went back inside. He slowly closed the curtains and relocked the door. It was time to head to the Abbey. Someone needed to tell the family.

Jarvis and Mrs MacBain left the Colonel's room after he'd told them the most fantastical tale.

'Do you believe him?' asked Jarvis quietly.

'I'm not sure. Parts of it ring true, but not enough to believe it all. I don't believe for an instant that anyone put him in charge of anything.'

They walked in silence, digesting what they'd just heard.

The Colonel had been sent to watch over Bella; that much was true. But he hadn't been sent by her husband. He'd been sent, he said, by the Foreign Office, to recover a jewel that Edmund had stolen and was smuggling into England.

The Colonel's job, he said, was to find the jewel and get it back to the Embassy in London, so they could hand it back to the Chinese Government. He needed to stay in the Abbey until he had the jewel.

'You don't have it?' Mrs MacBain said, her head snapping up in surprise.

The Colonel looked chagrined. 'I thought Mrs Blackwood had it, or that her nephew might. He's been searching for it since we left Shanghai. When he grabbed that suitcase in Marseilles, I thought that was it, that I'd lost it forever. But then he reappeared in Paris, and continued the journey, which meant—'

'That it still had to be in Lady Annabella's possession.' Mrs MacBain was trying to digest it all. 'And what happened when you arrived in London and found Bella missing?'

'Mrs Blackwood was surprised, a bit angry, so she sent her nephew to Paris to find Lady Annabella. I figured he'd reappear when he found it, so I followed Mrs Blackwood here.'

'Was it you who searched Bella's room, here in the Abbey?'

The Colonel sighed. 'Yes. When the nephew arrived the next day, and they didn't leave, I knew he didn't have it, so I searched her room. Found nothing.'

'You assaulted her maid.'

'That was an accident. She startled me. Sneaking up silently. Could give a chap a heart attack.'

Mrs MacBain gave him an exasperated look and was about to chide him when Jarvis jumped in.

'How did Mrs Blackwood even know about the jewel?'

He looked down as he shuffled his feet. He cleared his throat and looked back to Mrs MacBain, still sitting on the edge of the bed. 'There are no secrets in Shanghai when money is concerned.'

Mrs MacBain stared at him, not quite believing what she was hearing. 'Eyes and ears in the best houses.'

He coughed softly. 'Yes.'

They left the Colonel in his room and stood outside the door for a moment. Mrs MacBain stared up at Jarvis and shook her head.

'How do we figure out who's telling the truth?' he asked when they were some distance from the Colonel's door. 'We can't verify either story.'

She sighed heavily. 'Well, they can't both be telling the truth. But both of them could be lying.'

'What do you mean?'

'There is one other person who was in Shanghai with them, and that's where we need to go next.'

Jarvis looked at her, confused, but followed her silently as she made her way through the corridors and down the main stairs.

Stepping into the Armoury, Mrs MacBain was surprised to see Ross, looking quite solemn, and Lady Elspeth, who was pale.

'What's happened?' she asked as she approached.

Elspeth looked away, leaving Ross to deliver the news of Hugh's death.

The shock of it etched itself on to her face, and she leaned against a chair for support. 'Heavens.'

It was a moment or two before Ross addressed Jarvis. 'I can take you up there, Inspector.'

Jarvis looked at his watch. Nearing five o'clock. No wonder he was hungry; it was time for his supper. 'Yes, take me up there. But can we go through the kitchens? I've had nothing to eat today, and I've had so many cups of tea, I'm vibrating.'

'Oh, Roddy. I'm so sorry, I hadn't thought,' exclaimed Mrs MacBain. 'Yes, by all means, stop and grab something.'

As Ross and Jarvis departed, Mrs MacBain stepped to Library door and surveyed the family. They all looked suitably devastated but Angus was ashen and looked as if he'd aged twenty years.

Mrs MacBain took a deep breath and pushed her shoulders back. She stepped into the room and addressed them. 'I think we could all use a good night's sleep. I know it's early, but no one slept properly last night and today has been quite emotional. I'll have trays sent up for anyone who wants one. But I think this day needs to be finished. Shall we?' She placed an arm around Angus's shoulders and escorted him to the door.

One by one, they followed her out of the room. After seeing Cecil and Elspeth mount the stairs, she asked Lockridge to take Lady Georgina home to Thistledown Cottage and asked a footman to escort Angus to the Tennis Pavilion.

Before dinner service began, Mrs MacBain gathered the senior staff in her office, much like they did in the old days. As a matter of habit, Mrs Burnside brought in day-old cakes. 'I can't send 'em upstairs,' she said each time. No one ever objected. Even two or three days old, her cakes were always welcome.

'Firstly, we need to fire Colin, the footman,' Mrs Mac-
Bain began. 'He's been spying on guests for money.'

A horrified pause went through group, broken by Hudson.

'How dare he?' It was a scathing response, and all gathered felt the same revulsion and betrayal. 'I shall do it at
once.'

'Make sure the entire staff knows we've sacked him and
why. No second chances for something like this.'

Hudson nodded gravely.

'Now, I'm sure you all know that Mrs Blackwood was
found dead in the Small Library this morning.' Everyone
nodded. 'We need to keep a very close eye on Mr Parker –
he's the one in the white linen suit – and the Colonel, whom
you all know. We cannot allow either of them to disappear.'

'You think one of them offed the woman?' asked Mrs
Burnside, eyes wide.

'Quite honestly, I don't know. But they've given us con-
flicting stories and we have no way of knowing which one,
if either of them, is telling us the truth. The Colonel is
already threatening to leave, so we need you to keep an eye
on them as you go about your day.'

'You want us to spy on them?' asked Lockwood, a twinkle
in his eyes.

'Erm . . . well, yes.' A chuckle went round the room.
'They're both suspects in a murder inquiry. And I feel
Jarvis and his constables are a bit overstretched. We'll need
to help, but very quietly.'

They all nodded.

'The Colonel,' she continued, 'is rather dangerous. So
please be careful of him.' She described the violence Bella's
maid had suffered at his hands; gasps and shocked looks
flew between them. 'He has no respect for servants, so tread
lightly, please.'

She paused, unsure she wanted to continue, but summoned her resolve. It had to be done.

'Now, Sadie,' they turned to look at the Housekeeper, 'I need you to do something, but you've got to be invisible when you do it.'

'Erm, certainly. If I can, Mrs MacBain,' she replied, hesitation in her voice.

Mrs MacBain nodded. 'I need you to search some guest rooms.'

Sadie's eyes flew open, and the rest of the staff looked at one another, clearly confused. It was a sackable offence to snoop in the guest rooms and everyone knew it.

She handed Sadie the list of Mrs Blackwood's blackmail victims. 'But – and this is critical, Sadie – they cannot know. Find an excuse: delivering extra towels, someone complained about an overflowing bath, anything. But you need to search the rooms for two things: a brass skeleton key for the Small Library and Mrs Blackwood's cane. The one with the green flower on it. I don't know if the key exists, but the cane does and whoever has it . . .' She left the rest unsaid.

Sadie nodded, but the disquiet in her eyes was clear to the entire room.

Mackay cleared his throat. 'We'll go together. I can stand guard in the corridor.' Mrs MacBain was about to object when he held up a hand continued. 'They see me on the guest floors all the time, so it wouldn't be out of character. I can hold my own, needs be.'

She thought about this and then nodded. 'Thank you. Now, I'm sure you've all heard about Hugh's death. It appears that's who was stealing from your larders, Mrs Burnside. The family is in shock, understandably.'

'Do we know how he died?' asked Mackay.

'I don't, no. I suspect Roddy Jarvis will be back up here tomorrow and I can ask for news then.'

'What are we to tell people when they hear the news?' asked Lockridge. 'Two deaths in as many days. This won't be good for our reputation.'

'I can't even think about our reputation just now. We've got to find whoever killed Mrs Blackwood, so no one else gets hurt.'

'Do you think the same person killed Hugh?' asked Hudson.

Mrs MacBain looked at him. She hadn't allowed herself to think about that. 'I don't know. We need to work out why he was here in the first place. He was supposed to be in Spain.'

'Spain? But there's a war on!' shouted Mrs Burnside.

'Yes, and there's going to be one upstairs when the guests find out about Mrs Blackwood. No one is allowed to leave the Estate. People are not going to be happy, and we need to do our best to keep them calm. The last thing we need is panic.'

They all nodded mutely, each aware of the dangers of being engulfed in scandal.

'Talk to your staff tonight. I want every single one of them saying the same thing to our guests: tragic accident and the police have it well in hand, but we need to let them finish their investigation before anyone goes home.'

They dispersed to go speak to their staff. Mrs MacBain watched them go, hoping against hope that it would be enough to keep them from sinking.

One Day After the Murder

The following morning brought an unsettled feeling. *How is it possible so much happened in a single day?* Mrs MacBain wondered. She found herself drawn to Mrs Blackwood's room.

'Good morning, Tommy,' she said to the footman. Hudson had assigned footmen to stand guard at the door, until the room could be put back together. 'Long night for you.'

'Good morning, Mrs MacBain.' He looked fresh as a daisy.

The advantages of youth, she thought. 'Do you mind letting me in?'

Tommy opened the door and very quietly shut it behind her. Standing in Mackintosh, she took in the destruction.

It had been thoroughly ransacked, and nothing had been left untouched. She picked her way into the room, surveying the detritus. Clothes, shawls, bed linens. Even the pictures on the walls had been searched.

She opened the wardrobe and got a whiff of Mrs Blackwood's scent. It was what she remembered from that first night, floral and slightly musty. She pushed some dresses back and saw the large trunk sitting open, clothes hanging over the side of the exposed edge. She stood and took a deep breath. *Wait a minute, where is Mrs Blackwood's second suitcase?*

She rifled carefully though the wardrobe but didn't see it. It was definitely missing. Had someone taken it before or after the room was searched? she wondered. She didn't recall looking in the cupboard when they'd discovered the room. She took a step back to close the wardrobe doors, but the heel of her shoe caught on the rug. Before she knew it, she'd fallen over and pulled the bedside table down with quite a crash.

Tommy opened the door. 'Okay in here, Mrs MacBain?'

'Yes, thank you. It's nothing.'

But it wasn't nothing. The lamp had broken, a vase of flowers was spilling water out on to the floor. She pulled the table back up, but the drawer fell out, tossing the contents every which way. Kneeling to retrieve it all, she noticed Mrs Blackwood's passport on the floor. And a second passport. Both of them in Mrs Blackwood's name.

Elspeth and Imogen were installed in Rowan Tree, trying to make sense of it all.

'Why wouldn't Hugh come to the house?' Imogen mused aloud. Elspeth busied herself with the tea service. 'He's family.'

'Yes,' Elspeth said, handing her a cup of tea. 'But the family isn't best pleased with him at the moment.'

'No,' she replied thoughtfully. 'That's certainly true enough. I can't say I'd want to face them either. But to stay in a bothy. . .'

The door opened and the ladies looked up as Mrs Mac-Bain came into the room. She was surprised to see Imogen but delighted to see the baby Tessa.

'Fergus told me what happened and I thought I'd come see how you're all coping,' said Imogen.

Mrs MacBain nodded and took her place on the sofa.

'That's very kind. I'm glad you here, actually,' she said. 'I wonder if you can do a bit of snooping for me.' She handed Imogen the two passports, and Imogen handed her the baby.

Imogen opened both passports. Looking up at Mrs Mac-Bain, her confusion was replaced by a shrewd look. She nodded and put them in her pocketbook. 'I'll make some calls.'

Mrs MacBain bounced Tessa on her knee, making cooing noises at the delighted little girl. 'Is Fergus coming up to the Abbey this morning?' she asked Imogen.

She nodded. 'He needed to speak with Lady Georgina about something, so he's gone to Thistledown Cottage. He'll come up after.'

Mrs MacBain nodded. 'Lady Elspeth, when you were in Mackintosh yesterday, did you happen to notice the wardrobe?'

Elspeth froze for a moment and thought. 'I remember the doors being ajar, but that's about all. I didn't open them; I was trying not to touch anything.'

'Hmm . . . '

'Why?'

'One of Mrs Blackwood's cases is missing. I wondered when it disappeared.'

Elspeth set a cup of tea in front of Mrs MacBain and the women sipped in silence, each lost in their own thoughts.

'We were talking about Hugh,' said Elspeth at length. 'Such a tragedy.'

'Yes,' said Mrs MacBain heavily.

'I didn't even know he was back,' Imogen said softly.

'No one did,' murmured Mrs MacBain. 'Or that he was staying in the bothy.'

'Oh!' shouted Elspeth suddenly. 'I did.'

They stared at her, aghast.

'No. No, no. Wait. I didn't know it was Hugh, but I did know someone was staying in the bothy. I saw smoke when I was on the ridge, shortly after I arrived.'

'But why did you never tell anyone?' queried Mrs MacBain. 'You should have told someone.'

'I presumed it was outdoorsmen. Or vagrants.'

'You should have told someone,' Mrs MacBain scolded.

'Hindsight being what it is, yes. But in the moment, there was no reason to assume it was anything sinister. The whole point of a bothy is temporary shelter for anyone who needs it.'

Mrs MacBain silently conceded the point. But if Elspeth had seen smoke shortly after she'd arrived, that meant Hugh had been in residence for at least ten days. What had he been doing here?

Mrs MacBain fell back into the sofa cushions, shaking her head gently. 'Bothies are so primitive. Hugh wasn't the most rugged individual. It's a cold, damp hut at the best of times.'

'It's quite cosy with the fire lit.' Elspeth let the words escape without thinking. 'I should think. I couldn't say, obviously,' she stammered, blushing furiously and silently berating herself.

Imogen looked at her curiously.

'Erm . . . yes,' said Imogen, clearing her throat. 'But why stay in a cold damp hut when there are two great houses nearby? It seems unnecessarily punitive.'

Mrs MacBain untangled her necklace from Tessa's hands and handed her a silver teaspoon instead. With the child placated, she looked at Imogen and Elspeth. 'Put yourself in Hugh's place for a moment. You abandon your children and go to Spain; then remorse hits – presumably – and you board a ship to England. Once there, you board a train to Loch Down. That's quite a long journey. And once you reach Loch Down, you decide you aren't quite ready to face the family. What do you do?'

There was silence as each woman played it out in her mind's eye.

'Stay locally and screw up the courage?' suggested Imogen, hesitantly. No one was convinced by that.

'Perhaps,' said Mrs MacBain, 'but why not stay at the pub?'

'You'd be recognised,' Elspeth said simply. 'There's no way Hugh could have stayed anywhere in the village without word getting round.'

Imogen nodded. 'Then why not stay on your family's Estate?'

'It doesn't belong to them any longer,' objected Elspeth.

Imogen nodded. 'That's true, but it is empty. It's just sitting there, abandoned. One look would have told him that.'

'Tons of space, running water, and not another soul for miles. Yes, that's a much better place to hide,' Elspeth said. 'So why the bothy?'

Mrs MacBain thought about this. A memory came from long ago. What was it, ten years ago perhaps? Hugh had got separated from the New Year's stalking party, and no one had noticed until they'd returned to the Abbey at the end of the day. Ross began to mount a search party, but as it was a new moon, it was too dark for a search. They went out first thing the following morning and found him in a bothy, cold and hungry, but safe. Once back at the house, however, Hugh complained bitterly about it for the next two weeks.

He nearly froze to death, he was near starvation, he heard bears at the door. As if there were bears in Scotland! The way he had carried on, anyone would have thought he'd been gone days instead of hours.

No, thought Mrs MacBain, *he wouldn't choose to stay there unless it was absolutely necessary.* Then what, or who, was he waiting for?

Lady Georgina was having her morning tea when Fergus arrived at Thistledown Cottage. His face conveyed the seriousness of his visit.

'What is it? Is it news of Edmund?' she asked breathlessly, a look of genuine concern on her face. Since Bella had arrived in Loch Down, she'd been bracing herself for unwelcome news. Having lived through several wars, she knew how often the men simply did not come back. *Do they still ransom men of rank?* she wondered.

'No news, unfortunately,' answered Fergus, sitting in a nearby chair, 'but it is Bella-related.' He quickly explained the Foreign Office men and the money issue and then fell silent, waiting for her to absorb it all.

'Is that all? Well, you needn't worry about that,' said Lady Georgina breezily.

He stared at Lady Georgina, shocked.

'Forty *thousand*, Grandmama. It's a tremendous sum. The hotel didn't make nearly that last year.'

Lady Georgina threw a dirty look at her grandson. 'I do understand numbers, thank you very much. I ran the Abbey for decades, you will remember, and quite successfully.' She shifted in her chair and straightened her skirt, both of them aware that it had been nowhere near successful. Efficient, yes, but successful? Not by a country mile. 'But you needn't worry. Bella asked me to keep the money here in Thistledown Cottage. She spent a bit, yes, but there really was quite a lot left. It nearly didn't fit in the safe.' Her voice was positively giddy at the memory.

Fergus gaped at her, confusion crumpling his face. 'You have a safe?'

Lady Georgina looked surprised. 'Yes.'

'Where? Never mind where, when? When did you get a safe? I don't have a safe. Why do you have one?'

'It's rather irresponsible not to have a safe, Fergus. Surely there's one in the Gatehouse. Well, if not, I'd suggest you get that sorted straight away.' She shifted in her chair and straightened her skirts again, rather deftly avoiding answering his queries.

Fergus gaped at his grandmother like a goldfish, mouth opening and closing in surprise. 'When did this happen?' he asked, feeling slightly left out. 'And why didn't Bella put it in the hotel safe?'

'I had her bring it down after the trouble with her maid.'

'The maid? In Marseilles?' He was thoroughly confused.

She tutted. 'No. At the Abbey. Do keep up, Fergus.'

Frustrated, Fergus huffed and asked, 'When did this happen? Before she broke her leg?'

'Shortly after they arrived, I believe. We were at tea and Bella told me her maid had walked in on someone rummaging round her things. After the trouble on the train and in Paris, she wanted to know if she should do as Mrs MacBain suggested and switch rooms.'

Fergus digested all of this. 'Mrs MacBain knew about all this?'

'That woman misses nothing, as you well know,' replied Lady Georgina severely.

Fergus couldn't refute it. 'Bella has so few possessions, how on earth did they miss the money?' Fergus had no idea how large the pile would be, but he presumed it would be substantial and easy to spot.

'It wasn't lying about in her rooms, Fergus. Give Bella a bit of credit. Even she knows a suitcase full of cash on a journey like that is dangerous. No, her maid kept it on her.'

Fergus dropped his teacup. Swearing and sputtering, he mopped it up with a linen napkin. 'Her maid had it? Her maid carried forty thousand pounds? How?'

'When they left Shanghai, Edmund had it sewn into a sort of slip that the maid wore under her . . . costume.' Lady Georgina evidently didn't approve of the girl's native clothing.

'Which is why she wouldn't wear a maid's uniform,' he said slowly, 'and why Bella insisted the girl sleep in her dressing room.'

'Quite so.'

Fergus sipped his tea pensively. He was relieved Bella hadn't spent all the money, but it threw up another problem. 'The stickier issue remains,' he said hesitantly. 'What do we do with Bella if she has no money?'

Lady Georgina glanced up from her teacup, consternation slowly settling on her face. That, she felt, would take several pots of tea.

Bidding the ladies goodbye, Mrs MacBain stepped into the Armoury. Word of the deaths had clearly reached the general population of the hotel. Jarvis and his constables were standing in the middle of a crowd of guests, explaining that no one could leave until he'd finished his investigation. No One.

It was barely controlled pandemonium. She wondered if they'd ever recover from this. People don't tend to stay in scandal-tainted hotels. Not outside of London at any rate. She signalled to Jarvis who nodded his head and let out a loud and shrill whistle, which echoed in the vast space of the Armoury. The shouting stopped instantly.

'Now, I don't care what your title is, or what tickets you have for shows, no one is to leave the Abbey or its grounds until I say so. There will be guards posted at the gates and anyone who tries to leave risks being arrested. I suggest you all go back to doing . . . whatever it is you do all day here.'

And with that, he stepped away from the crowd and moved towards Mrs MacBain.

'Good morning,' she said.

He answered gruffly, 'Pack of hyaenas.'

She suppressed a laugh. 'Come.' She turned and walked towards the East Wing. Jarvis followed. 'Where we going?'

'I think it's time someone spoke to us.'

Jarvis looked at her. It was an odd thing to say. But he followed her and didn't ask for an explanation. They passed through several rooms before Jarvis realised where they were going. They turned down the final corridor just as Bella stepped through a door, a breakfast tray precariously balanced on her arm.

'Mrs MacBain. Inspector. What brings you here?'

'I need to see your maid, please.'

Both Jarvis and Bella stared at her, confusion on their faces.

'My maid? Whatever for?' Bella stood aside as Mrs Mac-
Bain opened the door and proceeded into the room with
Jarvis behind her. Bella followed them and set the tray on
a nearby chair.

Compared to Bella's room, the maid's room was quite
empty. She occupied one of four metal beds with a table to her
right and a chair. The walls and floors were bare. It was down-
right chilly, and the girl only had a thin blanket. Mrs MacBain
felt ashamed that she hadn't checked on the girl sooner.

She walked towards the maid and sat down on the bed.
'I thought it was time we spoke.'

The girl looked terrified and shrank back into the thin
pillow behind her back.

Bella looked between the two of them, confused. 'She
doesn't speak English, Mrs MacBain.' It had been an
eventful twenty-four hours, but for Mrs MacBain not to
remember something so fundamental was unbelievable.
Perhaps she is losing her touch? thought Bella.

'Now, we know you're not Bella's maid, but would you
care to tell us who you are?' She said it brightly, and then
smiled at the girl.

The maid looked between them; the uncertainty on her
face was plain. She stared at Jarvis, clearly unsettled by his
presence.

'Forgive me. This is Detective Inspector Jarvis of the
Loch Down Constabulary.' Jarvis nodded his head. 'You
are perfectly safe. We just need to know who you really are.'

It was a long moment before the girl spoke. Her voice
was lightly accented but had perfect diction. 'My name is
Wen Mai Ling. I work for the Foreign Office.'

'You speak English?' shouted Bella. She pounced on her
maid, grabbed her by the shoulders and shook the girl, shouting at her. 'All this time you've been able to speak English?!'

'Bella, please!' Mrs MacBain and Jarvis prised her off the maid. 'She's injured enough.'

Jarvis wrested Bella to the end of the bed and Mrs MacBain moved the chair to the wall opposite the bed. She pointed, much as someone would to a dog. 'Sit.'

Bella glared at Mrs MacBain, indignation rife in her face, but Mrs MacBain gave her a warning look that clearly said, 'Don't you dare.' It reminded Bella of Nanny and she meekly folded herself into the chair.

Mrs MacBain turned back to the maid, who was wincing from the pain. 'Lord Martin sent you to protect Lady Annabella?'

'Not much protection like this, am I?' she said wryly. 'I told him we needed someone else. I'm not trained to fight.'

They looked at her, confused. 'So why are you here?'

She looked at them tentatively and fell silent.

'Look here, miss,' said Jarvis gruffly, 'we're in the middle of a murder inquiry—'

'Murder?' she breathed. 'Who?'

'Mrs Blackwood.' Mrs MacBain watched her carefully. She was taken aback, but Mrs MacBain could see her brain was whirring. 'Now, why are you here?'

She stared between them for a long moment and then began slowly. 'I'm supposed arrange with the Foreign Office to have the Colonel taken into custody.'

Jarvis's mouth fell open. That was not at all what he had been expecting her to say.

Mrs MacBain was caught off guard and struggled for a moment before asking, 'What? Why?'

'Fraud, largely. He's spent years taking bribes to falsify official documents from the Consulate. Lord Martin sent a report detailing the activity, and I'm to deliver it to the Home Office.'

'It couldn't be posted?'

'A lot of the supporting documents are in Chinese and Lord Martin didn't want to take any chances they'd be advantageously mistranslated by one of the Colonel's chums.'

'Right,' said Mrs MacBain slowly. That fitted with Bella's statement of him having friends in very high places. 'And he sent you as a maid so you wouldn't draw the Colonel's attention?'

She nodded. 'I couldn't go as a Chinese national on British transport, so Lord Martin sent me as Lady Annabella's maid.'

'Does the Colonel know about this report?' She could see the Colonel being blissfully unaware, but equally, she could see him being quite dangerous if he did know.

'Not at first. He genuinely thought he was sent to protect Lady Annabella, but by the time we arrived in Paris, he'd worked it out.'

'What do you mean?'

'He thinks Lady Annabella has the papers since Lord Martin gave her the consulate money. That was very against protocol, and it made the Colonel suspicious. He searched our train compartment but couldn't find anything. When we finally arrived here, he waited for me in our room, grabbed me from behind. He started shouting at me in Shanghainese, telling me he wanted the report. I feigned ignorance and he threw me into a wall.'

Mrs MacBain shuttered at the thought.

'Before he left, he told me to find the papers for him, or he'd kill me.'

They contemplated this in silence. The Colonel was clearly not the bumbling buffoon he played at. He was out to save his own neck and that made him dangerous, very dangerous indeed.

'Where are these papers now?' Mrs MacBain asked at long last. She wanted to put them in the house safe.

'Hidden, in a safe place.'

'And you won't tell me where, I suppose,' ventured Mrs MacBain.

The girl shook her head apologetically. 'It's too dangerous and Lord Martin has worked for years to get the evidence on the Colonel. I can't ruin it for him.'

'Why did he send you? I understand your language skills, but given the nature of the task, surely someone who was trained to fight would have been more suitable.'

She sighed heavily. 'Edmund said I was the only one he could trust.'

'Edmund?' Bella carped. 'How dare you call him that? You are a maid.'

'I've always called him Edmund, Lady Annabella. We've been friends for years.' Mrs MacBain looked enquiringly at her. 'We were at Cambridge together.'

Mrs MacBain nodded; school ties were everything where the upper classes were concerned.

'She's lying!' scoffed Bella. 'What on earth would a maid be doing at Cambridge?'

'I'm not a maid!' shouted the girl. It startled the room. 'I'm a highly trained linguist employed by the British Foreign Office. I speak six languages, and four dialects of Chinese. I was never a maid.'

'But,' whimpered Bella softly, confused beyond belief, 'I rang for you, from my bedroom. I watched Edmund load the money into your clothes while we were at the house. How can you not be one of my maids?'

'Your problem, Lady Annabella, is that you think of maids as interchangeable pieces, one the same as the next. If you'd ever bothered to look at your maids, actually see them as people, you'd have realised instantly that I was never one of them. For god's sake, I'm not even Chinese, I'm Malay.'

Bella looked suitably chastised and sat down meekly on her chair. As she struggled to regain her dignity, Mrs Mac-Bain turned back to Mai Ling.

'How does the ruby fit into all of this?' She didn't understand why it had been stolen and sent to Scotland in the first place.

Mai Ling stared hard at Mrs MacBain, desperately trying to work out what she should do.

'Miss Mayling, a woman's died because of this ruby and from what you say, you're the only one Lord Martin trusted. It stands to reason that you are responsible for it being here.'

She turned her head to the wall, in a silent denial.

'Fine. If that's the way you want to play it,' said Mrs MacBain, disappointment in her voice, 'Detective Inspector Jarvis will have to take you into custody.'

The heads of both Jarvis and Mai Ling whipped round to stare at her.

'Custody?' sputtered Jarvis. 'What for?'

'Impersonating a maid!' shouted Bella, leaping up and pointing a finger at the girl. Jarvis gave her a sidelong glance and Bella returned to her seat.

'Smuggling. Receiving stolen property. And probably antiquities theft. If it's been in the imperial family for generations, as Mr Blackwood said, it's a national treasure. The question is whether the UK government will protect you or turn you over to the Chinese authorities.'

Mai Ling stared at her, eyes wide, trying to decide if Mrs MacBain was bluffing.

'Well, if that's your decision. Inspector.' She waved a hand towards the girl and Jarvis, doing a double take between them, stood slowly. He adjusted the waist on his trousers and cleared his throat as he walked to the girl.

'I'm arresting you on suspicion of smuggling and antiquities theft. Anything—'

'All right!' shouted Mai Ling, wrenching her uninjured arm from Jarvis. She sighed, irritated to have her hand forced. 'Technically, I didn't bring it into the country. Lady Annabella did.'

They all looked at Bella, who was offended by the very idea. 'I did no such thing!'

'How?' Mrs MacBain was baffled. 'Everything she had was searched. Several times, apparently.'

Mai Ling grimaced. 'Not everything. Edmund knew she'd be searched and that it was risky to hide it in her luggage, so he had her maid – your actual maid – sew it into her hat.'

Bella gasped. 'The flower!' her hand automatically went to her head.

'Yes. As long as you were wearing it, it was protected. No one would have checked it. So, to make sure you wore it constantly, he deliberately sent you with nothing to change into.'

'Oh . . . ' breathed Mrs MacBain, 'that's very good.'

Bella stared at her with her mouth open. 'I can't believe he did that to me.' She sat down, stunned. But whether it was her husband using her to smuggle the gem or her husband depriving her of clothing, no one was sure.

'I was supposed to wait in London with the ruby and the report. But then we got separated from the group when we stopped in Paris.' She glared at Bella. 'And I started to panic. I had the ruby but no idea where the Colonel was. Then Mrs Blackwood's nephew broke into the hotel, and I realised he was searching for the ruby.

And if Mrs Blackwood knew about it, the Colonel knew about it too.'

'Because they're business partners,' said Mrs MacBain slowly. This was exhausting. Why was no one who they said they were?

'Exactly, and if the Colonel had the ruby, he could use it to blackmail Edmund into withdrawing his report.'

'So, now he's searching for the report and the ruby.'

'Correct. But the first thing Lady Annabella did when we arrived was to change clothes and give the suit to your maid.'

'Who gave it to the Vicar's wife,' said Mrs MacBain slowly.

'Yes. It took me days to work out where it was. I'd searched everywhere but couldn't find it.'

'So you were searching for it as well? How did no one realise that?'

'Because I was looking in places where the suit might be, like the laundry, and the attics. They never realised it was in the hat. You've no idea how relieved I was when the Vicar's wife showed up with the damn thing.'

'You must have been beside yourself when she took it back.'

'Frustrated, certainly, but at least I knew where it was. The next morning, I sneaked out early to the church and got it back.'

'Wait, that was the morning you went down the stairs?'

She nodded. 'When I got back to the house, the Colonel was just coming back from . . . somewhere, he was outside at any rate. He spotted me and gave chase. Luckily, he was still in evening dress, and can't run very well in those shoes. He doesn't look it but he's swift. I ran into the kitchens, hoping he'd leave me alone in front of people. I didn't know the layout of the kitchens, so when he caught me, I had turned into that niche where the stairs were. He grabbed me, I struggled, trying to scratch him, punch him, anything. But then the door popped open, and he threw me down the stairs. As I was lying there, he searched my clothes and when I wouldn't tell him where it was, he kicked me, breaking my rib. I passed out and came to just before Sadie found me.'

Mrs MacBain gasped. 'You poor thing! Well, that explains why he was in the kitchen. He told me he wanted to request Toad-in-the-hole for luncheon, but the kitchen maids told me he was inspecting the breakfast trays.'

'He was. I couldn't have him find the ruby on me, and I knew he was going to catch me, so I put it on Lady Annabella's breakfast tray. Except . . .' she paused, looking chagrined '. . . I got the wrong tray and now I have no idea who has it.'

'Mr Hudson? A word?'

'Yes, Mr Mackay. What can I do for you?' They stepped out of the main hallway and into the staff dining room.

'Have you seen Mrs MacBain? I've been looking for her everywhere.' Hudson shook his head. 'Well, I need to get back upstairs. If you do see her, please relay this for me: we finished searching the rooms and Sadie didn't find anything. No cane, no key.'

'Ah, that's where I can help,' replied Hudson, pulling something from his breast pocket. Hudson unfolded his handkerchief to reveal a brass skeleton key. Mackay stared at it, eyes wide with surprise.

'Is that the one?'

Hudson nodded. 'I just verified it myself.'

'Where was it?'

'I got to thinking: the police only searched the Small Library, and not any of the adjacent spaces, and I wondered if it might still be there. So I sent one of the footmen to scour the area. He noticed the lid on one of the fire buckets was askew and looked inside. There it was.'

The men stared at it for a moment and then jolted in surprise when a voice assailed them from behind.

'If you're gonna stand there chatting, make yourself useful and lay the table for staff lunch!' shouted Mrs Burnside.

The men both made their excuses and scurried out of the room. Mrs Burnside sighed and then went to find a kitchen maid to lay the table.

'What!?' Mrs MacBain, Jarvis and Bella shouted in unison. Jarvis leapt to Mai Ling's side again, startling the girl. 'You put it on the wrong tray?'

'I didn't exactly have a lot of time,' she said defensively, 'he was coming into the kitchens and saw me at the trays.'

Mrs MacBain stared at the girl. The ruby was lost in the Abbey and there was very little way of knowing who had it. And whoever it was certainly wasn't telling anyone about it. What sort of person would get a precious jewel on their tray and just keep it? She shook her head, disgusted at the idea.

'In truth, being thrown down the stairs was probably the best thing for us.'

They all stared at the girl, whose body was broken and battered. Jarvis wondered if she still had concussion. How long did those things last, anyway?

'What I mean is, being moved here, to these rooms, the Colonel hasn't been able to find us. I don't doubt he's still looking. And as long as he's looking, both Bella and I are in danger.'

Mrs MacBain agreed wholeheartedly. She paced the room, muttering softly to herself. None of this even touched on the fact that someone, probably the Colonel, killed Mrs Blackwood. But she couldn't see why he would do it.

'Did you know Mrs Blackwood at all?' she finally asked.

'Of her, yes. But until this trip, I'd never even seen her. She's renowned in Shanghai. The Foreign Office keeps a close eye on her and her clients.'

'We've been told she was going to open a brothel in London with the Colonel, and that they needed the ruby to pay for the property. Does that sound plausible to you?'

Mai Ling thought it over for a minute and then shook her head slowly. 'I can't see that. It's too much work for him. And it's also too visible. He loved life in Shanghai. It's cheap, it's glamorous, he's a big fish in a little but very important pond; and it's far from the prying eyes of the Home Office. If anything, I would have said he would be stumping for another post, someplace foreign, like India, or Argentina.'

'Can you think of any reason why he would kill Mrs Blackwood?'

'She and the Colonel have been working together for the best part of twenty-five years. It would have to be something quite serious to cause that kind of fallout. But her hostile nephew, well—'

Mrs MacBain broke in, 'Not her nephew, as it turns out. He's her bodyguard.'

'Ah,' she said softly. 'That changes things. Well, if he had killed her, you would not have found her body.'

Mrs MacBain was on the verge of asking why, but then realised she didn't want to know any more details about how things operated in Shanghai.

'Thank you, Miss Mayling.'

'Wen.'

'When what?'

'No, my name is Miss Wen. Mai Ling is what you would call my Christian name.'

'Ah, my apologies. Miss When, thank you for your honesty today.'

Mrs MacBain left the room with Jarvis in tow. When they'd closed the door behind them, she looked at Roddy, a troubled expression filling her face. 'As long as the Colonel is free, that poor girl is in grave danger. Can you take him into custody?'

'What for?'

'He's assaulted her twice, putting her in the hospital. Can't you arrest him for that?'

He thought about it. 'Yes, but we wouldn't be able to hold him for long and then he'd know she gave him up.'

'And then he might really kill her.' Mrs MacBain shuddered. How could humans be so cruel to one another? 'We can say one of the kitchen maids witnessed and reported it? There were plenty about that morning.'

'Yes, that could work,' he said hesitantly. Jarvis really did not like the idea of arresting the man and keeping him in their cell. The Loch Down Constabulary only had one cell, and it was positioned across from the tea station. Anytime he wanted a cuppa, Jarvis would have to stand in front of the Colonel to make it.

Bella entered the hall, with the tray under her arm again. Mrs MacBain grabbed it. 'Give that to me. You cannot, under any circumstances, leave that girl alone. Not even for a minute.' Bella was about to object. 'If he finds her, Bella, there is no telling what he'd do to her. You have the protection of your husband's position; I don't think he'll harm you. But she has nothing. He clearly thinks she's disposable.' She studied Bella's face carefully, to see that the weight of the situation was sinking in. 'I'll send footmen to come sit with you both until we can get him into custody, but she can never be left alone. Do you understand? This is life and death, Bella.' The last part was emphatically stated.

'Perhaps you should send a police constable to stand guard then?' Bella said in a calm voice. It was the first time Mrs MacBain could ever recall hearing her so rational.

Mrs MacBain shook her head. 'No better way to telegraph where you are than a constable at the door. Besides, I doubt there are enough of them to be here round the clock.'

'You could keep her in the jail?' suggested Bella, betraying her newfound sensibilities.

Mrs MacBain gave her a look of disdain. 'I'll arrange for footmen to come sit in the room with her. But you'll still need to take care of her, Bella. She cannot be left alone, even for a moment. Her life is in your hands, Bella.'

Bella nodded, a mixture of glum and terror on her face. But she returned to the cold, spare room.

Jarvis and Mrs MacBain started the long walk back to the Armoury in silence.

'You know, Roddy,' she said as they were entering the main part of the Abbey, 'the more I learn the less I understand.'

He looked at her. She had a troubled look on her face, which he'd never seen before. He sympathised. He understood very little as well, but that they were dealing with some seriously unsavoury characters.

'We've learned all this information about these four people and yet none of it puts us any closer to solving who killed Mrs Blackwood. It is frustrating.'

'I still think we need to speak to the other people she was blackmailing. Perhaps we are making this too complicated.'

She shook her head. 'Lady Beaumont's been dallying for years behind her husband's back. I'd bet quite a lot that this isn't the first time she's been blackmailed.' She sighed softly. 'And the others, well, if Mrs Blackwood lived here, that would be different. But she was on her way to London and would be out of their lives in a matter of days. They'd have just paid her and been done with it.'

They continued in silence until they passed the Music Room. 'We know Miss When couldn't have killed her. She's too battered and broken to move on her own. And I think we can believe what she's told us about the whole affair.'

'But how do we know that? She could still be lying. We only have her word for it that she's with the Foreign Office.'

'True. But let's pretend she's telling the truth. If what she says is true, then neither she nor Mr Blackwood – Mr Parker – killed her, leaving the Colonel as our only suspect. So, let's say he did kill her.'

'Okay.'

'Why would he kill her? According to Miss When, he wouldn't run the club in London, too visible. He'd be more likely to take another foreign post. Perhaps Mrs Blackwood really wanted the Colonel to stay in London. They fall out over it. Is that enough reason to kill her? According to Mr Parker, she needed the Colonel to open the club, not the other way round. So if anyone was going to be disappointed, it was Mrs Blackwood, not the Colonel.'

'But let's say, for argument's sake, that he did want to run the club, but he wanted to cut her out of it?'

'You've met him, Roddy. He's a lazy man. He gambles, eats, and sleeps late. Running that club was going to be work, hard work, and from what everyone has said, he was a man who did extraordinarily little work of any kind.'

'True enough. So where does that leave us?'

'Nowhere. She has no club without the ruby, and he has no career without the report. Once they found both items, they could go their separate ways if that was what they wanted.'

'But he doesn't need to wait for the ruby, does he? He only needs the report.'

Mrs MacBain thought for a moment. 'No,' she said slowly, 'he doesn't need to wait. Which puts her in a vulnerable position. And she is not the sort to go into something unprepared.'

Jarvis looked at her, a thought forming in his mind. 'She convinced him that she had the report?'

Mrs MacBain cocked her head. 'Perhaps. We know she was blackmailing people, why not the Colonel as well? He went into the Small Library that night. She needs him; he doesn't need her.'

Jarvis got excited. 'Let's say she threatens him, saying he's got to open the club for her and then she'll give him the report. He's unhappy about it, kills her, then goes to her room, ransacks it and then—'

'Doesn't find the report.' Mrs MacBain let out a sigh of irritation. 'She was a shrewd woman. They knew each other for decades. She would not have issued an empty threat.' She stopped suddenly. 'Unless she threatened something else.'

'Like what?'

'Well, if the Colonel double-crossed her, she could always turn him into the Foreign Office herself. She's a witness. She could attest to his business dealings.'

'But that would implicate her in a raft of crimes.'

'Crimes that were committed in a foreign country. She's a private citizen. They couldn't prosecute her for that. But he is a government employee. It's different for him.'

Jarvis thought about this and nodded slowly. 'That is something worth killing for.'

They reached the Armoury. It had calmed down significantly, although Lord Ashdown was complaining heavily to Thompson about something. She hadn't the strength to go see what it was. There was lots of wild gesticulating.

'Before I forget, I'm want to speak to Mrs Burnside and see who ordered a boiled egg for breakfast the morning Miss When broke her leg.'

He looked at her as if she'd lost her mind. *Boiled eggs? What is she on about?*

'Miss When put the ruby on a breakfast tray, and later that morning, Mrs Burnside slipped on a boiled egg and fell, nearly taking out her eye on the way down. I'd wager that Miss When put the ruby in an egg cup and tossed the egg on the floor. I'm narrowing down those orders with boiled eggs, and hopefully that will tell us something.'

Jarvis shook his head in wonder. Only Alice MacBain would think to check the breakfast orders for a clue to a missing jewel. He hoped she did find something. Or, rather, that only one person in the hotel ordered boiled eggs that morning. He knew that was a long shot, but still, it'd be nice to have something be easy on this case.

'How many could there be?' he asked, fearing the number wouldn't be small.

'We generally send up between thirty and forty trays each morning. But still, it might tell us something useful.'

That evening, Fergus went to Bella's room before dinner. He wanted to talk to her about the money issue.

'Bella,' he began cautiously, 'you told the Foreign Office men that Edmund closed out your Shanghai accounts.'

She looked at him though the dressing-table mirror. 'Yes. What of it?'

'Do you know if that was his only account? Does he still have a bank account here?'

'No idea. I never looked at the accounts,' she said. 'This choker looks dreadful with this hair.' She removed the fake pearls and picked up an equally fake sapphire pendant instead, handing it to her brother.

'How can you not know the name of your bank?' He tried to keep the annoyance out of his voice, but it was such a ridiculous conversation to be having.

Bella noted the annoyance and returned it. 'You will recall, dear brother, that I am a woman. And as a woman, I am not allowed a bank account unless I am married. And even then, it is in my husband's name alone.'

Fergus paused. It had never really occurred to him. 'But how did you pay for things?'

She leaned her head to one side so Fergus could place the necklace on her. 'Edmund gave me an allowance each week – oh yes, the necklace is much better – but the rest went on account. It's quite a good system, really.' She patted her hair and stood, turning to face her brother.

'So, you have no idea where your money is?' Fergus was mystified. 'Or if you even have any?'

'I'm a woman, darling. Men have worked for centuries to keep us in the dark on this matter.'

Once everyone had retired for the evening, Fergus found himself in the Library with his grandmother. He recounted the conversation with Bella about their bank accounts, and Lady Georgina was quietly furious. Fergus stretched out his legs and leaned back in the chair. These were the moments he wished he smoked. It looked better than staring into empty space when thinking.

'I warned her,' she said slowly, her voice at once sad and angry, '*He who controls the money, controls the marriage*. I told her to keep her own money and to be ruthlessly involved in the finances.' She paused and huffed. 'I had dearly hoped, after seeing Elspeth and her mother, that Bella would listen to me.'

'What do you mean?'

'When your mother and father were engaged, I fought hard to have her dowry put into a trust that she alone could control. But of course, I was overruled; it went straight to your father. But with Elspeth, I was successful, and her dowry has been in her control their entire marriage.'

Fergus shook his head. He wasn't sure why they were talking about dowries. 'What does this have to do with Bella?'

'When a woman has her own money, it goes better for her in the marriage. Look at the difference between your mother and Elspeth: one hollow shell, one vibrant woman.'

The idea shocked him, but he had to admit, she was right. Nothing kept Auntie Elspeth down. She travelled, had heaps of friends, and was always lively company. But his mother, for as long as he could remember, had been, as Lady Georgina put it, a hollow shell. His father had controlled her for their entire marriage, and she had had no recourse, because he had her money. She lived on his handouts.

Fergus looked hard at his grandmother and wondered, for the first time ever, what she had been like as a young bride. He could barely see her that way.

Had she been happy to marry into the family? Did she like living at Loch Down, with no family, no friends nearby? What about her dowry? Did she keep control of it or had Grandfather overruled her? She was no Shrinking Violet, that was for sure.

He doubted anyone had ever asked her these things. And it made him wonder about Imogen. Her family wasn't near, exactly, but they weren't far away, only a half-day's travel by train. And she had moved to Loch Down on her own steam, taking a job as Lawlis's secretary. She was keeping the job, even after the baby, a fact that shocked the village gossips, but didn't bother Fergus in the least. Imogen was happy, and that was all he cared about.

He stood slowly, still watching his grandmother. 'Edmund always struck me as a fair and sensible chap. There will be something for her and we will find it. Once we do, you can teach Bella how to stand on her own feet.' He kissed her gently on the forehead. 'I'll have Lockridge take you home.'

Two Days After the Murder

Jarvis was back the following day. They were in her office, discussing both deaths.

'Mrs Blackwood was stabbed with something thin and long, and exceedingly sharp but it was double-edged, so not a *sgian-dubh*. Time of death was between midnight and six a.m., which we knew.'

Mrs MacBain nodded but said nothing.

'Hugh Dunbar-Hamilton died between twelve and twenty-four hours ago and there are no obvious signs of the cause. We've sent off for tests to be run, and they should be back in a couple of days.' He shifted in his chair. 'What have you been finding out?'

She glanced up at him.

'I know you've not been sitting here doing needlework.'

She sighed heavily. 'One of the footmen found the key to the Small Library. It was in a fire bucket near the baize door closest to the Library.' She opened her desk drawer and handed it to him, still wrapped in Hudson's handkerchief. 'No cane, however.' They were silent, contemplating the next move.

'I'd like to go speak to the footmen that were in the Oak Room the night of the ball. If the Colonel was at the tables until dawn, as he claims, he couldn't have murdered her.'

Jarvis, though, wasn't willing to give him up just yet.

'What if,' he began slowly, 'he went for a cigar when the band finished, and slipped into the Library in the commotion? He could have gone out into the garden, back to his room, changed his clothes and then come back again before the commotion of the departures died down. If anyone asked, he was smoking and chatting.' Jarvis looked pleased with himself.

'You're forgetting the garden doors only lock from the inside. The issue isn't how they got in, but how they got out of the room without being seen. We really need to know who this last meeting was with. That person would have been in the room between three and three thirty, when all the commotion of the departures started.'

'Then maybe it was Mr Blackwood – sorry, Mr Parker. He could have doubled back in the crowd or sneaked back and come in the garden. Lady Elspeth said he was always outside in odd places. Maybe he was familiarising himself with the layout, so he could escape.'

Mrs MacBain looked at him, thinking hard about this. They had discussed it before, but neither of them could find a motive for him to kill Mrs Blackwood. If what he had told them was the truth, he wanted her alive and suffering, not dead.

Just because we can't see a motive, she thought to herself, *doesn't mean there isn't one. But how do we find it?*

When Fergus arrived at the Abbey that morning, he immediately rang Lawlis and explained as much as he could about Bella's situation.

'It isn't my specialty, you understand. I'm a solicitor, not an accountant,' he said nervously. Having dealt with the Inverkillens for decades, he knew how sticky financial matters could get.

'I do realise that,' answered Fergus, quite reasonably, 'but I have a feeling we're going to need someone with a legal mind to get to the bottom of it. Bella doesn't seem to know a thing about his banks or investments and I wondered if you could help.'

Lawlis replaced the telephone receiver and sighed heavily. *It's like finding a needle in a haystack,* he thought, *without knowing if there's even a needle. Or a haystack.*

As Jarvis and Mrs MacBain walked into the Armoury, Thompson waved her over. She approached the desk and her pace slowed. He handed her a telegram, edged in black.

Taking it from him, she read the name and a deep sigh escaped her.

'Find someone from the family. Not Angus. Find Fergus, or Lady Elspeth, have them come, quick as they can.' She crossed over to Jarvis. 'I've got to deal with this. You'll have to speak to the footmen on your own, I'm afraid. Hudson should be in the Morning Room; ask him to gather them for you.'

In ten minutes, she was knocking on Bella's door.

'Come,' a voice called.

She entered the room to see Bella sitting on the sofa, writing letters on a campaign desk. She glanced up and said defensively, 'I didn't leave, the footmen fetched this for me. She's perfectly fine.'

Mrs MacBain walked slowly over and sat opposite Bella.

'You look dreadful, Mrs MacBain. What's happened?'

Mrs MacBain took the telegram out from the pocket in her skirts and handed it to Bella. Bella looked it but made no move to receive it.

'I can't,' she said hoarsely. 'You read it to me.'

Mrs MacBain opened the telegram and read it quickly. She looked at Bella and said: '*Regret to Inform Lord Edmund Martin Missing Presumed Dead.*'

Bella erupted loudly. 'What does that mean? I don't understand. Have they given up searching for him? What if he's just in a hospital somewhere?'

'I'm not sure, Bella.'

She grabbed the telegram, stood up quickly and bolted for the door. Mrs MacBain, surprised, watched her head for the door. *Oh no.* She quickly followed.

Bella wrenched the door open without a knock and in two steps was in the room, thrusting the telegram at Miss Wen. Miss Wen, for her part, looked startled and cowered in the corner of her bed, nearly falling out the other side.

'What does this mean?' demanded Bella, thrusting the telegram at her.

Miss Wen took the telegram and read it quickly. A faint 'oh god' escaped her lips.

'Well?'

She looked up at Bella, then to Mrs MacBain, and back again. 'It means he's not coming back.' She handed the telegram back to Bella who refused to take it.

'How on earth would they know? They could be wrong, couldn't they?'

'They don't issue this unless they are quite certain.'

'What do you mean by quite certain?' asked Mrs MacBain. It was a strange turn of phrase to her mind.

The linguist squirmed a bit and eyed Bella. 'In this case, it means they know he's dead, but they have no body.'

Bella melted slowly into a chair, shock and disbelief on her face.

Mrs MacBain read the telegram again. There were only two other lines.

Regret to Inform Sir Edmund Martin Missing Presumed Dead. Consulate Bombed 18 Aug. No survivors.

Bella stared at her. 'What am I meant to do now?'

Miss Wen's voice was hollow. 'I don't know.'

Mrs MacBain looked at her. The girl was nearly as shell-shocked as Bella was. She looked between the two women several times, her brain whirring.

'Miss When,' she began slowly, waiting for the girl to acknowledge her, 'what happens now, with regards to the Colonel and the report?'

Mai Ling shook herself to the present with some difficulty and then finally turned to Mrs MacBain, focusing slowly on her face. 'Erm . . . Nothing, most likely. Without Edmund to drive through the report, I don't know who would take up the case. I'm not important enough to be listened to, so the Colonel's friends will bury it. He'll go on to another post.'

Mrs MacBain kept her train of thought to herself. If Edmund's death essentially invalidated the charges against the Colonel, he no longer needed the report. Or the ruby. Which meant his knowing about Edmund's death would keep Miss Wen safe. It didn't absolve him from battering the girl into a hospital bed, and it didn't mean he didn't kill Mrs Blackwood. She needed to tell him; that much was clear. With luck, it would keep Miss Wen safe.

A knock at the door interrupted her thoughts. It was Fergus. 'You asked to see me?'

Mrs MacBain ushered Fergus into the hall, explaining the situation. 'Bella's in shock, I think. She's not really reacted normally.'

Fergus looked in the room. Both women were staring vacantly into space. 'It seems to have shocked them both.'

'Yes. Miss When, that's Bella's maid, was a long-time friend of Edmund's.' Fergus's eyes shot open in surprise.

'They went to Cambridge together. Look, I don't have time to recount everything just now. Suffice it to say, she speaks perfect English. Can you stay with them, please? I need to go speak to the Colonel.'

Fergus was confused, but a request from Mrs MacBain was not to be refused. 'Yes, of course I'll stay with them.'

Mrs MacBain sped off, hoping she'd discover Jarvis on the way. She didn't fancy spending a moment alone with the Colonel. He had proved himself to be dangerous in the extreme.

Passing the Dining Room, she narrowly avoided a collision with Mrs McCready, but the woman recoiled violently and nearly toppled over. As Mrs MacBain was apologising and grabbing for the woman, a gallant arm came from nowhere to steady both women. Turning to look at her rescuer, Mrs MacBain was surprised to see Cecil.

'Mrs MacBain! Didn't Nanny teach you not to run indoors?' Cecil's eyes twinkled as he spoke.

'Major! Thank goodness! Come with me. My apologies, Mrs . . . ' but she sped off, grabbing Cecil by the arm and dragging him into motion.

'My dear woman, whatever seems to be the rush?' he asked, trying to wrest his arm from her grasp. He was wearing a new suit, and he didn't want the nap of the tweed crushed. 'Where are we going?'

'I need to speak with the Colonel and frankly, I'm relying on there being safety in numbers,' she said cryptically.

'Safety in numbers?' Cecil looked at her, confused. 'I wouldn't have said he's dangerous. Careless, certainly, but he's not the type to hurt a lady.' He stopped and looked up at her seriously. There had just been a murder. 'Is he?'

'Considering he threw Bella's maid down the stairs, broke her rib, and threatened to kill her, I'd say yes, he is exactly the type.'

Cecil digested this for a moment, then nodded sharply and continued walking.

When they finally reached the Colonel's room, Mrs MacBain knocked on the door urgently and waited, breath held fast. Glancing up and down the corridor, she knocked again. Nothing. Cecil tried the handle and the door swung open. He stepped in tentatively, leaving the door open, and looked around.

'It appears no one is home,' he said at last, stepping aside to allow her to enter the room.

The room was indeed empty. Not only empty, but it had clearly been vacated in a hurry. The wardrobe doors stood open, gapingly empty. She pulled open the dresser drawers to find only drawer liners and lavender sachets.

Cecil peeked into the attached bathroom and slowly shook his head. 'He's gone, all right. Nary a toiletry left. Dear me! I think he liberated most of the loo roll as well.' Cecil tutted his distaste. Poor breeding outed in the strangest of ways.

Mrs MacBain sat down on the bed and swore softly. *How long has he been gone?* she wondered. *And how did he disappear without anyone noticing?* The man was loud, she reflected; people generally heard him before they saw him. How did he manage to simply vanish?

'I presume you didn't realise he'd gone,' said Cecil opening the wardrobe and peeking in, as if the Colonel was merely hiding behind a timber clothes hanger.

'No. We spoke to him yesterday several times.' She suddenly remembered how evasive he'd been the second time they visited. He'd clearly been packing when she and Jarvis arrived. 'I needed to tell him that Edmund has been declared dead,'

Cecil gasped lightly.

'Bella got the telegram this morning. But I wanted to Colonel to know, because it meant Bella's maid would no longer be in danger.'

Cecil tried to follow the logic, but it eluded him. Clearly, she knew more about what was happening than he did. Then again, she always knew more about what was happening than anyone else did. He left it alone.

'What now?' he asked, studying her closely.

'We'll need to tell Jarvis. He won't be happy. The Colonel is our main suspect in Mrs Blackwood's death.'

Cecil's head snapped up, shocked and surprised. 'The Colonel? He killed Mrs Blackwood? But why?'

Mrs MacBain stood slowly and walked to the door. 'We have a theory involving blackmail, but we've not a shred of proof.'

'I take it, you don't agree?'

She looked at him, in thought. 'I'm not sure. We're missing something. But for the life of me, I can't see what it is. Other than her cane.'

'Her cane?'

'It's missing. I think whoever killed her took her cane.'

'So, find the cane, find the killer?'

'Perhaps. We searched the rooms of everyone we know she was blackmailing, and we came up empty-handed. It's been very frustrating.'

Cecil wondered briefly if she knew about Angus. But not knowing how to ask, without further implicating his nephew, he simply held his silence.

They walked into the hallway and stood, looking at the traffic flowing back and forth. She glanced up and considered the large portrait on the wall opposite the Colonel's door. It was Bonnie Prince Charlie, dressed as a woman, being escorted by Flora MacDonald to freedom.

Cecil stood beside her. Following her gaze, he remarked, 'Ghastly painting, isn't it? I've never liked it. The colours—'

'It appears the Colonel also sneaked away to a life abroad.'

'I thought the police had guards at the gates. Surely, they'll catch him. Or start a manhunt?'

Mrs MacBain shook her head. 'I don't know how many men Jarvis would have available to search. They're over-extended as it is.' She turned to leave but her eye was caught by the frame. Was it her imagination or was the left side standing away from the wall? She stepped across the hall and touched the silver frame. It moved. A groan threatened to escape her. Looking around, they had a solitary moment. Gripping the frame, she pulled it forward and it swung open, revealing a narrow tunnel.

'How did he know about that?' she gasped, glancing into the tunnel.

Cecil gaped at the opening and then a flash of a memory overtook him.

It was the night he, Mr Rosenthal, and the Colonel went back to Thistledown Cottage for cards with Angus. It had been late and there had been much, much drink.

'Lemme ask you something,' Mr Rosenthal slurred slightly, *'are there really secret passages in these old houses? Or is that just in cheap novels?'*

'Secret passages?' asked the Colonel, struggling to lay his card in the centre of the table. He closed one eye and dropped the ten of spades.

'Priest holes,' replied Angus, 'he means priest holes. Yes, they're real.'

'The Abbey is littered with them,' Cecil contributed to the conversation, tossing his card and hoping for the best. It slid across the table and onto the floor. 'I'll show you tomorrow, if you like.'

'Fascinating,' said Mr Rosenthal, as he knocked his drink over, whisky flooding the cards. 'Oops.'

Cecil snapped back to the present. 'I've simply no idea. We best close it before anyone else comes along.'

They pushed the painting back into place and Mrs Mac-Bain gave Bonnie Prince Charlie a dirty look before they moved away.

They arrived back in the Armoury in silence. When they reached the bottom of the stairs, she bid him goodbye.

'One moment, Mrs MacBain. If I may?' He cleared his throat nervously. 'While I am loath to help anyone who would injure a helpless woman, I feel it my duty to tell you that I can offer the Colonel an alibi.'

Her head snapped up, and he could see she was disturbed by his comment.

'What? You can?' She again grabbed his arm and dragged him towards Rowan Tree, shutting the door roughly behind them, before rounding on him. She stared at him shrewdly. 'Tell me.'

'Well, the simple fact of the matter is, he was at the cards table all night.' Cecil shrugged apologetically.

'We know he was at cards during the ball. What we need to know if the Colonel left the room after the band finished playing.'

He looked surprised. 'I'm sure he didn't. A man that loud always draws attention.'

'This is rather important, Major,' she said, urgency in her voice. 'You need to be absolutely certain. There is no room for a mistake, so please take a moment to think.'

Cecil concentrated. 'He was two tables away when the band stopped. Most of my table retired for the evening, so I took the opportunity to stretch my legs. He joined me on the terrace for a cigar. When we went back in, he sat down at his table, most of his players returned, and I sat down about three tables away. But he was in my line of sight most of the evening. He did excuse himself when Lord Ruthven retired – that must have been about four, four fifteen – but he wasn't gone long, only long enough for a loo break or a quick whisky.'

'And you don't recall him leaving at any other point in the evening?'

Cecil thought for a moment. 'No.' He shook his head. 'I'm afraid not.'

'You're absolutely positive? No chance you're wrong?'

He considered it for a moment. 'I did not see him leave that table until the footmen threw us out with the dawn chorus. I'm sorry, Mrs MacBain. He was in my eyeline, and I would have seen the movement had he got up from the table.'

Mrs MacBain sat back in the chair with a discontented sigh.

'But, now that I think on it,' he said slowly, 'there was something. I didn't think anything of it at the time.'

Mrs MacBain straightened up, all ears.

'I'd forgotten my cigarette case on the table and doubled back for it. The room was empty by then, even the footmen had retired.'

'What time was this?' she asked urgently.

'About a quarter past five, I'd wager. I'd got nearly to the Stone Passage before I realised it was missing.'

Mrs MacBain nodded, visualising the pathway from the ballrooms to the main house. They had been connected by tunnelling through the ancient stone wall of a previous era. It must be about a three- or four-minute walk from the Ballroom wing. 'Continue.'

'Well, just as I was sliding it in my pocket, I heard something. I looked up and saw a swoosh of fabric disappear into the servants' stair.'

Mrs MacBain inhaled sharply. 'Male or female?'

Cecil closed his eyes in concentration, trying to picture the evening. The footmen had been polite enough when the clock chimed five. There had been one table that wanted to finish a hand. Cecil wandered towards the patio where two or three gentlemen were smoking. When the hand finished, the footmen swept everyone out of the rooms, much like beaters on a shoot, and then closed the doors behind them. When he returned, the room was empty. But then the sound of the door drew his attention. *What had he seen?*

'Gown. Decidedly a gown.'

'Colour?'

He screwed his eyes up, as if squinting to see. 'It was pale. White perhaps, or maybe soft grey?' He slumped down and shook his head. 'I can't say for sure. But it was a gown. That's all I recall.'

She nodded, her brain whirring. 'What time was this?'

Cecil thought for a moment. 'I remember the clock chiming the half hour.'

Mrs MacBain fell back in her chair. 'Well, that is very helpful, Major.'

She took her leave and walked back to her Below Stairs Office. She needed to find Jarvis. Here was confirmation of Mr Parker's story of a mystery meeting. And it was with a woman.

She found him in her office, enjoying a cuppa and her latest copy of *The Lady*.

'Here you are, thank heavens,' she said, genuinely relieved to see him.

'I spoke to the footmen,' he said. 'After the band stopped, a lot of tables emptied out, so there was a lot of movement in the room. People chatting, people leaving, new tables forming. Twelve or fifteen men stayed on to play cards. No one noticed the Colonel in particular. But he was there when they swept the rooms at five.'

She nodded, a satisfied look on her face. She kept smiling. It was a little unnerving. He started to feel like the ground beneath him was slipping away. 'What is it?' he asked hoarsely.

She hesitated, knowing this was going to be difficult for him to accept, 'We can rule out the Colonel as a suspect. He has an alibi.'

Jarvis set his teacup down roughly on the magazine. 'What? Who?' he demanded.

'The Major can vouch for him.' She replayed her conversation with Cecil, ending with a large sigh.

Jarvis made a disgusted noise. 'So, after two long days of investigating, we have zero suspects, and one late-night meeting with a mystery woman.'

'Yes.'

'Well,' he said after a long pause, 'to my mind, seeing a skirt means one thing: we need to look at Lady Annabella again. She's the only woman in the place who knew Mrs Blackwood.'

'But Lady Annabella's gown was deep blue. There is no way he could have confused that for a pale grey or a white.'

'Dressing gown?'

Mrs MacBain shook her head. Bella was still wearing Sadie's dressing gown and it was red tartan. 'It can't have been Lady Annabella.'

'She was blackmailing a few women; could it have been one of them?' Jarvis was clutching at straws and at this point and there were very few left. 'We should be searching the rooms of everyone on that list.'

'I already had Sadie do that; she found nothing.'

They were silent for some moments. Jarvis slurped his tea. It made her shudder slightly.

'And to top it all off . . .' she hesitated. '. . . the Colonel has done a runner.'

'What?!' He shouted it loud enough to startle a kitchen maid passing by the door. She dropped a silver gravy boat with a clatter. Mrs MacBain went to close the office door and then returned.

'What d'ya mean he did a runner? We have men posted! So do you!'

Mrs MacBain was deeply unsure she wanted to tell Roddy Jarvis about the secret tunnels in the Abbey. He was hardly discreet, and if he knew, the entire village would know by sundown. But how else to explain?

'The Major and I were just in his room, and it was quite clear he'd left and left in a hurry.'

'Does that mean he's got the ruby?' Jarvis asked.

'That I don't know. But I'm sure he disappeared last night, before anyone could accuse him of murder.' She sat down and stared at him. Without thinking about it, she made herself a cup of tea. It wasn't a great start to the day, but it wasn't the worst.

'Mrs MacBain, can I have a word?' It was late in the day and Imogen had just finished work. She had a very satisfied look on her face.

Mrs MacBain smiled knowingly. 'Certainly. Let's step in here, shall we?' They made their way to Rowan Tree. Closing the door to the din of the Armoury, Mrs MacBain looked at Imogen with expectation in her heart.

Imogen held up a passport. 'This one's real.' She handed it to Mrs MacBain.

'Are you sure?' she asked, breathless, looking at the cover.

'Positive. The British passport is definitely a forgery. After I got the news, I rang the General Register Office and asked about birth certificates and marriage licences as well. There are no records for a Mrs Fenella Blackwood in the whole of the United Kingdom.'

'Well done, my dear.' She beamed at Imogen. Flipping the passports open, a faint suspicion fluttered deep inside her brain. 'Can I ask another favour?' She handed Imogen the authentic passport.

'I've already started.' Imogen smiled, clearly pleased with her efforts.

Three Days After the Murder

Mrs MacBain was knocking softly on the door of Lawrence Parker's room, hoping to have a quick word. It was early and she was unsure what time he woke, normally. She waited a moment and then turned to go. Three steps later, she heard the door open.

'Mrs MacBain?' came a voice, still a bit sleep-laden.

'Oh, Mr Parker, I'm sorry to have woken you. I should have come at a later hour.'

'Not at all. Come in.' He stood back and held the door open for her. He'd pulled on shirt and trousers, but his feet were bare. 'What can I do for you?'

'I was in Mrs Blackwood's room yesterday and noticed that one of her suitcases is missing. The Colonel has disappeared and I wondered—'

His eyes flew open. 'Which case? The large trunk or the small suitcase?'

'The large one is still there but I couldn't find the smaller one.'

His face broke into a wide grin and he chuckled. 'Of course he did. The bastard. Excuse me! Well, he deserves everything that's coming to him.'

'What was in the case?' She eyed him carefully.

'Erm . . . her winnings and the blackmail money.' He paused, as if there was something else but did not want to disclose it.

'Mr Parker?' she prompted. 'Was there anything else in there?'

He nodded slowly. 'Peat.'

'Peat?' She nodded slowly. 'For the fire? Why didn't you put it in the log basket?'

'It wasn't for the fire.' He squirmed uncomfortably and then sat in a chair by the window, elbows on his knees. Mrs MacBain wasn't sure where this was going but she nodded.

'After I heard about my wife, all I could think of was getting revenge on the old woman. The ruby was really the only thing I could hold back from her. But the morning after I arrived, I went on that Distillery tour – the one Lord Inverkillen led? – and I realised that I could cripple her in a way she would never suspect.'

Mrs MacBain felt her feet start to go numb. She was entirely certain what he said next would not be good.

'The peat you use, for the fires in the Distillery, well, it looks an awful lot like opium.'

A buzzing noise filled her ears. 'Are you saying that she brought a suitcase filled with opium?!'

He nodded. 'Good for the punters, good way to subdue the girls.'

Mrs MacBain shuddered at the implication. 'And what exactly did you do with this opium?' she asked, a nasty feeling in her stomach.

'I wasn't sure how to dispose of it safely, so I took it to the peat store, unwrapped it and rolled it in the dirt. Then I stacked it.'

'It's in the peat store?' She was outraged. 'How reckless can you be? What if they use it?'

'It's at the very back, they won't get to that part for ages. I'll have found a way to destroy it before they even get close.'

Mrs MacBain was speechless. She stood and paced, agitated tremendously. What had they done to deserve so much chaos and ill-doing? 'Right, this is what is going to happen. I'm calling the police and you'll help them retrieve it from the peat store. Hopefully, if you turn it in, you won't be in trouble. Do you know how much is there?'

'Yes, eleven bricks.'

'Oh my word. I'll go call Jarvis now. You get yourself dressed and out to the Distillery straight away. Do you understand? Right away!'

He nodded meekly and Mrs MacBain walked as fast as her feet could carry her.

She had just reached the Armoury and was praying Jarvis was in his office, when a voice called to her.

'Mrs MacBain, well met!' It was the doctor. 'I'm looking for Jarvis. I was told he's up here and I have the toxicology report for Hugh. I told them it was linked to Mrs Blackwood's death and asked them to rush it for us.' He waved a file in the air, looking pleased with his subterfuge.

'And?' she snapped. She grabbed the file from his hands, giving him a paper cut.

The doctor was shocked. He wondered what had her in such a foul mood.

'Oh dear lord.' She grabbed his arm. 'Come with me!'

Before he could process what she'd said, she had walked through a concealed door, and was heading down to the kitchens. The doctor followed her, curious where they were going. She headed straight out the servants' entrance and into the side of the service yard without slowing down. She turned to see he was keeping up and, satisfied he was, started on a path through the woods.

After what felt like miles – but was, he realised, only minutes – he lost her behind a bend. He leaned over, putting his hands on his knees. He had a rather painful stitch in his side, but he kept going, holding his side and trying his best to take deep breaths.

'Ross! Where are you?'

The doctor could hear her shouting ahead of him, and it spurred him on. When he finally caught up with her, she was in the Distillery yard, shouting for Ross, bringing all industry to a halt. 'Where's Ross?' They pointed to the office door, eyes wide at the spectacle she was making.

Ross appeared a moment later, looking confused and alarmed. 'Alice? What's wrong?'

She caught her breath. 'You said Hugh broke into your peat store, yes?'

'Yes, MacAlister found a door we didn't know about.'

'It wasn't just Hugh. Mr Parker has been in there as well, switching out bricks of peat for bricks of opium.'

Ross's eyes flew open in alarm.

'And now the doctor's just informed me that Hugh died of a massive overdose of opiates. Hugh thought he was stealing peat from your store, but it was opium.'

Ross disappeared into the office without a word. A moment later, he reappeared with a torch and took off across the yard, heading for the peat store.

Mrs MacBain shouted to the nearest lad. 'Go to the Abbey and fetch Mr Parker. Bring him here kicking and screaming if you must. And find Roddy Jarvis!' She sprinted after Ross with the doctor close behind her.

When they caught up with him, Ross was examining the peat nearest the side door that MacAlister had discovered. He was shaking his head. 'It looks all right to me.'

'He said he rolled it in dirt so you wouldn't notice,' she told him, trying to catch her breath.

'He did well then,' said Ross, running the torch over the stack slowly. 'I can't see any difference.'

'I told him to dress and come straight here. He'll be the only one who knows which are peat and which are opium.'

It was an agonising wait.

'You might be able to smell it,' suggested the doctor. 'It won't smell like peat.'

Ross looked at the doctor for a moment and thought about this. 'The bothy did smell odd. Like nothing I've ever smelt before.' He leaned in and sniffed gently, several different places. 'No, smells like peat.'

Mrs MacBain tsked involuntarily. They waited longer.

'Erm, can I ask . . .' Ross cleared his throat '. . . what, ah, what happens when you overdose on opium? What kind of death did Hugh have?'

The doctor looked at him and thought for a moment. 'Well,' he began hesitantly, 'it's used in medicines as a sedative and opium addicts are known to sleep for days. He'd have just drifted into a deep sleep. It would have been peaceful, not painful.'

Oddly, it didn't comfort Mrs MacBain. Poor Hugh. Putting a log on to keep warm and then never waking up.

A few minutes later, led by Ross's lad, Jarvis and Lawrence Parker arrived at the peat store.

'What's all this then?' asked Jarvis, face red with exertion, looking between Mrs MacBain and the doctor. Mrs MacBain waved to the doctor.

'We got the toxicology reports back for Hugh Dunbar-Hamilton.'

'That was quick!' said Jarvis.

'I might have over-exaggerated the importance of it, so they'd rush.' He paused for a moment and then pulled his shoulders back slightly. 'Hugh died of a massive overdose of opiates.'

Mrs MacBain looked directly at Mr Parker, who glanced from the doctor to the peat store and back again. He blanched white just before his knees buckled. Jarvis grabbed his arm and supported him.

'What am I missing?' Jarvis asked thickly.

'Mrs Blackwood packed her second suitcase with opium.' She walked into the door of the peat store. 'Mr Parker has been switching out the opium with peat from here. But Hugh broke in and took one of the opium bricks, thinking it was peat, and took it back to the bothy with him, where he lit it and crawled into bed for the night.'

'And died,' finished Jarvis softly. 'Poor sod.'

'I was trying to keep it away from people!' Lawrence cried. 'I didn't want her to be able to ruin any other lives.'

Mrs MacBain sighed heavily and looked at him with sadness etched on her face. 'I know you meant well, but this was reckless in the extreme.'

'Which of these bricks is opium?' asked Ross, 'and how do I destroy it without killing anyone else?'

Jarvis raised his hand. 'I'll need them for evidence. Now, Mr Blackwood, or whoever you are, which of these are you responsible for?'

Mrs MacBain stepped back and watched as he began to sift through the stack. She wondered if they'd get all of them.

'I'll burn the entire stack when he's finished. Don't worry,' Ross said, quietly walking up to her.

'Can you do me a favour? Have the family gather, so we can tell them. Somewhere private, like the morning room.'

Ross nodded and watched her start to walk off. 'Where are you going?'

'To the Tennis Pavilion. Angus needs to hear this in private.'

Ross did as he was bid and gathered the family in the old Morning Room. They hadn't been together in this room since the day the Abbey had been up for auction, some three years ago. It had been an explosive afternoon.

They sat, some impatient, some bored, all waiting for Mrs MacBain to arrive. Angus was the only one missing. Fergus paced back and forth slowly behind the sofa, unsure what she wanted to see the entire family about, but given Ross's demeanour, he wasn't anticipating good news. Lady Georgina and Bella sat on the sofas by the fireplace. Elspeth sat in the window seat, which she'd never done; it had always been Iris's domain. It was a beautiful view of the garden, she had to admit. Ross kept trying to catch her eye, but she refused. The room was too crowded.

After fifteen minutes of waiting, Lady Georgina broke the silence. 'Shall we at least have some tea while we wait?'

Bella stood and pulled the cord to call the servants. *Staff!* she reminded herself.

Moments passed, a footman entered and was given the order. They resumed waiting. Cecil, who'd been thumbing through a poetry anthology, moved to the piano and played a simple sonata.

The tea came and they tried to enjoy it, but without knowing why they were there, or for how much longer, it was difficult. When the tea grew cold, Lady Georgina finally snapped.

'I demand you tell us what this is about, Ross! I can't stay here all day. I have things to do, you know.'

'I'm sorry, Lady Georgina. I'm following orders. I'm sure she'll be here soon.'

'And where is Angus? Why isn't he here?' she continued, as if he'd never even spoken. 'Has anyone seen him today?'

There were murmured answers of no, and Lady Georgina sighed. Cecil started a piece by Sibelius.

When the clock chimed half past, the door opened, and Mrs MacBain finally entered the room.

'I'm sorry to keep you waiting so long. I was with Angus, telling him what I'm about to tell you.' She looked around and walked to the fireplace, standing just to the side of it. How she hated the idea of breaking the news again. But she must, or rumours would easily fill the void.

'The doctor came this afternoon with news about how Hugh died. He suffered a massive overdose of opium.'

She had half expected them to start shouting, but they were silent. Confusion clouded their faces.

'Mrs Blackwood came to England to open her new business. We know she needed the ruby to buy the townhouse, and that she blackmailed people for money. We also know that Mr Parker wanted nothing more than to stymie her efforts and was hoping to keep the ruby from her. But he also decided on a second revenge. Mrs Blackwood brought with her a suitcase filled with opium and Mr Parker stole that opium, replacing it with peat from the Distillery storehouse.'

She paused to see everyone was still with her. The entire room looked dumbfounded.

'Now, what this has to do with Hugh is quite simple. Hugh broke into the Distillery storehouse, took a block of what he thought was peat but was actually opium. He lit it in the bothy and went to bed. According to the doctor, it was a very peaceful way for Hugh to pass. Opium is a sedative, so he would have just drifted to sleep and then passed into the great beyond.'

The room was silent but for the clock ticking.

'Poor Hugh,' murmured Elspeth.

'I will murder that man!' Bella jumped up and bolted for the door. Ross caught her by the shoulders and held her as she struggled against him.

Bella! Don't say such things. What man? the family exclaimed.

'Mr Blackwood Whatever-His-Name-Is! He has destroyed everything he's come into contact with: my maid, my jewels, my future. And now Hugh. Lovely, stupid Hugh. What are my children to do without a father?' Tears were streaming down her face.

No one had expected her to react so strongly. Ross guided her gently to the sofa, where Elspeth moved to put an arm around her shoulder.

'What will happen to him?' asked Fergus. 'Mr Blackwood - I mean, Mr Parker?'

'I'm not sure. Jarvis has taken him to the police station. It was an accident, but a man is dead because of his actions. He'll have to answer for it.'

A grumbling of agreement wafted softly around the room.

'Such a pity it turned out this way,' said Lady Georgina. 'I always liked the Dunbar-Hamiltons.'

The entire room turned to stare at her.

'What? There's little point in speaking ill of the dead. The living however, that's quite another matter.'

Four Days After the Murder

Lawlis rang Fergus the next morning. The Foreign Office had information regarding Edmund's arrangements. Fergus broke the news of Edmund's death before Lawlis had a chance to speak. Lawlis was silent for a moment or two.

'Oh dear. First Hugh and now Edmund. What a tragic week for Lady Annabella.'

'Yes, she's still in a state of shock.'

'And that does change things a bit. Edmund does have a bank account here in Britain but it's in his name only. Because they met and married abroad, he never had a chance to add her name to the accounts.'

'Not liking the sound of this, Lawlis.'

'Admittedly, it's not great news. She has no right to the account unless he gives her access.'

'That doesn't bode well.'

'No. But Home Office did share the name of Edmund's solicitor here in the UK. I've been in touch and asked him to come to Loch Down. Edmund left a will so, hopefully, it will settle something on Lady Annabella. Either way, we should have a path forward for her by the end of the week. I've booked him a room at the pub in the village. With all that's happening up there, I thought it would be easier.'

Fergus murmured his agreement. 'Erm . . . ' He hesitated. 'You aren't, by chance, Hugh's executor, are you?'

'No, I'm afraid not. He worked with a firm in London; we'll make some inquiries. I'm sure he left something for the children.'

Fergus hadn't even had a chance to think about them. Their father had just died, and their mother was penniless. How was anyone going to take care of them? It was becoming a Dickens story after all.

Mrs MacBain rose late that morning. She bathed and dressed carefully and then went down to the kitchens. Staff breakfast had finished, and the maids were clearing it all up. Mrs Burnside looked up when she entered.

'Morning, Mrs MacBain. You feelin' all right?'

'Yes, thank you. Why?'

'In all the years we've worked together, you've never missed staff breakfast. I was about to send someone up to check on you.'

Mrs MacBain gave her a small grimace. 'I'm fine, thank you. Could I get a cup of coffee?'

Mrs Burnside's head snapped round. She stared at her for several seconds. 'Coffee? Not a cuppa?'

'I could use something stronger. I'm a bit cloth-headed this morning.'

Mrs Burnside continued to stare at her as she walked to the door of the pantry. 'Maisie,' she shouted without taking her eyes off Mrs MacBain, 'can you get Mrs MacBain a cup of coffee?'

'Does she want milk?' a voice called back.

'No, thank you, Masie. Black will be just fine,' she called to the disembodied voice.

Mrs Burnside's unease was growing. First no breakfast and now a cup of coffee. 'You sure you're all right? What happened yesterday?'

'That's a very long story. I can't even begin . . .'

Maisie handed her a cup of coffee and Mrs MacBain drifted off towards her office. She settled into her favourite chair by the fire and sipped the bitter coffee.

What would they do now? Cecil's alibi, together with the footmen's recollections, exonerated the Colonel from Mrs Blackwood's death. But he had assaulted Miss Wen, and then stole Mrs Blackwood's winnings. Jarvis had a lot he could charge the Colonel with, provided they could find him.

But the larger issue remained. They had no viable suspects. Perhaps Jarvis had been right; they were trying too hard. It could easily have been one of the other blackmailed persons. She took out a piece of paper and pen and wrote the list of names as she remembered them.

Lady Beaumont, one of the sons of the Earl of Carrick, Lady Matthews, and who else? Lord Burridge, that made perfect sense. Mrs McCready? *Good lord what could that woman possibly have done? She's halfway to senile.*

She ordered them, deciding to start with Lord Burridge, but couldn't decide how to figure out which of the Earl's three sons was most likely to have been caught doing something sordid. They were all so unsavoury. And a dressing gown on one of the gentlemen could easily be mistaken for a woman's gown.

It made her head hurt. She put down the pen and sipped more of her coffee. She'd been positive that the killer had kept the cane. But Sadie hadn't found it in any of the blackmail victims' rooms. If they hadn't kept it – it would be damning evidence – then what had they done with it? Hidden it in the Abbey? Left it in the woods somewhere?

Tossed it in the river? Lord, it would be halfway to Oban by now. A knock at the door roused her.

'There's someone to see you, Mrs MacBain. I've put her in Rowan Tree for you.'

'Thank you, Tommy. I'll be right up.' She took one last sip of her coffee and put the list of names in her skirt pocket. They'd have to wait.

Sitting in Rowan Tree, in the seats by the window, was Imogen.

'Oh, good morning, Imogen. I'm glad you're here, actually. Could you ask Lawlis if he knows where the Dunbar-Hamiltons are? They need to know about Hugh.'

'He's already working on that, don't worry.' She set a folder on the table and slid it across. She looked seriously at Mrs MacBain. 'I heard from Immigration and the records department.'

Mrs MacBain gasped. 'Mrs Blackwood, you mean?'

'Yes. Most of what she told you was true. She married John Blackwood when she was eighteen and moved to Shanghai. They had one daughter, Abigail Frances Blackwood, who died when she was twenty-two. She's buried in Canada. But then there's this.' She opened the folder and pointed to a piece of paper.

Mrs MacBain picked it up and read the contents twice, looking back and forth between the paper and Imogen, her mouth agape. 'Is this true? It can't be!'

Imogen frowned and nodded her head. 'I rang them last night, to be sure there was no mistake.'

The women stared at one another for a few moments.

'Does this mean what I think it does?' Imogen asked softly.

'I'm afraid it might,' Mrs MacBain said. She sounded hollow.

Imogen watched her carefully. 'Now what do we do?'

Mrs MacBain looked up at her, regret filling her eyes. 'We call Roddy Jarvis.'

Imogen, Jarvis and Mrs MacBain stood outside the door to the suite. No one spoke as they waited. The door was finally opened by Mr Cooper.

'Good morning, Mr Cooper. May we come in?'

Slightly confused, he nodded silently, and let them into the Stuart Suite. He was still in his dressing gown, a pale oatmeal colour.

'Who is it, darling?' Mrs Cooper called from her dressing room.

'It's Mrs MacBain.'

As Mrs Cooper walked into the living room, the smile disappeared from her face. She swallowed hard. 'Won't you please sit down?'

'What's this about then?' asked Mr Cooper, reading the tension but not understanding.

'It's about Mrs Blackwood.'

Mr Cooper pulled a face, confused. 'The woman who died?'

'Yes,' replied Mrs MacBain. 'You left the ball early, didn't you?'

'Erm . . . yes. I came up about one, I think. After the breakfast buffet.'

'And did you sleep in your dressing room?'

An audible gasp went up from Mrs Cooper. 'Why do you need to know that?'

Mrs MacBain looked at Mr Cooper. 'Did you sleep in your dressing room?'

Mr Cooper stared at her for some moments, trying to work out why she wanted to know. After a brief silence, he answered her. 'Yes, as a matter of fact, I did. I wanted Emily to enjoy herself. It was her first ball and I wanted her to stay as long she wanted.'

'So, you didn't see her come in that night, did you?'

'What? Erm . . . no.'

'Which means she didn't see you either.' They stared at her, confused. 'Neither of you has a proper alibi for the time Mrs Blackwood was killed.'

A guarded look replaced the confusion on Mr Cooper's face. 'Why on earth would we need alibis? We hardly knew the woman!'

'That's not strictly true, is it?' she asked quietly, looking at Mrs Cooper.

There was silence in the room as the women looked at one another. Mrs MacBain handed Mrs Cooper a folded slip of paper and Mrs Blackwood's Canadian passport. 'Would you like to tell him? I presume he doesn't know.'

Mr Cooper looked back and forth between the women, confused. 'Tell me what? What's happening?'

Mrs Cooper stared at the paper for a long moment and then looked at her husband, tears brimming.

'What is that?' he asked, slightly rudely.

'It's a telegram from the Canadian Embassy.' Mrs Cooper looked at her husband, remorsefully. 'It says Mrs Blackwood was my grandmother.'

'But you said you had no family.' Mr Cooper was fighting his emotions and a great deal of confusion. 'You said you grew up in an orphanage.'

'Convent. Not quite the same thing.'

'So you never knew who your family was?' Mrs MacBain asked.

'My mother was sent to the convent as punishment for getting pregnant with me. She raised me there. So, I knew her, but no one else. Until we came here.'

'How did you know Mrs Blackwood—'

'I didn't, not at first anyway. That's why I tried so hard to befriend her. But she avoided me like the plague.'

'The headaches,' murmured Mrs MacBain.

'And then one night, I overheard her tell her nephew that they were leaving Loch Down after the ball. I panicked. I knew it would be my last chance to find out, so I sent her a note, asking to meet. I didn't hear anything back, so I figured I'd ambush her at the ball, but she wasn't there. At least, I thought so, but then we saw her nephew coming out of that room. Do you remember?'

'Oh, yes. I do remember,' gasped Mrs MacBain.

'And I figured if he was there, she had to be as well. I mean, they were never apart. I said goodnight to you but I didn't go to bed. I sneaked back and listened at the doors. I could hear a female voice, so I slipped out to the garden, to make sure it was her. It was, I could see her talking with Lord Inverkillen, so I waited. When he left, she just sat there, waiting for something, so I went in through the French doors.'

'You were her last meeting.'

She nodded. 'It seemed as if she was expecting me.'

'Tell us what happened when you got in the room.'

The Night of the Ball

'I know who you are, you can stop pretending,' said the old woman. She was sitting in a chair next to the fireplace. There was a silence as the women inspected one another. 'You look just like her, you know. It's remarkable, really, as if no time had passed whatever.'

The girl quietly closed the French doors behind her, remaining silent.

'I presume you know who I am?' The voice was unfeeling.

The girl crossed the room and sat on the sofa. 'Yes.' She said it quietly, nearly in a whisper.

She nodded. 'I am curious how you knew? What gave me away?'

The girl reached for the cane, hesitating until the old woman handed it to her. 'It's beautiful,' she said softly, staring at the jade flower as she twisted it in her hands. 'She always said it was.'

'I should have known.' She laughed derisively. 'Your mother was obsessed with my cane. She begged me for one for years. It was the only thing she asked for on her sixteenth birthday.'

'But in pink.'

'Yes!' Her eyes twinkled. 'Yes. That was the moment I looked at her, really saw who she'd become. She was no longer my little girl; she was a young woman, with ideas of her own; a very pretty, young woman. Shanghai could be a dangerous place for women, so I hired Emmett to protect her.'

The girl's head snapped up, shock registering on her face.

'She didn't tell you that part, did she? Of course not. Always selecting her story carefully. Yes, Emmett was her bodyguard. Much older than she was, very experienced. He came highly recommended. That was before I knew how wicked she'd become.'

'Wicked? You're hardly one to be throwing stones,' spat the girl.

'Now look here, I married into the business when I was as young and naive as you are now. By the time I realised what the business was, it was too late; I had a small daughter to think about. What was I to do?'

'You could have gone back to your family in Canada and told them what he was.'

'Oh, my dear girl, times were very different then. The shame would have been mine for leaving him. And that shame would have extended to my daughter and to my family. It would have ruined our lives. No, scandal was never an option. I had to make the best of the situation.'

'And making the best of it meant running an opium den for thirty years?' She was incredulous. 'You ruined countless lives, including your daughter's.'

'Oh no, she did that all on her own.' Her voice was suddenly hard. 'Don't you dare pin that on me.'

'She was a sixteen-year-old girl who fell in love.'

'That was not love, no matter what she may have told you. That was spite. She seduced a servant just to enrage me.'

The girl looked affronted.

'Oh please, don't be so protective.' She jolted off the sofa and crossed to the fire, staring at the empty grate. 'I found out about it when she fell pregnant and came crying to me to fix it. As if I could make it disappear. Oh, that girl! It still makes me so angry.'

Turning round to face the girl, she let out a tense sigh. 'You have no idea how hard I worked for her, to get us accepted into polite society. It took me years of flattery, bribery, outright blackmail; but I did it. I did it so she could go to the right schools, meet the right people, and be seen in the right places. I had her all but engaged to a Slavic prince. She would have been a queen! But no, she was in love! She wanted to marry Emmett and have his baby.' Her eyes raged with contempt.

'So, to punish her, you shipped her to a convent in Canada, run by the most sadistic and cruel woman known to man.'

'How dare you!' She turned abruptly and shouted, 'That woman is my sister.'

The girl was visibly shaken. 'Sister Thomasina is your sister?' She looked at the old woman, horror clearly etched on her face.

'Ha! Yet another thing your mother failed to mention, I see.' She was smiling cruelly at the girl. 'Tommy was the only one I trusted to bury the scandal, so I sent her off before she could elope with Emmett.'

'But she was so cruel to mother.'

The old woman merely tutted impatiently. 'She was lucky Tommy took her in. Your mother brought shame and scandal on herself. She ruined any chance of a respectable marriage, of a respectable life. If she'd been in the least bit virtuous, none of us would have been in that situation.'

'A bit rich for the drug dealer to be occupying the moral high ground.'

'And yet, I do. It is the only hard and fast rule of the upper classes: don't get caught.'

'You sent her away,' the words were strangled, 'because she got caught?'

'I sent her away because she was a *woman* who got caught.' She moved quickly and paced behind the chairs, agitated. 'Women do not come back from this type of scandal. A man may father ten bastards and still be welcomed as a hero, but the woman will always be treated as vile and contemptible. The scandal is always hers to endure alone. I sent her to my sister, to be taken care of and then returned to me once the baby had been born. A long trip abroad I could explain, but a baby? No.'

She leapt to her feet and rounded on the old woman. 'I can assure you, they did not take care of her.' The women stared at each other, hardness in both of their eyes. 'They tormented her. Bullied her, shamed her. I grew up hearing daily that my mother was a whore and going to hell. Your daughter wasn't being looked after; she was being tortured.'

'She was free to leave at any time and come home. She chose to stay.'

'She chose me. She chose to stay because she wouldn't give me up for adoption. You might have happily abandoned her to a life of misery, but she wasn't going to do the same to me.'

'Oh.' The woman looked callously at the girl. 'But didn't she?'

The girl fell back, dazed as if she'd been punched. She steadied herself with the cane and breathed unsteadily. Tears splashed across her cheeks. 'She couldn't take the abuse any longer. Do you have any idea how broken she was?' The old woman picked at an invisible hair on her sleeve. 'Of course you do. Sister Thomasina kept you well informed. Monsters. You are both monsters.' She walked quickly to the door and stopped, turning back to face the old woman. 'Did you even think of what my life was like? You left me there to rot, too.'

'I left you there to be educated. So you wouldn't make the same mistakes.' She crossed the room and said in a low growl, 'I left you with Tommy because you were the last hope of making any good of a bad situation.'

'Make good? There is no good in this situation.' She stepped back from the old woman and stared at her in disgust. 'Your sister hounded your child to her death. Your daughter killed herself because she couldn't take it any longer.'

'She killed herself because it was the right thing to do.'

The shock made her gasp and double over.

'Do you honestly think you could have married so well if she'd been alive?' The woman looked down at her, imperiously. 'No. She did you a favour.'

'A favour?' The words escaped in a hollow whisper. She stood slowly and looked at her grandmother. The old woman stared blankly back, neither of them sure when the blade had entered her stomach.

'Don't . . . get . . . caught,' she said, labouring hard to get the words out as she slumped to the floor and her life slipped away.

They were silent for a long time, taking in the story that had unfolded.

'Where did the knife come from?' asked Mrs MacBain gently.

Mrs Cooper's head jerked back into the present. 'What?'

'Where did you get a knife?' Mrs MacBain repeated slowly.

'Hmm? Oh.' She appeared to be in a bit of a trance. She stood and walked into the wardrobe. They heard rummaging and then she reappeared, holding Mrs Blackwood's cane. Taking it in hand, Mrs Cooper twisted it and then pulled the flower. She put it in the palm of her hand and held it up for all to see. A hidden stiletto gleamed in the light. 'This was her protection, not the cane.'

'How the deuce did you know about that?' asked Jarvis, flummoxed.

'Mother told me,' she said simply. Looking at her husband, tears welled up and started to fall. 'Oh, darling, I'm so sorry. I didn't mean for any of this to happen. Honest I didn't.'

Mr Cooper stared at his wife, ashen-faced and silent; horrified.

'You must believe me.' She knelt in front of him, looking up at him earnestly. 'I didn't even know she was alive until I saw her cane. I had to know if it was really her.'

'That's why you asked to meet her?' said Mrs MacBain.

'Yes. I had to know that it was really her, and if it was, I wanted to confront her about Mother. I hadn't expected her to be so callous about her, so cruel. She was entirely uncaring about her own daughter. It shocked me. I didn't know I'd stabbed her until she fell.'

Mrs MacBain asked gently, 'And when you did realise you'd stabbed her?'

Mrs Cooper thought for a moment, her eyes focused in the past. 'I panicked. I cleaned the blade with her skirt and put it back into the cane. That's when I realised I had blood on my dress, so I locked the doors, drew the curtains and then burned my dress in the fire.'

Mrs MacBain nodded, remembering the ashes in the grate. 'Yes, I thought it was odd. It was such a hot night for a fire.'

'I couldn't take the chance of it being discovered.'

'Then what did you do?'

'I waited, tried to figure out how to get out of there. I had hoped there was a servants' door, like I'd seen in so many of the other rooms, but I couldn't find one. I couldn't go out into the garden, I'd be seen. It gets light so early here! I really had no choice but to wait until the footmen broke up the cards game. Once I heard them leave, I waited a few minutes, until I was positive everyone was gone, and slipped out, locked the doors behind me, then took the servants' staircase. I buried the key in a fire pail and made my way back to here.'

'In your petticoat?'

She nodded. That was clearly what Cecil had seen, not a gown but a petticoat.

'You took a big risk using the back stairs. What if someone had seen you?'

She shrugged. 'I don't know. It's not like I planned it, any of it. I only wanted to speak to her. It just . . . all spiralled out of control.' Tears threatened to spill.

'That's why you wanted us to leave,' Mr Cooper said hollowly, 'that morning, you kept insisting we go back to Paris.'

'Yes. Some small part of me hoped we could be gone before anyone found her; it's such a remote part of the Abbey, and the doors were locked. Your staff is just a little too efficient, Mrs MacBain.' Turning to her husband again, she smiled as tears fell down her face. 'I do love you, Alistair, and I did really want to have children with you. I'm sorry I've messed it all up.'

'Oh!' shouted Mrs MacBain, leaping forward to grab the girl before she collapsed to the floor. 'Call the doctor!' But it was too late. Her blood spread slowly from the jade flower on to her pale pink nightdress.

Part Three

Seven Days After the Murder

That afternoon, Mrs Burnside brought in the pile of breakfast orders with boiled eggs. It was thick, as Mrs MacBain had expected.

'Forgot about those.' She smiled weakly. 'I appreciate this.'

'Can you tell me what it's all about?' Mrs Burnside asked, curious.

Mrs MacBain looked at her and wondered where she'd even start. 'When things settle down, perhaps. I haven't the strength just now.'

Mrs Burnside had the grace not to look as disappointed as she felt. She closed the door softly, leaving Mrs MacBain to her pile of slips.

Slowly, she worked her way thought them, placing them face down as she read. About three-quarters of the way though, she stopped. *Yes,* she thought, *I suspected as much.* Well, what to do now? She set it aside and continued though the rest of the slips. Sitting back in her chair, she pondered her next move.

Guest: Major Cecil Ogilvy- Sinclair
Room: Serramuir, First Floor West
Delivery time: 8:15
Black pudding
Bacon
Mushrooms
1 Boiled egg, 3.5 minutes
1 order toast, white
Tea

Oh, Major. Would he be brazen enough to keep such a valuable object, quite obviously misdelivered, and not say a word? Was he really that unscrupulous? It seemed so much riskier than anything Cecil had attempted before in his life. A pilfered piece of family silver was nothing compared to this.

She sighed heavily, knowing that proving he had it would be nearly impossible. How on earth was she meant to handle this? *But maybe,* she thought, *just this once, it's not mine to sort out.* She stared out the window in deep thought. When the clock chimed the quarter of the hour, she rose slowly, stacked all the slips together, and tucked them in the back of her top desk drawer. If Roddy Jarvis asked to see them, she'd produce them.

Edmund's executor, Mr Rosemont, was an altogether superior cut of man. Lady Georgina could tell from a single glance. Better cut of suit, better shoes, better manners. And judging from his demeanour, they could relax a bit. She poured the tea.

'Thank you for accommodating me on such short notice. I must say, I had no idea the Abbey was so grand.'

Lady Georgina tittered as she passed his teacup. Bella inwardly rolled her eyes. She hadn't wanted to serve tea, but Lady Georgina overruled her. Tea just prolonged what she knew would be doleful proceedings.

'Now,' he got straight to business, much to her relief, 'I will need a copy of the wedding certificate. It's a formality, but the marriage must be verified.'

'Why?' asked Fergus.

'His will predates the marriage and nominates "any future spouse" as his sole beneficiary.'

'How prescient of him,' said Lady Georgina, rather amused by his planning. 'And if he were unmarried?'

'Everything would revert to his family, of course.' He placidly picked up his teacup and took a sip. Chinese, if he wasn't mistaken. Oolong, perhaps? 'Now, the marriage certificate?'

There was a queer pause. Looking over his cup, Mr Rosemont saw the family exchanging puzzled looks.

Bella broke the silence. 'Edmund doesn't have any family, Mr Rosemont. It's one of the reasons I married him. I have quite enough family in this family.' Her grandmother and brother turned to her, clearly offended.

Rosemont put his teacup down, consternation on his face. He flipped though some pages and finally nodded his head. 'Yes, here it is. His mother's still alive; Graciella Santa Rosa de la Paz-Martin. She lives in the house in Madrid.'

'House?'

'Mother?'

'Madrid?'

There was another queer silence and then they all spoke at once.

What do you mean, Madrid? As in Spain? Was he Spanish? Did you know about this, Bella? I most certainly did not. You mean he never told you he had family? I thought he was an orphan. Did you know he was Spanish? How could he have been in the Foreign Office if he was a foreigner? None of this makes any sense. Why would he buy a house in Spain if he lived in Shanghai? He never mentioned Spain to me. Who is this mother of his, with that ridiculous name?

Mr Rosemont's head went back and forth between the questions, trying to answer but unable to get a word in edgeways. Lawlis, having been on the receiving end of the Inverkillen Barrage many times, chuckled to himself and then held up his hand for silence.

'Please!' he said loudly. 'If you will let Mr Rosemont speak, he will have answers for you.'

They subsided and after Mr Rosemont blinked once or twice, he shook himself back into form. 'Lady Martin, am I to understand that you didn't know Edmund was half-Spanish?'

Bella was visibly startled. 'No. I didn't know that.'

The room looked at her, shocked. 'How,' intoned Lady Georgina, 'can you know so little about the man you married?'

'What? He said he went to Eton and then on to Oxford. It doesn't get more English than that.'

'No, it certainly does not,' murmured Lady Georgina. She aimed a shrewd look at Rosemont. 'Unless he was lying?'

'No, no,' assured Mr Rosemont. 'He did attend Eton, and he did row for Cambridge. His father was English, his mother is Spanish. I acted for Lord Neville until he died – he was quite a bit older than his wife – and Edmund, as only child, inherited the Estate.'

The family digested this information. Fergus reached for a ginger biscuit and nibbled it thoughtfully.

'And would that be a substantial Estate?' Lady Georgina asked hopefully.

'I wouldn't like to speculate on your idea of substantial, Lady Georgina,' he said, glancing around the room, 'but it encompasses the house in Madrid, which I believe holds a prominent position on one of the more important squares in the city.'

Lady Georgina made an admiring noise.

'The house and grounds in England were sold and the funds put into a portfolio of stocks and shares.'

Bella looked up brightly.

'But he mostly invested cautiously, long-term gains. He didn't have the stomach for financial speculation.'

'But I thought financial speculation was the reason one entered politics,' Lady Georgina said earnestly. Lawlis and Rosemont stared at her, uncomprehending. 'To have the inside track on what to invest in, so as not to risk the family fortune. It's just good sense, really.'

Rosemont turned, nonplussed, to Lawlis, who, for his part, was breathing out slowly.

'Erm,' hesitated Fergus, wrenching his confused gaze from his grandmother to Mr Rosemont, 'you said there was a house?'

'Yes.' He flipped through the papers again. 'Yes, it's in the Salamanca district, but I'm afraid I don't know much more than that. Dona Martin resides there currently and I believe she keeps a rather large staff.'

Lady Georgina murmured appreciatively.

He spent some minutes detailing the investments that were solid but not brilliant, various accounts with small annuities, life insurance policies, and the Foreign Office pension. Bella, it seemed, would have a modest but stable income. Fergus breathed a sigh of relief.

'And then there are the vineyards,' he said.

'Vineyards?' asked Fergus.

'Yes, outside of Madrid, they have a vineyard that pro-
duces rather excellent red wine. I receive a case every year
for Christmas. I'm unclear if it's a commercial venture,
however. Edmund never took any income from it, so I presumed it was for the family cellars only.'

'Maybe we can sell it in the restaurant,' Fergus suggested.
Rosemont hesitated. 'If it survives, yes.'

'Survives? Why on earth wouldn't it survive?' asked Bella.

The question flummoxed Rosemont. He gaped at Bella
for a moment and then ventured a hesitant response.
'Because of the war?'

'The war? In Shanghai?' demanded Bella. 'Surely that
has no bearing on Spain.'

Rosemont stared in disbelief. *Surely, she'd read about it
in the papers*, he thought to himself. Taking a deep breath,
he said, 'The civil war in Spain, Lady Martin. Madrid has
been under siege since last year?' No response. He turned
to address Fergus. 'Once the war is over, we can take stock
of what's left of the vineyards, but until then, there's no
telling what will survive the fighting.'

'Are you telling me,' Bella said slowly, trying to control her emotions, 'that I've lost two homes in two separate
countries because of two separate wars, neither of which
has anything to do with me?'

Rosemont reluctantly nodded. It was the most extraordinary coincidence. 'Now, if you can just supply me with
the marriage certificate, I can advance you funds.' He took
another sip of tea. Yes, most certainly Oolong. He approved.

Bella blinked at him, silent horror on her face. 'I don't
have it. I didn't think to bring it. Everything happened so
quickly.'

'Ah, that complicates things.' He saw the tears starting
to form in her eyes. 'Never fear. Complicate was the wrong

word. If you provide me with the date and location of the marriage, I can get a copy of the certificate. But it might take a week or two.'

'As long as it happens, I don't think we care much if it's this week or next,' said Lady Georgina. 'Unless, of course, it takes several months. She has existed in limbo long enough.'

Rosemont appraised Bella carefully. *Yes*, he thought, *she certainly has.*

Jarvis had sent a constable early that morning with news that everyone was free to go and not one guest was wasting time in leaving. Mrs MacBain wondered vaguely why Jarvis hadn't come himself, but she supposed he had his hands full. She certainly did. She watched the ensuing pandemonium with trepidation. By teatime, there were very few guests left in the Abbey. The family had a quiet dinner together and then went through to the Blue Drawing Room. In the silence, it almost felt like it was their home once again.

'Bridge tonight, Mama?' asked Cecil.

'Hmm? Oh, no,' she replied, looking up at him. 'I can't bear the thought of not partnering Mrs Blackwood. She was such a fine player. I dare say my winnings will look quite small in the future.' No one wanted to explain that Mrs Blackwood wasn't a fine player, she was a strong cheater.

Cecil turned and addressed his nephew. 'Billiards, Angus?'

Angus stood and stubbed out a cigarette. 'I'm afraid not. I'm leaving early in the morning.' Cries of surprise went up among the family.

'Leaving? Where are you going?' Fergus finally managed to ask, the surprise showing in his face.

'I'm headed to New York with Mr Rosenthal. He's offered me a job.'

A thousand questions came at him at once.

A job? New York? Were you even going to tell us? You can't live in America. When did this happen? I suppose you thought a postcard would be fine notice. What about the children? What sort of a job? Not tennis, I hope.

Angus waited until they subsided and continued. 'Mr Rosenthal owns a hotel, quite fashionable from what I understand.'

'But what are you going to do, Angus?' asked Lady Georgina.

'I'm not entirely clear on that, if I'm honest. He wants me to be the resident aristocrat. *Class up the joint,* as he put it. I'll live in the hotel, he'll pay me a salary, and I just, erm, spend time there like I do here.'

'That's a job?' asked Cecil, incredulous, but mostly jealous.

'He likes the idea of an Earl mingling with the guests.'

'So, you'd live and work in the hotel? How claustrophobic,' remarked Lady Georgina, pulling her wrap higher on her shoulders.

'Ah, there you all are!' Mr Rosenthal entered the room, all smiles and charm. 'Did you tell them yet, Angus?'

'You own a hotel?' Fergus asked, annoyed that he hadn't known but Angus had.

'Yes, just near the Park.' Having never been to New York none of them had any idea of the significance of his statement, and they looked at him blankly. 'A bit like over-looking Hyde Park in London.'

More blank stares. 'I'm also opening a second hotel next year, so I hope to be seeing a lot more of you.'

Fergus felt his hand go numb and nearly dropped his glass. 'What? Why is that?'

'I bought the Dunbar-Hamilton Estate.'

Lady Georgina and Cecil were having a nightcap in the Drawing Room at Thistledown Cottage. They were discussing Angus's latest news.

'Well, I'm quite proud of Angus for finding a way to support himself finally. But I worry he'll become too crass and American.'

'I sincerely doubt that will happen, Mama.' He swirled the liquid against the fire, admiring the colour. 'At least not for a while. When he visits, you can remind him of his heritage.'

Since Angus announced his venture, Lady Georgina's mind had been occupied with her son. Here he was, back in Loch Down, in no hurry to get back to London, to his wife. She had watched with some concern how he was comporting himself among the wealthy widows staying at the Abbey. She'd seen the behaviour before. It was how he met his first wife.

'Cecil, is everything all right with you and Eva?' she asked as she sipped her sherry, eyes never straying from his face.

'Whatever do you mean?' he asked cautiously.

She set her glass down and looked at him. 'I'm worried your marriage has ended.'

Cecil was surprised by her directness. There was little room for evasion, as she well knew. He considered lying to her but could see little point in it. He may very well need Thistledown Cottage soon, and it wouldn't do to burn the few remaining bridges he had. He sighed heavily and sat across from her.

'Eva sued me for divorce.'

'And you came home to lick your wounds.' It wasn't unkindly said but it did sting. 'Oh, Cecil, what are you going to do?'

'I always land on my feet,' he said, somewhat petulantly.

'No, Cecil, you don't. You land on someone else's feet. Feet that are richer than yours.'

'And what's wrong with that?'

'Oh, Cecil,' she tutted, 'I have no doubt Eva's father will fiercely protect her assets and you, once again, will be left penniless and homeless. Which, tragically, is where you were when you married Eva. You do not have a talent for fortune hunting, whatever you may think. Quite frankly, I can't watch you go through it again. It's time you found a way forward that doesn't involve rich wives.'

Cecil gaped at her.

'You need an independent income, Cecil. I don't know what or how, but you need to focus your considerable energies on that, not another wife. I'm not going to be around forever, you know, and when I do go, I'd like to know that you can take care of yourself.'

They were silent for quite some time while Cecil digested this. Lady Georgina watched him carefully, to see if her words were taking root. But when he excused himself and left the room, she was unsure they had.

Eight Days After the Murder

Mr Rosenthal and Angus were leaving on the first train the next morning. Fergus had come up early to say goodbye. He was in the office with Mrs MacBain, telling her about the developments of the previous night.

'He bought the Dunbar-Hamilton Estate?! When?'

'It's quite a tale, actually. When Hugh's parents left, they emigrated to Canada, and met—'

'Mr Cooper?' she asked, incredulous.

'Yes. He's Canada's largest whisky producer and wanted to use the Estate to make Scotch, as he called it.'

'Which is why he was always out in the woods.'

'Yes. He was spying on Ross, to see how he does it, checking out the property, making sure he could use the river. But then, after what happened with his wife, Mr Cooper confessed to Mr Rosenthal that he couldn't bear to see this place again, so Mr Rosenthal offered to buy it from him.'

'Just like that?' Mrs MacBain gasped. 'Over whisky after dinner?'

'Just like that. Apparently, Mr Rosenthal is from one of the richest families in New York.'

Mrs MacBain was stunned. *Mr Rosenthal was wealthy?* He certainly didn't act like the rich families she knew, the ones that stayed at the Abbey. He was, to the contrary, kind and considerate, positively down to earth. Most of the upper classes she'd dealt with had been cold, imperious and, frankly, rude. She shook her head, bewildered by it all.

'And now he's opening a hotel next door?' That part worried her greatly.

Fergus nodded, equally worried. 'He called it a *sister hotel*. He'll send his clients from the New York hotel here and bring European guests to the hotel in New York.'

'Is Loch Down big enough for two grand hotels?' she asked.

Fergus shrugged. 'Well, we'll see. He's not offering stalking or shooting, so we'll keep a lot of our clientele that way. And they don't have a ballroom, that I remember.'

'I'm in no hurry to stage another ball, if I'm honest.'

Fergus nodded, a wry look on his face. 'He'll have to renovate it, so that will buy us some time. He's got some grand plans. An indoor swimming pool, for a start, bathrooms in every bedroom, central heating.'

'We can't compete with a modern hotel.' He could hear the worry in her voice. 'Together with the rumours that we know will be doing the rounds . . . '

'Ah, but you're forgetting one important thing.'

'What's that?'

'It will be overrun with Americans. And no one likes to holiday with them.'

Bella wheeled Miss Wen to Rowan Tree. The exertion left her red in the face and gasping for air. Mrs MacBain shook her head slowly at the pitiful sight. She stepped forward to hold the door as Bella struggled. When they were finally in the room, she turned and gestured to the men on the sofa.

'Miss When, these gentlemen are with the Foreign Office. They're going to take you back to London and get you to the Consulate.'

The men bobbed their heads in recognition.

Miss Wen looked worried and Mrs MacBain continued, 'We've rung the Foreign Office and verified their identities. You can trust them.'

Miss Wen exhaled a long and shaky breath, nodding her head slightly.

'Do you have the money?' the taller of the men asked Bella.

Miss Wen patted a suitcase on her lap. 'It's in here.'

He took it and set it gently on the coffee table. The two men crowded around the case, but Mrs MacBain could just see though a gap between them. She gasped softly when they opened it. So much money, it was unbelievable. It took quite a bit longer than Mrs MacBain would have expected to count and transfer the money to the new special case they'd brought with them. They snapped the case shut, the two locks were secured, and then one of them removed a set of handcuffs.

'Are you arresting me?' asked Miss Wen, terror in her voice.

The men stopped their movement and looked at her. 'No. Why would you think that?'

She indicated the handcuffs, and the men chuckled. 'It's not for you, it's for us. We handcuff ourselves to the case for transit.'

'Oh,' she said, not looking entirely relieved.

'All set to go then?' the shorter man asked. Miss Wen nodded.

'Gentlemen, would you give us a moment, please? To say goodbye in private?' Mrs MacBain ushered them out of the office and shut the door behind her. She turned to see both Bella and Miss Wen looking at her, confused. 'I have to ask you one thing, if you don't mind.'

Miss Wen looked at her guardedly, and Mrs MacBain figured it was now or never. She sat down, eye level with Miss Wen, and took a deep breath. 'There's one thing I don't understand. Why did Edmund want the ruby?'

Miss Wen thought it over and gave a small, bitter laugh. 'I suppose it doesn't matter now. It was to fund the war in Spain.'

'What?' It came from both Mrs MacBain and Bella.

'Edmund had a contact who could smuggle the ruby into Spain. From there it would be sold, and the funds used to purchase guns. But the meet with the contact was here at Loch Down.'

Mrs MacBain's brain started to tingle. 'Here? Who was this contact?' She held her breath.

'I'm not sure. Some writer, or journalist he knew.'

'Hugh!' shouted Bella. 'Is that why Hugh was here?'

'I don't know who it was. My part was to keep the ruby until Edmund came for it. You're only told the parts you need to know, and I didn't need to know a name.'

Mrs MacBain's brain was whirring. Hugh, who wanted to be a journalist and wanted to be taken seriously. It made absolute sense. What better way to prove his credentials than to provide arms and funding for a war and then write about it?

Oh Hugh, she thought, *how vainglorious*.

Mrs MacBain shook her head, still a bit confused. 'Why would Edmund fund the war in Spain?' she asked.

'Edmund was Spanish, on his mother's side.'

Mrs MacBain looked at Bella, who nodded. 'I only just found out,' she replied.

'And is this ruby really a national treasure?'

Miss Wen nodded. 'Oh yes. It's part of the Qing dynasty, and it's been displayed at the Imperial Museum since the war. How Edmund got a hold of it, I'll never know.'

'What if whoever has it tries to sell it?'

'They'd have to sell it on the black market. Any legitimate seller would consider it a looted antique.'

'So an auction house, like Bonhams, wouldn't agree to sell it?' Mrs MacBain held her breath.

Miss Wen shook her head. 'It has no provenance, no papers of ownership. Even if they didn't know what it was, they'd steer well clear of it.'

'But someone could keep it, in their private collection, yes?'

She thought about this and nodded. 'Yes. But it'd be dangerous. The Chinese government, once they realise it's gone, will pursue it relentlessly. The best thing that can happen is that it's turned into the Foreign Office, or a museum, and then returned to China. Imagine if someone came to England and stole the Crown Jewels. That's what we're talking about here.'

Mrs MacBain thought about it and she doubted she'd ever see it. She stood and straightened her skirts. 'Well, thank you, Miss When.' She opened the door to the office, watching as Bella groaned, and pushed the former maid into the Armoury. 'Good luck. Be careful.'

Miss Wen smiled up at her and then looked to the Foreign Office men. 'Shall we, gentlemen?'

Elspeth was packed and ready to depart, but she had one last thing she needed to do. As she picked her way through the woods, she wondered how she should start. She hoped the Distillery yard would be empty. When at last she arrived, mercifully, it was.

It must be elevenses, she thought. She made her way to the office, and then knocked on the door.

'Come!' said a gruff voice.

She opened the door and smiled, as Ross finished what he was writing. 'Where is everyone? It's quiet as a church-yard out there.'

Ross's head snapped up, and a smile crossed his face. 'They're out burning the peat from the storage shed.' Elspeth cocked her head questioningly. 'I didn't want to take any chances.'

An awkward silence ensued.

Elspeth cleared her throat gently. 'What you said at the ball—'

'No, I shouldn't have pressed you. It was a big night for Delphine. You needed to be there for her. It's what mothers do.'

'You were right. I was avoiding you.'

Ross looked at her, curious, hurt, and surprised.

'I was on the ridge by the osprey's nest the day I arrived, and I saw the smoke from the bothy. Thinking it was you, I walked out. But it was empty, and all I could see was an unmade bed.'

'And you decided I was there with someone else? Oh, Elspeth . . . '

'Why shouldn't you have someone else? Someone you can have a future with. My life is in France, and I can't change that. Why should I have sole claim of you?'

'There has never been anyone else for me.' He stood up and crossed the room to be nearer to her. 'I know you had no choice in who you married. I made peace with that a long time ago. But there is no one I'd rather be with than you. I can't deny that I'd like to see you more, but life is what it is.'

'Are you sure?' Elspeth looked up at him, tears threatening to fall.

'Yes.' Ross gathered her up in his arms. 'Unless you ask me to dance again.'

Mrs MacBain was in the Armoury, watching the few remaining guests depart. Not everyone had been lucky enough, or fast enough, to get a train ticket the day before. In fact, the train carriages from Loch Down had never been so full, which led to heated arguments, accusations of queue jumpers and fabricated seat reservations. It had caused two successive services to depart late, something the station manager took to heart. When he returned from his final trip of the day, Lockridge reported breaking up more than one scuffle on the platform. Today's lot of passengers, she hoped, would be more reasonable.

Heading back towards her office, she heard her name across the din of the room. It was Imogen, hurriedly picking her way among the trunks and cases.

'Have you seen this?' she cried, thrusting the local newspaper, the *Loch Down Tribune*, at her. 'I will kill that man if I see him!'

An audible gasp went up from those around her. Imogen looked around, apologetically. 'Unfortunate choice of phrase, my apologies.' She shook her head and murmured quietly, 'But a good hiding wouldn't go amiss.'

Mrs MacBain barely heard her. The colour had drained from her face and her knees buckled. Imogen only just managed to catch her in time.

'Let's go into your office, shall we?' Imogen led the shell-shocked Mrs MacBain across the Armoury and into Rowan Tree. Settling her into a chair, Imogen held her shoulders and looked critically at the woman. 'Tea? Or brandy?'

Mrs MacBain looked up from the newspaper and merely blinked.

'Definitely brandy.' Imogen poked her head outside the door and gave the order to the nearest porter. She returned and sat down opposite Mrs MacBain.

'I've not had a chance to speak with Mr Lawlis yet, but I'm positive we can sue them. Libel, slander, defamation,' she checked them off on her fingers, 'a whole bunch of things. They cannot be allowed to print gossip as fact!'

Mrs MacBain looked at the headline again, screaming at her in large bold typeface.

'ONLY MURDER IN THE ABBEY'
By Hamish MacTamish

Loch Down – After days of rumours, a reliable source close to the inner workings of the Abbey corroborated three murders occurred at the Highland Ball.

When asked about the deaths, Detective Inspector Roddy Jarvis of the Loch Down Police Department confirmed that the body of the Honourable Hugh Dunbar-Hamilton, noted local and celebrated author, 'has been found dead in a bothy on the Estate, as well as two women from Shanghai and Canada.'

When asked what assurances the police could give that the citizens of Loch Down would be safe in the woods that surround the village, after three murders in a bothy, DI Jarvis responded:

'Oi! I never said that. I . . . erm . . . misspoke. There was no murder in the bothy! You hear me? No murder in the bothy, an accidental drug overdose. The only murders were in the Abbey. Erm, no; one was a suicide. But that was the girl who murdered the old woman, who was blackmailing people, so she might have had it coming . . . But to recap, only murder in the Abbey, and just the one.'

Just the one? She had it coming? Are we to feel safe in our homes when those in charge of our safety are so casual about murder? I took to the streets to ask your opinion.

The article went on, but she didn't read it. She was flabbergasted. Not only had he managed to put 'murder in the Abbey' into the newspaper, he'd managed to do it twice. It was the perfect quote to ruin them.

Mrs MacBain sighed morosely. 'How could Roddy have been so . . . thoughtless?'

'We'll force them to print a retraction,' Imogen said.

'Oh, Imogen, it wouldn't do a blind bit of good. Retractions are printed in the back pages, in very small print, so no one can read them. Besides, it's all true!' She shook the paper angrily and threw it on the table. 'No, the damage is done; our reputation will be ruined.'

A knock at the door sounded and a footman brought in a tray of brandy. Imogen poured a large measure and handed the snifter to Mrs MacBain, who took it and stared at the liquid.

'I'll ask Lawlis. I'm positive he knows the reporters for the *Inverness Courier*. We can issue our own story to them, and hopefully that will be what the *Scotsman* picks up. Not . . . *this*.' She picked up the newspaper, glanced at the headline contemptuously, and then threw it back down again.

Mrs MacBain closed her eyes and sighed heavily.

'We'll find a way to fight this. I promise you. It might injure the hotel in the short term, but we won't let it damage you permanently. Not while I draw breath.'

Mrs MacBain appraised her carefully. Imogen was spoiling for a fight. And she didn't look like the type to back down. It was a bit terrifying, to be honest, but luckily, they were on the same side.

Once again, Mrs MacBain gave silent thanks for women that surrounded her. 'Okay then,' she breathed out at last. 'What do we need to do first?'

Epilogue

It was a fine September day in London, crisp and fresh. Autumn was in the air. Thomas Kettering was reading *The Times* and sipping his morning tea, Darjeeling, with a splash of milk. His wife, Iris, entered the room and kissed him lightly on the forehead.

'Good morning, darling.' She settled herself across the small round table in the Morning Room. 'I'll be in late today; I have to take the twins for a doctor's appointment.'

He murmured something, having remembered the appointment.

Thomas Kettering was an art historian and ran a team of eight, who authenticated artworks for private clients. He'd been in his professional capacity when he met Iris, having been called to a crumbling great house in a village called Loch Down, Scotland – so remote and unfamiliar, he'd had to consult an atlas – to cast his eye over a collection before it went to auction. Iris had been a ward of the Inverkillens, and the task of guiding Thomas around the Abbey had fallen to her. Her observations and notes on the artworks had impressed him and he quickly found himself relying on her impressions. When he was finished with the job, he returned to London having secured her, not only for his wife, but also as the newest member of his team. She'd proved to be a valuable asset over the years.

Iris poured herself a cup of tea and opened her preferred newspaper, the *Scotsman*. It kept her connected to Scotland and though it didn't contain much of importance for her life in London, she refused to give it up. As she looked over the front page, she gasped. 'Three Deaths at Exclusive Highland Hotel!'

'What?' he asked, looking up suddenly. 'Loch Down?'

She nodded as she read through the article quickly, her jaw dropping. 'A woman from Shanghai came to stay and was killed during the ball. A young Canadian woman several days later, and – oh! – Hugh Dunbar-Hamilton has died as well!'

Thomas leapt up and came round to read over her shoulder. It was unbelievable. 'I thought Hugh was in Tangiers?' He grabbed the paper from his wife, who was staring across the room, tears starting to form in her eyes. Hugh was, after all, her brother-in-law, sort of.

'*Found dead in a bothy on the Estate. Both women stabbed, murder-suicide.* What on earth happened?' He walked around and sat down, reading the article closely.

'I must ring Mrs MacBain. This must be so upsetting for her,' Iris said thoughtfully.

Thomas set the paper down and looked at his wife. 'Yes. Perhaps you should take the day off.' He proceeded to flip through the pages of *The Times*, searching for any mention of it. 'Nothing in *The Times*, at least.'

Iris looked at him and nodded with relief. It was a small mercy. 'I should telephone her.' She leapt up from her seat and was nearly to the door, when it opened. Morgan, their butler, entered the room with a small brown package on a silver tray.

'Madame, this just arrived for you.' He offered the tray to Iris. 'Special delivery.'

Iris stopped moving and both she and her husband looked at the package. It was a perfect cube, brown paper, tied neatly with dark green gardening string. 'Erm, yes, thank you, Morgan.' She took the package – it weighed next to nothing – and the butler bowed and left the room quietly.

'Were you expecting something?' Thomas asked, seeing the confusion on her face. Special deliveries weren't unusual – many clients sent smaller pieces directly to them, but they were sent to the office, not to their home.

'No, not at all.' She set it down on the table and took a seat.

She pulled on the string and tore the paper off to reveal a black box. Opening it, she peered inside.

'What's that?' he asked, trying to peek into the box.

'I'm not sure,' she answered, pulling out a note and reading it aloud.

'This came to me quite by accident. I know I can trust you to return this to the proper authorities when the time is right.'

She handed the note to her husband, who studied it with a frown. 'The proper authorities? Who are the proper authorities? And who sent it?' He turned the card over, looking for a clue to the sender but found none.

Iris carefully reached in and pulled out a golden egg. It dazzled in the sunlight, causing her to gasp with wonder. 'What is it?' she asked, turning it to the left and then to the right.

He examined it carefully. 'I think this writing is Chinese, just here.' He pointed to the base of the flower. Iris set it carefully on the table, where the egg blossomed. It was a lotus flower, and inside the petals sat the most spectacular ruby either of them had ever seen.

Acknowledgements

It seems like I thanked everyone I ever met in the last book. I thanked family, friends, strangers with particular sets of skills; anyone I could think of, I thanked. Mostly because I presumed it would be my only book. One Hit Wonder, me. And I was happy with that. Until I wasn't. Turns out, the Inverkillens don't go away that easily. Lady Georgina kept waking me up, demanding more lines in the next book.

So here we are.

Firstly, I must thank Monty, who really does all he can to make it possible for me to live in my imagination most of the day. Pity him, folks. He has spent the past year listening to me bang on about the Abbey, rail against characters, reel from plot twists I hadn't seen coming; I spoke to him as if it were real life, real people. And through it all, he smiled and encouraged. So thank you, my darling.

Secondly, I must thank Charlotte, Rachel, and Melissa, who read multiple versions – quickly, often dropping everything in their lives to do it – and came back to me with feedback and suggestions. What you did was invaluable, even if I didn't use all of your ideas. Without your support, your excitement, and your critical eye, I'd still be stuck on version 1.0.

Lastly, I must thank the Literary Team. Greg, my agent, without whom I'd still be a bored dog-mom, frustrated designer, and unfulfilled creative. Cara, my editor, who breathed much-needed life and enthusiasm back into me and the book when it was sputtering. And Hodder &

Stoughton for giving me another chance to spend time in this lunatic world I created. I appreciate you all for what you've given me.

Till next time!
B.

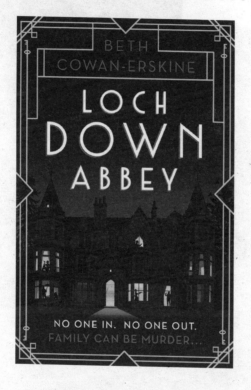